LAZARUS CITY - BOOK FOUR

ROTTERS END

MELISA PETERSON LEWIS

To you, the readers.
Thank you for being part of this journey.

one

Shelby

THE NIGHTMARE REMAINS
FULL OF YESTERDAY'S DANGER
THIS FEAR NEVER WANES

I pull out the community college catalog and place it on the desk between me and Mrs. Quinn, an angry twenty-something who doesn't want free college. She doesn't want handouts or charity either.

"Mrs. Quinn. The grant will pay for your associate's degree and contribute to your education beyond those credits." My role as a community outreach liaison is not as rewarding as I imagined. I bridge work and education gaps for Lazarus City survivors, and things have slowed significantly.

She squints her dark eyes through tangled bangs. Mrs. Quinn's stench is enough to set my nostrils on fire, and I force myself to breathe through my mouth. I check the time; it's already past five o'clock, and I should head to happy hour to meet my roommates, but I'm going back and forth with this young woman who doesn't want my help.

Her palm stretches over the table, and I believe she's going for the catalog. I exhale with relief until her fingers wrap around my reusable water bottle. As she pulls it to her lips, her mouth opens to reveal gray teeth, and I want to offer her a hygiene gift bag full of all the essentials, but she won't take it.

"Keep it." I gesture to the bottle.

"The trains will operate again, and soon. More of us are coming out," she hisses. Then, with a loud whack, the bottle slams onto my desk. "Must be nice to sit in the air conditioning all day." She leans in closer than I'd like. Then she takes a box of tissues from my desk, scoots back her chair, and walks out the door, leaving my bottle.

After two years of survivors reentering society, those who wanted aid received it. Now I'm left with the mentally unstable, the lost, the forgotten, and my contract is for another three years. Why did I need to serve this group so badly? I should have taken the assistance provided and reinvented myself.

I've learned to leave the job behind when I walk out the door. And that's precisely what I do.

My legs burn on the leather seats when I enter my car, and the music isn't loud enough to drown out what I'm most worried about. When I pull up to an Irish pub, the weekend can truly begin. There's a push for a new Baltimore to be created. Between surrounding cities like Frederick, Washington, D. C, Philadelphia, and Wilmington, most businesses have tried to reestablish their grounds. We have satellite offices in each location, but I've made Frederick my home because it's the least congested.

Inside, I find my people. Angela waves me over, and Jeronimo pulls up another barstool so I can sit.

"If you think your day sucked," Angela says, "imagine being on the highway for three hours in this heat." Her dark hair is shaved close to her head, and I notice she hasn't changed out of her EMT clothing yet.

"Car accident?" I ask.

"Yeah, pretty messed up too." She takes a long swig of her beer to finish the bottle. She has a higher tolerance for seeing the unimaginable than most.

Jeronimo belches. "I gotta piss. Oh, I let Jessie out before I came and fed her, so she's good for a while." He stopped home to change out of his suit and tie. I'm not exactly sure what he does, but it's something for an insurance company. He hates it.

"Wait." I reach for his arm to grab his attention. "Did you hear anything?"

"You know I'd tell you." He swirls his finger in the air. "Get me another round?"

I take the seat and try to avoid Angela staring at me. The baseball game is on the television. The Orioles moved to a small field in Frederick, which caused a big stir in the sports world because the Raven's football team went to their practice facility on Ownings Mills, meaning their stadiums aren't side by side like they used to be. I haven't been to any games, knowing the crowds would trigger my anxiety.

"Why do you do that to yourself?" she finally asks.

I think she can read my mind for a second, and she's talking about how I avoid stadiums. "What do you mean?" I ask.

"If Jeronimo hears from anyone inside, we'll be the next to know."

How can she be so sure? The news reports how successful the cure is, and they've been doing ration drops again for months. Yet the world is so divided on this. People mostly fear survivors, including those who were never sick and received the vaccine. We're no threat to anyone, yet society discriminates and harasses survivors if their identity is discovered. Some groups treat survivors well and try to lend a hand. When I meet someone new, I avoid mentioning Lazarus City in any context. There are things I'd like to avoid getting people's opinions on.

Jeronimo returns, and we order dinner and sit at the bar for longer than we should. Soon it's growing dark, and my scrambled thoughts remind me of this painful time of the day.

"I should get going. Jessie will need to go out." I hand Angela my card. "Will you run this when you get the bill?"

"Slow down. Slow down," she says. "It's getting late, and we can go home with you."

Jeronimo waves at the bartender. "Check?" Then he turns to us. "Drinking cheaper beer at home sounds like a good idea."

I watch the sky turn from blue to navy in a few minutes. The bartender brings us the bill and chats up Jeronimo about the game on the television.

"Can we move this along?" I check my voice and can tell it sounds nervous.

Angela's head swivels to the window. "Oh, I didn't realize how dark it's gotten."

I put my credit card back in my wallet and sign the bill. Each minute ticks closer to total darkness outside, and I have a few miles to drive home. "Did anyone leave lights on for us?"

"Of course I did," Jeronimo says. "Still afraid of the dark, Shelby?" He asks carefully, understanding my fears. Angela hates the smell of barbecue after she accidentally ate cooked human outside of the rations area, and Jeronimo sleeps with a hunting knife under his pillow.

"I'm not. It's Jessie. I need to get home." Nothing like throwing your dog in front of your true feelings to set your friends' suspicions going.

He reaches out and clasps my hand. "You're okay." His large dark eyes find mine, and I realize he's right. "I'll drive you home, and we'll come get your car tomorrow."

"No. I'll take myself home." I pull my large purse off the back of the stool and storm outside to show them. Jeronimo grabs the purse's strap and pulls me closer to him and Angela.

"You don't have to pretend with us. If you're scared, I'll go with you," he says.

"I'm not." I twist away from him and plant a smile on my face. "See," I say as I point to my mouth. "I've totally got this. I'll see you two at home."

I turn out the door and into the parking lot, which is well lit from all angles. People are walking to and from their cars without care. If they can do this, so can I.

A feeling comes over my shoulders. Is someone behind me, watching me, waiting for me? Do they hear my heartbeat and wonder what I'll taste like? My knees lock, and I try to force my hands to unzip my bag in search of keys, but they aren't listening.

"Shelby?" Jeronimo taps my shoulder. "Let me drive you home."

Tears form, and I shake my head. "I want to do normal things."

"We get there at different times."

But when will it be my time? Angela and Jeronimo may have some paranoia left, though it doesn't cripple them as it does me. My dad tells me we all heal and need to give ourselves the grace to work through our trauma without comparing progress to others. So much easier said than done. What does he know? He never slept on top of a bus while the infected streamed past, hoping to find their dinner. He's never been on the menu.

"Okay," I say.

Angela stands next to me and takes my hand. "We're a team. We've got you."

Together, we walk to Jeronimo's Jeep and pile in. It smells like old hamburgers, which, for some reason, comforts me. On the drive home, he turns the music off so I can watch my imagination roll through what's hiding in the dark places along the street. We drive out of downtown and towards our home nestled near a large park. It's a brick cape cod facing another row of houses. There's a small backyard Jessie defends from bunnies and squirrels.

Jessie barks before our keys even jiggle the lock. My sweet girl is getting old. She has some pep, but she takes her time getting up and sleeps more than before.

I let her out back and turn on the lights we've set up that create a daytime glow in the small backyard. Our neighbors must hate us, but they leave us alone.

Jeronimo hands me another beer. "It'll get easier."

I exhale, listening to the tree frogs and bugs orchestrating the night. "Maybe it won't?" I ask, hoping he'll have an appropriate answer.

"Maybe it *won't*? That's a shit way to look at it." He laughs, trying to tease the tension out of me.

"Jerk," I say.

"Yeah, that could change too.

"Probably not." I hold up my beer, and Jeronimo taps the neck of his with mine.

We swig our beer, standing by the door so I can step back in at any minute. Lock out the night. There are others who can't, though. The subject has been tossed around briefly. The trains are taking people out again. Every survivor able to leave the city has a second chance.

Will Dean be on one of those trains? The only way would be if he were cured, and I have yet to hear if he's received a suitable version. I want to help again if I can. They've talked about moving some of us to the airbase where survivors first report. I've lived through coming out of Lazarus City with nothing but a ten-pound bag of belongings.

"You're thinking about the train?" Jeronimo says. "You want to know if Dean will be on it?"

"I do."

"You'll need to talk to Jason then."

Pain pings my heart at the suggestion. A lot can change in two years.

two

Shelby

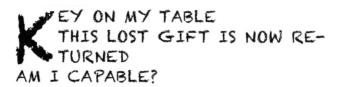

KEY ON MY TABLE
THIS LOST GIFT IS NOW RE-
TURNED
AM I CAPABLE?

"Coffee," I groan. The robust smell of Jeronimo's coffee wakes me every day. Being from Puerto Rico, he insists the beans come whole from the island. He'll find no argument from me.

I throw on a pair of shorts and a sweatshirt, then pat Jessie, who sleeps near my feet. She's nestled in pretty well, so I leave her. When I open my door, I catch a familiar voice that doesn't belong in my house. It's a woman. At first, I think this is another of Jeronimo's conquests. The revolving door of strange woman in the morning is expected; I stay out of his business. Angela and I mostly keep to ourselves, our hearts healing from the damage Lazarus City caused.

Our kitchen is a small, yellow-painted room containing a metal breakfast table and four chairs. She's out of place standing with Jeronimo.

"Hi, Shelby," Lindsay says. She glows. Her hair is highlighted and cut above her shoulders, and her makeup shows off her blue eyes and soft smile. We were friends once, but we took different paths even after forgiving each other. She's wearing a navy floral dress and is bringing a cup of coffee to her nose; something I do every morning, like a button to start the day.

"Lindsay?" I want to ask if everything is okay. She and her husband, Chad, reunited when she got out, and she sought medical attention for the long-term effects of April's poisoning. Then I notice something else about her; she is very pregnant.

When my eyes go to her stomach, she rubs her hand over the bump with a smile. "Yep. It's number two since I've been out of Lazarus City. Another girl."

"Wow, congratulations." My cheeks grow warm, and I'm unsure what emotions are coming through. She's creating life after all the death we've witnessed. It's too surreal to imagine myself in her situation.

"Thank you. I'm here because I want to talk to you about something." She looks at Jeronimo and says to him, "Do you mind if I talk to Shelby alone?"

He grabs his coffee and hugs Lindsay. "Take care of yourself."

"I will," she says.

Jessie finally catches on to the fact that we have a visitor and strolls into the room. Lindsay reaches down and pets her carefully. "She's so sweet."

"She's not a puppy anymore, but she still chases the squirrels." I want to ask her why she's here but don't want to seem rude. "Do you want to sit?"

"Sure, but I can't stay long. I just wanted to give you something." She sits at our small table, her belly rubbing against the tabletop, making it wobble. I catch her coffee to make sure it doesn't spill. Then she brings something out of her bag.

"What's this?" I ask, addressing the large brown envelope she places on the table.

"That's what I'm here about. I'm not sure why I held onto it, but now the trains are going again." Her fingers slip beneath the fold, and she pulls out my map of Baltimore City.

"Oh my god!" I gasp at the sight of it. Jason added notes and drawings on top of mine. The edges are torn and frayed as if it's been opened and closed hundreds of times.

It all floods back. The running, hiding, worrying if I'll have enough food, trying to find a cure, seeing my friends die. I can't look away, but my hands won't reach for it either.

She slides it closer to me. "Are you alright?"

"How do you have this?"

"The night April shot Jason, she was probably looking for this. It marked all of our hidden locations, where we stored guns, and the new tech house. Shelby, it has everything. Some of the information is still accurate. After everyone left, it's not as though we were running back to get our guns. Nobody cared anymore."

"But why do you have it?" And why has she brought it here?

"Jason let Mona borrow it." She unfolds the map, trails her finger down to the Rec Pier, and then taps another downtown point marked with a blue star. "Mona passed away a few months ago."

This brilliant woman's passing creates a sadness I've yet to shake. "I attended her service."

Lindsay smiles. "Me too. There were several hundred people there. No wonder I missed you." She sips from her coffee, places the cup down, and taps a blue star on the map again. "I knew this map was important, and Mona was adding something to it."

"So important that April would have killed us for it."

"She was going to give it to Fat Man," Lindsay says.

If burning the Rec Pier didn't take us down, dismantling all our outposts and safe houses would have. This map began with squiggly lines and Xs marking the areas I couldn't pass. It morphed into so much more. I smile, thinking about Jason's first reaction to the map when we met. He was impressed with the areas I'd been to. I wonder if it pushed him to explore territories he hadn't before. The idea of Jason fills my stomach with uncomfortable flutters.

I reach for the map and spin it around so it's facing me. "You haven't told me why you have it. I mean, why do you have it here in my kitchen?"

She adjusts in her seat and then reaches for her phone to check the time. "Mona was tracking something. I think it has to do with how the virus started and who is behind it. I didn't get to ask her about it before she died, but we worked on ideas while still inside. I pushed this away when I got out because I wanted to be with Chad. But after Mona died, this was delivered to me."

"So, you're here because of Mona?"

"Shelby, I don't want to go back inside. Even when the walls come down, I'm done with Baltimore." Lindsay folds her arms in front of her defensively. She almost lost her life several times, not that I didn't, but I imagine being a new mother sways her decision.

"I get it. But what exactly was Mona pinpointing with these blue stars?" Upon closer examination, I see several tiny stars around the city's center.

"It may have information about VioTech or the government. I'm sorry, I don't know more, but it's important, and Mona specifically wanted you to have this." Lindsay flips the envelope over, and I see it physically addressed to Lindsay, but it has my name on it.

"What?" I can hardly believe what I'm seeing. Mona and I were acquaintances at best. Why would she entrust me with this?

"Jason. You two split up?"

"Why are you asking?" My voice sounds defensive, and I try to reel it in.

"It's that..." she trails off, and I'm suddenly the last to know some big plan is already in motion.

"What the hell is going on?"

She exhales and reaches for my hand. "They're going back inside and leaving you out. Dean is there, and if it were Chad, I'd go in without wasting a second. This map will do more than help you navigate the city. Do you understand? This could be what prevents Lazarus City from happening again."

"Wait. Who is going back in, and what do you know about Dean? We haven't spoken since I left the city." My mind races past the map to the unanswered questions lingering years later.

"Jeronimo, Angela, and Jason are going in to organize a mission for the infected. They will cure those they can, free survivors, and after that, the military will sweep the area, killing or arresting any-one left behind." Her voice is rapid, as if she's running out of time.

"How do you know all this? Why would they go into the city without me? Did Dr. Warren tell you?" I tried to stay in touch with Dr. Warren and Mike early on, but they didn't return my calls, so I've stopped.

"Jason and I talk sometimes," Lindsay says. "But he doesn't know I have the map."

My head jerks up. "Why me? What is this map going to do? There has to be someone else more qualified." Jason, Angela, and Jeronimo would be more qualified than me, and apparently, they have a free ride back inside.

"Mona said you!" Lindsay tears up, and I reach for a napkin to offer her. She dabs her eyes and then looks at me. "Don't under-estimate Mona. Her reach goes far beyond what you can imagine. There isn't more I can tell you, but whatever she has planned, it's important. My guess is she chose you because of your connection with Dean, and she has reason not to trust others."

"Who doesn't she trust?" I beg for more.

"I don't have all the answers you need, Shelby."

"I have to go back inside?"

"Yes," Lindsay says.

I fold the map and put it in the envelope in case Angela and Jeronimo walk in. The traitors knew they were leaving but didn't tell me. Why would they keep this from me? My suspicions point to Jason trying to control my safety even now.

"There isn't time to cure the entire city, is there?" I ask.

"Not even close."

"All those people are going to die?"

She nods slowly, and I see we have similar feelings toward the infected. These lost souls are trapped in a body that forces them to rage and eat. They could be saved, but there's not enough time, manpower, or people who care. The danger of the infection break-ing out far exceeds the desire to save everyone.

"I don't know how to get in or what to do." This is crazy. Does she think I'll climb the wall to investigate these random blue stars on a map?

"This might be your last chance to see Dean and find out what Mona needs from you. I'm not sure how you'll get in, but I can tell you it won't be with Jason. Why is he so adamant about that?" She crosses her arms over her belly and examines me.

I refuse the bait. "Thank you for all this. I'll have to figure it out alone, I guess."

She leans in and whispers, "No one knows about this map but me and you. No one."

"I understand." We thought it was lost in the fire. Jason hasn't questioned its whereabouts, and we've all worked hard to put the city behind us, that is, until now.

Lindsay stands and takes another sip of her coffee before placing the mug in the sink. "I should go."

Angela bursts into the room, holding a dozen grocery bags looped over her arms. She shuffles forward and pushes them onto the counter. "I got your freaking Pop-Tarts without icing, you weirdo." When she turns, she finds Lindsay, and her mouth drops open. "Lindsay, no one told me you were coming over."

The two embrace, and over Lindsay's shoulder, Angela mouths the words, "What is happening?" When she releases Lindsay, she forms a smile big enough to fool anyone. I slide the envelope into the back of my shorts and cover it with my shirt protectively.

"Just checking in on an old friend." Lindsay grins back, and Angela cocks her head suspiciously.

"You told her, didn't you?" Angela asks Lindsay while my head bobs back and forth between them.

"She has the right to know."

"Well, I was going to tell her when I had more details!"

I raise my hands and step in. "It's okay. Really, it's fine. I need time to wrap my head around my roommates disappearing."

"Shelby," Angela says, her eyes already pleading. "You flip out at night. You're not ready for a doomsday part two, okay?"

"I get it." My temper flares, and I stand from my seat. "You can be honest with me."

"I didn't lie. I just withheld the truth until I had more information." Angela steps forward, and I avoid her by going to her groceries and looking for my fantastic Pop-Tarts without stiff, gross sugary icing.

Jeronimo walks in, making the kitchen overcrowded.

Lindsay squeezes past him. "Okay, well, it was nice to see you all, but I'm going to get going. Chad and I were just passing through town."

"That explains the dude in the car out front." Jeronimo reaches into the grocery bag and takes out meat and eggs to put away.

"That's him. Bye-bye now." Lindsay leaves the house smiling as if she didn't drop the quest of a lifetime on my lap. I scoop Jessie some food before I get lost in thought.

Jeronimo puts a gallon of milk into the fridge and then closes it. "She told you we were going back in?"

He grabs my hand when I move past him, but I pull it away. "It's none of my business anymore. Just make sure rent is paid, or whatever."

I leave the room as fast as I can without looking like I'm running. My heart thunders in my chest. Dean could be killed, along with hundreds of infected. How will I get into the city? The walls are as protected now as they were three years ago when they went up.

I close my door and lock it. The envelope pokes my skin under my shirt. When I carefully pull the map out and spread it over my bed, I see how soft it's become from overuse. I count the stars, and there are five, which seems reasonable. There has to be a key here. Something showing me what Mona's plan for me is. One thing is clear: no matter how terrified I am this minute, I am returning to Lazarus City.

13

three

Dean

NIGHT ENCLOSES ME
LAZARUS CITY, MY TOMB
I'LL NEVER BE FREE

The life of a hermit. I'm not responsible for anyone. The burden of keeping someone out of trouble is gone. This city is mine to do whatever I want. Sours either died or were cured, so they are none other like me. Who would want to be like me, anyway?

My phone rings, and I forget I charged it yesterday. If it works, then they pester me. I don't like to be pestered. The cracked screen shows its Aisha, which means she'll want something.

"What?" I bark.

"One of our back doors is damaged and we can't fix it from the inside." Her tender Pakistani voice runs an angry chill down my neck.

"So, fix it tomorrow morning."

"Dean, there are rotters trying to get in Sinai again. We need you to redirect them. Please," she begs.

Please is the magic word, but I don't jump to it anymore. "Close off that area and deal with it tomorrow." It's not like she isn't used to working with rotters. They've been curing them, one small group at a time.

"You answered your phone," she whispers.

This is the one promise I made to them. If I answer my phone, I'd intervene with rotters. It's just me, after all. I'm the only one left. Why did I charge my phone? It's been dead for over a week, and I made myself accessible again because I was considering calling

Ivan, my brother. He's the only one I keep up with, and it's just to let him know I'm alive.

"Why are you even working at this hour?" I grumble, reaching for my sneakers and my hatchet.

"Night observations on a new group of rotters. Rob is here. He's been asking about you."

It's been two years since the first group of survivors left Lazarus City. Shelby, Dr. Warren, and her staff, and every member of the Rec Pier were on those trains. They left behind most sours as we scrambled for the cure. I say most because Kenny and Lion got out on the last train.

Lion, the traitor. He was supposed to stay and help lead the efforts to cure rotters, but no, he selfishly chose to leave with Kenny. I don't blame Kenny, in fact, I encouraged him to go. Aisha tells me he's where we'd hoped he would be. Going to college, in therapy, and trying to move on with his life.

"Rob should know this isn't something I need to get involved with," I say. I turned Rob into a sour by accident. It was self-defense. Over the next year, before his symptoms attacked his body and caused deterioration, it was the two of us. The guy is pretty funny. But now, he's one of the cured, and I don't hang out with those.

Aisha grows impatient. "Don't be a jerk about this. It will take fifteen minutes out of your precious busy schedule to come redirect these rotters."

"See you soon." I hang up and regret answering my phone once again. Could it be me, or is Aisha coming up with jobs so she can check in?

I lace up my shoes knowing perfectly well I am going to go no matter what. My days are quiet, and I sleep. My nights are long and boring. Jessie, my faithful dog, is on the outside with Shelby, so I don't have anything or anyone who needs me. If I don't move, I don't need to eat a lot. There are times I forget how to get out of bed. My energy wanes, and any purpose is shadowed by sadness, frustration, and anger. I'll never leave this city. Ever.

To keep these depressing feelings in check, I've developed a quadrant around the city. Each night of the week, I check a different area. What the hell I'm looking for is anyone's guess, but it keeps me moving.

It's summer, and the bugs are screaming as I venture out of the mansion at the zoo. The animals are long gone, though I have a few chimps who come back to their dwelling every night. We coexist as they return to their wild instincts of providing their own food and water.

The jog up to Sinai doesn't take long. The grass around the building has completely grown in. The door she's referring to has a dozen rotters pushing inward, and I'm guessing there are cured on the other side bracing the door, so it doesn't fall in.

One of the rotters snarls and lunges at the door. I shove him, hoping to redirect his attention. The summer air is muggy, and the rotter's skin feels like a chilled orange. He slips and falls to the sidewalk. Then the others behind him push forward and trip over his body so I've got a pile of rotters laying at my feet.

"Great." I need to get their attention. There's a truck nearby, so I scurry over and punch through the glass window, then slap the horn. It takes time for them to get up, but eventually it draws their attention.

"That's right, you mindless idiots. Let's move!" When they draw in, they hover around me, unsure what to do next. If I stop blasting the horn, they'll be back at the door in no time.

The rotters' faces are blueish gray, rotting teeth, and terrible breath. They want to speak to me, but they can't. Their hisses catch the air around me and I do the only thing I can think of. I tie their shoelaces together so they can't get up.

Comically, each one falls and inches around like a worm. I can't leave them like this until morning, but it'll give the cured folks inside a chance to fix the door.

I run back up to the hospital and sniff the air, detecting more rotters on the way. All appears good for now, so I call out quietly,

"The rotters are tied up. Fix the damn door, and I'll be back in an hour to untie them."

Rob opens the door further. He's not as muscular as he was when he was a sour, but he's still fit and tall. "Hey, man. Thanks for this." In his hand is a drill and new hinges. "I'll be quick."

"Take your time. I'm going for a run."

He looks as if he wants to say something more but doesn't. It's not his fault he needed the cure. I'm not sure if he'd choose to be running the night shift with me over this. I'll never ask.

"Wait!" Aisha pushes past Rob with a backpack in her hand. "Dr. Warren keeps sending you food. Please take some."

"Got it." I take the bag and put it on my back. I know they cook whatever I don't take, so nothing goes to waste.

"Dean, do you want to come in? We can catch up. Lion would like to hear from you."

"No." I shake my head, acknowledging it came out more abruptly than I intended. "No, thank you. I have to go."

My attention turns to my usual route before anyone can stop me. It's Monday, the start of the week and my schedule, so today I go north. I catch my pace and wander up the empty streets overgrown with weeds and trees struggling through the cracks. In the dark corners, green moss grows thicker every day. The city is lost to nature. Being witness to this fascinates and terrifies me. What if nature consumes me one day, too? What if I'm just like the cars now covered in honeysuckle and invasive vines, dead and hidden?

I used to brush these ideas away, but I find comfort in thinking something might hold me. I could belong somewhere. Even if it's pulling me to the ground.

Tonight the moon is out, and it's high, so I know I've a good amount of darkness left. My brother must think I'm dead again; it's been too long since I reached out. I should, but I don't.

A bird's squawk catches my attention. Birds singing isn't exactly something I'm used to because I'm a night dweller. I check my surroundings and even in the moonlit street; I don't find a bird.

I shake my head in case I'm hearing things. The neighborhood is full of large homes and overgrown landscaping, making it difficult to locate doors and porches. Wings flap against something from inside one of the houses. I breathe in, catching feathers and dandruff faintly coming from a white home bordered by two massive oaks. Briars cross over the porch, making a makeshift barbed wire protection.

The flapping stops.

Decay and rot trickle into my nostrils and I realize the bird has caught more than my attention. I'm so tired of dealing with them tonight. When I turn, there are three rotters standing almost right behind me.

"Jesus!"

I stumble backwards, staring at their black eyes. As always, they garble groans. Even though it's clear they want to communicate with me, I've lost interest.

"I don't know zombie-talk," I remind them.

A tapping at the window shifts the rotter's attention to the house. I follow their gaze to the second-floor window where a dark bird is pecking. The glass is framed in blood and my heart drops. I should want to hunt and eat this bird, but something else is happening.

The rotters stumble past me towards the house, but they get close to the sticker bushes and their clothes snag on the thorns. I let them be.

Tap. Tap.

As curiosity pulls at me, I circle the home, looking for a different way in. The side of the house is equally tangled in vines and grass so high it reaches above my waist. I take out my hatchet and use it to create a path to the basement door.

"That smells horrible." I roll my eyes. "Why am I talking to myself?" It's going to be flooded, as so many homes are. I take off my shoes and backpack and leave them on the top step. The door is locked, but a small window allows me to punch through and undo the latch. My skin itches as it heals instantly. These abilities grow stronger. It makes me grateful and hateful.

Black water stretches out on the basement floor. A few narrow windows keep the inside dark, even by my standards. I step into water about four inches deep and the floor is slimy from algae growing. With luck, there will be a snake or rat to make a meal out of. I slosh through and make my way up the stairs. The house is perfect. The cushions are arranged on the couch, a magazine sits on the kitchen counter, and the only thing catching my nose's attention is dust, damp basement, and feathers.

The house has grown silent, and I wonder if the bird died of its injuries. If that's the case, it will be dinner.

I creak up the steps to the room I'd seen the bird in. There are swaths of blood on the comforter, window, and wall, but no bird. I crouch down on the floor, thinking it can't fly any longer. There's no bird under the bed or furniture. When I stand, a black mass flies at my head. The bird caws again and lands awkwardly on the dresser. Its dark eyes blink, studying me.

I gently raise my hands. "Hey, bird. What's wrong?"

One of his wings has crumpled feathers and the other wing is spread out like he can't draw it back in. I put my hands by my side and carefully take a step closer to figure out what's happened. Then I see it. Wrapped around his body is a small gold chain. When I quickly check the room, I notice a vanity with women's jewelry tossed over the tabletop. The curious bird must have gotten entangled.

This will not be easy. I grab a pillow from the bed.

"I'm going to assume you are a crow, since you're smaller than a raven, but maybe you're a blackbird. Blackbirds aren't crows, right?" I talk steadily to keep him from getting too worried, though my heart pounds in my chest as if the bird is a bomb.

I shake the pillow out and hold the pillowcase so I can toss it over him. His black head pivots and he hobbles forward on the dresser.

"It's okay. I promise I won't eat you."

19

Just as I lunge forward, the bird caws and darts toward me. He hops to the ground, flapping his good wing, screaming at me. I drop to my knees and chase him. He's surprisingly fast for having little legs and being unable to fly.

"I said I *wasn't* going to eat you."

He tries to fly but only manages to leap out of my grasp several times before I finally wrangle the pillowcase around him like a taco. I haven't been this close to a bird I wasn't trying to eat in a while. The thought amuses me.

"Stay calm," I say again to either remind myself or comfort the bird.

Carefully, I turn the taco bird around and discover the necklace, coated in the bird's blood, is too tight to pull off. I walk with him into the bathroom and locate fingernail clippers to snip the chain in a few places until I can pull it off. Once done, I keep him in the pillowcase so I can take him outside with me. He doesn't squirm or call out any longer. Like a baby, he closes his eyes and rests while I carry him down the steps and into the kitchen. There's a broken window with a tuft of black feathers and in the sink is a slice of petrified pizza.

"Is that what you were after? Pizza." I touch the rock-hard slice. "Nobody's eating that."

I find a can of corn in the cupboard. I place the bird on the counter and let the fabric fall from him. Half expecting him to fly, I brace myself for his wings to go wild, only they don't. He stretches them and walks in a few circles, but he doesn't get away.

As soon as I pull the top off the can, he jumps at it. I dump half the corn out and he marches around in the corny water, chomping up the kernels as he goes. I miss Jessie at this moment. Whenever humans were too much, I could always rely on my dog to sit with me. I try not to spend my nights guessing what Shelby and Jessie are doing, but I'm alone so often it's hard not to think about those who filled the void.

He caws at me slowly, making a ticking sound, and I worry he'll draw more rotters in.

"Done already?"

He stretches his wings again but doesn't fly. I realize he's grounded, and without a way out, he'll die.

"Me and you both."

I take the blood splattered pillowcase and gently put it around him. He squats down without resisting. With the bird under my arm and a can of corn in the other, I head out through the flooded basement. Before we go home, I untie those rotters at Sinai.

four

Dean

THE CROW GOES CAW CAW
AS INTRUDERS COME INSIDE
EXPOSING MY FLAW

The caw-cawing of my new roommate breaks into the room like a siren. He settles for a while, then tries to fly at the curtains.

"I should have left you to the rotters."

He screams at me again, and I throw my pillow in his direction. I expect he'll continue hollering at me, so I cover my ears with the other pillow until he grows silent. I sit up to find him at the foot of my bed. His tiny black talons grip the wood frame. Then he cocks his head and blinks. I'm not sure how I know this, but I sense he's hungry. He gingerly walks onto the bedspread, past my feet, then stops at my knees.

"Fine."

My phone shows it's only two in the afternoon. I've miraculously kept the solar-powered mansion running. I gave up on any outbuildings long ago. It runs enough power to charge my phone overnight and keep the refrigerator cold for meat.

The room is muggy, so I don't bother dressing. Unfortunately, the power is not sufficient to run the air conditioning.

"Come on, bird." I reach out my arm so he can climb on. He has no trouble pricking my skin with his talons and walking up to my shoulder. So now I'm a pirate.

"You need a name."

He clicks at me from deep within his throat.

"Albert? No, Barry? Or how about something traditional like David?"

He remains silent.

We walk through the dark hall and down to the kitchen area. Still running on solar panels, the mansion has some luxuries. I unwrap the food Aisha gave me last night and take a sniff to find its pork. I take a plate out of the cabinet, cut up the leftovers nice and small, and set the bird and the dish on the table like he's my date.

His beak taps the plate every time he snatches the meat. I have a friend to eat with for the first time in over a year. The thought is sad and irritating.

Even with all the shades drawn, I can tell it's sunny as shit outside. I pull on a hat, push flip-flops on my feet, and step out the back door when I find someone walking up the parking lot. It's Aisha, and she's got Rob with her. Perfect. I'm standing in my briefs, with sunglasses and a hat as my only accessories.

"Dean?" Aisha calls from about fifty feet away. "Are you naked?"

"I'm not naked, but I'm not dressed. Give me a minute." I rush inside and put on a pair of running shorts and a t-shirt. When I go back downstairs, Aisha and Rob are huddled in the kitchen corner with the crow on the counter. His wings are spread lopsidedly from his injury, and his beak is pointed directly at them.

"Pizza, chill out!" The name slips out when I remember the stale, dry pizza he was trying to get at.

Pizza lowers his wings with the injured one, taking more time to fold in.

Aisha looks at me with wide eyes. "Are you playing with your food now?"

"He's not food."

Rob moves to a stool next to the butcher block island. "Cool. Does he do tricks?"

"Um, no. Well, I'm determining if he'll even stick around. I found him injured last night, so I brought him here. Now I'm Dr. Doolittle or something."

"Pizza?" Aisha stands against the wall as if the crow might change its mind and jump at her.

I shrug. "Can we skip to why you're here?" What do they need this time? My abilities haven't waned like the others. Instead, they've grown freakishly stronger.

"Lion wants to speak to you," Alicia says.

"Why?" I pick up the plate with pools of watery blood from the meat Pizza ate. Hopefully, he's got a full belly now.

"Well, if you'd check your cell," Aisha rolls her eyes.

"I told you I don't want to be involved." It's clear the cure only works if the suppressant is taken first, but Nick's reaction to the drug confused the doctor, and there's no solution. I watched him take his last breath at Sinai, and I don't want that to happen to me. I'm unique or damaged. There are two ways to see it.

Rob tries to pet Pizza, who screeches and bites his finger. "Ouch!"

"Careful. He's a wild bird," I remind him.

Aisha moves away from the wall and closer to the door. "Lion isn't the only one who would like to speak to you."

"Why stir anything up? Dr. Warren sends notes when she sends food." Nothing new, again and again. She tells me she's trying, but my condition isn't like the others. It's as if there is a Lazarus virus type C, and I'm the only living person with it. She's hypothesized that the same rotter infected Nick and me. But even after capturing and curing hundreds of them, we have yet to find one with a similar DNA match. And we may never.

Aisha steps closer to me, and Pizza squawks at her as if warning her not to come closer. I can't resist grinning at my new guard bird. She continues speaking to me slowly while her eyes stay locked on Pizza. "I'm not just talking about Dr. Warren and Lion. Ivan and Shelby are out there. I'm sure they miss you."

"What do you need, Aisha?" Her guilt trip is getting old.

Aisha is clearly scared of the crow, so Rob steps in. "They're using the trains again. More survivors are getting out now that Dr. Warren can prove her cure works, and Lion needs you to call him."

"Right," I say, unimpressed.

Aisha growls frustration. "We want you to get out too!"

"Lion is a janitor the last I checked. There's no escape without a working cure. You get that, right?" I'll be left with nothing.

"Pick up your phone and call Lion." Aisha points to my phone on the table. "This isn't just about you. They'll send the military to clear the city once the survivors are out. It's all over the news. You'll be hunted down like the rotters we can't save."

The conversation turns darker, and I imagine lying in bed when a bunch of uniformed military personnel storm through the mansion. If I'm captured, and they realize what they have, I understand what that means. Fat Man might be dead, but he wasn't pulling the strings from the outside.

"It'll be bad?" I ask.

"VioTech has tested the Lazarus type B strain on animals, according to Dr. Warren. So the infection is already on the outside. They'll inject humans before long, and they'll be able to stabilize this virus if they find you." Making this virus stable has never been Dr. Warren's focus. It's always been to cure and eradicate it.

"Okay. Okay." I slap my hand on the phone and pull it towards me. What choice do I have? I'm a freak with a cool virus that strengthens me, allows me to heal quickly, run super-fast, and my sense of smell could probably pick up a bomb from a mile away. I'm the trophy they don't know exists yet. Or do they?

Aisha steps closer and puts her hand over mine, holding the phone. "Do you want to see your brother again? Work with us." She hesitates because she's not sure how to make this happen.

"I am working with you. I've provided blood when asked, hair samples, and I've pooped in a fucking box and had a drone fly it over the wall. Every night I run laps around this city, ensuring there isn't a breach in the walls or something out of order. I trap rotters when you need them. I'm more than proving myself to the cause."

"Speaking of," Rob interjects, "we can use about ten new ones. Preferably ones who aren't falling apart and gross." He frowns, and

25

I consider some of the badly hurt rotters I've brought in. While it's hard to turn anyone away from the cure, it's evident that severely injured rotters die once they become healthy again. Shouldn't it be the opposite? You cure someone, and they get better, but the virus freezes them in time, preserving them. They hardly bleed or get cold. When they're cured, their blood runs warm and catches up with the months of abuse. Often, they succumb to their injuries fairly quickly.

"I'll bring ten tonight. Look at me! I'm participating." I grin, hoping to lighten the mood.

Aisha opens the door to leave. "I'll have your participation trophy ready. Please call Lion." She walks outside, but Rob hovers for a second.

"What's up?" I ask.

"Lion works for VioTech."

"As a janitor," I remind him.

"He has news he hasn't shared with Dr. Warren yet. He said he would only talk to you, man. So best call him for all our sake." Rob grins convincingly.

Lion's position at VioTech can't give him much access, but Rob's warning intrigues me.

Pizza walks to the end of the counter and keeps his eye on Rob as he leaves.

"They aren't so bad," I tell the bird. "I'm not like them anymore, or they aren't like me."

I put my arm out so Pizza could walk onto it again. His claws dig in as he wanders up to my shoulder. With my free hand, I pick up the phone and open it. There are a few numbers stored, and I scroll through them: Lion, Aisha, Kenny, Dr. Warren, Shelby, Ivan. It has been a while since I've spoken to anyone on the outside.

"Let's check the zoo and go back to sleep." It's strange hearing my voice so often since Pizza joined me. I don't have to speak out loud, but I sense he understands somehow. I adjust my cap and glasses and step into the sun. As my flip-flops smack the ground,

I realize I've become accustomed to a life of disconnection. News reports never tell the full story, so I've tuned them out. Recent events have me reconsidering my disconnection from society.

I walk the road to oversee the border and find nothing out of place. Pizza sits squarely on my shoulder, bobbing with every step I take. We wander around, and I let Pizza explore some overgrown grass in the old turtle exhibit. Then we head back to the mansion so I can sleep. But, before I do, I hold the black phone in my palm and consider calling Lion.

The former leader of the zoo was bitten and became a rotter during our battle with Fat Man. He was the first rotter, who was a former sour, cured. He all but disappeared until recently. Does this man deserve my time? After the blood we'd spilled together and the trust we carried, he quickly turned away from me to save his ass. I'm not sure I want to welcome him back.

I put the phone on the kitchen island and kick off my shoes.

"I'll figure it out tonight," I tell Pizza, who turns his head and peers at me as if he comprehends this prison we're in together.

five

Dean

SHAMBLE ON THE STREET
ROPES TIGHTENED ON YOUR THIN WRIST
THE CURE WILL DEFEAT

"Come out, rotters!" I shout as I drag the metal bat across a wrought-iron fence. A loud clang rings into the otherwise still night.

Their groans are muffled behind a group of row homes. I turn the corner, finding several near the back lot.

"You're not hiding from me, are you?" I smile as if it's a game. The rotters continue to be unresponsive to my presence, making this part of the job easy. Dragging their damn bodies to the van is another story.

Three women huddle together peculiarly. They each wear black leggings and dark jackets, which is unusual since most rotters wear clothing from the summer when the infection first hit. I get closer, and they sway together with their heads down. I search my surroundings, feeling eyes on me from somewhere hidden. One woman has black hair knotted in a clump on her frail back. I examine the rotters before I use the tranquilizer, so I put the bat under one arm and twist her around so I can see her. Her teeth are rotten, her eyes resemble coal, and her skin is washed of pigment. There's something about her. Her sneakers are black, and even her socks are black. This isn't from the grime of the city, it's the color of every article of clothing she wears. She's a former runner.

When the Rec Pier burned, many of their runners were lost. Jason and I are the same in this way. Our connection to those we led was rattled and torn down so quickly. I want to save all three rotters for him because he would do this for me. Former leaders understand one another, even if we didn't leave things on the best terms.

Carefully, I turn the other two around so I can examine them. Their clothing is black from head to toe, and their physical ailments are similar, though one has a gash in her leg so deep I glimpse bone behind the mangled flesh. I should turn her away, but I don't want to reason with myself tonight. They could talk in less than a week, and the vaccine prevents them from getting sick again. I could give her a chance at life. How do I take that from someone?

"Come here," I say to her.

I take a thin rope from my pocket, tie it around her wrist, and do the same with the other two, so they're on leashes. This is the best way to get them to the van. I accidentally sedated them too far from the van once and paid the price of carrying rotters' limp bodies a few hundred yards.

More rotters stumble into view, hovering outside my reach. I walk up to a young man with a broken nose and missing an eye, but the rest of him is intact, so I grab his hand to add him to my collection.

"Okay, who else?" Five at a time is the reasonable amount I can leash. More than that, and they trip over one another. If one falls, they all tumble like a string of dominos. While this is entertaining, it also slows me down, and I don't want to be doing this shit all night.

Beside this guy are several others, but some are too far gone to save. One older woman is missing an arm that could bleed out. Another fella has trails of red veins growing up his arm and neck, showing a severe infection. He'd probably already be dead if he weren't infected. Behind this group of sad individuals is a much younger rotter. He's a thin young Black teenager stealing my breath because he reminds me of Skiddle and how badly I wish he were here. The nights I spend with Pizza only scratch the deep-rooted pain stretching into depression. Skiddle was a young man with his life ahead of him. He never got to finish school or learn to drive or thousands of other big and small milestones that come with maturing.

I walk up to this kid and check him for injuries, only to find a puncture wound in his stomach. While I can't be sure how deep it is because the rotters don't bleed like an average person, it looks significant enough to be life-threatening. I already have a guy missing an eye.

"Fuck it," I reach for the child's icy hand, kneel to the ground in front of him, and slip the rope around his thin wrist. "All I can do is try, right?" I whisper.

Careful not to move too quickly, I tug on the ropes to get my collection moving. Three women, most likely former runners, a guy who looks like someone spooned his eyeball out, and an injured boy who's tugging at my heart. This is the first of several groups I'll encounter tonight.

They follow my lead with no struggle, and as their eyes fall on me, trying to catch my attention the way they always do, I make a silent promise that this will be the last night they spend on the street.

Once at the van, I drug them and ease each one's fall to the ground, so they don't further injure themselves. Then I give them a better pat down to ensure something isn't missed, like sharp objects that could hurt the staff. I find a cell phones in the women's pockets. I always leave these because once they're cured, they can connect with someone on the outside. The man has a gun, and I pull it out to find it fully loaded.

"Well, that's something."

Only a few of the people I search have guns. Most weren't loaded. I take it from him and put it on the passenger seat. With my former threats being dead or released from the city, I don't need to carry a weapon, but I hold on to them on the off chance another enemy rises.

I drive them to Sinai hospital where Aisha and Rob live. Several former members of my community and cured rotters meet me outside with gurneys to take the infected inside. Each one is strapped to the bed tightly in case the drugs wear off, a lesson I only had to learn once. Tonight Aisha is there making it impossible to dodge her.

"Five?" she asks.

"It's my first trip. Watch the young one. I'm not sure he'll make it."

Aisha examines him and makes the same heartfelt connection I did. Our Skiddle. The one we were supposed to protect and guide through this fucked up place. It could be him; only that would be impossible.

"We'll do what we can."

The staff is generally not from the medical field. All the doctors, scientists, nurses, and other medical persons fled on the last train. Dr. Warren's team provides assistance and support through virtual sessions. The team at Sinai have become nurses, doctors, and surgeons through trial and error.

"Alright, see you in another hour," I say.

"Wait!" Aisha reaches for me, but I step back so she can't curl her fingers around my arm. "Sorry," she says, knowing I don't like to be touched by salts. I realize they can't get infected by brushing against my skin, but their warm touch reminds me of what I can't have; the sun without pain, regular food, or someone to hold at night. The list could go on.

"What is it?"

"I promised Lion I would call when I saw you. So, here!" She pulls out her phone and dials his number, then as soon as it rings, she holds it up to me.

I try to move away. "Um, that's okay. I don't want to...."

"Hello?" Lion's voice slaps me, and fear and guilt curl in my stomach. Though I'm not sure what drives either.

Aisha waves the phone at my face. "It's on speaker so he can hear you."

"Dean? Are you there?"

I scowl at Aisha for ambushing me and swipe the phone to turn off the speaker option. "We're no longer friends," I hastily joke with her.

"I can live with that," she says in her sweetest voice.

With the phone held next to the hatchet on my hip, I walk outside for privacy. I wait until I'm in the van to speak.

"Lion?"

"Dean, it is you. Man, it's good to hear your voice. How are things at the zoo?"

The pleasantries are not reciprocated. "How's life? It's great. I live alone in your abandoned mansion, thinking of how this cure won't work on me. How's it going for you?"

Lion didn't leave just the sours; he left his entire family here. I've searched for them, hoping to capture and bring them in, but as I check the wallets and IDs I find, I've learned how far rotters have traveled over the past few years. They're constantly searching for food.

"I understand there is bitterness between us, but you have to understand—"

"Oh, I get it. You saw your chance to put Lazarus City behind you, so you left with Kenny."

"No. I wanted to protect our community from the outside. All our threats were evacuated. And who would watch those assholes out here? What VioTech is doing should scare you." He sounds sure of himself. I'm instantly brought back to the war room where we'd strategize about taking down Fat Man.

"You're a janitor the last I checked."

"Not any longer. I oversee the lab animals at VioTech, and I've got news."

I can't stifle my laugh. Of course Lion found a way to work with animals again. A former zookeeper, animals are his passion. I have a feeling he wants to ask about the residents at the zoo, but the answer won't be what he wants to hear.

"So, what, you have access to their secret lab?" I ask.

"Something like that."

He's not bluffing, but some of this doesn't fit together. Somewhere, a file with his name on it identifies him as a survivor or even a sour.

"I don't want any part of this. I'm already rounding up rotters like a zombie cowboy."

"You're already involved, Dean. You think Fat Man was the biggest problem? Ha! You haven't met his wife."

"Courtnay Baby?" When we tortured Fat Man, his phone revealed a contact for *Courtnay Baby*. When we answered, we discovered his wife on the outside. She never indicated she was part of the same organization as him.

"Courtnay Baby, in the flesh. She's something else too."

"Does she realize who you are?"

Lion hesitates a moment before speaking, and now I know how he got a job there. "Marcus gave them information. They identified me as a cured survivor of the type B Lazarus virus and have asked for blood samples. I complied. They know everything, Dean, but from what I gather, they don't understand how unique you are. There is a mission to round up any sours left."

Marcus, the former leader of the aquarium, killed Skiddle, and then I put a bullet in his head. Months later, every sour deteriorated rapidly, and had to be cured in order to survive. "There aren't any sours left."

"You are a sour, Dean!"

"No one is going to find me. I know every inch of this city." My mind circles around the possibility of a group of scientists getting their sterile hands on me.

"Trains are running again. They will come for you."

This is the second warning regarding my safety. I am taking this seriously, but if the trains are running, they're not taking survivors out yet. I have time.

"I appreciate the warning," I say.

"You should see this facility. VioTech is cooking up a lot more than over-the-counter pain medication and shaving cream. There are so many divisions and subsidiaries, it's hard to keep track. I work away from where they're doing tests on our virus, but I have an idea where it is." Lion could keep this conversation going for hours, but I have a job to do.

"Look, man. I have to round up a few more rotters for Aisha tonight. I'll check out the train station soon to see what's going on." I start the van and rest my elbow on the windowsill. His voice confuses my gut reaction. Lion's been a trustworthy leader, and someone I wanted to follow until he left the city. But I'm not his loyal groupie anymore.

"Right. You're working. I'm going to get closer to where they're studying the virus and then fill you in. If you see them setting up headquarters in the city, I recommend staying the hell away from there."

"Got it. Talk to you later." I hang up as I hear Lion trying to squeeze in a goodbye. Then I toss Aisha her phone since she crept closer toward the end of my conversation. She grins and walks off, satisfied that her job to get me on the phone with Lion is complete.

If Lion and I mend our friendship, it's not going to be over a twenty-minute phone call. His work whereabouts are interesting, and if he gets access to the area he's speaking of, I'd like to learn more. Until then, it's zombie rodeo time.

six

Shelby

BALTIMORE CITY
I'LL FIGHT MY WAY THROUGH TO YOU
YOU'LL KNOW NO PITY

"Are you wearing black?" I ask Angela as she stuffs her backpack with necessities.

I'm off the guest list because they see me as weak. This is their error. I might be petrified and uncertain, but the calling is too strong. Sometimes we have to do things we're scared of.

"No, but I get a badge to identify myself. Pretty cool." She pulls out an identification card with a centered blue and green emblem. It states she's Rescue Mission Personnel, her name, and an identification number.

"Nice."

My friends are plunging back into the city. I should be grateful not to be forced into that world again. Any normal person would think so. And I've toyed with all the reasons I shouldn't accept this mission from Mona. She had her reasons to choose me, and I cannot ignore her.

I've pondered this for the hours and days leading up to Angela's departure, and I reason Mona chose me because of my relationships with multiple people. Dr. Warren ushers in the cure, while Mike continues to find cracks in the conspiracy leading it to the government. Dean is my husband, and the only remaining sour. Finally, Jason, who Mona may have thought was still my boyfriend, directly leads efforts to maintain order in the city.

"Are you taking food?" I ask, trying to bring myself back to the moment, and knowing how hard it will be to return to a place with sparse rations. There can only be a little left in the city after all this time. Cans of food, perhaps, but anything else would be rotted away.

"Just a few things. They won't let us take our weapons, but I'm stashing a few small knives in my bag."

I remind her, "There are old stash houses you can visit."

"If the cured haven't discovered them already."

Angela works to pack what she's laid out on her bed, and I watch in silence. Will she make it out a second time? Will any of them? Some of the infected died off, and others cured, but the city isn't rid of them. Not by a long shot. I leave the room only to wander into Jeronimo's across the hall. He's already packed, his bag sitting near the door, and he's on his computer intently looking at the screen.

"Am I interrupting?" I ask.

He spins in his office chair to face me. "No. What's up? Feeling left out and sad?" he asks, always right there to the point.

"Yes. I'm having a pity party."

"Party of one."

I laugh. "I would join you if you asked. Is that crazy?"

"Not at all, Shelby. You were right there with us. I never thought I'd help the infected, but the cure changed how I see everything."

Our reasons cross paths, but they're different. "I've always wanted to get the infected healthy again. When I pushed for the study at Johns Hopkins, I saw it was possible to bring them back."

"Joi killed Yeji," he says flatly. His disdain for Joi, our infected patient who showed us the truth, is always a tongue slip away.

"It wasn't Joi's fault. She turned because the hospital stopped treating her."

He waves me off. "We'll never see it the same, but it doesn't matter. We want the same result."

"A city without the infected?"

"Yep," he says. "Jason is coming with us. You two are in a messed-up place, but you should call him. You know what it's like in there, and he could use your support."

I look away when he brings up Jason, and my gaze lands on his clock, showing me how late I am going to be to work.

"Shit! I got to go. They're preparing us for new survivors."

Jeronimo stands and walks over to hug me. "I won't be here when you get back, but I'll make sure Jessie is let out and has food in her bowl."

"You love her, don't you?" I tease.

"Yeah, I do. Dang dog!" He laughs and squeezes me.

"Be safe," I say as I pull away. "Text me if you can?"

"You bet."

I marvel at the obstacles Jeronimo and I have overcome. I used to think he was made of stone, but he's just as damaged as the rest of us. His need for control makes him stubborn, and even mean. Friendship and belonging brings the best out of him. We needed time to let that happen. After Jason and I ended things, Jeronimo was quick to invite me to live with him and Angela. He jokes it's more about Jessie, but I know different.

Before I leave, I run into Angela's room, finding her sitting on the floor with Jessie curled next to her. Angela's hand glides over Jessie's white fur and tears stream down her cheeks. I kneel next to them.

"Are you okay?" I ask.

"I'm stupid crazy, right? What am I doing going back to that nightmare?"

All my fears bubble to the surface, and I burst into tears. "You don't need to go."

She wipes her wet face with the back of her hand. "I do. I have to do this. The infected killed Megan, and I can't let her death mean nothing. She cared about everything and everyone. This is for her." Megan was a lead nurse who helped the infected until she was killed. Angela's wife died without her nearby, which has always haunted her.

I bring Angela in for a hug, and we sit on the floor together until Jeronimo pokes his head in the door.

"Shelby, get your ass out of here," he says.

"I know. I know. I'm late for work. Miss you already. Please be careful." I stand beside Jeronimo, and he gently punches me in the shoulder.

"We will be," he says.

I use my sleeve to dab the tears off my face and walk away, because if I stand there one more second, I'll cling to them until they pry me off.

My vision is blurry from tears the entire ride to work. The steering wheel takes most of my emotions because I squeeze it until my knuckles cramp. Once I pull up to the building, I take a few minutes to sip some cool water and look at my face. It's red and blotchy from crying, and any signs of makeup are washed away.

I want to believe they will survive this, but Lazarus City has taught me that nothing is fair or predictable. My fingertips rub the mascara that's crept out of place, and I open my door into the hot summer day.

The air conditioning blasts my skin once inside the office, so I pull a sweater out of my bag immediately. My co-workers are mostly fellow survivors with various backgrounds that make them good at our jobs. We're not licensed, but we underwent extensive training on what we can offer those seeking support. I scramble past everyone and head to the break room, where I unload my lunch into the refrigerator. I can let myself fall apart when I'm alone tonight and consider Mona's gift, but now I need to work.

Or I need coffee.

I brew a new pot and pour it into a mug, letting the heat bite my fingers through the ceramic. My heart rate rises without warning as the uneasy sign of anxiety trickles through my body. Why am I letting them go without me? The story and all the terrible endings that could happen replay over and over again.

Stop. I have to stop this carousel of intrusive thoughts.

What if I faced this fear again? I left Baltimore because that's what Renee wanted. If I returned, could I find the closure I need?

"Shelby? You working today?" my manager calls from outside the break room.

"Coming!" One more sip of hot coffee, and I tell myself it's okay to leave these thoughts for now. I pinch my eyes closed and say a silent mantra; *everything will work out how it's supposed to.*

I turn to leave the room and run directly into someone. Hot coffee leaps from my cup. "Shit!" It burns my fingers.

"Holy fuck! Hot!" the man yells. He pulls his dress shirt away from his body, so the scorching coffee doesn't rest against his skin.

"Oh, my god! I'm so sorry." I put the coffee in the sink and quickly wrap ten paper towels around my hand to dab the man in front of me. His light blue shirt is ruined, and coffee is dripping off his chin.

"Leave it. It's fine!" he says, and when he looks up, my heart drops. It's Jason Foley. His dirty blond hair is trimmed short, and he's wearing glasses again. There's no longer a scraggly beard hiding the dimple in his chin.

"Jason, what are you doing here?" I ask.

"Getting coffee thrown at me, apparently." He unbuttons his shirt and pulls it off, revealing a stained white shirt underneath.

"I'm really sorry."

He looks at me and grins. "Sure that wasn't on purpose?"

I laugh effortlessly and then shake my head. He always diffuses a situation with a single line. It's a gift. And he's clearly kept up with working out too, so, yeah. The reasoning side of my brain hums, and it all floods back.

We wait for the other to say something. I want to ask Jason why he won't take me with his team, but he'll smooth talk some sweet answer to convince me he's right.

"Do you have another shirt?" I ask.

"There's a set of gym clothes in the car. I'll go change." Before he leaves, he steps closer to me. Closer than he's been in a long time, and then says, "Follow me."

"I'll tell my boss I need a few more minutes."

We leave the break room, and the floor is busy with people standing with ticket numbers in hand. My boss is a short older woman with curly white hair. She's been doing social work long enough to recognize I need a break before asking.

"Don't be long. We have a full day here," she says.

"I won't."

Jason leads the way out the front door and into the sun, which seems too bright to be real. The summer humidity quickly transforms my cold, air-conditioned, stricken body.

I can't imagine what Jason has to tell me. He's already apologized for what happened, though I'm not sure he has a reason to do so. I forgive him. I wanted him to move on and leave without guilt or anger over our failed relationship.

We stop at a silver truck, and he unlocks his door to get to his gym bag in the backseat. He pulls off the stained and wet undershirt and throws it in the back of the truck. My cheeks warm at the sight of his torso.

"That's going in the trash," he says. Then he pulls on a fresh navy poly-blend t-shirt and looks down at his pants. "I don't think shorts would go over well." There's a brown stain around his crotch, but the khaki pants hide it well.

"Again, I'm sorry," I say.

"You're pissed, right?"

My mind jumps from Jason breaking up with me and then to his team going into the city. "I understand why you didn't ask me to go back in with you," I try to sound convincing.

"The government is running supplies into the city. Soon they will start a massive campaign to cure the infected. Anyone who isn't on that train will die or be imprisoned." He jumps right into business.

I've heard this before. The timeline is unknown, but there are hundreds, if not thousands, of infected who need the cure before the final train runs.

"Why the brute force? Can't they get on board with the cure now that Dr. Warren showed it works?" Those trials are saving hundreds of people already.

"Um," Jason mumbles and rubs the back of his neck. A tick of his when he's stressed out or angry.

"Here we go again," I say. He has more information, and I either have to pull it out of him or find the answer elsewhere. "This is why we can't be together, Jason. You keep too many things from me."

"No, we can't be together because you're in love with Dean."

I hug myself protectively. "Of course I love him. I will never stop caring. What we had was different."

"You can't have Dean as your husband and me as your... whatever the fuck we were doing. Our relationship was going nowhere because you're hung up on Dean getting out of the city."

"Hung up on Dean's freedom? What are you fighting for? Why are you going back inside if you're not hung up on getting people out too?"

"That's different." Jason steps back and looks around the parking lot in case our fight is drawing attention, which it is. He closes his truck door and jerks his head to the left, signaling me to follow.

"Why, so we can fight in private?" I snap.

"No, because I actually have something to tell you that doesn't have to do with us."

"Oh."

We walk down the sidewalk and towards a picnic table under a tree. The breeze and shade break up the heat better than the blacktop.

Jason sits first, and I sit across from him. His grin reminds me of the more leisurely days we had when we moved into an apartment together. We fell into a routine too easily. Work, dinner, Jessie, not that he took Dean's place because there is no comparison.

41

Even though we're far from others, Jason whispers. "I still have the ring."

"I thought this conversation wasn't about us?" A lump forms in my throat, and I force down the screaming tears that want to burst free.

"Shelby, I can't take you inside because you're not built like the others. You need to take orders better. I mean, you overthink everything."

"Wow, you are digging yourself deep!"

"Fuck." He laughs with me. "I love you, okay? There's no fucking way I'm bringing you back into that city."

"Jason, we've hardly talked in over a year."

He shrugs, and I know I hold the same torch for him. When he tried to give me a ring, I froze. How could I marry someone when my husband was fighting for his life in a decomposing city? It didn't seem fair, but there's more than our love for one another to consider.

"I need to get to Dean," Jason surprises me. Their relationship was always curious, and he never explained what happened with Fat Man's death. "Dr. Warren told me he's the last sour, and if the wrong people catch him, it'll be bad."

I've been putting this together, but not quite to this extreme. "Dean never answers his phone. Does he realize what's happening?"

"He does, but I'm not sure he knows what to do about it. I'm going to cure as many infected as possible. We're opening the convention center and bringing beds in from local hospitals. That's the mission everyone will see, including Angela and Jeronimo. Dr. Warren has also tasked me with keeping Dean off the radar."

"Can he get out?" He can't board a train and ride home with others. They do a health check and run stringent records on everyone who leaves.

"I'm working on it."

"There's more, isn't there?"

He grins. "Always."

"I want to go in with you." If I don't say it, there could be doubt in his mind.

Jason reaches across the table and cups his hand over mine. "I know you do."

seven

Shelby

HE WILL COME TO KNOW TRUE TERROR THAT NEVER DIES WELCOME TO THE SHOW

"How long has it been since they left?" my sister, Carley, asks as we set the table for Sunday dinner at my parents'. A headband holds back her short blonde hair, and she's got streaks of guacamole on her shirt from one of her daughter's tiny fingers.

"Over two weeks." Jessie circles my feet, hoping I'll drop food from the table.

Outside, my dad handles the grill wearing an apron that says, "License to Grill." He flips the hamburgers onto the plate and will be through those doors in a matter of seconds.

"Any word from Dean?" Carley asks.

"No. Can we table this for now?"

She shrugs. "Why haven't you called Ivan? Those two probably talk all the time."

My dad interrupts us by placing the platter of food in the center of the table. "Talk about what?" he asks with a curious smile.

"Nothing," I say to avoid this conversation. Anytime Dean is brought up, it's a topic that circles the room for hours. Everyone finds it necessary to tell me what Dean is most likely doing. He's fine, they say. He's probably running the show; they seem to know it all. Dean will get out one day, they assure me.

Carley rolls her eyes. "Dean hasn't reached out to Shelby, but Jason is supposed to find him."

Sisters can be the best and worst within minutes.

"Dad," I say, "can we avoid this topic tonight?"

"Sure, sweetie. Nothing to talk about. Let's eat dinner." My dad, always good at avoiding uncomfortable conversations, claps his hands and calls out to others. "Dinner! Come and get it while it's hot!"

The grandkids burst through the door, their cheeks kissed by the sun and hands dirty from playing in the garden. Renee waddles in, pregnant with her second child, as Roscoe bolts past her, trying to keep up with his cousins. My mom and my other sister, Anne, carry large baskets full of green beans and head for the kitchen.

"Let us wash up," Mom says in a sing-song way.

Anne scoots the kids to the sink after she's dropped off the basket. "Say the alphabet, the entire thing. Your hands are filthy." Her long brown hair is braided, and she's wearing a straw hat to block the sun. She looks just like me and Renee, which is ironic because Carley, my bossy twin sister, looks nothing like either of us with her lighter features. My mom jokes that if we weren't born on the same day, she'd think Carley was switched at birth.

Thomas and my brothers-in-law are golfing, so tonight is special. It's just my parents, the kids, and sisters—a sense of belonging changes when it's the original six of us. I can't put my finger on it, but I pretend more in front of the men. The kids roar into the room, arguing over who sits where. After a few minutes, we settle in, and they banter while my gut twists with nerves.

I should talk to Ivan. It's possible he's heard more than me. This map that Mona gave me could be dangerous, and I'm trying to figure out how to bring someone into that.

"Shelby?" Anne asks. "Did you hear what I said?"

"No, repeat it?"

"Have you seen the news? The cure has been all over it. They're dropping more rations because so many need them. The train is taking in the military. Any word on Dean?"

And there it is again. I can't be around family without Dean's ghost sitting next to me. No wonder Jason left. He's constantly walking in the shadows of a man he hardly knew. I don't think they mean to do it. They took to Jason, but how many lovers have been in this situation? It's territory we're entirely unequipped to travel.

"Carley suggested I reach out to Ivan, and I will. Tomorrow, of course, since it's already getting late."

Carley, perking up after she hears her name, jumps in. "I'll take you right now."

"What? That's crazy. We just sat down to dinner." Why is she so invested in this?

Renee laughs uncomfortably. "Carley, this isn't a reality TV show. This is Shelby's life."

"I know that, *Renee*," Carley says her name slowly to drive the point that she's irritated. "Ivan probably knows when Dean can come home. Others are getting out, so why not him?"

I've never told them Dean is sick. Who would they slip and tell? What questions would they ask? They wouldn't be able to see him in the same way. Renee and Thomas agreed to keep it between us, which keeps the secret of sours close. They think he's in a leadership role and he chose to stay behind, only he's become hard to reach.

Anne smiles at me weakly from across the table, feeling bad for bringing it up.

Renee picks up an ear of corn and shakes it at Carley. "Ivan isn't a box of locked knowledge. He's just a guy mourning his mother and lost brother. You should leave him out of this." She takes a bite to avoid saying something that will stir the conversation in an ugly direction.

"And how would you know?" Carley folds her arms over her chest and examines Renee.

This is dinner at the Bolger's house. Five women coming together and getting into each other's business, but usually, it comes from the right place. The two go back and forth, not making any sense until my mother interrupts.

"Girls. Let's take a breather." Mom turns to me with a soft grin. "Shelby, darling. Dean is a special man and honorable for staying behind. We love him and want to see him freed. So whatever we can do to support you, please tell us." My mom's gaze circles my sisters. "You girls are not being helpful."

Anne quietly says, "Sorry. It's interesting how they're getting more people out after all this time. This time next year, we could eat dinner next to the harbor again."

They haven't seen the city like me. I witnessed one year with no one taking care of the streets and buildings, and it took a toll. Having restaurants open anytime soon is a dream made up by outsiders. Still, I smile at her, and I hope she's right.

Dinner continues when Carley asks Renee questions about the nursery she's putting together. It's a more joyful topic than my depressing situation.

We clear the table once we're done and put dishes away. My dad comes to me and gives me a nudge.

"Come with me for a second. I want to show you something."

I put down the dishtowel and follow Dad into the garage. It smells of wood from his crafts and oil from the lawn mower stored in the corner.

"What's up, Dad?"

"Honey, I know you want to go back."

My jaw drops open. I've stared at the map for hours but never mentioned it to anyone. I feel betrayed in some way. How have I given myself away?

"No, I don't." The lie spills out too easily.

Dad grimaces and hums when thinking of what to say next. "Yes, you do. You've been through a lot, dear. More than I could ever imagine. Truthfully, I'm impressed by how much you and Renee keep it together."

"Dad, do you know what you're saying?"

"I do." He rubs his arm and looks at the ground. "There are fewer infected now, and I trust Jason to keep you safe. He's a good man, and I'm sorry things didn't work out for you two."

"That means a lot. Thank you."

"Look, honey. Don't tell your mom I said this, but do you see that black box in the corner over there?" He points to a dinged-up metal box under his workbench. "There's a handgun and a few extra rounds. If you need it, the code is 1234. Yeah, not very original of me."

My eyes stay locked on the box my dad keeps hidden in plain sight. He's not much of a handgun person. Most of his hunting rifles are locked away in the safe they keep.

"I couldn't get into the city if I wanted to," I say.

"Oh, I bet you'd find a way. Maybe you and Ivan can find closure to what happened to Dean. I saw him at his mother's funeral all those years before. It was a sorry sight." I imagine Ivan had thought he had lost everyone in his family. The isolation must be difficult.

"I'll think about it." I reach over and bring my dad in for a hug. "Thank you for being so open-minded about this."

"1234. Take it with you," he whispers, as if he already knows I'm leaving.

Trees line the long driveway, and the evening sun shines through. Ivan hears the car pull up, and he walks out the front door to greet us. His dark brown hair is wet as if he just got out of the shower, and he's wearing athletic attire showing off his titanium prosthetic leg. Ivan was injured during an overseas drill when he was in the army. He lost his lower left leg, from the knee down, and was forced to come home for rehabilitation. It was almost ten years ago, and today Ivan lives alone in a cabin deep in the woods. I miss seeing him. Not just because he reminds me of Dean with his laid-back disposition, but they look so much alike with tan skin, dark eyes, and thick brown hair. The type of features that say kindness, strength, all while being men of few words, with a lot to say. Maybe I read him this way because he reminds me of Dean so much.

"Shelby and Carley. It's rare that a set of twins shows up on my doorstep." He grins wide, revealing dimples under his scruffy beard. Jessie darts over to him, and he kneels to pet her.

"Cute," Carley says, smiling back. I considered coming on my own, but I wasn't sure how long I'd be here, so I need a designated nighttime driver. "We're here on business, though."

Ivan rubs his chin. "Your text didn't mention business, but I guess we need beer."

We follow him inside the small single-level cabin and join him at a wooden table. I'm thankful for the air conditioning and the cold beer he places next to me. This place is, by all means, the typical bachelor pad with no curtains on the window, mixes for muscle gain on the counter, and a row of dirty sneakers next to the door. Ivan is a reader with shelves of books lining shelves in the living room. He'll happily discuss the classics. A conversation I can rarely follow in depth.

I address him carefully to butter up the conversation. "I'm sorry I haven't been by in a while, but it's good to see you."

"Likewise. Without Dean around, we've fallen into our habits." Ivan takes a drink from his beer, and I watch the condensation drizzle down the dark bottle.

"Are you keeping busy?" I ask.

But before he can answer, Carley interrupts to rush us along. "Ivan, Shelby wants to get into Baltimore to find Dean and bring him home. Jason is inside, so he can help."

"Carley, really? Jason isn't part of this." I wish she wouldn't bring up Jason in front of Ivan. The two met, but it was hard to tell what they thought of one another. Then again, it's convenient that Carley assumes a man is my only reason for wanting to return. Does she think I make all my decisions with my heart?

He slowly raises his hands. "No, it's okay. You can't wait for my brother forever. I don't think we can call this your typical breakup situation, right?" Ivan knows Dean is a sour, but this is kept in a tight circle.

"You love Dean," I say.

"I do." His eyes fall on me sincerely.

"You haven't talked to him in a while?"

"No. I was hoping you did?" Ivan confirms what I expected. Dean has pulled away from both of us.

"I haven't."

Ivan shakes his head. "I think it's tough. He knows he's stuck in there forever." Ivan finishes his beer and places it on the table. I find his gaze more serious than before. "I want to get him out. So if you need my assistance, then let's do it."

"Dean is not stuck in there forever!" Carley yells, startling Jessie. "You can get him out and then move past all this."

I stare at my sister, deciphering her suggestion. "Is that what this is about? You think I'm hung up on Dean?"

She stumbles for words and looks out the window to avoid me. "What you and Renee went through is impossible. Dean should be moving on too."

While I agree Dean deserves to be here, like everyone else trapped inside, what waits for me is chaos, terror, and nightmares beyond Ivan's imagination. Can I bring him into this?

I face Ivan. "It's bad inside." He needs to be prepared.

"Are you worried about my leg?" He's not angry at me, but that's not my point. I don't doubt he could keep up if not even leave me in the dust. But he has to rest his leg and take the prosthetic off. If we had to run when he wasn't prepared, that could get him killed.

"They come out at night. That's when we're most vulnerable, so we must travel during the day. If we're on the street after dark, we need to get as high as possible or find a working door. Do you snore?"

"What? Me?" He smirks. "Never."

I pound my fist on the table, causing them both to flinch. "I'm serious! If you snore, they detect you. They will stop at nothing to get you." Rage unexpectedly builds in my throat. "I've been in a house when they've heard me. They ripped away the plywood we nailed to the window frames. After they broke through, they swarmed into the house. They don't care if they are hurt, cut, or whatever else. They keep coming!" Images of moaning, hissing, infected, overtaking the space I thought was safe fill my head. Their teeth ripping at my friends. If he doesn't take it seriously, it'll be impossible to go inside with him.

Carley waves a hand in front of my face to get me out of the panic daze I'd entered. "Maybe this is a bad idea. I guess I thought you would be okay, you know? Stay off the street at night and find Jason to protect you."

I jerk my head in her direction. "Stay off the street at night? If you make the slightest sound in a quiet city, they will track you down and won't stop trying until the sun rises again. Jason can't protect me from that."

"Shit," Ivan says, his face paler than ever.

My gaze sways over them. "Carley, don't you say a word to Dad about this. It's not as simple as outsiders make it out to be. But Ivan, you need to be ready for this."

Ivan scoots his chair back and walks out of the room. I glance at Carley, and she shrugs. When Ivan returns, he has a red gym bag he drops on the table with a loud clunk. Then he unzips it to reveal a pile of guns, hunting knives, and gadgets I can't name.

"I've been waiting my whole life for this." He grinds his teeth and breathes deeply through his nostrils. "If my big brother needs an escape plan, you can count on me."

"Wow," Carley says, reaching for the zipper to close it. "Can we take this off the table, please?"

Ivan removes the bag and places it at his feet. "I mean it, Shelby. You're not going into that concrete maze without me."

"I need you," I admit. "There's a lot more to share." He deserves to know about the map, but not in front of Carley.

"A few of my buddies worked with the train system the last time this happened. They can reach out to them, but security is

tight. You'll need to tell me where to go when we're on the inside."
Ivan says.

"There's someone I can call."

It's not that I haven't reached out to Mike. After the last train arrived two years ago, and we ushered hopeful survivors through the system, we didn't get intel suggesting Fat Man's people were convening on the outside. If I get in front of Mike, he might be interested in what I could find in the city. He's always been a man of means.

eight

Dean

A TICKET TO LEAVE AND EXTENDED BY YOUR HAND MY FINAL REPRIEVE

Pizza squawks and stretches his wings while we sit on the wide steps of the yellow mansion. The clouds are rolling in this afternoon, and a clap of thunder rumbles in the distance. The sweet scent of rain is growing stronger.

"Just another summer storm, Pizza."

He caws and clicks in his crow ways before flapping and flying into a nearby tree. This bird has been able to fly for a while but doesn't leave. Can't say I mind. Someone keeping me company in this deserted place is nice.

From his perch, he continues to caw louder. It may be the storm bothering him or something else. The wind picks up, and I can tell it'll be significant. I don't check my phone to avoid more responsibility. While I want to be there for others and continue providing them with protection, I'm figuring out what to do with Lion's information.

The sky brightens and dims in the distance as the lightning grows closer. A gust of wind kicks up dust and knocks my hat off.

"Come on, Pizza," I call, but he stays on his branch, cawing his little head off. "What's your deal?"

Then I notice someone walking up the road toward the main entrance. The cloudy sky allows me to focus my gaze, and Jason's bushy hair, along with his two friends, comes into view. I heard they were here, but I wasn't sure how soon they'd visit or *if* they would.

"Dean?" Jason shouts over the thunder and wind.

"Come inside," I say reluctantly.

The three of them march up the steps after me, but Pizza won't have anything to do with it. I usher Jason and his crew through the door, glancing back for Pizza. He's a wild animal, and he'll be fine outside in a storm, yet I hold on to the feeling that he'll leave if I turn my back.

The wind picks up leaves and debris from the sidewalk and carries them up the steps as gray clouds tumble above. A flash of lightning raises my arm hair. Pizza is silent in the tree as it sways frantically in the rough breeze. I wave to offer him shelter, but he remains in his place.

"Dean, you coming?" Jason says from inside.

"Yeah." I let the door slam shut by the wind. Pizza will have to be okay. "We can meet in the banquet area. It might provide enough light for you all." I lead them down the hall to an open space where weddings and formal events were held. The exterior walls are windows from top to bottom, which is why I don't generally come in here.

"Nice setup," Jeronimo says. I've never trusted this guy, and now he's living with Shelby. It's a mystery how that arrangement came about. I get the sense that Shelby and Jason are no longer an item. I can't say I hate the idea, even though he's decent enough.

"We used this for meetings when others lived here." I point to a table and set of chairs. "You should ride out the storm, anyway."

Angela smiles, unsure of how to address me. From what I remember, she's good friends with Shelby. I want to ask her about Shelby, but I want to see how formal this meeting is.

"You don't sleep during the day anymore?" Jason asks.

"Oh, I do. At least once a day, I circle the property." I hate small talk. Can we get the uncomfortable question out of the way? "Why are you here?"

Jason eyes me, a bit surprised. "We're accelerating the numbers of cured before the trains stop running. They'll only run for a short time before the military sweeps the city."

"And that'll be bad," Jeronimo adds.

"What do you mean bad?" I ask, wondering if they have the same information Lion does about my condition and how others might come after me.

Jason opens his bag and pulls out a laptop. He shows a color-coordinated map in different shades of blue. "This is where the infected population used to be high." His finger trails along the darker blue areas downtown. "But that's not where they are now." Next, he points to the outskirts of the city; all areas I'm familiar with.

"Well, downtown is where runners and sours were stationed. Maybe we pushed the rotters out?" I suggest.

"Or Fat Man removed them." Jason widens the map so we can see the entire border around the city.

"If he relocated them," I say, "it's the only good thing he did."

Angela shakes her head. "No, dude. We think he killed them."

"Yeah," I say sadly, recognizing how stupid my statement sounded. The fires that Fat Man and his team would burn replay in my mind. Marcus, our fallen leader who turned against us, showed me their grotesque trick. They coaxed rotters into small buildings and then lit them on fire.

Jason turns off the screen. "The infected population is less than we originally thought."

"How did you get these images?" I want to know which team Jason is playing for. He may have been a runner, but something tells me he's in here with more power than when he left.

A clash of thunder makes us all stare out the window. Rain pelts against the glass and the trees dance fiercely. Nothing out of the ordinary for a summer storm in Maryland, but it's always enough to get me on edge.

"These are from the military," Jason says. "They've provided some information so we can aid their efforts. There will be more than one operation going on."

So he's with the government now.

"Tell me more about sweeping the streets?" I ask, curious how much he'll spill. There's also a part of me that wonders if Jason and his two runners are here to take me down. Lion said someone might come after me. Could it be the team that helped bring Fat Man down? I run my hand down to my hip, touching my hatchet.

"There are cured, and others who evaded the trains because they didn't want the vaccine or didn't have the means to travel to the train. Whatever the fuck their reason is, they're out there. The military wants anyone without the infection to be on a train soon."

Angela speaks up. "They will use force."

"I'd expect no less," I say.

"There's more," Jason continues. "The infected are being cured, but not all of them will make it. We're ramping up our efforts until the cut-off date, yet to be released. After that, any remaining infected will be removed."

I snort. "Removed? You mean shot on sight?"

Jason's voice raises. "You realize some of the infected are too far gone to heal, and the end goal is to reopen the city? We can't save everyone."

I lightly tap my fist against the table. Everything we fought to prevent Fat Man from doing will happen anyway. They're going to kill whoever is left over. What if one of those people is me?

"No doubt you have a hard job," I say. "I won't kill anyone that doesn't deserve it."

"I didn't ask you to."

"So, why the hell are you here?" He hasn't gotten to the point, and I'm sure they need my help with something. Gathering more rotters, probably.

"You're the only sour left. How long until that information is public knowledge?" Jason asks.

Here it is. This is where he tells me my life is in danger, and he gives a shit. "Maybe others already know," I say, trying not to sound defeated.

"What if I guarantee you a safe exit?"

My interest is piqued but guarded. How much control does Jason have here?

Another clash of thunder catches my attention, but the clouds are breaking up, and it will soon be over.

"I'm listening," I say, simply because no one else has presented me with options. Escaping on my own would be difficult, given the security around the perimeter.

"VioTech," Jason beings. "They have a lab and want to talk to you."

I jump out of my chair and back away from them—my hand lands on my hatchet. I shouldn't have let them in! They were so calm this entire time only to deceive me. "Get out of here!"

Jeronimo is up in a flash and holding a gun in my direction.

Angela stands slowly with her hands up. "Whoa. Whoa. What is happening?"

"Your boss wants to sell me to the highest bidder, that's what!" I shout, unhooking my hatchet and poising it to throw at Jason's head.

"No!" Jason shouts and quickly rattles off new information. "VioTech is working alongside the military, and so is Dr. Warren. She said we should use caution around these groups. I am working with Dr. Warren, just like before. Jeronimo, put your gun down."

Jeronimo hesitates before lowering his gun and holstering it. "You should warn me before springing news like that."

"Yeah. Okay. Well, I didn't think Dean was so amped up, and I didn't want to alarm you that VioTech was here," Jason says.

Angela's head twists back and forth as we are talking. "Seriously, what the hell is going on? VioTech is going to be inside with the military?"

"What are you saying?" I slowly lower my hatchet.

"Dr. Warren needs you to stay away from military operations. You can't go to Sinai or help with that mission anymore. If you do, you'll be on everyone's radar," Jason says.

"And that would be bad," Jeronimo repeats.

"I get that, thanks." I walk to the table to ease into my chair; everyone follows my lead. "How many bosses do you have?"

Jason rubs the back of his neck and scowls. "I've gotten myself in some trouble with VioTech. They tried to blackmail me into sharing information about the sours. I would never do that." He taps his finger on the table to drive in his point. "Dr. Warren helped me lead VioTech away from her studies. She's more advanced in the cure than they are."

"Why should I trust you?" I ask, trying to keep my frustration inside. If he's working for Dr. Warren again, I need to ask her about that.

Angry now, Jason says, "I took a bullet to protect my people. Fat Man came from VioTech, but there are worse out there, and I'm getting to know who they are. His wife, for one. She's the brains behind every move he made."

"That's what I've heard," I growl.

"Are there places you can go that wouldn't be expected? The zoo is targeted, and so is the aquarium." Jason puts away his tablet, suggesting our conversation is ending. "So is your old house on Patterson Park, and the row home you lived in outside of Hopkins. You can't go back there."

"I should become homeless?" I'm not taking orders from this guy.

"It's for your safety. I won't mention this to anyone. Not Aisha, Rob, or any of your crew. Shit, I didn't mention it to these two because I was afraid they'd tell Shelby."

Shelby. I'm silent and wonder if this is where he tells me how she is. Does she talk about me anymore?

Angela smiles at me. "While I am offended that Jason didn't inform me, Shelby and I are good friends, and I understand why he'd want to keep this from her. She and Jessie came to live with me and Jeronimo after..." she trails off.

"After what?" I ask.

Jason swings his backpack on and exhales loudly. "After she turned down my proposal."

"She did what?" I grimace. Something twists in my heart, but then it releases, and I chuckle. Before I can stop myself, I'm laughing so hard my cheeks hurt. She turned down Jason's proposal. My strange jittery laugh trails off when I think of Shelby remaining locked in our marriage when she should move on. That guilt quickly mixes with the idea that I could fix our marriage. Can zombies with superhuman abilities be married to regular people? Probably not.

Once I get my shit together, I say, "I'm sorry, Jason. I don't even know what to say."

"Yeah, thought you might get a kick out of that."

I wipe my grin clean when I notice that the tenderness of Jason's news remains fresh with him. How long ago was this? He's never given me reason to question his motive, and I realize I should heed his warning and make myself scarce. At the very least, it would mean I don't have to deal with Aisha or Jason for a while, and it'll give me time to call Dr. Warren.

"Okay, well, you need me to disappear. How long do I have?" I'll discuss Shelby later. For now, she's got a home with Jessie, and she's safe. That's enough for me to sit and process for another time.

"Now," Jason says.

"Today?" I run my hand over my hat and pull the brim down to cover my face more. "This is happening fast."

Angela interrupts. "We're here for you. Aren't we, Jason?"

"Honestly, Dean, it's better if we don't know where you are." Jason dips into the bag he's carrying and pulls out a phone. "This has a few important numbers programmed, and I guarantee it cannot be tracked. Throw out any other phones you have."

I take the phone from him and spin it on the table. What important numbers did he program?

"Can I think about it?"

"Not really." Jason walks to the exit, and his team follows. "We can't tell anyone we saw you today. Dr. Warren will talk to you when you're settled, but don't mention your location. We'll coordinate a drop-off nearby if we need to get you supplies and food."

I walk them to the front door, staying within the doorway because the storm has broken up, and the sun is bright.

Angela walks over to me and gives me a hug. "Shelby would have wanted me to do that." I wrap my arms around her and squeeze because it feels one degree closer to Shelby.

Jeronimo bounds down the steps, but Jason pats me on the back before leaving. "We're going to get you out of here."

"I won't hold my breath." I wave them off as they continue through the parking lot.

Before I close the door, a dark feathery figure sweeps down from the side of the building and flies into the mansion. Pizza is wet.

"Time to pack," I tell him, to which he caws as if he understands.

It's night, and time for me to leave. I search the mansion for anything I want to take. My hatchet, a few handguns I've collected, spare clothes, food for Pizza, and the new phone Jason gave me. He suggested the old phone was traceable. So I dump it in a bucket after I transfer a few more numbers.

This nagging feeling that I should call Dr. Warren picks at me, but I hesitate. Let's find a new home first. I'm not fearful of someone coming after me, but I'm curious about what they'd do to.

Pizza paces the front porch. I let him crawl up my arm and onto my backpack where he settles in, and together we leave the mansion for the last time.

The ghosts of those who lived and died here visit as I step through the main gates and into Druid Hill Park. There's no turning back now. Every evening I kept busy with made-up jobs or gathering rotters for the team. No more.

Jason promises me a way out. How strange it would be if this city wasn't my prison?

Pizza rests while I walk through the woods. I stare into the night, wondering where my first stop should be. Then I decide it'll be directly north. The quickest point to the wall, and I'll walk the perimeter until I figure out what to do next.

My new phone vibrates in my pocket, and Dr. Warren's name appears, so I answer. "Hello."

"Mr. Kaplan?"

"You got me."

"The phone is operational. That's good. Don't tell me where you're headed, assuming you left your previous residence."

"No problem," I say.

"Very well. I understand Jason Foley visited you, and I wanted to ensure you understood the danger."

I don't want to brush her off, but if one more person tells me there's a mysterious threat coming my way, I might lose it. "Message received."

Frustration grows in Dr. Warren's voice, but it isn't directed at me. "I've worked closely with our federal government to release the cured and survivors within Baltimore City. Getting those trains running again has taken a substantial amount of time and research."

"Why are you telling me this?"

"I've not had tremendous luck reviewing your symptoms from this distance. My progress on a cure for your unique strain is not going well. What I need is DNA from the original host."

The original infected host could be dead or a rotter too damaged to save. For all I know, it's someone who didn't turn at all, and they're on the outside living it up. If this is what she needs to cure me, it's hopeless.

"Sounds like I'm a sour for life."

Dr. Warren groans, which is very unlike her. "An opportunity will present itself; when it does, I am prepared."

But will I be? "Is there anything else?" I ask, eager to get off the phone.

"Yes! Shelby has contacted my brother, Mike Gillespie. I believe she plans to break into the city with your brother, Ivan Kaplan. He's a veteran of the armed forces, correct?"

"What?" I snap. Shelby and Ivan together? What is Shelby doing coming back here and dragging my brother with her? "Is she looking for me? Are they inside already?"

"I can't be sure, but I was certain you'd want this information. She asked for Aisha's phone number, which was provided to her."

"Stop them!" I shout, and Pizza flies off my backpack, his dark wings brushing my forehead. "You can't let them in here." I was so close to breaking off, and now this. How could Shelby be so stupid? And Ivan? He has no idea what he's walking into. The rotters move in herds searching for food. Shelby and Ivan will die if they don't have a secure place to stay.

"Mr. Kaplan, I'm not sure that's possible. I'm not involved with security and want to avoid causing attention to people entering the city without proper authority. If I were you, I would call them and tell them not to enter."

"No shit?"

"Your language is not appreciated."

I determine the one place anyone trying to find me would go, including Ivan and Shelby, is my real home. The one on Patterson Park that I lived in with Shelby.

I say, "I have to hang up," and pull the phone away, but I hear Dr. Warren shout, so I listen again. "What did you say?"

"I am working on a plan to transport you from the city."

"There is zero chance of me leaving here without Shelby and Ivan." I disconnect and change the course of my path.

The phone rests in my palm. It's obvious my next step is to call Shelby and Ivan. When I do, they don't answer, so I leave a message. I send them a text identifying myself, but they don't respond.

My eyes stay glued to the phone, waiting for something to happen. Why wouldn't they get back to me?

"Fuck!" I growl.

I have to find these two and keep them safe. My chest fills with fear and frustration. Why are they coming in here?

"Come on, Pizza!"

I stomp back to the mansion I just said goodbye to, ironically. Pizza flies ahead, knowing where to go. Did Jason put Shelby up to this? I send him a text because if I speak with him, there won't be anything good to say. It's in the middle of the night, but he responds quickly.

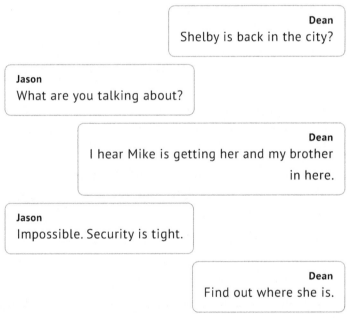

> **Dean**
> Shelby is back in the city?

> **Jason**
> What are you talking about?

> **Dean**
> I hear Mike is getting her and my brother in here.

> **Jason**
> Impossible. Security is tight.

> **Dean**
> Find out where she is.

He doesn't respond, but I know I've ruined his restful sleep. Why does Shelby want Aisha's phone number? I'm trying not to overreact by calling everyone to locate my wife. I don't want to be what drove her back here.

Once inside the mansion, I throw my backpack on the ground and prepare for a run. I have a few hours left, and I'll need to visit a few places: the train station to see if it's running again, and my old home.

nine

Dean

I T SMELLS LIKE SOUR
I'VE CERTAINLY FOUND SOMETHING
EMBRACE THE HOUR

The night ends quickly, and my brain is wired from hearing Shelby and Ivan are entering Lazarus City. There's only one thing left for me to do, and it's against everything I've been told. After I eat, I put on my hat and the special glasses Dr. Warren made. They make going out during the day easier on my eyes with UV-blocking technology beyond normal sunglasses. Dr. Warren said she's working on contacts that would do the same.

Pizza screeches at me as I leave the mansion for Sinai. He doesn't follow because I've exhausted him from the previous night. I wave him goodbye and sprint away.

Sinai isn't too far, but the hospital is eerily quiet once there. Aren't there supposed to be hundreds of rotters being cured here? I walk around the building without a soul emerging, so I text Aisha.

When she doesn't respond for a few minutes, I text Jason. But he's also silent.

Unsure where to go, I decide the train station might be an interesting place to check out during the day. Last night it was empty, but the tracks were clean of debris, indicating they'd been used recently. There's fencing and protective barbed wire surrounding the tracks, so people don't rush the train. They've learned from their previous mistakes.

When I arrive, there's a train sitting under the roof with passengers getting off and military in the area. As I draw closer, I can smell their cotton uniforms, their salty sweat, and the rubber on their boots. This could be the group to stay clear of. I want to look closely at them to know what I'm dealing with. They're each armed, and they carry canvas backpacks with supplies. Teams are unpacking boxes marked as medical equipment.

I need to figure out where my wife and brother are and then get them back outside. After that, I can tag along with their exit; better yet, they haven't made it inside, and I can worry about myself.

Aisha finally returns my message with a phone call.

"Dean, where are you?" she asks.

"I went to Sinai, but no one's there. Now I'm at the train station watching the military unload."

"We moved our patients to the convention center, but we'll begin operations at Sinai again soon. They're more equipped where the primary operation will be. You shouldn't come here! I've spoken with Dr. Warren and Lion."

Everyone knows I'm in trouble. "I need to see Jason. Is he there?"

"Yes. His team is planning their night raids to capture rotters. The military relies heavily on those of us who stay inside. Why do you need Jason?

"Tell him I'm on my way."

"Dean. Do not come here!"

I pull my hat low and run towards downtown where the convention center is. It's a large building, not very tall, but it has roadways around all sides for unloading for events. It's a good place to set up. They must be planning on rounding up hundreds of rotters.

The cars are dusty from being parked for years, but I notice more are to the side than before. The military is clearing a path from the train station to the convention center for easy access.

Outside, the building is crawling with military and those I suspect are cured survivors helping the cause. I don't have a good plan, and nothing comes to mind, so I set off on a direct path to finding Jason, reasoning if I look like I belong here, I'll blend in.

As I get closer, I can smell the salt on everyone, making me more nervous. I keep my head toward the ground and avoid eye contact. To the left, I find Jeronimo directing those with supplies. If he's close, so is Jason. My fist tightens. What ideas did he put in Shelby's head to get her in here? What promises did he make her? Or knowing Shelby, what is he leaving her out of that has her so desperate to get in? Either way, he had direct contact with her and could have prevented this.

Organized chaos is the only thing I can use to describe what's happening inside the building. There's a large open entrance with old signs for the last event. A gem and jewel show by the looks of it.

The air conditioning must have been turned on recently because the musk and humidity are slowly lowering. I search my surroundings and notice people with badges clipped to their clothing. As I walk through a crowded tight spot, I slip one off someone's belt and clip it to mine. To gain access to the lower level, which appears to be where they're setting up beds, I flash my badge, and someone waves me in.

In the distance I find Jason, and then about twenty feet away is Aisha walking over to him with her fists pumping. No doubt to tell him I'm on my way.

She reaches him and pulls him in to whisper. Jason, looking intrigued, raises his brows and searches the area.

Our eyes meet, and Aisha follows his line of sight that falls on me. Her face turns red with anger. I'll admit, I'm a little afraid of her when she gets this way.

A voice comes from behind me. It's a man, and he's not pleased. "You need to get the hell out of here."

I turn to find Jeronimo's angry glare burrowing into me.

"Not until I talk to Jason."

"We gave you a phone for that. You walked into a hornet's nest, idiot!" Jeronimo takes my arm and tries to lead me away, but I rip away from his grip and push him against the wall.

"Not until I talk to Jason," I repeat.

Jeronimo shoves me back and hisses close to my face. "You're putting yourself in danger, and everyone trying to help you. Get the fuck out of here, or I'll make you." He nods toward his ribs where guns are attached to his side. I'm significantly faster and stronger than him. That gun could be in my hand before he knew better.

"If you touch me again, I'll put that gun in your mouth and pull the trigger." I reach for his weapon, pull it from the sleeve, and point it at the ground just to show him what I'm capable of.

"Wow!" Angela jumps in from nowhere. "This isn't going well." She carefully reaches for the gun and takes it from me. With a nervous laugh, she hands it to Jeronimo. "Nice trick, buddy."

Before I realize it, Jason and Aisha have caught up to us.

Aisha steps up to me and, through gritted teeth, she murmurs, "Do not draw attention to yourself." She looks around the room. Others are busy setting up the operation, and we're undetected within the commotion.

"Shelby and my brother are trying to get into the city, or are already here, and this asshole knows something he isn't telling me." I point at Jason, ready to punch his ugly face.

"Hold up, boss," Jeronimo presses his fingertips into my chest, and I swat them away. "Shelby was not invited on this mission. She's home with Jessie and hopefully paying our rent."

I cock my head towards Jason. "That's not what I heard."

Aisha, the voice of reason, holds up her hands. "Meeting room, now. You are not airing your complicated relationship with this woman here." Then she leans in to whisper to me, "You need to be out of this main area."

"Fine. Lead the way," I say.

"Not everyone, just the two of you. The rest of us are busy." Aisha shakes some paperwork in her hand at my face.

Jason turns to leave, and I follow without saying another word to those gawking. Angela, however, walks with us to ensure there's peace.

They lead me to an office on the second floor, and once there, Jason punches the desk. "Are you insane? About fifty people here want to tie you up, drug you, and throw you on the next train out of here in a box labeled VioTech."

"Not my concern right now. Shelby is trying, or maybe she already is, inside this city. What do you know about it?"

"Nothing! We told her to stay away. Didn't we, Angela?"

Angela backs into a corner of the room and gives us a fake smile. "I mean, we suggested that very strongly."

Jason creeps closer to me and says, "I don't want her in here anymore than you do. I'll make sure security looks for her and your brother. There's only one way into the city, and that's the train."

I shove Jason back, so he'll give me my personal space. "You haven't told Shelby I'm being hunted, have you?"

"Of course not. I called her last night and this morning. She isn't answering my calls. Angela also tried but couldn't get through. She's avoiding us."

Or she's wandered into a pod of rotters, and they killed her. I need to find her, but I don't know where to go. I've left notes at all the places she might visit, and the phone calls are going nowhere.

"Did you try Renee?" I ask.

"Not yet. Look, Dean. If you choose to come around here, you need a better disguise." He turns to Angela. "Can you get him a military jacket and cap? If Shelby shows up here, you'll be the first person I tell."

Jason is trying to be cool. It's why I know he's an alright guy, but I still want to punch him. I agree to his terms, and Angela sets out to get what Jason suggests.

The two of us are silent until Jason says, "You love her?"

This got uncomfortable fast. "Yeah. But not like you think."

"We were engaged, or I proposed, and she said no. I dropped to one knee, asked her father for permission, and lit an entire room of candles."

Wow, this guy is more romantic than I am. I'd dropped to one knee outside a bar on New Year's Eve. I'd carried the ring around all night, sweating nervously.

"She said no?"

"Well, she didn't say yes. Because of you."

I sit on the desk, surprised. "Me?"

"Shelby can't be on the outside while you're in here. It completely consumed her. After we broke up, I cut off contact. I thought it would be best if I took myself out of the puzzle." Jason rubs the back of his neck and exhales. "I love her. I would never let her in this place."

My heart sinks, and I realize I've played this all wrong. "We need to find her."

"Yes, we do," Jason says.

Angela returns with military fatigues, a cap, and an ID card that says Robert Redford.

"Really?" I ask.

"I panicked, okay? There are people everywhere." Angela drops the items on the desk. "You're welcome."

"Thank you."

"You've calmed down, I see." Angela walks back to the door. "Time to go. Another group of military just arrived, and they look fierce."

I put the button-down shirt over my t-shirt and pull the pants over my shorts. This is what Ivan used to wear. For a second, I recognize how lucky I am that he's traveling with Shelby. He's trained, smart, and quick.

Before I leave, I say to Jason, "I'll see you soon."

"Dean. You've got to keep a low profile. If they get a hold of you, your strain of the virus will eventually be duplicated. We don't want that."

69

"I hear you. Robert Redford might stop by again, but I won't do it unannounced."

With more pressure sinking in around me, my goal has shifted. Find Shelby and Ivan. Make sure they aren't trapped in this city. Then get out of here for good.

Nothing will be resolved today.

I walk away without an escort, which would be more suspicious. On the way through the crowd, I catch the scent of something familiar. I take a second to place it, but it reminds me of a rotten orange cooking in the sun.

Sour.

There's another sour here.

My heart quickens, and I scan the room, inhaling as I do. If there are sours here, they can also smell me. It can't be anyone from my old group because they're cured or dead.

The front of the building is built with glass doors, so there are multiple ways to enter and exit. Standing near the far side of the room is a group of individuals who have a look to them. Their skin is tighter, their muscles pronounced even under their fatigues. These humans were made in the lab. I can tell from here they weren't plucked at random on the street like my community was. They were hand selected. The men are giants, and the woman similar. Notably, there is one man who is over seven feet tall. He is a Black man with a shaved head and eyes so dark I wonder if these are the contact lenses Dr. Warren referenced.

They are me, and I am them.

Given there's a group of them, they won't pick up my scent outside of their own. A chill runs down my spine. It's been a long time since I've seen another sour.

I rush from the building. As soon as I'm out of sight, I sprint so unnaturally fast it would draw attention.

If this is who is hunting me, I have a real reason to be afraid.

ten

Shelby

**TIME FALLING LIKE SAND
RETURNING ME TO THE PAST
A FEROCIOUS LAND**

The computer screen flashes to life in front of Mike. It adds contrast to his dark features and thick beard. Ivan reaches for his reading glasses and the three of us sit at his kitchen table to discuss our plan.

Mike resembles the Johns Hopkins version of himself I'm most familiar with. He's gained his weight back and has a rounded belly, thick black hair, and darting eyes full of deep thought. I worry if I'm his equal, or if I'll always be catching up to him in some way.

"Here," he points at the screen showing us the convention center downtown. A building not easily missed. "This is where they're running the cure non-stop. It's intended to treat thousands of infected by this fall. Before the end of the year, the military can clean it out."

"Wow, that's fast." Ivan slurps his soda and keeps his eyes fixed on the screen. "I have our garb."

He's referring to the military fatigues he's picked up from friends, complete with made-up names sewn to the breast. We have boots, hats, and even canvas bags that match the professionals.

"Good." Mike pulls out two large envelops from his bag. They're marked with our initials. "Your identification. You'll need these badges and paperwork for the train. We'll figure out how you'll return once you find Dean."

His interest in Dean warms my heart. He knows how important he is to me, and our common goal is to get as many cured out of the city as possible. His sister developed the cure, and Dr. Warren is who I first met when I got to Johns Hopkins all those years ago. Dr. Warren's a strict woman, but brilliant, and I have faith in her abilities.

I slip my hand into the envelope and pull out my identification. This is real. It's happening. I'm going back to the city.

Anxiety sits heavy in my gut, making me have to pee every ten minutes. I've completely stopped eating until my body shakes, demanding food. Between Dean and Mona's stars, I'm unable to turn away from this. Sometimes we do things even if we're scared, and this is one of those times.

"Here are new phones," Mike says, pulling out two black flip phones from his bag. I haven't seen a flip phone in a while, and I smile at the mechanics. "These will protect your screen more, and they're compact. And they aren't traceable by anyone except me. If you get in trouble, call me, and I can find you. You've already turned off your personal phones, and you'll need to leave them here. I've programmed my number, and both of yours. That's it. Questions?" He's so serious that it takes me back. I've given thought to what we're walking into. A massive government operation to free an infected city from the crippling effects of rage, hunger, and death.

This has global attention. No precaution is too much.

Ivan gets up from his chair and brings over his bag of guns. "I couldn't secure military issued weapons, but these will look close enough." There are several Glocks, a first aid kit, rations, compass, and a few things I can't identify.

I run my hand over all the gadgets, but when I see it trembling, I pull back.

Mike looks at me. "Shelby, are you prepared to use these?"

Ivan interjects. "We'll go over it and the plan again tonight."

A cold flush runs through my bones as the men stare at me. "I'm fine. Just feeling jittery." A knock at the door causes me to jump.

Ivan stands and walks to the door. "It's your sister. She's here to get Jessie."

I'd forgotten Carley was coming by. I'm relieved to see her for another moment, but I also worry that she'll see how frightened I am. I can't be talked out of this. Not when I'm already on the verge of a panic attack.

Carley walks in and kneels to pet Jessie. "Hi old girl. You're staying with me for a while." She walks over and wraps her arm around mine. "Can we talk outside for a minute?"

The sun is high this warm afternoon. I willingly go outside and suddenly wish I had a cigarette, which is bizarre because I haven't smoked since college.

My sister reaches for my hands and stands in front of me. "You good? You look like you might faint."

I force a grin. "This is happening so fast. I'm just worried we won't find Dean." I'm worried no one will be able to protect me from the murderous monsters. I can't say that to her. She has to know the chances of me coming out of Lazarus City twice aren't good odds. The infected are being herded, but they aren't off the streets.

"Stay close to Ivan. He'll help you find Dean. You said you have places you're checking first, right? We're all rooting for you."

"Yes. And once we find him, we'll have to figure out an exit strategy." My family has rallied behind me to go find Dean and bring him home. If only they understood the full reason why it has to be me. It could take time to find Dean, and I've got no idea what condition he's in. The end of this plan will have to remain open, even if I'm not comfortable with it.

Carley reaches into her purse and pulls out something wrapped in burlap. She carefully unfolds the layers of fabric to reveal my dad's handgun. "He insisted I bring this to you."

I take it from her, check if it's loaded, which it is, and wrap it up again. "Thank you. Ivan has what we need. It has to match what the military carries." I miss my knives. They sit on the top of a closet along with Yeji's gun in the last house I lived at in Baltimore. "Tell Dad I'll be okay." I hand the gun back to her.

"Okay, I don't like long goodbyes, and this isn't a goodbye because I'm going to see you again soon!" She jumps toward me for a long, tight hug. Then she takes my hand, squeezes it four times, one for each sister. My tension gives way for an instant. Maybe it's Mona's spirit telling me this is going to be okay, or my sister's reassurance. My anxiety rests for a moment, and then my stomach gurgles.

Carley laughs. "Are you hungry?"

"I must be." I pull away from her and dab at the tears dampening my cheeks. "Get out of here with my dog. Take care of her, and Mom and Dad. I love you."

"I love you too."

I stand by the minivan and watch her get Jessie into the car. Jessie has a sad look on her little white face, and her brows rock back and forth as she tries to read the situation. I walk over and give her another pet and a kiss on the head. "I'll be back soon. And I'm bringing Dean with me." She wags her tail and licks my face.

They pull away, and Jessie watches me from the back window. We stare at each other until my sister turns the corner out of sight.

"You going to be okay?" Ivan asks from the porch.

"I'll have to be."

"We're going to do some practice tonight." He's referring to target practice. I've been to the range with Angela. The controlled environment heals the trauma of using a gun to defend myself. The problem is, I won't be in a controlled environment.

Images of April's body jolting when I emptied the gun into her body flash before me. "I know how to use one," I say. "I'd do it again if I have to."

"Let's hope not, but we'll be prepared. Come back in when you're ready. Mike has a few more things."

I follow Ivan inside to find Mike with a map on the computer screen again. When he sees I've returned, he points to several areas around the city. "This is the train station. You'll arrive early in the morning, but so you aren't suspicious, you'll have to unload cargo and walk to the convention center. From there, you'll slip away."

Ivan points to the screen. "We should go to the aquarium. It's not too far from there and it's a place Dean visited."

Mike shakes his head. "That place has been long emptied. My sister says to try the zoo first. Then any other place you may have seen him, Shelby. We'll need your help here."

I point to an area near Johns Hopkins, and then to the home we used to share near Patterson Park. "He could be in one of these areas. Can we ask Aisha if we see her?"

"I'd rather not let others know you're coming in."

Ivan groans. "Why doesn't he just answer his phone?"

"I suspect he has a new one." Mike stands and stretches. "Well, friends. I should get going. You have what you need from me. The rest is up to you."

"Sure is," Ivan says.

After Mike packs up and leaves, Ivan and I flop on the couch to sit in the fear of uncertainty.

I pull my bag close to me, waiting for the right time. "I have Aisha's number if we get stuck, but I'd rather try to find him ourselves. If we call a bunch of people, then they're going to be tipped off we're coming inside. Also, there's something I haven't told you." The map that Mona gave me screams for attention, and I realize it's time for me to tell Ivan why I'm playing along with some of Mike's overly cautious rules like a phone that only has two numbers programmed.

I fetch the map from my bag. Ivan sits on the edge of the couch, curious.

"What's that?"

"Something no one knows about. Not my family, or Mike, or anyone." I spread it on his coffee table and tell him why Mona left it for me when she passed, and when Lindsay brought it over. Then I sink further into the mystery. "I'm not sure what we'll find, but it could shut down VioTech. I looked up the locations of these stars, and one of them was a small lab in Canton, another was at Johns Hopkins. It must have connections to VioTech."

"What in the world, Shelby?" Ivan groans.

"Okay, this sounds crazy, but hear me out. I was involved in a trial to test a suppressant, only I took it to another level with Mike's support. That drug is phase one of the cure. Mona knows I've been involved with things outside of the Rec Pier." I smooth the map out over the coffee table and point at the stars again. "This could bring down whoever is behind the creation of Lazarus City."

"Well..." he trails off. "Well. Well."

"This is pulling you into something bigger, and you're questioning some of my tactics for finding Dean." Straight and to the point is all we have time for, but I'm trying not to lose him.

Ivan goes to the fridge and takes out a brown bottle of beer. He cracks it open and takes a long sip. "I won't have this in Lazarus City."

"No."

"I'm drinking one more, then." He grabs a second one and brings it over with him. It's late afternoon, so I consider having one myself. A so-long to a world I just returned to, with all the demons dancing in my head.

"Ivan, you can back out, but I will be on that train to bring Dean to safety and solve the clues on this map."

He hums and takes another sip. "This is kind of a big deal, yeah? This is protecting the world sort of stuff, and not a simple rescue mission." He grows quiet as he puts the bigger picture together. After several sips of his beer, he looks to the ground and says, "I agreed to protect my country when I joined the armed forces. If this is my next mission, then I accept. But you have to be honest and open with me. I cannot do this without all the information. Get a beer. Sit down."

I do as I'm told, taking a seat across from him in a brown cushy armchair. And then I start from the beginning. I tell him about what it was like when the virus first hit, and how I found Renee after

Dean went missing. What life was like in the hospital, and then at the Rec Pier before the fire. The details about friends I lost are difficult, but I share that too. He already knows about the sour's abilities and Fat Man through Dean. But my version of the story takes us well over an hour, and he has pizza delivered before he asks questions.

When I get to the part where I'm outside of the city, and welcoming newly released survivors, Ivan is stunned.

"You saw Lindsay when she first got out, and she didn't mention the map?" He has a good point, and one I've considered.

"I'm not sure Mona, god rest her soul, completed the map by then. She probably continued this mission when she left quarantine." I hope I'm capable of living up to her expectations.

"Do you want to find Dean?" His voice catches when he asks. Ivan thinks I'm abandoning his brother.

"Of course! Dean is the reason I want to nail VioTech. If it weren't for this virus, Dean and I would be together." Dean would want the organization that was responsible for the Lazarus virus to pay just as much as I would.

"My brother is why I'm going in, but I'll see to your map situation after we find him." He points to the map. "What are these stars?"

"That's what we need to figure out."

We spend the final hours before the sun sinks reviewing the map and having last-minute target practice. We'll look for Dean first and then use the map to carry on our secondary mission.

The next morning, we have to move quickly. Reporting to the train is at 0500 hours, according to our itinerary. Ivan drives us to the train station a few miles northeast of the city border. I'm shaking from nerves and not eating breakfast. If we're caught, we'll be imprisoned. If we're not caught, we'll be back inside with monsters.

When we arrive, I follow Ivan, trying to mimic his speech, walk, and confidence. There's something stiffer about him. The expression on his face reads business, order, and certainty. I have none of those feelings.

A group of others dressed like us are walking to a meeting area. Time is warping around me strangely. While the line takes an hour, it seems like only a few minutes. They ask for my identification and my numb hand pushes it at the desk person.

She stamps something, hands me a badge, and points me to another area. "Get your vitals checked, and you'll receive your full duties for today, as well as directions on leaving the city."

I didn't realize they had already scheduled people to leave. It's comforting, even if I won't be on that train.

"Thank you." I search for Ivan, who has been separated from me. Mike suggested we act like we don't know one another, so we plan to sit apart and keep to ourselves.

It's like a floodgate of people moving to different parts of the train station. Their feet follow in line, and I stay with them as best I can, keeping my head down.

After more debriefing, we're asked to board the train. I search for Ivan and find him a few rows head of my seat. I appreciate that he's in view.

Mike sends me a text to remind us to be careful, not to trust anyone, and to keep him up to date on what we find. He shouldn't worry. I plan to do all those things. It'll be helpful to have eyes on the outside, especially with his connections.

The train jerks, and as if I'm on a roller coaster cranking the carts up for a big drop, my stomach flips. What lies ahead for me? This map, my old key to figuring out the city, will again serve me.

eleven

Shelby

FAMILIAR PLACES
NATURE CONSUMING IT ALL
DIFFERENT FACES

All goes black, and then the sun flashes sharply. We pass through the last tunnel into Lazarus City. It's a jungle in the middle of summer. Trees and shrubs have taken over backyards, and vines swallow entire blocks. The weeds are taller than the average adult, breaking through the concrete and pavement. The city has been reclaimed by nature. It seems unrealistic we could ever save it.

The train passes by signs. Some are old, but others new. *Help Us! Survivors here!* Mark some of the front steps of row homes we pass. There are people here who want out. They've been inside for three years, and a portion was probably spent infected. Their physical health must be awful.

We pull up to the train station and those around me gather their things. I search for Ivan and see he's doing the same. He must be careful not to let anyone notice his prosthetic leg, which would be a deterrent for letting him serve in this capacity.

The train empties.

I'm here again. I stand and move to the exit.

Lazarus City.

My chest tightens, and I jump when the doors behind me close.

"Unload supplies over there," a man calls over the crowd on the platform. "Load the trucks in front of the building."

Someone pushes past me and bumps into my shoulder, then another one. I need to walk, but my legs go numb.

"I got you." Ivan takes me by the elbow and gently encourages me to move with him. "Look busy and no one will suspect," he whispers.

I do as I'm told, with tight lips and a warmth in my face that suggests I'm flushed with fear. Nausea picks at me, but I swear I'll throw up if I eat or drink. Everyone around me is calm. If I break this illusion, it'll be obvious I don't belong.

The boxes are marked with different medical supplies. Unloading takes several hours, and when we're done, they call for a short break where rations are provided.

"Force yourself to eat," Ivan says as he thrusts a box into my hand.

The food is bland but calms my nerves more than I anticipate. I don't speak, and I keep my head down. Someone comes over to converse with Ivan. I let them be social without me.

After the short break, we finish loading and securing boxes in several large trucks. Then we're instructed to walk to the convention center by following a leader. There aren't enough modes of transportation for us to catch a ride.

Those who haven't been in here before keep their hands on their guns, and their heads are in a constant swivel. The walk takes thirty minutes, and the afternoon heat is making it unbearable. No one reacts to the rising temperature. Another illusion, I suspect.

At the convention center, there are several teams of people moving about. I instantly search for someone I know, but there are too many faces, and no one stands out.

We're directed to large garage doors at the back of the building where we move the supplies in. It's painstakingly slow, and I'm almost at my end when the last few boxes are packed inside a storage area.

Ivan walks up behind me and whispers, "They're going to assign us different projects."

"If we go inside, it'll be harder to get out." I imagine everyone here has a purpose and a place to be. It won't take long for them to notice we're missing.

A man in charge directs us to take a break and to receive more rations inside before reporting to our next assignment. We hang back, pretending we're talking about something, and slowly drift away from the group.

Ivan points to a church across the street with a small park. "We need to ditch this clothing but keep it somewhere we can return to it if needed."

We carefully run across the street and behind the building, checking to see if anyone followed. There isn't anyone around, so we strip out of our hot army garb and into something easier to run in. In the packs we carry, I have a trash bag to keep our boots and fatigues in. I stash them inside a bush. Ivan and I look like everyday citizens, and I hope this doesn't draw attention to us this close to the convention center. I'm eager to move.

"The zoo." I wave my hand for Ivan to follow me, and we start off in that direction. The sidewalks are lined with grass tufts and sharp weeds that catch our shoes and scratch our legs. When I left the city, it was unruly, but this... this is unlike anything I imagined. I wonder if the wildlife is completely eaten, or if some of this brush has provided additional coverage.

"It'll be over an hour if we take small roads," Ivan says. He's familiar enough with the city to get to and from major points of interest.

"But if we take the main roads, we'll be spotted more easily, assuming people are still around in these areas. My biggest concern is getting us to the zoo. If Dean isn't there, we'll need to move on quickly. It's already later than I'd like."

The sun isn't setting for another few hours, but time will go by quickly. Once the sun drops, it does so without remorse.

"I'll follow your lead," Ivan says. He's become one of those people whose head is on a constant swivel.

Up ahead, a few people stand on the street. I can tell they aren't infected by their normal speech and mannerisms. When we pass, I keep my mouth shut.

"Where are you going?" An older man says. He's so thin, I can see his shoulder bones poking through his dirty t-shirt.

Ivan taps his gun. "Don't mind us, just passing through."

"I ain't gonna bother you. Just wanting to know where you're going." The man is irritated, but I get the sense that he means us no harm, so I interject before Ivan causes a scene.

"Druid Hill Park. I'm looking for an old friend."

Behind the thin man are to other men who appear in similar shape. Their teeth are the color of corn and broken. These are former infected.

The man speaks again. "You're from the outside?"

"We are," I say. "But I was here the first year. Now I'm back, looking for someone important to me."

He scratches his chin and purses his lips as he studies me. "Hope you find 'em. Watch out for the park. Them rotters are still wandering around pretty heavily at night."

Rotters. The insiders have adopted the sours lingo. I'll remember that to blend in. "I know what happens at night," I return carefully.

"Maybe you do." He passes his hand in the air. "Not all of us cured are friendly. Careful with yourself."

Ivan steps forward, but I put my hand up. "We'll leave you be." I tug Ivan's backpack, so he follows me.

When we're a fair distance away, he says, "They smell horrible."

"You get used to it."

We continue our walk and notice the men are following us. Ivan whispers, "Follow me. Let's lose them."

Walking down a narrow street, Ivan quickly ducks down another alley and then we zigzag through the city until we're out of breath. My heart is pounding, and I've no idea where we ended up.

"Do you think they're gone?" I ask.

"They were too weak to follow us that quickly." Ivan seems sure of himself, rubbing his knee from the extensive activity we've been through already. I don't mention anything because I know he'll speak up if his prosthetic is bothering him.

I get the map and find a road sign to figure out where we are. The city is like a maze, and we took a wrong turn. I twist the map around, trying to pinpoint our location.

"Are we here?" I point to an area south of the park.

Ivan looks at the sky and then down the street. "We need to go this way."

I've never walked this path before. I observe the row home doors for a secure spot for the night. We may have to come back this way.

Finally, we break through to the park, and I know the zoo is close. Ivan points us to the left, and I follow him through a field of overgrown weeds and shrubs. The thinner running paths are completely consumed by brush, forcing us to stick to the roads.

A beacon of hope emerges ahead. It's the arboretum, which is just outside of the zoo.

"Where was he in here?" Ivan leads us through the main gates of the zoo, and we walk past the gift shop, which has broken windows and vines crawling up the side.

"At the mansion. This way." I jog, hoping I can catch Dean before we have to scurry in another direction.

When we arrive, it looks the same as it did before. Nearly untouched by the city falling apart around it. He must be taking care of things. Dean has always been handy, and busy work gives him purpose. This place is drenched in Dean; I can feel it.

I run to the doors and throw them open.

"Dean!" I call out. "Dean, are you here? It's Ivan and Shelby."

Ivan bounds up the steps after me and we search the downstairs area quickly. Then, I run up the steps to the rooms on the second floor, calling out his name, but there's no answer. He'd probably be asleep, preparing for whatever his nightly plans are. Where could he be if not here?

I call down to Ivan, "He's not here." My voice shakes. "This is where Dr. Warren said Dean would be. Where is he?" I'm shouting at Ivan like he knows something I don't.

"Shelby, let's search the property before we panic, but it's getting late. Maybe we can stay here tonight."

"Let's go outside. The mansion is safe, and maybe he'll return."

Outside again, we go through the main animal exhibits. Each cage is either opened, or there are gray bones left where animals died. The polar bear exhibit is one of these. I remember seeing the dead bear when I first came here with Jason. The poor thing didn't make it, and now his bones are picked clean by rodents and birds.

"Should we split up? Cover more ground?" Ivan asks.

Separate.

I calmly take a breath in. I can do this. The zoo is abandoned. There aren't any sours or animals left to draw the infected. It's probably pretty safe, but I hate that word.

"I'll take North America. It's smaller, so I'll work my way around your area."

Ivan agrees, and we go on our different paths. As soon as he's gone, I realize how very alone I am.

Thoughts of terrible things happening crawl into my mind and make my scalp itch with dread. There could be infected hiding in one of the smaller buildings. The wind picks up and catches the dry weeds.

"Dean?" I call out weakly.

Could I hear footsteps? A tapping of something makes me whirl around, but it's a trapdoor in an animal cage caught in the breeze.

Not a human. Not a monster.

The trail I follow is kid friendly, with big turtles to climb through, a giant nest, and other obstacles that would entertain them. I jog through, tired, and my legs are growing weak. The sun is turning the sky an orange color, and I know we need to get indoors quickly.

I'm about halfway through the exhibit when I hear animal screams high in the trees. Chimpanzees. They're free from their pen, and I worry other animals might be too. It causes me to run faster, searching the area for any clues of a living person, but there's nothing.

Only empty cages and moss-covered railings keeping me on the path.

I come to the end, disappointed there was nothing, and search the trees again for the chimpanzees. They're following me. I hope they stay where they are. I don't have food, and I don't consider myself to be food.

The large rhino exhibit marks the African exhibits. I search for Ivan, but don't call out because I fear it's getting too close to dark.

I am over halfway through and cannot find Ivan. The trail veers off and goes down to an elephant pen. Maybe that's where he is. Before I go in that direction, I stand quietly, tilting my head in different directions to see if I can hear something I missed before. A sound, a clue, something.

Then I hear a scream. A man's voice comes from down the hill.

"Ivan?" I shout, hoping to get a response, but nothing is returned. Only the rustling of leaves high on the giant trees.

I walk toward the scream and find a large structure behind the elephant house. There are no animals in the yard.

The sound of a people struggling against each other could be made up in my head, or it could be Ivan. The building is brown and dark, with several windows broken and the doors hanging open.

A soft grunt. Hiss. "Ah. Ah. Shhh." The siren of the infected.

There is a pop once, then twice. It's a gunshot, I'm sure.

I run toward the door, knowing Ivan must be inside, but it's so dark I freeze. A tomb for the infected. A hive. The echoing sound of hissing vibrating groans bounce off the walls. A shuffle of unsteady feet come closer to the door where I stand. I listen. I watch.

A gray hand with dark veins grabs the door frame, and a face appears so hollowed and sickly I can't believe this person can stand. A woman with black eyes and tangled white hair screeches into the fading day, knowing she can't come outside yet.

85

Tears break free. Could my death be a gift for things haunting my nightmares?

"Ivan?" I murmur softly towards the door. "If you're in there, I need a sign." God, please don't be in there. Please. We don't have much longer until they'll be after us.

There's a crash around the side of the building, and when I rush over, I find Ivan laying on the ground with broken glass around him. Arms reach out of the window after him, and I grab his backpack and pull him several feet away. He's covered in blood.

"Are you a bit?" I scream in a shaky voice.

"No. No. It's from the window."

A large gash runs from his temple into his hair, and his shoulder has a puncture wound. "Can you walk?" If we don't move, we'll never make it back.

"Yes." He groans and stands, limping. "I thought I heard someone in there, so I called out for Dean."

"You never go in a dark place!"

"Shit! I'm sorry, okay." Ivan breathing heavily through his teeth. He sees Lazarus City for what it is now.

I tug on him to move faster as the sun drops lower in the sky. The mansion is about a quarter mile away, and the hissing of infected waking for their nightly terror grows.

Their feet thump closer as they break from the building to follow us. Ivan's pace is slowing us down. He falls, and I yank him upright with strength I didn't know I had.

"Faster," I say quietly, hoping the infected have lost track of us. He drags his leg but keeps up as I pull him along. The blood from his head is seeping down his cheek and neck, soaking into his shirt. I wonder if they can smell it. Dean would have been able to.

"Shoot them!" he shouts, pulling his gun from the holster.

"No, it'll only make more come. This is a small group we can keep out of the mansion."

We reach the mansion, and I scurry to the main entrance with Ivan close to me. The doors are big, but they close easily. My fingers fumble with the locks, but I get it done. Then I drag nearby furniture to put in front, and we race up the steps to one of the rooms. I lock the bedroom door, and Ivan collapses on the tiled floor of the ensuite bathroom.

I hold my shaking finger to my lips and allow him to see the full terror of my expression. They'll kill us. Snuff us out of this world by ripping us open with their teeth.

Shut up.

Hold still.

Noises outside tell us the infected are there, rummaging around for an entrance.

Ivan groans, and I slap my hand over his mouth. His head is bleeding badly, as head wounds often do. I find a towel and press it to the cut. It could use stitches.

Carefully, I pull back his shirt to look at his shoulder. The puncture is deep, and I see fatty tissue bubbling out. I only know to put pressure on things like this, so I find another towel and hold it in place. Our first aid kits have gauze and tape, but nothing more substantial.

I whisper, "We stay here."

He nods.

Welcome to Lazarus City.

twelve

Dean

HELLO THERE, FELLOW
MANNERS WERE GONE LONG AGO
TEETH BROKE AND YELLOW

That sour man's face. He was something out of a science-fiction book. Tall, muscular, and the way he moved was mechanical yet graceful.

I have no doubt they have intel on all the places I've lived in Baltimore, but if Shelby is looking for me, these are also the places she'll go. I've put her in danger.

I'm in a home at the far east end of the city. It's not clean or comfortable, and it's been looted several times over. There's a bed that smells like pretzels and mildew, but it kept me far from the center of attention.

It's almost noon but sleep won't come. Tonight I'll go somewhere else. Somewhere more comfortable. How long can I do this? I text Dr. Warren to ask for a drop off somewhere in the east side. One thing I don't want to worry about is food. She'll respond with coordinates for me to grab and go. The drones are quiet and don't cause attention.

My phone vibrates with an incoming call, and I see it's Jason. He confessed to loving Shelby, and that feeling sits like a peach pit in my throat.

"Hey," I answer.

"Dean, I have news. Are you somewhere that you can talk?"

"Go ahead."

"I assume you saw them at the convention center," Jason says. I instantly know he's going to mention the gigantic sours that came in.

"Those sours were created in a lab, right? VioTech is my guess."

"Last night, VioTech provided us with night hunters, or that's what they call them. They say it's a different version of the vaccine that's being tested, and it makes recipients repel the infected."

"Sounds like a sour to me, only that team is bigger and stronger than anyone I know." I try not to let the concern in my voice come through.

There's a pause in the conversation, and I suspect he's going to tell me to keep hidden. I have no reason to cross paths with them unless it's to find Shelby.

Before he can give me a pep talk, I change the subject. "Why isn't Shelby answering her phone? I can't get through to my brother either. It's like both of them lost their phones at the same time."

Jason laughs nervously. "That's the real reason I called. A group of new recruits came in yesterday. They ran a manifesto before bed last night and discovered two cadets are missing. After reviewing surveillance, I suspect one of those was Shelby."

"You saw her face?" I need to be sure.

"It wasn't a clear picture, but I recognize her build. Trust me, it's her. The man she is with had a skin tone similar to yours. I'd say he was a little taller." Jason waits for me to say what he's already suspecting.

"It was Ivan Kaplan, my brother."

"Seems it could have been. We searched where they went off camera and found clothing with different names, but my suspicion is the same."

They've been in the city for one night. Shelby is smart enough to keep them out of trouble, but where would they go first?

"What is the military doing about it?" I ask.

"Nothing. Everyone is too busy. The night hunters are working. It would be better if you get to them first. I can't get out now, not with more teams coming in and our first groups of infected coming in."

They would notice he's missing. I get it.

"The zoo will be my first stop," I say. "Then I'll circle around to other places Shelby might know. I'll check in."

"Before you go, I wanted to mention Mike gave Shelby a new phone, but I don't have her number yet. As soon as I get it—"

"Mike?" That lunatic brother of Dr. Warren's? What's his position this time?

"Yeah. He got Shelby and Ivan in here with fake identification."

"Damn it!" I guess I can't be mad at Jason any longer. "Who's Mike working for?"

"I don't have the answers, Dean, but we have the same questions. I'll hook up with Dr. Warren and dig around a little. Let's touch base later. I might be able to get up to Sinai for a meeting. Keep you posted."

He hangs up, and I fall back on the bed. Shelby is here. Someone is hunting me. Mike. What the fuck is that guy doing in this? Wouldn't Dr. Warren know if her brother was stirring shit up? I feel like she would have warned me if so.

I stretch and groan. The hatchet is next to the bed, and I strap it on my hip. Its weight is safe and secure, but those beasts of sours would be more than a match for my little blade. I'll need to keep a gun on me and ready at all times.

My sunglasses and hat are fixed to my head, and the sun is miserable. This summer is humid, sticky, and unforgiving. I run hot as it is, and it feels like I'm cooking from the inside out.

I run to retrieve the food drop off Dr. Warren texted about. It's a tight white plastic container secured with a latch system. Inside will keep my food cold for a few days, but then I'll need more. Keeping my strength has become a priority. I flex my muscles and consider how small I am compared to the sours at the convention center. The women are thicker than me, the men giants. In a hand to hand combat, I would be at a disadvantage.

With VioTech creating sours, I wonder how many there are. If there's a handful in here, that means there are more out there. The world isn't safe. Those sours aren't safe unless they discovered a way to maintain the infection.

After eating, I envision the city in my head. My first stop will be the zoo, which is far, but the most likely place Shelby would go. I run in the shade, and while my strength is good, my legs are noodly, and I'm forced to take several breaks.

There's no wind. The air clings to my skin, causing me to sweat. When I make it to the entrance, my arm hair goes up on end, and I take a deep breath into the air, trying to catch what's going on. The flutter of wings catches my attention, and I find Pizza floating down from above. He lands on a trashcan and caws at me, like he's angry that I left.

I give him my arm, and he walks up to my shoulder and over to my backpack where he settles in. This bird is flying fine, but I suppose he likes the free ride.

"What did I miss?" I whisper. I walk past the mansion and notice the door is open. Upon entering, I find misplaced furniture, and I smell salt. Blood is a distinct rusty and copper scent; it's different from the salt that I pick up from healthy people. And there is most certainly fresh blood somewhere in this house.

I follow my nose and find droplets of dark red blood going up the steps. The path isn't hard to follow, and it leads me to one of the rooms I haven't used in months. In the bathroom, I can't believe what I see. Blood covered towels are in a corner, and a makeshift bed in the bathtub.

My body goes numb. Shelby or Ivan, or both, are hurt badly, but they aren't here now. I can't catch the fresh scent of a person any longer.

"Shelby?" I call out anyway, hoping my senses are off and she's here.

No one answers. I run from room to room looking for more evidence that someone was here, but I don't find anything. Where would they go next?

Before I leave, I jog the zoo paths to search for them in case they're hiding. The only suspicious area I find is near the elephants, where there is broken glass and red spots going down the trail.

This place has rotters, I know it does, but they don't bother me, so I let them nest there. Like lazy residents that don't pay rent, they keep away unwanted visitors at night in case anyone gets brave enough to come find me.

That won't work with sours hunting me.

The door is open, and it's dark inside. I pull my glasses off and walk in. The stench always gets me, and I gag. My wrist blocks my nostrils as I try not to breathe them in.

"God, you stink."

I search the floor for any signs that they had a fresh meal, but I find nothing. Rotters hover in the corner in a lazy hibernation stance. There's a broken window in one of the offices. Could Shelby or Ivan have come in here? Shelby would avoid places like this.

The building isn't providing me what I need, so I finish my quick tour of the zoo with Pizza flying overhead.

"Pizza!"

He comes down and rests on my backpack. We head out of the zoo and into Druid Hill Park. The next stop is the aquarium, which was abandoned after the food was eaten and anything we didn't eat was tossed into the bay.

What didn't we eat? Not much more than jellyfish and a few strange fish that weren't edible.

I walk, I don't run. I don't want to rush in case there's something worth catching. A scent of a salt. A voice from someone nearby tipping me off. Pizza flies off ahead of me. And then I see my first witness.

"Hey, man," I call to a group of three old guys sitting outside fanning themselves with their hats.

"Hey, young feller. Hot one, ain't it?"

"Sure as hell is. I'm looking for a woman, about five foot five inches, with brown curly hair. Her friend was a guy that might look kind of like me." I study him, and I see the gears turning. We don't get a lot of people walking around anymore, so if he saw her, he'd remember.

His buddies stand next to him but don't make eye contact.

"Sure. They went that way just yesterday. Was it yesterday?" He turns back to his friends and one of them nods but keeps his chin facing the trees behind me.

"How about this morning?"

"Nope. We just got out here. Inside is like an oven."

"Not much better out here, sorry to say. Thanks for your help." I nod at him and flash a smile to be friendly.

He doesn't so much as respond but squints. Before I wait for a further awkward conversation, I decide it's best to depart.

Two blocks later, I smell them following me.

Were these the men who hurt Shelby and Ivan? Did they follow them all the way to the zoo and attack them? It's a bit farfetched, but they aren't friendly either.

I walk quicker and take a turn down an alley, then lay flat against the wall.

Soon the man and his two friends come into the alley and cross my path. I slam the first to the ground, and his head thumps on the concrete. I need to ease up, or I could kill him. I grab another by the throat and push him against a brick wall.

"Easy feller," the old man who does the talking says as he backs away. "We were just curious. Not gonna do nothing. Nobody really comes around here."

"I'm around here all the time, but you don't see me."

I release the man and shove him towards the others. Then I give them a fair amount of time to slowly back away.

"If you see that woman or man again, tell them to go to our house near the park. They'll know what I mean."

"Yes, sir," the leader says, and then they turn and hustle away.

Pizza flies in once again and lands on my pack. I duck my head, so his wings don't catch me.

"That was interesting."

We're back on our path and headed to the aquarium. The shade is minimal around downtown with the sun high. So I take it slow once again.

thirteen

Dean

HOME, I'M GETTING THERE
BLADES OF GRASS CATCHING MY SKIN
OBSTACLES TO BEAR

The aquarium is tightly sealed, as I expected, and so is where I stayed near Hopkins. My final stop is our home at Patterson Park, and after this, I can't imagine where she would have gone. The blood at the zoo adds to the worry I hold. If it's theirs—a pain in my heart tightens. I can't allow myself to go to dark places.

The last two years were spent exploring this city. I've been to every corner and unique place this city offers. The worst thing in here is the rotters, but this changed once the military arrived with their designer sours.

A scent in the air startles me. I exhale thoroughly so the next breath can gather the complex smells around me. It's summer. There are wildflowers and grass, but also brick, asphalt, and metal. Something else too. The wind is hitting my face from the west, so whatever I'm getting is located in that direction.

There's a fire escape crawling up a nearby building. I reach the bottom rung and hoist myself up without lowering it. As I climb, I continue testing the air for new clues. I smell aftershave and spice, like a man from a shower.

I also smell sour.

The top of the building looks out over the park and parts of the harbor are over a mile away. The sour is down there, and he's searching for me.

Pizza lands on the roof near me and cocks his head, trying to figure out what the fuss is about. I bend down and say, "Someone is coming."

He stretches his wings and flies out over the streets in front of us. I see him swoop from one street to the next until he lands in a tree a few blocks away. With the sun out, my vision isn't great, so I lose track of him.

I crouch low on the black tar roof. My skin tingles as the sun tries to burn my arms, but I heal too quickly for sunburn.

After a few minutes, I see something moving on the street below. Their scent comes and goes based on the wind's direction, but I can tell it's them.

I hold my position, unsure of what to do. The sours wouldn't detect me up here; at least, I don't think they would. The wind is always a factor to consider, and I'm up nearly four stories above them.

Pizza takes off from the tree and takes a long path to return to me. He walks up to my shoes and pecks at the laces. I can't say he wants me to leave this roof, but if he does, the feeling is mutual, so I go back down the fire escape to the street and run in a direction that would keep my scent away from them.

I sprint fast, paying little attention to where I'm going, only ensuring it's away. Pizza disappears for a while but occasionally flies into view.

When I stop to rest, I'm not exactly tired, but wanting to gather my senses and figure out where I am. There are train tracks ahead, and I recognize the scrap metal yard. There are a lot of woodlands tucked into this area too. I move onto the tracks, and they take me to a small river. It's unfamiliar to most because it disappears into smaller streams until it's nearly invisible within the denser residential areas. This area has spread out single-family homes, making it feel sheltered from the city.

Pizza and I reconvene in the overgrown neighborhood. He takes bugs out of the air while perched on my backpack—quite the life of luxury he has.

I search for a home that doesn't have broken doors and windows, and I'm surprised that quite a few are in good shape. A yellow house with white shutters looks comfortable and unoccupied, so I break through the back door using my shoulder. The bolt cracks the doorframe.

"Anyone here?" I should have knocked. "I'm just trying to lie low. If you're here, I'll be gone in a few minutes."

I breathe in, catching dust, but no mildew. This house is not lived in anymore, but it's in good shape if the owners return. They're fortunate, and I'll do my best to repair the door on my way out, or at least not have it look like it's broken.

The couch welcomes me to sit, and I take off my backpack, so Pizza can walk onto the floor. This day has gotten too long, and my body needs rest. I pull my hat over my eyes and fall asleep with Pizza nesting in a chair across the room.

My dreams are restless. I'm being chased, but I can't tell who's behind me. Still, I run. I run until my legs feel like sand; thick and heavy. Then, I go slower until I'm hardly moving. Whatever is behind me is getting closer. I can feel the coldness of it creeping in. When something reaches for me, I jolt awake, knocking my hat and glasses from my face and trying to remember where I am.

A house in Rosedale. An area I've only jogged through but have yet to stay. Pizza stands on the coffee table with his wings spread slightly. I must have scared him.

Outside, it's dark. I reach for my phone and find it's after ten o'clock at night. The sun must have worn me down.

"We need to eat something," I tell Pizza, who purrs in the strange way that crows do.

I'm thankful for nightfall. Everything is clear and easier on my eyes. It has a green and sometimes a blue hint, but the images are crisp. I search for canned food and find a few cans of dog food under the sink. I open one for Pizza, and he devours it. Crows will eat almost anything.

I break into my stash and have a healthy portion of what Dr. Warren left. The package is cold, which makes it a bit chewy but satisfying.

A tingling stretches over my neck and trails to my shoulders and gut. Food is fuel, and I'm getting ready for a long night. Unfortunately, I didn't get to check my house at Patterson, so I'll be going back.

I'll take a chance on the sours hanging around.

After repacking and taking an extra can for Pizza, I stretch. Pizza isn't a nocturnal animal, so he'll be looking to roost somewhere. Maybe even here. I worry about him finding me again. My attachment to this bird has become weird, but I'm unwilling to psychoanalyze it.

Before I leave, I open a window and take out the screen so Pizza can go when he wants. At this moment, he's content on the chair.

I fix the door enough that no one would notice I broke in, and I leave my backpack here so I can run faster without it. The hatchet is where it needs to be, and although I haven't felt the need for a gun in two years, I take one tonight.

The train tracks glow in the moonlight as I retrace my steps. Cicadas and crickets sing, and the smell of rotters comes from ahead. Pizza should be safe, though a scratch of worry stays with me.

Several blocks later, I come up to the park, and on the other side is the house I shared with Shelby. This is the last place I can imagine she would look for me. If she's not here, I'll start calling everyone. Until then, the crisis of my missing wife and brother can remain between Jason and me.

The park is terrible to cut through, with weeds sometimes reaching my shoulders, but it's direct, so I take it. I feel itchy by the time I get to a hill overlooking our block. There are no lights in my house. I hide a key above the door, but that would be too high for Shelby to reach. Not too high for Ivan, though.

A shuffle and murmur of conversation make me freeze. I drop down into the weeds to stay hidden. Breathing in, I find sour and salt. This must be the night team Jason spoke of.

Shit. My forehead forms beads of sweat, and I know my scent is everywhere.

The talking stops for a minute, and I hear someone give an order. A shuffling of feet goes past, and then the sounds of air pistols unloading.

Groaning and hissing bodies drop to the ground. They're collecting rotters for the convention center.

I hope they focus on rotters, but if the sour in the group has any clue what to look for, they'll be able to find me.

A few minutes later, a van pulls up, and the rotters are moved in. A door closes, and those on foot continue away from me. It's quiet again. I breathe in, still catching them in the area. I tell myself to wait a few more minutes until it's safe.

My legs cramp. Bugs crawl up my neck and down my arm, but I wait.

When a breeze picks up, and I no longer sense of anyone near me, I slowly stand.

I nearly fall back over when I notice him. The Black man I saw at the convention center is on the other side of the street. Eyes as dark as mine burrow into me.

We hold our position. Neither of us reaches for a gun. I couldn't say if there were others around, but as the wind hits the back of my head, I realize how unfavorable it was to detect him.

I don't know what to do, so I speak. "Hi, there." I sound stupid.

"Are you who I'm looking for?" the man says. His bald head catches the moonlight above, and his nostrils flare as he takes in my scent blueprint.

"Probably not." I shrug casually, trying to play it off like I belong here, in the weeds, on a hill, in the dark. My feet dig into the ground to push off into the park anytime. I've been a sour longer, so I should be faster and more robust by theory, but he looks mighty big.

The man cocks his head and eyes me suspiciously. "You don't smell like a cured or a rotter." He's using my terminology, which irks me.

"I haven't showered in a while." Is there anything I can do to get him to go away? "What's your name, big guy?"

"Omar."

"Well, Omar. It's been great chatting, but I don't want the infected to get me, so I'm heading home. Which is on the other side of the park, far away."

He steps forward with a grimace. "If you're cured, why are you out at night?"

"I'm..." I trail off. What am I doing? "Looking for a lost friend?" I'm not sure why this comes off as a question, but when his fists tighten by his side, I know he'll pounce.

I bolt.

The unexpected transition stuns him for a second, and he doesn't come after me immediately. It's only a few moments until his feet hit the crunchy grass, and he's climbing the hill.

I'm at an advantage because I know this city better than he does. There are ins and outs. With every turn, something different, the landscape has changed since the city fell.

Through the park I go, my arms pump in front of me, speeding so fast I overshoot the turn. Nevertheless, I need to be downwind of Omar, so I take a large U-turn going back through the park on the other side.

Briars catch my legs. Occasionally, I step on something hidden deep in the grass that threatens my speed, but glancing over my shoulder, I see I'm gaining distance. Omar is swift and steady but slower.

I need to get off the street, or he'll be able to follow my scent now that he has it. So I climb a rickety fire escape after cutting a sharp corner into a narrow alley. Before he enters the street, I'm up on the roof. I watch him below. My chest heaves from the run.

Our hearing isn't exaggerated like our sense of smell, but in the stagnant night, I wonder if he could catch my heart pounding in my chest. I step back, watching him walk into the alley to search for me.

He stands still. His shoulders sway as he determines what happened to me. Then, his chin dips down, and his shoulders rise as he sucks in the air. I've confused him, but only for a minute.

His head shoots up, and his black eyes fall on me.

Damn it!

I run down the roofs to the end of the block and leap over to the next block. I run once again to the end and jump again. My knees crunch, and my feet slap into the tar roof. This one was further, and I roll to avoid falling. I'm figuring out where Omar is now, but he's not gone as high as me.

Ahead is a street too far to jump over, so I'll have to get down. But, before I move, I hear Omar.

"Dean," a man says in a sing-song voice. "What's the matter? I thought we'd be friends."

He knows my name.

My head rotates left and then right. Where is he coming from? The street isn't safe, and the roof isn't safe. There's only one other place I can go right now. I go back two houses to one that has a rooftop deck. Following the spiral staircase down, I kick open the door that leads into the house.

It smells of salts. Shit, someone's living in here. I run through the house, hoping they stay out of my way, and then there's the sound of a gun being cocked and aimed.

"Stay where you are," a man says.

I slowly turn around, my face dripping with sweat. "The street. I can leave, and no one gets hurt."

The man is familiar to me. He's a Black man about my height with a neck tattoo of someone's name. I study him; he lowers his gun and makes the same connection.

"Dean?" he asks, pointing the gun toward the ground.

"Yeah. Mack?"

He smiles. "Man, it's good to see you. It's been a while. What's wrong? Why are you running?" Mack was a security guard at the aquarium. At first, I wasn't sure we'd get along because he was tight with Marcus, the asshole who used to lead the group. But with time, we grew close. He's a cured sour waiting for his chance to leave the city.

"Someone's chasing me, and he's not the friendly type."

"You can hide here. Go to the basement and lay under the tarps. It's musty down there and should confuse his senses." Mack turns to lead me away from the steps.

I put up my hands and shake my head. "I can't do that to you." Omar is dangerous, and this would put Mack in a bad place.

He snorts. "You killed Marcus. He forced us to eat people. Do you remember that? Marcus told us this was the way of our kind. I hated myself every day since then, but when you killed him, I could put it behind me. You were our leader, and I owe you." He stands firmly with his lips tight.

"Marcus was a monster." So was Fat Man, and now I have his crazy wife and Omar threatening me.

He points to the stairs, and I creep down with him. A knock at the front door suggests I've been found.

"Go," he whispers and opens the basement door for me.

It's dark and muggy, as he suggested it would be. There is a gravel and dirt floor with plastic flooring to prevent water seepage. We had something similar in our Patterson Park home. I regret every second of crawling under the plastic because it coats me in filth. If Omar comes down here, he shouldn't be able to detect my scent.

The door opens, and Omar tells Mack to lower the gun, but he refuses. Mack says he's cured and knows his rights. He throws out Alisha's name and tells Omar she's overseeing operations at the convention center.

After a bit of back and forth, the door closes, and footsteps come closer to the stairs.

A whisper from the resident reaches me. "He's gone for now, but he'll be back."

I get out from under the plastic, dust myself off, and run up the steps. "The roof might be safer after all. I'm sorry about your door."

He waves me away. "Go on. I can fix the door later. That guy is like you. I can tell by his eyes." I nod, and Mack swings his fist into the wall. "So they're doing it anyway? Are they experimenting with our type? God, this will never end."

"We'll see how far they get."

"You got to keep our condition away from them. Too many sours died at Fort McHenry."

The grave site of over two dozen of our members remains there. Fat Man captured and penned them in an abandoned structure without food or water. The air inside was of death, and no one survived.

Though, my mind recalls someone living. A person or large animal ran out of the building when Nick and I discovered it. But I was never able to piece that together.

"I'll do what I can to protect our community."

"Even if you're the last one." Mack smiles and lightly punches me in the shoulder.

fourteen

Dean

PIZZA IS A BIRD
UNDERSTANDING SPOKEN WORD
HE LIKES TO BE HEARD

"Is it safe here?" I ask.

Jason waits outside a back door at Sinai. "As far as I can tell. Pick up anything?" He gestures to my nose.

I breathe in. "We're good. Does the military come here?"

"Not routinely. The convention center and hotels close by are where everyone is staying. Have you found Shelby?"

My shoulders relax. "No, but I didn't get to check our old home. I was going to do that after visiting here."

Pizza circles us, then lands on my backpack to roost and stare at Jason.

"New pet?"

"Something like that."

I follow Jason inside, but Pizza doesn't like it, so he departs before we go through the door. The hospital is dark enough to take my glasses off, and Jason leads me down the hall to a meeting room. Inside is Rob, Jeronimo, and Aisha.

Curiously, I ask, "No Angela?"

Jason answers, "We need to leave someone behind, so no one misses us."

There's a display screen on the wall, and I put my glasses on to block the light. Aisha is controlling a satellite view of Baltimore.

She addresses the room. "Dean, I heard you met the sours last night?"

"It was just one, and he called himself Omar. He already knew who I was." The man's image sticks in my head. His smell, behavior, and mission make me shutter.

"The night hunters are staying here, separate from the military." Aisha uses a laser pointer to mark the areas on the map near the convention center. "I understand you run different areas each night, and it appears they're splitting up to do the same. They're searching for rotters, but I suspect they also want to find you."

"Shelby and Ivan are in here too." I wonder how many know of this new dilemma.

Rob interjects, "Shelby is back? I didn't realize. Where is she?"

"Good question," I respond.

I recap the areas I've searched and the findings at the zoo. The group offers to check other places, but I turn them down. If they work closely with the convention center, someone will notice if they're missing.

Jeronimo appears more agitated than when I walked in, and he finally speaks up. "Lindsay visited us right before we left. What if she said something to Shelby that got her thinking she needed to come in?"

"Like what?" I ask.

"I'm not sure. She's been involved with survivors since her first day out of quarantine. The people she's met and worked with is enough to keep fueling your nightmares, that's for sure." Jeronimo opens his palm toward Aisha, asking for the laser pointer. He circles it around a few places, including the row home Shelby lived in after the Rec Pier burnt, Hopkins, and the gym in Canton. "These are places that were familiar to her. Not just the places she may look for you, Dean. I would check those as well."

Hopkins would surprise me because it's boarded up pretty well and completely lifeless inside. If she's hurt, though, it's possible. I make a mental note of these places and agree to run to them after the meeting.

"Who can I call if I run into her?" I ask, considering she might be injured.

Rob and Jason both speak up. But it's Rob who gets his word in. "I'd like to know if she's okay, and Jason isn't always available."

"I'll make sure a message gets to you. If they're hurt, I'll need someone."

"And I can handle that." Rob pulls up a medical bag next to his chair. He always has it close.

Things are strange between us. What do you say to someone you spent nearly every hour with, but after he got sick, we weren't the same anymore? I can't say who initiated the divide. It wasn't fueled by anger, and there is no bad blood between us. These are unsaid words we need help putting together.

Aisha waves her hand to get our attention. "We're not done yet. We didn't bring you here to talk about Shelby. The night hunters target different sectors, and we know their schedule." She uses the pointer to show me Patterson Park, where I was last night, and nearby areas around the harbor. "This is what they hit last night."

"That's where I was. I ran into Mack, who may have saved my life." I could smell others living in the home with him; there could have been children.

"Tonight, they'll split up and search these areas." She swings the laser over far north points. Nowhere near where I need to be. "Stay clear of those areas."

"No problem."

She clicks her tongue. "Are you taking this seriously? Just because they'll be in the north doesn't mean they'll be easy to avoid."

Worry creases into her beautiful face, and I realize how stressful these last two years have been for her. Aisha led Dr. Warren's creation of the lab at Sinai and cured several hundred rotters. She's been a crucial part of the success.

"Aisha, chill out," Rob says. "I think our man here has an idea. He was chased last night."

Oh no. Rob pulled the pin on the hand grenade known as Aisha. A few of us at the table look away or step back. Her eyes drill into him, and her cheeks turn red.

"Chill out? If VioTech gets our man here, those sours walking around will be stable forever."

Her words punch me in the gut, and I consider interrupting her, but I can tell she's just getting started.

"You have been a sour, Rob! You know what kind of power that gives you. Imagine if a company like VioTech could bottle that. Sell it to anyone. Our enemies overseas, gang members, stupid rich idiots who think this will make them indestructible. This could bring down society as we know it. Do you want society to end, Rob? Dean has sensitive feelings, and I get it; we all do. But you will shut up unless you want the world to spiral out of control." Aisha punches the table with the butt of her fist. "Dean!" she growls. "Say it out loud. Tell me you understand how serious this is." Her voice shakes at the end, and she looks at everyone in the room.

"I hear you. I understand," I say slowly.

Rob coughs to break the tension. "Is it just me, or, um, do we need to get you the hell out of this city?"

"I can't go until Shelby and Ivan are safely removed too," I say.

"Then we had best find them! Not all of us have to go back to the convention center. I'll come with you." He breaks into a smile, shifting the tension in the room, and I recall our times running the streets together. "I may not be able to keep up, but in case you didn't know, I'm basically a surgeon now."

Aisha laughs. "You are not a surgeon!"

Aisha, Rob, and others learned a lot over the last two years. They trained in the field, with some of their experience treating unique and traumatic injuries the rotters bring back.

"Dr. Rob, they call me. I have a pack with supplies right here. If someone is hurt, I'll be prepared."

"Okay, Dr. Rob," I say. "You can come with me."

He rubs his long fingers over his chin and says, "You won't regret this." Then, with an evil laugh, he leaves the room to gather more supplies.

I turn to follow him, but Aisha catches my attention. "I'll take Jeronimo and Jason to check Hopkins, but we can't be gone any longer."

"It's pretty boarded up," I say.

"Trust me, if someone wanted to get in, they could. Remember where the sours will be tonight. Stay off the street. Stay up high so they can't catch your scent as easily. Stay—"

"Aisha, I get it. I'm a sour too, in case you forgot. The wind, height, thick walls, I'm equipped to handle this sort of thing."

She stumbles into me and hugs my torso tightly. "Be safe." Then she lets me go, Jason and Jeronimo say goodbye, and I go find Rob.

The gravity of this terrible situation weighs on my shoulders more than when I arrived. Aisha's speech caught me off guard, and she's probably been talking to Dr. Warren. Those two have an interesting relationship. Aisha quickly became Dr. Warren's right-hand woman in here. The two are direct, honest, and driven, so it's not surprising that their personalities clicked almost immediately.

Though, I get the impression she's been downgraded at the conference center. The team is meeting off site. They have the military's plans, but they aren't delivering the action.

Minutes later, I'm outside with Rob.

"Hot as a magnifying glass on an ant. Am I right?" Rob wears sunglasses, khaki shorts, and a t-shirt. He has his red medical bag slung over his shoulder. "Are you going to make me run in this heat?"

"Yep. But to show you how nice I am, I'll carry your bag."

I take it from him and sling it around my chest. It sits awkwardly with my backpack on, but I find a comfortable enough spot, making sure it doesn't rub against my hatchet.

We take off at a slow jog. The buildings around us cover the streets with shade on one side, so we stay in that area whenever possible. The heat is waning and growing each time we come in and out of the sunlit areas.

This was our routine. We'd run through the city. He'd talk about the craziest stuff, and our conversations always turned into something a little too serious. He'd ask me what I would do if I won the lottery, and I'd laugh because there's nothing to buy inside these walls. Then we'd talk about buying VioTech out and closing them down.

Tonight is no different.

"Your brother's in here? Did he bring food from the outside?"

"Yeah," I tease. "I'm sure he has a bacon cheeseburger in his back pocket." My stomach gurgles at the thought.

"That's torture!" He laughs and then changes his tone. "Why do you think they came in here? Really?"

"Good question. At first, I thought it was because they were looking for me, but now I'm unsure. Jeronimo said Lindsay visited Shelby, and you may remember, Lindsay was friends with us before the city fell. Those two seemed to have a falling out over something, but I didn't think it was repairable."

"Lindsay? She's a good person. Shelby accidentally had her ringer on at night, and when someone called her, the rotters broke through the window and swarmed the house. I hear they escaped from a deck coming off the back of the house. Her friend was killed, and Lindsay made it to the Rec Pier."

He's referring to our friend Scott, who was one of the last people I thought would be killed in the early days. I remember visiting Lindsay's house after it was ransacked. If Shelby was the cause, no wonder Lindsay was pissed.

"But they worked it out?" I ask.

"Before the Rec Pier burnt down, I'd say there were doing pretty well."

I don't know how else to respond to his story. Picking up little pieces of what Shelby had to go through always makes me uncomfortable. It wasn't easy, but she always had someone providing her with protection. In this case, right now, that someone is Ivan.

"Would she go to the front door or the back?" Rob asks. We stand at the bottom of the marble steps leading to a red door. The bronze crab knocker has a few rusted spots but has held up well.

This is home.

"Front door." I walk up and knock but don't call out. Rob and I stand in silence, the heat beating at our necks.

"Knock again?"

I do what he suggests, this time a little louder. After a minute, the door flies open, and Shelby is standing there with blood on her shirt and hair stuck to her sweaty forehead.

She launches herself out the door, and I catch her. "Dean?" she cries. "Ivan is inside. He's hurt." Her words are broken with sobs as her arms cling to me.

I release her and look at the smears of blood on her face. "How bad is it?"

"He jumped through a window, and it cut his face. There's a puncture wound on his shoulder too. They won't stop bleeding, and I wasn't sure what to do or who to call." Her voice is jittery, like she hasn't slept in days.

Rob pushes past us. "Where is he?"

I take the bag off and hand it over to him.

"Rob?" Shelby reaches for his hand and drags him inside. I close and lock the door behind us. "You're okay? I can't believe you're here!"

With a firm grip on Rob, she pulls us to the master bedroom and into the bathroom in the back. Ivan is sitting next to the toilet, looking pale and sweaty.

Rob kneels and puts on a pair of gloves. "Can you tell me your name and where you are?"

Ivan bats a hand at Rob. "Who's this guy?" he says breathlessly.

I bend down and get in his face. "It's me, Dean. This is my friend Rob, and he's going to take a look at your cuts. Hold still for him, okay?"

My brother's shirt is soaked in blood, and the gash on his head continues to pulse and bleed.

"Dean?" His eyes widen as he finds me. I bite back tears. This is the first time I've seen him in over three years, and he's injured beyond what I expected.

Rob sees my concern. "Head wounds bleed a lot. I'll get him stitched up, but he's a bit delirious, so I'll give him a sedative. Catch him when he goes."

I get closer to Ivan and watch Rob prepare a syringe with clear liquid. We have a lot of this in the city since we use it on rotters. The needle goes into his shoulder, Ivan's eyes roll back within seconds, and he crumbles into my arms.

"Spread him on the floor so I can get to him better. Can we open those curtains for more light?" He pulls out scissors and cuts off Ivan's shirt, revealing a deep wound on his shoulder. It's jagged and torn.

Shelby throws open the curtains and bends over to watch us. Rob hands her the bloodied shirt, and she throws it in the wastebasket.

"Um, can I get a little space? How about you two prepare a bed for him? Maybe get him some clean clothes?" Rob smiles to lighten the mood, and I notice how closely Shelby and I have been leaning in.

"Right," I say. "Shelby, let's get the bed ready." Something to keep us busy and our minds off my drugged brother on the bathroom floor with Dr. Rob.

The bedroom is dim, and I take off my glasses. Shelby sits on the bed, dazed. For the first time, I allow myself to really look at her. She's healthy, with some of her weight filled in from the last time I saw her, and she has a glow to her skin that was once lost.

"We were looking for you, and we split up. Ivan thought he heard something in that barn by the elephants, but it was a pod of rotters.

If I had been with him, I would have warned him. This is my fault." She wipes tears away and looks at me for forgiveness.

I sit next to her and change the subject. "You came here to find me?"

Her gaze finds mine, and she walks her fingers over to rest on the top of my hand. "I did. The house looks perfect, Dean. Did you do all this work?"

The careless and messy squatters who took over until they left on one of the trains didn't make it easy. It took a lot of time and effort, but I restored most of our belongings and removed whatever they left behind. When I say it took time, I mean it took over a year. I painted, cleaned, washed, rebuilt, and organized every inch of this house. It kept me connected to Shelby and Jessie, even if they weren't here.

"Welcome home," I say. "I tried to get things back to the way they were in case..." I'm not sure in case of what. If the city ever opens again? That seems unlikely.

"It's great." She reaches over and hugs me again. Her shirt sticks to her skin, where Ivan's blood soaks through.

"You need to clean up. Those drawers have clothing for you, and that dresser has things for me that Ivan can wear."

She walks over to her dresser and opens it. Inside are a few of her old things I could salvage and some new ones I picked up. The first thing she grabs is a Jimmy Buffett shirt. We bought it when we went to his concert a few years ago.

"I never thought I'd see this again." She holds it up to her, smiling.

"It might be dirty. I can find a new one," I say.

"No! It's perfect." She finds more clothing to finish her outfit and heads to another room to clean up. The water runs, but there is no power, and this house feels like a sauna without the windows open. I crack a few, so there is airflow, and then I busy myself getting things together for Ivan.

Carefully, Rob and I strip Ivan and remove his prosthetic leg so he can rest comfortably in bed. Moving a limp body takes work. He's taller than I am and solid. We manage to get his head on the pillow and the rest of him lying on top of the sheets. He has a bandage around his head and shoulder.

"He should rest for a while," Rob says. "And take antibiotics, which I don't have here. Do you think we could get him to Sinai? I can keep an eye on him better there."

"I'm sure we can figure something out once he can move."

"This house isn't safe. Those sours know where you live. The sooner you vacate, the better." Rob packs up his stuff and throws the rest of Ivan's clothes in the trash. "Get rid of any evidence that you were here." He thrusts the bag at me.

"I don't want Shelby and Ivan brought into this."

"Brought into what?" Shelby says from the doorway. Her hair is wet and tied back, and she's wearing the concert t-shirt with a pair of black shorts. Her standing in that exact place, in familiar clothing, makes my heart stop. I breathe in, catching myself from falling into the past.

Rob walks over and gives her a proper hug. "How are you?" he asks.

"Rob? I can't believe you and Dean are together. If I'd known, I'd have been less worried all this time. No one would talk to me. I felt so out of touch." She squeezes him harder and rests her head on his arm.

"Yeah, well, that asshole turned me into a sour. But, since all the other sours were cured, I had no choice but to hang out with him." He chuckles. "We had some quality moments. I understood this infection better and saw parts of the city I'd never been to. Dean saved my life because I was going downhill fast."

"Shut up." I throw a pillow at him, and he catches it.

"Be nice to the Rob," Rob jokes. "I just saved your brother's face. He's going to hurt when he wakes up, but he'll be okay." He opens his bag and hands Shelby a bottle. "Pain killers. Stay ahead of the pain."

"Got it," she says.

"Can't stay. I have to get to the convention center before some-one comes looking for me. Dean, give Shelby my cell so we can coordinate Ivan coming to Sinai." Rob gives a thumbs-up and walks out the door. "I'll let myself out," he calls up after us.

"Sinai? And what was he talking about when I walked in?" Shelby gestures for me to follow her to the living room downstairs, so we don't disturb Ivan.

We sit on the couch and twist our bodies to face each other. I don't want Shelby involved, but if I keep it from her, that could be more dangerous.

I begin, "Rob was sour for about a year, but then he had to get cured like everyone else. I've spent the last year alone and avoid-ing people as much as possible." She sits back and listens to every word. I tell her about dragging rotters in at night so Aisha, Rob, and their team at Sinai could cure them. I tell her how quickly things have changed now that the trains are bringing in people and supplies. Then, I tell her about Omar and his gang of sours. Their target is me, and I even tell her what Aisha said about the serious-ness of this.

Shelby doesn't speak. She gets up, walks to the kitchen, and returns with her bag. Her fingers fiddle with the zipper nervously, but she gets inside and pulls out an envelope.

"What's this?" I lean over the coffee table as she spreads a well-worn map onto the table. It has so many markings, and it's grown thin from use.

There are blue stars in several areas, and she points to each of them. "This is a treasure map given to me by Mona Denkins. She passed away a few weeks ago and left this to me. Lindsay thinks it holds clues to bring VioTech down."

"How?" I ask.

Shelby looks at me, concerned and angry. "Someone put this virus in here on purpose. And I'm going to expose who that was."

fifteen

Shelby

ISSIONS PULL AT ME
WHICH ONE IS MORE IMPORTANT?
ONE WHERE ALL ARE FREE

The house remains quiet until late into the evening. Everyone needed time to decompress and rest. We took different rooms until Ivan woke up, calling us from the master bedroom.

"Is anyone here?" he calls. I'm glad the sun is high. Otherwise, he would have alerted the infected to our location.

"Ivan," Dean says from the third-floor bedroom. He bounds down the steps to get to his brother, who is thrashing blankets away from him and searching for his prosthetic leg.

"Calm down." I make it to Ivan first and rest my hand on his chest. "It's Shelby, and we're in my old house. A friend stitched you up and gave you something that made you sleepy. Dean is here too, look." I point to Dean, standing at the foot of the bed. Tears soak his cheeks as he walks to the side of the bed and sits next to Ivan.

They reach for each other and embrace. I could never imagine the pain they hold. Their mother died, and Ivan thought Dean was dead too. He thought he would be without family forever, but Dean changed that. This is the first time they have felt one another in years.

Ivan cries openly with Dean, and I feel I should leave, but it's hard not to invest in these boys. I've known them both for so long. Dean runs his hand over Ivan's head to jostle his hair and then laughs.

"Little brother. What did you get yourself into?"

"Me? It was Shelby's idea." He jokes, but I am guilty of dragging him in here. If only I were more confident to do these things myself.

I sniff back the tears from falling and excuse myself. "You came voluntarily, the last I checked. I'm glad you're feeling better, and you should take your time getting up. I'll make us something to eat, but we must consider leaving before night falls."

The late summer sun is in our favor if we want to make it to Sinai tonight.

"Leave?" Ivan is confused and looks to Dean for answers.

Dean turns to me. "I'll fill him in. You pack up and get some food ready."

I leave so they can recover some of the time that's been lost between them.

My bag has a few provisions, but Dean may have more food in the kitchen. After that, we can go to Sinai because it's better for Ivan, but I need to search Mona's stars with or without help.

My phone has been charging using a solar battery I kept near the window. I take a look and notice there are a few texts from Mike. He's checking in. There is too much to text, so I call.

He answers, and I put him on speakerphone to prepare pasta and beans. Dean did a good job stocking the house with a few supplies. As a pan lands on the gas stove and the pilot clicks to life, igniting the burner, Mike answers in his deep voice.

"Shelby, is that you? I thought I lost you for a bit."

"We're here. I'm at my old house but not for long. Ivan was hurt. You'll never guess who came to give him stitches?"

"Who? Was it Dean? I didn't think he knew how to do those things." Mike pushes the conversation to get to something.

"It was Rob, your old roommate."

Mike puffs out air in disbelief. "I forgot he was working with the cure efforts. How is he?"

"Great. Rob is much better than when we left the city. Dean is here too, but left Ivan's injuries to Rob."

"Dean is there?"

I guess this means I completed the mission he put us on. "Yeah. He looks great, but there are people after him. It's not what I expected, so we must move until you find a way out. Are you working on that?"

"Honestly, you found him a bit sooner than I anticipated. I'll iron out the details, but you'll need to keep me posted on where you are at all times."

"Sure, I'll do that." My concern is getting Dean out and being able to look at the points of interest on the map. I could find a way to stay behind if Dean needs to leave today.

"Hey," Dean calls from the doorway. "Are you talking to someone?"

"It's Mike. He's on speakerphone if you want to say hi." I point at the phone and then open the can of beans to rinse.

Dean steps back and puts up his hands as if he doesn't want to speak, but Mike catches him.

"Hi, Dean. Good to hear your voice. How are things in the city?" Mike tries to sound chipper, which feels awkward.

"Great," Dean says. "My brother had a rough night, so I'm grabbing him some water. Good to hear from you." Dean fills a glass from the sink and takes it out of the room. He eyes me strangely as he leaves.

"Mike, I should go. We're getting something to eat and then heading out. I'll let you know when we get to Sinai."

"Sure, sounds great. Take care." Mike disconnects.

What was that all about? I add salt to the pot of water and run up to see what's going on upstairs. While Dean is remaking the bed, Ivan is in the bathroom with the door closed.

"Now you make beds?" I laugh. "The apocalypse has domesticated you."

"Well, I spent a lot of time putting this place back together. I don't want one visit from guests to go messing it up." He tucks the sheets in tightly and places the pillows in place. "Hey, what's up with Mike?"

"He got us in here, and he's going to get you out."

Dean takes off his glasses and rubs the bridge of his nose. "I don't trust him. Never have. Dr. Warren said she's getting me out with Jason's assistance. Everyone wants to know where I am, and I hate it."

"I'm sorry. Does it matter whose plan works first? Everyone is working on this."

Dean fluffs a pillow and throws it on the bed. "But everyone has different reasons for helping me. I'm not sure all of them are good."

He could have reacted better to the map, but having him close again makes my heart full. I don't want to argue over things that haven't happened yet. I can understand his reservation. Dean met Mona only once, and while he was friends with Lindsay, it's been years since they connected. So he's got no reason to trust either of them.

"So, where are we going first?" he asks carefully.

Ivan walks out of the bathroom, looking much more refreshed than before. Black strings are poking out of rippled skin where Rob did stitches. It will scar, but the bleeding has stopped.

I turn my attention to him. "How are you feeling?"

"Sore. Tired. But I can make it to the hospital if that's what we need. You cooking?"

"Crap!" I run back down the steps and find a boiling pot. The pasta goes in, and I call up to them. "Twelve minutes until we eat." Well, at least Ivan and me.

A few minutes later, we're sitting at the table. Dean has food from Dr. Warren, but it's the last.

"I'll tell her to drop something off so I can pick it up later," he says.

"I heard you talking about the map again." Ivan asks. "I'm not in the best condition to run around until my shoulder heals. It'll need at least a week, I think." He tries to lift it but can't get very far.

"I can go alone," I say.

"No way." They say together using the same tone.

"Why not? I know this city better than Ivan, and Dean has people chasing him." I shove food in my mouth before my voice has a mind of its own. There's too much at stake here. If I don't find out what Mona has, the virus will continue to be used by VioTech. Or if I'm not taking VioTech down, I can expose the responsible company.

Dean chews on a hunk of pinkish meat, and I have to avert my eyes. I've never seen him eat like this.

"You're on a mission you can't turn down? I get it," Dean says. "But things aren't like they were when you left. You still have the rotters, you have crazy cured people robbed of life for months or years, and you have the military doing rounds to clear this city. It's not safe for anyone to travel alone."

"You seem to get around fine." I point out.

Ivan's eyes dart between us. "Um, can we all hold hands and stare lovingly into each other's eyes again?"

We swing our heads toward him and glare.

"Or not. That's cool too." Ivan takes his plate and walks into the living room to give us the space to hash this out.

"Dean, this map is important. Do you see this handwriting? It's mine." I point to areas around Patterson Park and the prison. "I was trying to get to Renee after we were separated. Jason took it over when I joined the Rec Pier, and now it's back with me. This isn't a coincidence."

"The map didn't choose you, Shelby," Dean groans.

"But Mona did, and I'm going through with it."

He was mine, and I was his, but we are not each other's any longer. I've lived without him for this long, and while I might be scared to do this alone, I owe it to the world. The Lazarus virus creator needs to be exposed.

I shove food in my mouth and look away.

"I forgot how stubborn you can be." Dean finishes his plate and walks it to the sink. He rests his hands on the counter and groans. "This is important. You should follow it, but Ivan isn't in any condition. He lost a lot of blood, and we can't have his stitches breaking open."

"I can get to and from places without anyone noticing. It would be faster if I had a bike. I can avoid the infected, so they shouldn't be an issue." I regret mentioning the infected as soon as I say it.

"They won't be an issue again, you mean."

Ivan's injury is my fault, but who goes into a dark building with the infected lurking? Splitting up early was stupid, and I blame myself for suggesting it.

"We need to get to Sinai." I change the topic and finish eating. I pack and prepare to leave with a full stomach and enough water to last our journey.

The walk to Sinai is brutally hot, and we take several breaks to allow Ivan to rest. He curses himself for being weak, but I remind him he needs time to recover.

Ivan stands under a shaded porch and sips water before joining us on the street again. "The point of me coming in here was to protect you. How much further?"

"Another mile, but it's a lot of uphill," Dean says. "There are shortcuts, but it's through some overgrown areas. The streets are more clear."

We follow him, and I notice a shadow circling us. Large black wings flap close to my face. I screech and duck. When I look up, a crow is sitting on the back of Dean's backpack. He doesn't flinch with the wild bird pecking at his shoulder.

"What the heck is that?" I point.

"A crow. His name is Pizza." Dean reaches into his pocket and pulls out a bag with pasta. He feeds it to the bird over his shoulder.

"You have a pet?"

"I'm not sure, but I rescued him, and now he sticks around. I like the company."

Ivan laughs. "Of course you do. Something that doesn't talk back."

"What's that supposed to mean?" Dean grins. "I like people."

Ivan and I look at one another and smirk. "Sure you do," I say.

Dean hesitates in responding as he continues to lead the way. Something is picking at him, but I don't know what it is. I walk closer to him and hold his hand.

"Everything okay?"

He squeezes my hand but let's go. "I've gone weeks without hearing my voice. The past year has been full of solitude. It's not that I don't like people, but those around me always get hurt. People aren't my thing anymore. When I leave here, you and Ivan will have to say goodbye to me again. This time, it might be forever."

I'm blown away by his hurtful suggestion. "Dr. Warren wants to find a cure for you."

"There is no cure, Shelby. I will be a walking virus capable of starting the real apocalypse at any time. I can't be around others." His shoulders slump, and I recognize how far gone he is. Dean has always been friendly. While he's a man of few words, they are kind and funny, and people are drawn to him. But unfortunately, this isn't who he is anymore.

Ivan catches up to our pace. "That's a shitty way to look at life, bro. How about we tackle one day at a time? Right now, we go to Sinai. Tomorrow, we'll deal with the map. When it's time for you to leave, promise you'll talk to us before you make some macho decision to storm off into the sunset. Can you manage that?" He lifts his good arm and squeezes his brother's shoulder, but Pizza doesn't like Ivan getting close, so he pecks at his hand. "Ouch. Devil bird!"

Dean chuckles. "He's not tame. Careful." We walk a few more steps, and Dean finally addresses Ivan. "I won't go without telling you. Let's make sure we get out of here together."

It's the promise that will get me through these next few days, and we'll deal with forever when forever needs to be addressed.

sixteen

Shelby

FINGER TRAILS MY SPINE
YOUR HEAT COVERS MY BODY
EVERYTHING IS FINE

We arrive at Sinai, and I brace myself to see others from my past. Rob was a shock, but we didn't get to catch up. Jason, Angela, Jeronimo, and maybe others will be here.

Pizza flies into a tree when Dean takes us through the back door with a security code. The hospital has full electricity, so I see why people live here. As soon as I walk in, I notice the cool air conditioning. It's not on full throttle, but it's enough.

"Anyone here?" Dean calls out. Then he turns to us. "They're usually on the third floor with patients."

Every hospital feels like a maze with different halls going into sections for every aliment. We reach an area where people move from one room to the next.

"I thought they moved everything to the convention center?" I ask. While I didn't go inside, I could tell it was busy.

A beautiful woman with dark hair and tan skin walks up. Aisha, I could pluck her off a busy street. My confidence is constantly tested when I see her. Dean and this woman were together. The betrayal sits in my heart. This feeling isn't shaken no matter how many times I run through the reasons Dean was with her.

Jason is behind her, and things become more complicated.

"We're running smaller groups through here," Aisha says. "Every effort helps, and the convention team supports us when we have a rotter who is too injured for what we can do."

"Oh." I don't know how to interact with her. We're not friends, but we're not enemies either.

"Who is this?" Aisha's full lips crawl into a grin. I don't think I've seen her smile before.

Ivan reaches his hand out to her. "I'm Ivan, Dean's brother. And you are?" I swear he's blushing.

"You're the one and only Ivan? Nice to finally meet you." Aisha holds his gaze and keeps her eyes locked on him.

"Um," Dean says, uncomfortably. "This is Aisha. And this is Jason. At the end of the hall are Angela and Jeronimo. I don't see Rob."

Aisha speaks, but her eyes remain on Ivan. "We take turns going to the convention center. He'll be back tomorrow." She turns her head and studies Ivan's stitches. "Those are fresh. You must be who Rob sewed up."

"You got me." Ivan smiles, and the tension in the room takes on a new flavor. Are they flirting?

"I can't believe you walked here," Aisha says. "You must be tired. Let's get you some rest so I can redress your shoulder."

I hadn't noticed, but there were spots of blood bleeding through his shirt. The walk must have taken more out of him than I expected.

"Thank you." Ivan follows her away from us.

I lean close to Dean and whisper, "What just happened?"

"I'll figure it out another time. I have to go. It's not safe for me or you if I bring trouble." He brings me in for a hug and then is gone before I can remind him to stay in touch.

Jason stares at me from a few feet away. The last time we met, things weren't exactly comfortable. I haven't told him about the map, and there's this little voice in my head telling me to keep this away from him. Without Ivan being able to go with me, I'll need to go alone or bring someone in.

I say a quick hello to Jason, but I walk past and go to where Angela and Jeronimo stack sheets onto a cart.

"Angela," I get her attention, "can we talk somewhere?"

She jumps when she hears me. "I heard the rumor but couldn't believe it until I saw it myself. You little rat. You made it into the city without us." Angela throws her arms around my neck for an embrace. "You found Dean?"

"I did. You just missed him."

"He's got to watch himself."

"I know."

Jeronimo steps over and punches me lightly on the shoulder. "Can't keep you away from this shithole, huh?"

"Nope. I love danger."

I tug on Angela's shirt. "Can I talk to you in private?" Jeronimo looks insulted, so I quickly say, "I have my period," louder than I need to, but it works. He walks backward a few steps before getting back to his task.

"I have tampons. My bag is in room 204," Angela says.

"Come with me. I need to talk to you about something." I take her hand and drag her into the closest patient room.

Instantly, I realize we're not alone. There's a smelly woman strapped to the bed. Her hair is caked in mud, and under the restraints is a blanket that most likely hides her naked body. She's a rotter processing the cure. This woman's chest is heaving faster than imaginable.

"What's wrong with her?" I ask.

"She's had two doses of the suppressant and needs a few more before the IV with the cure serum. Her body is trying to fight it off. At least she's quiet. Some of these guys are like listening to dying puppies all day." Angela checks the tubes and a clipboard at the bottom of her bed. "Someone will be in here soon, so if you got something to spill, ya better do it."

"Right. Remember when Lindsay visited?" I pause and hold my breath. I should have started somewhere else.

"I remember." Angela's tone is deep, as if she's bracing for me to say something horrible.

"What I'm about to tell you cannot leave us. Okay? I mean it, Ang. You cannot tell anyone. Ivan and Dean know, but that's only because I thought they could assist me. Now I'm not so sure since Ivan is hurt and Dean is in danger." My eyes switch focus between Angela and the doorway. She has to understand how important her silence is.

"You're kinda freakin me out."

The raspy inhales of the infected woman pitch higher than before. Yet Angela won't remove her attention from me.

"Lindsay gave me something." I pull out the map and show her the stars that Mona wrote. "They're important, but I'm not sure why. Lindsay hinted that it would lead us to the cause of the virus and who's responsible."

She stumbles back and bumps into a chair. "Dude. What? You're inside for all of twenty-four hours, and you're stirring up some pretty serious shit. Mona had a lot of connections, but I can't believe that map is alive after the fire."

"Lindsay had it the whole time," I say.

"So what do you need me for? Other than to keep my big mouth shut. Which I'm not cool with. Jason and Jeronimo should know. Even Aisha could help."

I try to hide the strange feelings I have about Aisha. I don't think the two of us could ever be friends being we shared an interest in Dean. I am married to him. If that's not complicated enough, my almost-fiancé is working with her.

"You have to come with me tomorrow," I say.

"Um, come again?"

"I can go alone, and I will, but I think you're as invested in the outcome of this virus as I am." I smile wide and cheesy. "Please?" She could turn me in to Jason or Jeronimo, but knowing Angela, she'll find a way to come on this adventure.

Angela pauses. She hovers in silence, weighing her current workload with what I've thrown at her. Eventually, she says, "I'm in, but if it gets dangerous or to the point we find something worth mentioning we have to tell Jason."

Jason's head pops through the door, taking us both off guard. "Did I hear my name?"

Angela observes the infected woman again and then says, "I was explaining what we do here. You can pick up where I left off. I need to finish what I was doing with Jeronimo. Shelby, I assume you're staying here?"

"There isn't anywhere else for me to go."

Angela gives me the thumbs-up and leaves. Jason stands over the bed and checks the fasteners.

"Can't be too careful, but this one received enough suppressant that I don't think she'd attack us."

"I'd rather not find out. Do you mind if we find somewhere else to catch up? I'm sure you're pretty upset to see me." I try a sly grin, but he shakes his head.

"Fucking right I'm pissed. Let me show you to a spare room. I'll make sure Ivan gets one near you."

I follow Jason through the halls. While the building has power, most of the lights are out. The corridors are shady, and so is the stairwell we go up. They keep their patients on a different floor, which makes sense in case anyone escapes. I shudder at the thought.

He escorts me to a hospital room with one bed. The space is dark, and it smells like plastic and dust. I don't imagine anyone has stayed here in quite some time.

"How long are you trying to stay?" Jason asks. "You already found Dean."

I bite my tongue. The map has found its way to me and away from him. I have control over it for the first time, and I plan to keep it that way.

"I'll leave when I know Dean has a safe exit," I say.

"Then you can put this city behind you," Jason murmurs, as if he knows it's not true. But we'll never let it slip our minds. Our bodies took a beating the year we were here. My digestive system isn't what it used to be.

Jason walks to the window and pulls the curtains back, so the sunset brightens the room. It's orange, red, and purple—one of the more colorful ones I've seen. I walk up to him and rest my head on his shoulder. Why couldn't we make it? Why couldn't our relationship be as bold and beautiful? It's not that I didn't want it to be.

At this moment, my skin feels warm and prickles with excitement from being this close to Jason. The way he used to bring his body over mine and run his nose along my jaw up to my ear. He'd tell me he loved me. I believed him.

His arm carefully comes around my shoulders, pulling me closer to his side. I let my hands wrap around his stomach, and even though I'm trying to convince myself not to, I breathe him in.

Where did we go wrong? I know what went wrong, but I can't pinpoint when it started to decompose. Were we always doomed to live with Dean's ghost? Did I do this on purpose?

Why do I think about this? My mind races as my fingers dare me to run them up his back or to more secret places like down his pants. This city makes me want him. There's something wrong with me.

I pull away, but he maneuvers so I'm standing in front of him. If I look at him, we'll kiss. If we kiss, other things will happen. I turn my chin away from him, confused. What does he want?

His finger touches my chin and turns me toward him. Then he leans in but stays an inch away from my lips. Our relationship isn't a game. It's an unwritten agreement that sex isn't want binds us. There's going to be more. We've made this promise to each other before, and I recognize how important it is to him.

"Should I leave or close the door?"

I can feel the warmth riding over my body, craving him. This is not one of the reasons I came to this city. Is it?

"Close the door," I hear myself say.

His mouth is on mine, and my hands run through his dark blond locks. The scruff from not shaving rubs my lips, but I want more.

I push him away. "I said close the door!"

He picks me up, so I'm straddling him, and he carries me to the door. We spin around, so my back is against it as it closes. His teeth tenderly sink into my neck, trailing upward until his lips meet mine. He moves us away from the door and carries me to the bed. We fall into it together.

I lift his shirt to find the map of scars and chest hair I'm familiar with. His leg has healed from the gunshot, but there are a few things he eases into, like kneeling on the bed between my legs. With one tug, he removes his shirt and drops it to the ground. Then he raises mine slowly until I lift my shoulders and head so he can pull it off.

His green eyes catch mine again—checking in with our agreement. Today isn't a onetime sex cure. We will have to face the demons that pulled us apart instead of running from them. This city brings it all back. Worrying about Dean and the cure. Looking for answers that matter to the heart and the world. It's heavy. And it terrifies me to do it without him.

The room glows in all the colors of the sunset. My fingers find the button to his pants. Again, we move fast to undress one another. I keep my eyes on him so I can remember the curves of his body and the intimacy it promises. I remind myself this won't be our last day together. I agree with his unsaid terms and am curious where it'll take us. I'm not saying yes to his old marriage proposal, but I will give in to the moment tonight, tomorrow, and maybe the day after.

Our skin is bare. Jason nestles closer to me, and for a minute, we hold onto one another to feel each other's heat. Breathe each other's smells and remember every good second between us. What do we owe one another?

Jason groans in my ear. I part my legs and tilt my hips. Then, running my nails down his back, I wrap my legs around him as he rocks into me. I'm not sure how long I'll be able to hold onto him again. It could be as long as this city keeps us captive, or it could be forever.

seventeen

Shelby

DISCOVER A PLACE
WHERE MORE SECRETS ARE HIDDEN
PROVIDING NO GRACE

The trains run survivors out of the city, and I've lost track of time. I can't blame Jason, but our nights together and a chance to work with him again brought back every reason we began our relationship. When he's in charge, there's something about watching him organize and work that connects us. It's the man I fell in love with. He's so confident, and even when he's frustrated, he has this way of turning things into doable actions.

I've been here for almost two weeks serving their operation. The map sits in my bag, out of sight and out of mind. Angela hasn't pressed me, but I can tell she's wondering what our next steps will be.

Curing the infected is dirty, stressful work. Bringing them back from rage so powerful, witnessing their eyes adjust, their skin regain pigment, coaxing them into reality, is astonishing. There's an emotional component no human can turn their back on. Some of the infected have been this way for three years. They hardly remember the fall of the city and the harsh winters. We've borrowed a few nurses from the convention center to assist, but anyone with severe complications goes to where the main operation is. Jason took three of our patients there today.

It's the middle of the morning, and I'm transitioning the cured to recovery rooms. Most of them take this time to sleep and allow their bodies to catch up to their minds. We make connections on the outside when possible. Most are so dazed when they finally heal, they aren't sure who to contact.

Rob gave me a list of three rooms. I'm on the last one. I gently escort a young woman to a wheelchair so I can take her to a room without restraints and locks on the door.

She's lost three toes to frostbite and has several areas that need stitches. We always run antibiotics with their suppressant to ward off infection, but the sores around her mouth look tender and wet.

"Sit right here." I assist her into the chair. She's silent. I wonder if she's confused, grateful without words, or still healing. The suppressant returns their minds in time.

"Where are we going?" she whispers.

I've already told her, but I gently repeat it. "I'm taking you to a new room. One that's more comfortable. You'll be able to go home soon. Out of the city."

Her eyes trace the ceiling, and then she looks to the door. "Out of the city? My home is here."

I wheel her into the hallway when I pass Angela. Every time I see my friend, she gives me a one eyebrow-up glare, and a disappointed smirk spreads on her lips. Today is no different. She told me she would investigate Mona's stars, and I've put it off.

"Hey, you," she says. "Is this your last one?"

"It is."

"Come to my room after. I need to show you something." Angela keeps walking, but I watch her go down the hall until she's out of sight. What could she have?

I take the woman to another hallway off this one. The new room is too bright with the outside shining through.

"Too much." My patient points to the window, so I quickly draw the shades.

"Better?"

She stands and reaches for the bed. "How long will I be here?"

"Just a few days before they want you out of the city. A train will take you to a place for quarantine." She's a jittery, thin woman and her missing toes have her second-guessing her steps.

"I don't remember much," she says. "It's all so dark. The last thing was a house party on our street, and people acted crazy. My roommate and I felt so sick that we stayed in bed the next day. We'd call one another from our rooms. She called 911, but no one came."

Their stories are always unique. While many were turned at the stadium event where Dean was infected, others fell victim much later.

"The emergency system went down pretty fast once the infection took over. What part of the city are you from?"

"Pig Town. Not too far from the stadium." Her eyes flicker as she tries to stay awake for our conversation. I hold out my arm to help her settle into the bed.

"There used to be a delicious Ethiopian place over that way," I say, remembering the spongy bread and spiced foods we would eat in a tiny restaurant.

She pulls the blankets around her and closes her eyes. "That was a good place."

I tiptoe backward and close the door carefully.

A hand lays on my shoulder, and I yelp.

"Whoa, sorry," Rob says. "You were staring at the door, and I thought something was wrong."

I shake my head. "Hi, Rob. My last patient is in her bed. Can I get you anything?"

"Don't you wish we were going to the basement for Mike's moonshine?" He grins, and we walk down the hall together.

"Those were the good days in here. I may have complained that our jobs were repetitive, but we were safe, and now I see what a difference we made. The suppressant works." As soon as I speak, I remember how much Rob didn't want to be involved in my secret trial. "I'm sorry. I didn't mean anything by it."

"No, you're right. I was a headcase when I thought they'd found my wife, Judy. She runs through my mind whenever we bring in a new set of rotters. We may find her, but we may not. I wish I knew what happened to her. The not knowing is the hardest part. Well, this conversation blows." He laughs and throws his arm around my shoulders. "Let's change the subject."

Would he be there for me now if I confessed my secret? He could take my map to anyone. I like Rob, but we haven't talked in years, and it's too soon to trust him again. So I come up with a random question to change the subject, as requested.

"The trains are running. When are you leaving?"

"As soon as they let me. I understand that's not the most heroic answer, but I've paid my time here. If someone handed me a ticket, I'd be gone. You know I haven't had a hamburger or pizza in three years?" He pats his stomach. "I could use a few pounds back on my skinny ass."

"Yeah, you could." I poke him in the ribs. "I get it, though. Wanting to leave as soon as you can."

"You would, too, right? Do they even know you're in here?"

"Nope." And I want to keep it that way.

"They might evacuate Sinai before the final trains take people out."

"Oh." I hadn't thought that far ahead. We're a smaller operation than the convention center, so they would clear this out first. After that, I'd have to find somewhere else. Or it's time to get moving on this map instead of playing house with Jason again.

Rob turns us to the nurse's desk, where a few others are waiting for directions. "We can take a break. Let's meet back here to talk about it this evening. It's time for a new group of infected."

"I'll see you later, Rob." I wave and walk to my room. On my way up, there's a call from Mike. I could let it go to voice mail, but I've done that trick a few times. He's not happy I've let Dean wander away, but it's not safe for him here.

I answer reluctantly. "Hi, Mike."

"Hi, Shelby. Just checking in. Has Dean revisited the hospital?" He sounds annoyed, and I can only imagine he's thinking of everything he had to go through to get Ivan and me in here.

"No, but I was going to call him and ask if he'd stop by tonight." I lie, though it's not a bad plan.

"It would be a good idea to keep up with his location. We'll need to act fast if I can get him out of the city."

"I know. I'm sorry. There's so much work at Sinai that I've lost track of time. Ivan feels much better, so we'll reach out to Dean tonight. I'll let you know as soon as we hear from him."

"Sure. Sounds good. Everything else okay there?"

"Yep. It's similar to what we did at Hopkins. Lots of watching the infected for results, then shuffling them through to the next recovery room. We've been taking groups of them to the train every day."

"That's good to hear. Our efforts allowed this to happen. I'll catch up with you tonight."

He hangs up, and I brush off the feeling that he's only interested in Dean. I wonder if I've put him in some position by being here. I send Dean a text asking if he'll come by.

Angela stands in the hallway near my room.

"Lady. Where have you been?" she asks with her arms folded over her chest. I don't answer, but I walk into my room with her behind me. There's a rations box on my table that I rummage through. A chewy protein bar that resembles peanut butter is all that's left.

"Want to share this?" I hold it up to her, but she shakes her head.

"What are you doing? You came here like a bullet with one target, Mona's stars on your map."

"And to find Dean," I remind her.

"Which you did. Now you've bailed. The train is moving people out already. How much longer do you think you have?"

I chew on my bar. My teeth get stuck in the soft, sticky glob, making it hard to talk. The map is secure in the backpack I keep in the closet. I carefully pull it out and lay it on the bed before us.

"Look at these marks." Angela points to one near Fells Point. "It was so close to where we were. And this one is near the stadium."

I count the stars again, and there are five, mainly around the center of the harbor. It's possible to look into several of them in one trip. "What time is it?"

"Time to go for a stroll?" Angela grins. "Secret mission Blue Star. I have to run to my room, but I'll be back in ten minutes."

My mouth parts to say something. A protest, maybe? But nothing comes out. Angela leaves, and I scramble to find my running shoes and a hat to block the sun. I fill my water bottle before studying the map one more time.

Our journey will not be a short walk. We'll be several miles away from Sinai, and we need to be home by eight this evening before it gets too dark.

One star is at Johns Hopkins, and that won't be easy to get into. It's also a giant building, and there are only so many clues Mona left me. Another is in an apartment complex north of Fells Point, and yet another is close to where I lived with Dean. The other stars are on the other side of the harbor, and we won't have time to search for them. Each star has a number next to it, and I assume it's a building number to help us narrow in. We're about to find out.

Angela knocks on my door. She has a backpack on, and a gun strapped to her back, so it hangs near her rib cage. I put the Glock I carry in my bag.

"First stop, Hopkins?" I ask.

"Hmmm," Angela looks at the map laid across my bed. "Let's try for the furthest away first, so we're making our way back."

"That's a better plan. The first stop is somewhere south of Patterson Park, near Fells Point."

I fold the map, and we are on our way. I feel guilty about leaving Ivan behind, but Aisha has been keeping him busy, and he likes getting involved. Their relationship grows more intimate with every passing day, and I'd rather step away altogether.

Once outside, I immediately start to sweat. July will be over soon, but the summer sun is high and hot, with no rain in our future.

"How do you want to go?" I assume she's been running this for a while since the convention center is south too.

"Stick to the main roads. They ask the cured to relocate closer to the train until they depart. They should leave us alone if we show them this." Angela pulls her badge from her pocket.

I fiddle with the badge I keep in my back pocket. It's a fake name, and I say it over and over in my head in case anyone calls me by it.

"Do you think we'll see sours? The ones Dean is so afraid of?" So much so that he doesn't come to the hospital unless Jason clears it.

"I've only seen them once, and that was when they first arrived at the convention center. Talk about a group of muscle-stuffed individuals!"

We skirt several parks because they're so overgrown the vines would prevent us from pressing through. When we take an exit to walk on route 83, a main artery feeding the city, I notice how bare the highway is. No soil means nothing is growing, but there are cars layered with years of dust that we walk past. Most have their windows broken from those searching for supplies. The sun is unforgiving, but we continue until it becomes too much.

"Let's walk under the overpass," Angela suggests. It's a longer walk but much cooler. I haven't been on an adventure like this with Angela for quite a while. Our first solo trip was when she cut her arm, and I walked her up to Hopkins for antibiotics and stitches. Our friendship has grown so much since then. We've become survivors together; created new lives outside the walls with careers, happy hours, and confidants. We have friends on the outside that we invite to the bar or a baseball game, but for the most part, Angela, Jeronimo, and I stick together.

It's like we've become a secret unit of runners. I wonder if Jason would have been part of our group if we didn't break up. Did I take that option away from him when I moved in with Angela and

Jeronimo? I've considered that I have, and my need for belonging outweighs the guilt.

I wedged my way into Angela and Jeronimo's tiny house when Jason and I split. Fearful they'd turn me down and take their old leader's side, they welcomed me openly, and Jason stepped back to give me space.

Angela sees me randomly smiling at her. "What's gotten into you?"

"Thinking about everything we've been through together, that's all."

"Well, let's be sure this isn't our last Thelma and Louise adventure, okay?"

"I'm pretty sure they die at the end of that movie," I say.

"Okay, well. Let's not do that part."

We pass by a road that would have taken us to Hopkins and keep going. Everything is becoming more familiar as we move closer to Fells Point.

"Can we walk through so I can see it?" Then she'll know what I mean.

"I haven't seen the Rec Pier yet, either. Let's go down this way." Angela points us through Little Italy. "Over that way is where we'll find another star. We'll go there next."

Within a few more minutes, we come to the cobblestone that lines the streets of Fells Point. There are so many weeds popping up between the stones that it's easier to walk on the sidewalk. When we turn the corner, I see the remains of the tech house where Kory lost his life. We tried to put the fire out with buckets from the harbor across the street, but our efforts did nothing to save him. The building crumbled on top of him.

A few days later, there was an explosion at the Rec Pier. April shot Jason. I killed April. Lindsay was lost. It was a nightmare.

It's been two years since I saw the Rec Pier. I'm shocked at what's left when we come up to it. The front of the building is black, but some stone walls remain. Trees grow in the center. They reach for the sun and away from the charcoal and rubble ground.

It's almost completely gone.

So many runners drowned or were attacked by the infected. Everything slowed down after this until I got word that I was leaving.

"Hey, what do you think?" Angela says as we stand in front of the building, looking at the charred ruins of our old headquarters. The trees growing inside rustle in the wind. Its new inhabitants.

"I'm sad another historical building is gone, and for the destruction Fat Man caused. But I'm glad we aren't here anymore."

"Same." Angela raises her middle finger. "Fuck you, Fat Man. You turned April against us, murdered countless people, and other things."

"I'm sure we're just scratching the surface of what this guy stood for."

"Terrifying!" Angela shudders. "Let's go. What was that number on the map?"

I wrote it on my palm so I wouldn't have to pull the map out again. "2220 are the numbers. We need to move around the harbor more."

Our pace is slowing, and our heavy feet and overheated bodies protest. But finally, we make it to the first building. It's a long warehouse-looking structure turned into elegant offices. The outside is painted gray, and several signs over the door indicate more than one company is inside.

"Now what?" I tested the door, and it's locked. I can't imagine anyone would try to loot an office building.

Angela reads the signs to herself, her lips mumbling as she goes. "Newton Inc. sounds like a science type of company, right?" She punches the name in her phone and skims what she finds. "Yep, looks like a good target. I'll look up the others. Maybe we should break in through the back, so we don't draw any attention."

We split up and walk around the building in search of an easy way in. When we meet around the back, large windows make up one of the office spaces.

"That's a lot of glass." I look around for something to break it. A brick catches my eye. "This will work."

Angela gives me a thumbs-up and steps away. I throw the brick at the glass, then cover my ears, expecting it to shatter. Only it doesn't. It clinks, then falls to the ground.

"I threw that hard!" I protest.

"Let me try." Angela picks up the brick, and I put my hands over my ears again to soften the sound. I see her bicep bulge as she brings her arm back and then lets the brick sail into the window. It cracks but doesn't shatter.

She throws the brick again, and the glass webs across the window this time. We're getting there. It takes three more throws before the glass shatters. The noise echoes through the street.

"Let's get inside." I step in, calling out so anyone inside, including the infected, won't be caught off guard. Together, we draw our guns and walk into the office space.

"Which office are we in?" Angela says.

"We'll have to check the front lobby." The office smells like paper, plastic, and cleaning products. There's a company sign indicating this isn't the space we're looking for. Luckily, the door to the lobby isn't locked, and we get to the directory easily.

Newton is on the second floor. When we get up the steps, the door to the office is open, and inside, it looks like someone has been here. Papers are thrown around the small space inside, with cubicles and a few closed doors to offices. Filing cabinets spill over, and desks are overturned.

"This is a mess," I say.

"Yeah, but it tells me we're in the right place. Let's look around." Angela goes into the first office.

I'm lost in the clutter. What are we even looking for? Whatever it is, we aren't the only ones. I step over fallen chairs, trash cans, and cubical walls that are down.

The first office I go into is that of the CFO. There are files everywhere, but no laptop. Just by looking at the information scattered on the ground, nothing important glares at me. Every drawer and cabinet space is empty on the floor. I swim through it until I give up and move to the next room.

Again, it's a disaster, and again, nothing stands out. I make my way to another room and find it locked. I throw my shoulder into the door, and I'm painfully reminded that I'm not very strong.

"Angela. There's a locked door here."

"Guess what I found? Keys." She dangles them in her fingers and crosses the open space with cubicles until she gets to me. "It was taped to the underside of a drawer."

"How did you know to look there?" I'm amazed.

"Too many true crime shows, I guess." She tries several keys before one works. Inside is a windowless space that's too dark to see inside. So we both instinctively use the flashlight setting on our phones.

Cages. The first thing I notice are small metal cages.

It looks like towels are at the bottom, most likely bedding for an animal.

"I don't like this." I try the light switch with no success. Angela gives me a gentle push to encourage me to walk into the room, but my feet aren't convinced.

"I'll go first." Angela walks around me.

Our light moves over large metal tables, filing cabinets, chairs, and monitors, and then it falls on the cages again. As I lean closer, I realize those are not towels in the cage but chimpanzees that have rotted down to nothing but bone and fur.

"That's horrible. They starved in here, the poor things."

Angela shakes her head. "We have to be in the right place. But what are we looking for?"

"Lab results?" Movies make sleuthing look much easier than this. "We can't stay here forever. Let's grab a few things and study them later. The files in here aren't touched."

In a digital world, there isn't much on print, but we grab anything paper we can find—even calendars from the wall and notepads found in various locations. Something has to make sense.

"Let's try that second location. We can always come back." Angela is as discouraged as I am, but we stuff our bags with what we can carry. Before we leave, I find a phone directory taped to someone's desk.

"We can see if Google identifies anyone." I fold the form and put it in a side pocket.

We make our way out of the building, stepping over the broken window as we go. The overwhelming sensation that we walked several miles to find nothing eats away at me. I'll fail at this mission, and one of Mona's dying wishes will be for nothing. I promise to bring in Jason if I get stuck, but for now, I'll sift through what we found when I'm not worried about the incoming night and the terror it brings.

"The next stop is near those housing projects outside Little Italy," Angela says. "What will we find there?"

A man steps behind us and growls, "You're not going to find anything!" His hand grabs my backpack as I try to run. Angela whirls around and draws her gun. I duck, covering my head, expecting her to shoot.

eighteen

Shelby

HIDDEN CLUES APPEAR
LIKE A PUZZLE, MUST BE SOLVED
TO FIND THE TRUTH NEAR

Angela laughs sarcastically. "Ha, very funny. How did you find us?"

I look up to find Jason and Jeronimo. Only one of them finds this amusing, and it's not Jason who has a good grip on my bag straps.

"Let go!" I tug away while Jeronimo snickers at us.

"What are you doing here?" Jason says. "Aisha received a call that someone was breaking into a building."

Jeronimo grins. "We didn't expect to find you two screwballs."

Jason releases me and walks over to the door we smashed in. "You do this?"

"Angela did," I say

"Why?" Jeronimo and Jason ask together.

The map is secure in my bag, but so are about twenty pounds of random papers. I scramble over what to say, what story to conjure up that's believable—anything to get them to turn around and leave us alone. We have two more stops if we're lucky.

"I thought I heard someone inside," I say.

"So you went through the window?" Jeronimo asks.

Jason steps through the broken window and checks out the office space. "Someone better tell me what the fuck is going on, and now. I don't have time for your games or the runaround. So what are you looking for?"

Angela looks at me with a pathetic look that tells me she's about to spill everything. "They could help us."

"No," I say.

Jason comes back to the sidewalk and kicks glass from under his feet. "Shelby. You didn't come in here for Dean, did you?"

"Of course I did!"

"And?" Jason asks.

"Um." I stumble while Jeronimo and Angela patiently wait for words to come out. Do they expect lies? "I don't want to tell you."

Jason runs his hands through his hair and back to his neck. "For fuck's sake, Shelby! This is why it's so hard to help you. You keep things hidden, putting people in danger, and then the world explodes around you."

I'm shocked by his words. I haven't wrangled Jason into anything. "No! You can't do that. Your problem is you don't trust me to take care of myself. Well, I can do much more than you give me credit for. Save your hero act for someone else!"

I grab Angela by the arm and lead her away from them, trying not to cry.

"You okay?" Angela asks.

"He doesn't control me. He's not the law. There is no authority here. If I want to break into an office to look around, I can do it without his permission." Every instance he's kept me out of boils to the surface.

The pounding of feet catching up to us doesn't deter me from stomping on.

"Shelby, wait." Jason jogs in front of me and walks backward to get my attention. "I'm sorry, okay? You know what we've been through here, and when you shut me out, I worry."

I stop walking and shove him back. "I'm doing something. And it's important, but it's also none of your business."

Angela murmurs, "It's something Mona gave her."

"Mona? She's dead." Jason is interested, and it's all falling apart.

"She gave me a key," I admit. "It could lead to information about the virus."

"Mona?" Jason says again. "I saw her in her final days. She wasn't right in the head. Between dementia and the trauma, I wouldn't be sure about whatever she left."

Jeronimo puts up his hands to calm us down. "It's true. I heard she had a few screws loose in the end, but we all respected her. I think Shelby deserves to be heard out. If she wants to tell us."

His composure surprises me, and I'm tempted, but not without assurances. "I'm not sure I want to."

Angela encourages me. "Shelby, these guys are our friends. Jason might be a little hot-headed, but we can trust them."

I eye Jason, worried he'll throw me on a train at any moment. "You don't need to watch over me," I say to Jason. "This is important, and I need you to let me see it through."

"You're not putting yourself or anyone else in danger?" Jason asks.

"No, of course not." I feel as though that's mostly the truth, but it's hard to gauge.

He shakes his head, already apologizing for suggesting it. "I'm sorry. Let's see what you have." He's sincere because that's the type of man he is. If Jason wants in, this could go smoother, but if not, it's all over.

I kneel and swing my backpack in front of me. My fingers catch the zipper, and I open it enough to pull out the envelope with the map.

Carefully, I reveal it to Jason and Jeronimo, who swears in surprise.

"Is that my fucking map?" Jason asks.

"No. It's my fucking map. And if you support me, you'll take me to these locations on our way back to Sinai." I jab my finger at two stars, one at Hopkins.

Jason asks me several questions about the map. I explain that Lindsay brought it to me after Mona died and that Angela and I are leaving the first star, but there are more to follow. I share my assumption that Mona left it to me due to my connections with him and other key players and that it might show us who created the Lazarus virus.

"You've no idea what you're looking for?" He studies it closely, running his fingers over the fine-marked paper.

"Lindsay said they were tracking the virus and those involved from an early stage." I explain the papers in me and Angela's backpacks and our plan to look through them later.

"Okay. I support you." Jason folds the map and hands it back to me. "This is yours. It always has been."

"Thank you." I tuck it away so it won't be damaged.

Jason points us in the right direction. "We're running low on time, so I'm not sure we can check out Hopkins today. Anyway, there aren't any numbers listed there, and it's enormous." He helps me pack my things and gives me a hand so I can stand.

Jeronimo says, "She didn't tell you what to look for? This is like one of those themed escape room events, but in a city full of zombies."

"Something like that." I smile, and as a team, we walk down the street to the next location, which is in the apartment complex near Little Italy. It takes us a while to get there, and we contemplate the scenarios of what we're looking for and what it might lead to. I try to ignore Jason warning me that Mona wasn't of sound mind when she passed. This map could have been done at any time. Maybe even two years ago when she first left Baltimore.

When we come to the three-level condominiums made of red brick, small windows, and no porches or balconies, Jeronimo asks us to wait.

"There could be people living here."

"We know the apartment number," I remind him. "So we don't have to disturb too much."

There are tall weeds full of briars and mosquitoes we need to walk through. My bare skin catches and bleeds as thorns poke and tear. We swat at the bugs until we reach the landing going into the complex's main entrance. The door isn't locked, so we walk right in.

Before we move too far, we freeze at the sudden sound of groans from the basement level.

"Infected," Jeronimo whispers. "They suck at stairs, but we need to be quiet." He holds his finger up to his lips, and we all nod in compliance.

Carefully, we take two flights up to the top floor and find the apartment we need. I try the doorknob, and it opens. Inside looks as if it's currently occupied. No dust or trash is lying about. The couch has a butt imprint and a cup of coffee next to it.

"Is someone here?" I ask Jason, who's standing closest to me.

He shrugs and takes out his gun. We walk through the small living room and past the open kitchen. It smells like food, and a can of empty soup is on the counter.

"We should call out." I suggest as I tug on Jason's sleeve.

Jeronimo hears me and shouts into the room. "Anyone home?"

There's a shuffle in the room down the hall. The afternoon sun creates a dim hallway, but we walk down slowly, holding onto one another, with Jason in the lead and his gun drawn.

"Who's there?" Jason calls. "We're with the rescue mission and don't mean any harm. The trains are running. You can get out of the city."

I'm in the back of the group. My head is hiding behind Angela. I have my gun in my hand, but it's pointed at the ground, and I pray I don't need it.

A woman shouts to us. "I'm a cured infected! This home is where I grew up, so I came back here. I don't have any weapons. Please don't hurt me."

Jason calms his voice. "Come on out. We have guns, but we will lower them when we're sure you're unarmed."

A thin Black woman with a scarf around her head comes out of the room with her hands in the air. She's terrified, and behind her is another person, but I can't make them out.

"Who's with you?" Jason asks.

"A friend, but she's shy." The woman is dragged back into the room by a smaller hand tugging on her pink house dress. "It's okay," the woman says to whoever is behind her. "They won't hurt you, dear. They're with the rescue mission."

Jason flashes his identification badge so the older woman can see it. "That's right. Here's my ID."

Suddenly, the woman pitches forward and falls on the carpeted floor as if someone pushed her. I glimpse braided black hair, jeans, and white sneakers dashing away from the door. Then, a crash occurs, and the woman on the floor screams.

"They won't hurt you! Come back!"

A crash comes from the room. I push past Jason and step over the woman to get to the bedroom. A large sliding window is punched through, and blood is on the sharp edges. When I look outside, there's no one.

What was that? How did they survive a fall like that, or even have the strength to push through the window?

"No one's here," I call out to the others.

Angela comes in behind me and looks out the window. "Do you think it was like that before now?"

The blood on the window is red and fresh. "No, I don't. Was that what I think it was?"

Angela says what I'm thinking. "A sour. But how?"

Jason and Jeronimo take the distressed woman to the couch and get her a glass of water. It comes out brown, but she drinks it anyway.

"Want to tell us what's going on here? Let's start with your name." Jason asks.

"I'm Beth Jackson, and that was my niece. When I arrived here after they cured me, she had been living here. Said her father and mother were dead. She's special, you understand?"

Jason continues to speak softly. "Your niece, does she have a name?"

"Viola Jackson. She's just a girl. Please don't hurt her." The woman trembles so much that I sit next to her and take the water glass from her hand.

"I'm not hurting anyone. My name is Shelby Bolger, and I'm here to save the sours."

"Sour." The word rolls off Beth's tongue, and I can't be sure, but I think she's heard it before.

"That's what I think Viola is. Can you tell me if she heals quickly? Can she run fast and smell things you can't pick up? Does bright light hurt her eyes?" I sit back, giving her space to process my questions. Years of working with survivors have taught me one thing; they need to go at their own pace.

She fumbles with the hem of her shirt, and her eyes fall on me, capturing my full attention. "How did you know?"

"I'm a Lazarus City survivor, and I used to work at Hopkins."

Beth flushes and gathers her thoughts. "I was infected early on." She lifts her sleeves to show me bite marks on her arms. "I wish I knew what happened to my brother's family. Viola has been this way since before I was a bit."

"This is your house?" I ask.

"It's a rental property I have. It used to be my mother's. I moved in to fix it up right before the infection took over. I'd never planned to stay long term, but now it's home, and the infected can't get up here easily." Beth has calmed down enough for us to ask her more questions, but she's worried about her niece.

"Do you have a phone?"

"No, I'm sorry. But I'm here most days."

Jeronimo speaks up. "Not for long. They're going to want you on that train and soon."

Beth's expression falls. "I can't leave Viola. I'm all she has."

"I think there are others like her," I say. "Because someone I love is a sour too."

nineteen

Dean

BROTHERS ON THE MOVE SHARE WISDOM AND HISTORY WITH NOTHING TO PROVE

Fifty-five miles of beltway surround Baltimore City. That's over three-thousand square miles for me to hide, and I've not run into the sours in a week, so I feel comfortable visiting Sinai tonight. Aisha lets me know where the sours are expected each night, and I go in the opposite direction.

It's just after nine at night, and the sunset has faded. I go to the back door of the hospital and punch my code in as I always have. Inside is quiet, so I walk to where they run trials until I find someone.

Rob comes into view first. He greets me with a grin and a tricky handshake I can only attempt to follow. "Sup!" he says. "Here to lend a hand tonight? We could use a few rotters."

"I didn't know I was coming here to work." That's not Shelby's intention either, but I'll do what I can if they need me. And then I'll go back to hiding until Dr. Warren can get me over the walls.

At the end of the hall, Ivan and Aisha stroll toward me, looking cozy. They're smiling and joking about something. She slaps his arm and laughs. I recognize what's going on here.

"You're looking better," I say to Ivan, catching him in a romantic trance. Instinctually, I want to tell him Aisha is crazy, controlling, and bossy. But that would be my story and how we reacted together.

Ivan's a grown-up. I'll see how this plays out, as long as it's not in front of me.

"Dean! He walks over and throws his arms around me, thumping my back in a tight hug. "How have you been? Any trouble out there?"

"No. I've laid low, thanks to Aisha's tips."

Aisha blushes and takes a step away from Ivan. "Let's keep it that way. I'll let you two catch up. There are a few cured to move into recovery rooms. Rob, can you come with me?"

Rob follows her down the hall. "Sure, but Dean, we need more rotters while you're here. If you don't mind, that is."

"I don't mind."

"I'll come with you," Ivan addresses me. "My arm is doing much better. Did you want to go find Shelby first?"

"No, I can do that after. Let's go." Tonight is the first time we've worked together like this. I imagine his military training will kick in, and he'll be more of a help than most out there. I can leave him in the van until the rotters pass out. But just in case, I ask him to get his gun.

He meets me at the front entrance, and we walk outside into the twilight. The van I always drive is parked where they'll unload the rotters. It's a white moving van, nothing fancy. We can't repair the rusty tire wells and a crack in the windshield. It's always unlocked, and the keys are above the visor. Ivan climbs in beside me and notices where I keep them.

"No one tries to steal it?" he asks.

"There aren't cars moving around, so no one checks anymore. They have a drone and bring gas. Messy process." I turn the ignition, and we're off.

Ivan receives a phone call from Aisha and talks quietly with her. I drive slowly away from the main entrance and down the road, leaving the hospital while I wait for information from Ivan. The sours were supposed to be far from this area, but that could change. When we approach a stop sign, I stop. Then I almost turn on the blinker out of habit. How does that still happen after all this time?

"She said to avoid Mt. Washington and Hampden," Ivan says, hanging up the phone. Then he adjusts his seat and stares ahead as if he doesn't want to talk about something. I know exactly what it is, so I push that button.

"So, you're moving in on Aisha?" I turn the wheel, so we're heading east.

"No." He acts surprised that I would ask.

"You sure? Because things are definitely over with us. I mean, super over, no spark, never going to happen again kind of over." I side-eye him, trying to catch a reaction. Are his cheeks pinking up?

Ivan tugs on his shorts in discomfort. "She's nice."

A chuckle bubbles up from deep in my gut, and a laugh forms in my chest before it bursts out. "Aisha is an absolute gorgeous disaster. She's mouthy as hell, but she's usually right. Look, Ivan, if you like her and need my permission or something, then go for it."

"I thought you two were together."

"We *were* together. We aren't anymore and there's plenty of time between our breakup and now. She's firmly in the friend zone." Very firmly. Again, I should warn him, but that wouldn't be fair to either of them. Aisha was in a desperate situation, and she clung to me when all I needed was to be alone. We're both guilty of unhealthy relationship decisions.

"Firmly in the friend zone?" Ivan asks.

"Very firm. Vise-like, even," I assure him.

His lips part, and a grin spreads across his face. "Cool."

"Cool," I repeat. This is the deepest conversation we've had in a while, and while I wish it weren't about my ex-girlfriend, I'm glad to see Ivan taking an interest in someone.

The engine attracts rotters, and some trail out of the woods between residential areas nearby. This area of the city is spread out, with family sized homes, mature trees, and open space now covered in brush and overgrowth.

"Looks like we got our first customer," I say.

151

Three rotters walk into view. I quickly notice how clean their clothing is, and their faces aren't as pale as usual. Ivan grabs my arm.

"Those are soldiers."

They're wearing gray fatigues, but I can't find any points of injury.

"Stay in the van," I tell Ivan. "And keep it running in case."

"In case of what?" Ivan's eyes widen, and he slips over into my seat when I exit the car. I take the medical bag with me that has syringes ready.

It has been months since I've seen a freshly turned rotter. A few mishaps have happened while curing rotters, but it's seldom. And the team at Sinai are vaccinated, so most grow ill, but recover. At Sinai, we have all the tools needed to cure someone. Out in the field is different. Leaving Ivan's question unanswered, I creep towards the rotters for a better look.

Two men, one woman in gray t-shirts, and matching cargo pants amble toward me. Their boots are laced neatly, and the woman's hair is pulled back in a tight bun that isn't disturbed. They've turned very recently.

I've seen a lot of things in this city, so I'm cautious as I approach them.

The woman's black eyes fall on me, and she stops. Mouth gaping open, swaying in place, she's similar to the others with struggled moans making an "ah ah ah." I plunge the needle into her neck, then ease her fall to the ground.

Next, I focus on her buddies, the two men. They have wandered past me and are against the window trying to get to Ivan. My brother holds his gun to their heads, ready to shoot if they break the window. I run up behind them and quickly administer the sedative. They're sloppier than the woman and fall to the ground like limp spaghetti.

"Oops." I pull them away from the door so Ivan can get out. But before I let him open the door, I inhale to see if there are other rotters nearby. There is rot, but it's not close, and there is no wind. "Come out," I tell him.

Ivan steps out of the van and holsters his weapon. "How recently did they turn?"

"I'd guess within twenty-four hours. Something must have happened. Maybe these are scouts that made a stupid move. Let's get them back to the hospital."

"Wait. Are they injured? How did they turn?" Ivan carefully flips over one of the men, and we look for a bite mark. We pull up his shirt and his pant legs, not finding anything.

We search the other two, and they're also free from wounds based on a quick spot check.

This is suspicious, but they're rotters who need the cure. "Maybe Aisha or Jason will know something," I say. "Let's get them into the van and restrained."

Ivan and I carry the men to the back of the van and bind their hands and feet. The woman is light, and I easily run through the same routine with her.

"Let's get them back," I say. "Someone might be looking for them."

We drive to the hospital. Ivan is quiet for a while, but then he sets in on the questions. "Will they let them go home once they're cured?"

"Trains have been taking the cured out, so it's possible."

"Do you think Shelby has anything important with that map?"

I'm wondering how he's putting these things together, but I answer. "From what I understand, Mona had her connections, so it could be worth looking into. But you two need to be on a train soon." I'm not trying to scare him, but he could have been killed on their first day, and now we're seeing soldiers with the virus. It's always been unstable here, but this is a new height.

"Wait," I say, slamming on the brakes. A dark figure hovers in the shadows, but in a second, I recognize her. "Stay here." I jump out of the car and run to the overgrown yard where the woman stands. With no time to waste, I go to my text messages on my phone and scroll through until I find one Lion sent. It's a family picture of Lion, his wife, mother, and his daughter. They were living together in Druid Hill when rotters attacked them. Lion isn't sure what became of his family. I zoom in on the woman in the photo. She has a ruby ring instead of a diamond wedding ring on her left hand. Her cheeks are round, and she's petite like her husband.

I step over the briars and fallen limbs that separate me and the woman for a better look. She doesn't run, of course, because she's a rotter. It makes it easy to pick up her hand and find her ruby wedding ring. Tears sting my eyes, and I choke them back. I found her.

"You're going to be okay, Mrs. Stark. I'm going to take your hand and you lead to the van." I'm gentle, but she won't move. Then I notice her feet are caught in vines tied around her ankles. One vine is cutting into her so severely that the skin has swollen.

I remove my hatchet and saw away at the vines until I can move her. Parts of the vine are tightly in place, but I'd rather the medical team look at her injuries than pull it off myself.

Her steps are too wobbly, and I think she might fall, so I swing her into my arms like a husband carrying his wife over the threshold of a new house. She must have been standing in one place for days or weeks. If it were winter, she'd have died.

Ivan steps out of the van, but I yell at him to get back in. I'm not taking any chances. Lion's wife eating Ivan would ruin this moment, and she can't be trusted around salts.

I ask Ivan to roll down the window and give me a syringe. Then I quickly do what I did to the soldiers, binding her ankles gently.

As quickly as I can, I get in the van and get us on the road again.

"Who is that?" Ivan asks.

"It's Lion's wife. At least I'm almost certain it is. I've been looking for his family since he told me about them. When I got a new phone, I asked Lion to send me the picture again."

"Damn. That would be a miracle."

My heart thumps wildly at the possibility. Have I found this woman after all this time? His mother was much older, so I didn't think I would find her, but I'd kept my hopes up about finding his wife and college-aged daughter. I've also been looking for Rob's wife, even though he told me not to. I suppose there's something in him that knows she's dead, so I don't push him. Still, I look.

We pull up to the emergency entrance at Sinai. No one is outside because we have this routine down. I get out first. I inhale to test for rotters in the area, and then I circle the building as quickly as possible doing the same.

I run up to the glass and thump it hard enough to get their attention. The doors open, and Rob and Aisha come outside. They each have a gurney. A few cured sours from our community come out with more gurneys.

Rob opens the back of the van. "Only four? What's going on?" He's concerned and bracing himself for someone mangled inside. Someone incurable.

I point to the uniformed rotters. "Three of them are soldiers that we can't find wounds on. It's suspicious as hell. Then there's this woman." I step in front of Rob and into the back of the van. Carefully, I carry her out and place her on the closest gurney. The assistants quickly secure her to the bed in case she awakens.

Rob leans over her and shrugs. "She looks okay. We should be able to help her."

"Her ankles are in bad shape," I say. Be careful when you untie her." I look at Aisha, who is focusing on the soldiers. "Aisha, do you recognize this woman?"

"Let me see." Aisha comes over to examine the woman. Then she gasps. "Is this Pearl Stark? Oh dear god, Dean. If this is her," she trails off. "Get her inside! This could be Lion's wife." With that, several of our crew jump into action. Each of them knows Lion and feels the urgency.

Our group shares pictures of missing loved ones. Aisha is certain her family is dead because she witnessed it. There are friends of hers we look for, and occasionally we'll find people we knew, but this is special. We've not had a hit this close before.

Two assistants run Lion's wife inside with Aisha, leaving Rob and Ivan to move the other bodies onto a gurney and secure them.

We'll reunite Lion with his wife. I can't imagine how he'll react. Disbelief is my first guess, then gratitude and possibly mourning when Pearl realizes how many years she lost with her daughter, and mother-in-law gone. All sense of normalcy forever changed.

"Out of everything you've brought, these four are like nothing I've seen," Rob says. His attention turns to the soldiers. "No wounds? That's something else. We'll cut off their clothes and examine them closer." He puts a glove on and rubs his hand over the man's arms and legs. Then he pauses. "I don't want this to get weird, but I'm going to feel this guy's ass."

"Okay," I say slowly.

Rob runs his hand over the man's pants and around to his backside, then under his back as far as he can reach with the man tied to a stretcher. I watch curiously.

"Here. Feel this." Rob reaches for my hand and brings it to the guy's lower back. I almost pull away, but then I feel it. There's a little lump.

"What is that?" I let the nubby thing roll around in the man's skin.

Rob walks over to the woman and feels in the same area. "I saw this in a movie once. It could be a tracker."

An insane story comes together, and I say it out loud. "No bite marks. Recently turned. Tracker? Are we being set up?" I breathe in deeply, trying to catch trouble, and that's precisely what I find. "Fuck. Get inside!"

"What is it?" Ivan scans the night around us, drawing his gun. "I don't see anything."

"They're here. Watching."

The assistants return and run the rotters inside with Rob closely behind them. "I'll get others," he calls back.

"Ivan, go with them!" I pull the hatchet from my belt and walk away from the van. "Now!"

"Who is it?" He's frantically trying to understand what's happening. A gunshot echoes into the night, hitting the van close to Ivan.

"Get the fuck inside!" I growl like an animal. The veins in my arms thicken as blood pumps quicker, trying to keep up with the adrenaline coursing around me.

Ivan trips as he tries to run, but he rights himself and scurries inside. He won't leave the doorway of the hospital, though. On his knees, he points his gun into the darkness, waiting for the threat to present itself.

Their smell is more pungent now. Sours and rotters. Lots of them coming this way.

twenty

Dean

HATCHET IN MY FIST
TRUSTED AND NEVER FAILING
YOUR SKULL CAN'T RESIST

Jeronimo runs out with Jason behind him. A few of our assistants are previous liaisons and scouts from the old days, and they're ready for whatever comes at us.

"Dean, get closer to us." Jason waves at me, but I ignore him. This isn't their fight. Aren't the sours part of the rescue mission? So that means they're technically on the same side.

Jason, like an idiot, runs out to where I am. Without hesitation, Jeronimo and the others follow.

Jeronimo speaks first. "How many?"

"Rotters? Maybe twenty or thirty. That's not what's got me concerned. Sours, a few of them. Maybe five or six." My sight allows me to see them before Jason and Jeronimo. I point in the direction of the woods to the side of the hospital. "They're coming from there, but some might be on the street too. You need to secure the hospital. I'll lead them away."

"Man, that's a lot of trouble on your ass," Jeronimo says. "Let me take a few down."

Jason holds out his hand. "We can't shoot down the sours unless we have good reason."

"The fuck, Jason." Jeronimo keeps his gun pointed toward the woods. "Those sours are leading a herd of infected to our front door. Seems like a good reason." Moans of the infected reach us. Twigs snap in the distance as they rustle their way forward.

"The rotters are a distraction," I say. I inhale again, and the scent of sours surrounds me. There's no telling where they're coming from.

Jason barks orders at those around us. "Use tranquillizer darts. We can collect rotters like we always do, and if we hit the sours, then we'll treat them too."

Everyone holsters their pistols and takes out a longer barrel gun. "We'll need more," one of them says. Then, there's a quick discussion of who'll stay and who'll retrieve more supplies.

"Where are Shelby and Aisha?" I ask.

Jeronimo says, "They're inside. Let's worry about getting you out of this without them bagging and tagging you."

"That's fair." My fate affects everyone, as Aisha so kindly pointed out the other day. "Here they come."

Rotters, two and three at a time, come from the woods. Their clothes are tattered, their skin so gray it's as if they were rubbed in ashes. These are old rotters. Sick from the early days. But it's clear they've been rounded up and sent here on purpose.

Our crew is made whole again when others return with more supplies.

Jason shouts over the groans coming closer. "Use these on the good-looking ones but take out any rotters who can't be cured. If it comes to it, save yourself first." We all know what he means.

The pop of the tranquilizer guns sounds off as six of our assistants walk toward the mob. They aren't as scared as they would be if they'd never been this close to them. They understand how they move, and how not to get pinned into a group closing in around you. They're more intelligent than the soldiers brought here to work at the convention center or try to capture me.

Rotters wobble and drop as the sedative kicks in. At first, we're able to keep up with those coming close, but behind this group is another twenty. The largest hoard I've seen in a while.

Jeronimo shoots down the first rotter with a traumatic head injury. They had a split running from their forehead down to their chin, with bone showing through the coagulated skin. Then Jeronimo takes out another who has half an arm missing, and an exposed femur. They don't bleed. The virus won't allow their blood to run thin enough.

I step away from the group. The rotters are coming from the same direction, which suggests that those targeting me would sneak up from behind. With another inhale, I sense the sours are doing just that, so I run away from the group.

Jason calls after me. "Where are you going?"

"Sours are this way. Keep your eyes on the rotters." The sours would not hurt the people here, but the rotters would enjoy a late-night breakfast if they could.

I follow the scent, and it leads me around the hospital to the dumpsters. There are several in a line. I listen for someone close to me, but there's only guns firing on the other side of the hospital.

"Omar, you out there?"

This game frustrates me. I could run, but they would follow, and it's clear there are more sours.

A man steps out from behind tall pines a few yards past the garbage. "I'm here, Dean." When he says my name, it confirms how dangerous this has become.

I smile to be an asshole. "Where are the rest of you?"

"You don't have to run, Dean." Omar shortens the distance between us. "We want to talk."

"Yeah? Well, I like talking. What do you want to talk about?" He didn't answer where his friends are, so they're probably right behind me. Going back the way I came isn't an option.

"Let's make a deal," Omar says with a wide grin. "If you don't run, we won't hurt you. Then we can talk about what it's like to be infected like us."

"You feel strong, don't you? How long have you been like this?" I let him continue walking toward me, and he stops a yard away. "Did they tell you in less than eleven months you'll start to feel sick? Then in a few weeks, you'll die without treatment. Do they even offer you treatment?"

His eyes flash, and I've struck a nerve. "That's not true."

"How long since you turned? Three months? I'm faster and stronger than you, but you probably guessed that when I outran you the other day." I smile so he can see I'm goading him. Time living with this virus has given me an advantage.

Then he grins and nods slowly. "It's been about that long."

"Feeling like a king, are you?"

"It's time to come with me, Dean," Omar's deep voice rattles. He's the tallest man I've ever seen, with shoulders the size of watermelons.

There's shuffling behind me and over my shoulder are four sours dressed in dark street clothes. I take out my hatchet, lunge forward, and slice Omar's knee with all my strength. He falls, clutching his leg. I know it'll heal, but this gives me time to deal with the others.

A man with a big nose and long hair jumps on my shoulders, but I twist and drop him to the ground. I raise my hatchet and bring it down on his skull. It cracks and splits. He won't recover. Someone shrieks and grabs my arm, pulling me away. It's a woman with sharp nails digging into my arm so tightly she pierces my skin. Another man dressed in a dark jogging suit catches my other arm. He pulls the hatchet from my hand and throws it to the ground.

"You killed Sergio!" he shouts at me. Together they hold onto me while another young woman punches me in the face. My nose breaks, and stars flash before me.

"Fuck!" I groan. Then I raise my foot and kick her in the stomach. She doubles over, screaming.

The man in the dark jogging suit makes a mistake and gets too close to me. "You okay?" He leans in, asking the woman holding her stomach. I crack my forehead into his cheekbone and he releases me. I use my free hand to punch the woman with sharp nails in the throat. She grabs her neck, wheezing. I scramble to the ground for my hatchet, but a burning sensation rips through my calve.

Someone shot me.

I reach my hatchet and turn around to throw it at my attacker. It whirls through the air and lands squarely in the man's face. He drops his gun, his dark jogging suit spoils with blood, and he falls to the ground. My hatchet is out of reach and buried deep within him. There are two women remaining, and one of them lets Omar lean on her to stand.

I march to the man who's face holds my hatchet. I brace my good leg on the ground and press my other foot to his cheek so I can pry it free. The bullet went straight through my leg; it throbs so badly I feel nauseous.

In a hobbled jog, I run to the front of the hospital away from the sours. The women with Omar gain on me quickly.

Jason sees me coming. "What the hell happened? You're shot?" Then he sees the threat closing in. "Jeronimo, this way!" he shouts.

Jeronimo aims and fires his tranquilizer guns at the sours coming closer. One of the women staggers, and then drops. But he misses the other. Omar is healed enough to walk, and he yells to us. "This is not your fight, Sinai. We don't want to hurt anyone here, but we will if we need to. Dean comes with us."

"Nobody is going with you, boss," Jeronimo says, firing the tranquilizer at him.

Omar jerks out of the way and Jeronimo misses by an inch. Then the giant man pulls out a pistol and shoots. Time nearly halts. One second Jeronimo is standing next to me, the next he's on the ground with blood spreading across his chest.

I take the gun from Jason and fire at Omar and his accomplice until there are no bullets left. The woman falls with a shot to her face and chest. Omar takes one in the shoulder; I was aiming for his heart. Then another hits his arm causing him to drop the gun. That shot was on purpose.

Omar grunts, "I'll be back for you. This city can't keep us apart forever." Then he turns and wanders away. I run my hand over my hatchet, but he's too far for me to do enough damage, so I watch him walk down the hill too injured to come back tonight.

Jason is on the ground holding Jeronimo's head in his lap. "Dean, how many rotters are left?" He's level and calm. I've seen this in people when things crash around them.

I quickly count the rotters on the other side of the van. "Five, but your crew's got them."

"Tell one of them to get help. Jeronimo is bad, but he's breathing. We need to airlift him tonight."

"Tonight?"

"Yes!" Jason turns his head towards me, and I can tell he's not as calm as I thought.

I rush to the door and find Ivan dragging drugged rotters into the building and securing them. "Jeronimo has been shot," I tell him. "Go get Aisha."

He sees my leg. "Are you okay?"

"It'll heal, but Jeronimo isn't like me. He will die." My leg is hot as my body tries to repair itself. The blood has stopped, but there's a lot of damage to the muscle, and possibly my bone. This will take several days to recover from. I'll need to lie low somewhere. At least I know Omar is in the same situation.

Ivan darts from the room, and I make sure the last rotter he worked on is secure to the stretcher. He's done an excellent job. How has he fallen into this world so quickly? I should be impressed, but I'm terrified.

Within minutes, Aisha runs down to meet me. "What is it?" she asks.

"Jason says they need Jeronimo airlifted. Is that possible?"

"What? I don't know. Who do I call?" She holds up her phone, and I point her outside.

Together, we come up on Jason and Jeronimo. Jason's hands are slick with blood as he keeps pressure on the chest wound.

"I think it punctured a lung. Give me your phone." Jason uses one hand to dial a number. Then he shouts. "This is Jason Foley with US Mission Crab Shack Unit 32. We need an airlift from Sinai for medical attention immediately."

We're silent. Confused over what's being said, hopeful that whoever Jason's connections are, they're able to save Jeronimo.

Jason hangs up before I catch the rest of what he said. "Get a gurney. We need to prepare Jeronimo for airlift."

Rob runs out with Shelby and Angela behind him. "We were told to stay inside, and then someone said Jeronimo was shot?" Rob swings his medical bag around and drops to the ground to attend to Jeronimo, whose face is turning blue, and there's a trace of blood on his lips.

"Gurney!" Jason shouts. Shelby jumps and runs back to the hospital to return with what's needed. We lift Jeronimo and get him in place with Rob putting pressure on the wound over Jason's hand.

Jason and his team storm inside, leaving Shelby, Aisha, and Ivan behind. There are bodies all around us. Probably fifty dead or drugged rotters, and then the sours; one dead, one drugged.

Aisha is overwhelmed. "These are too many for us."

"Leave them. The drug will wear off and they'll be gone by morning. You might want to secure this one. She's a sour." I point to my enemy on the ground. "I'd appreciate if you cured her as soon as possible."

Shelby steps forward. "Dean, you're hurt."

I wrap her in my arms and hold her. "I'll be okay. I'm sorry about Jeronimo."

When I pull away, her lip trembles. "Where are you going? You have to let Rob or Aisha look at your leg."

"No. It's fine. I've had worse." This is true, but I don't usually walk several miles after an injury of this magnitude.

Aisha steps forward, her cheeks flushed with worry. "Take the van as far as you can before you go on foot. We'll get it tomorrow. Don't tell me no!"

"That's actually a good idea," I snicker.

"Don't act like I don't have good ideas!" She surveys the area, her stare falling on the bodies. "What a mess. You need to leave."

Ivan stands behind her and puts his hand on her shoulder. Her fingers run over his, and she smiles at me weakly. I return her smile, letting her know it's okay.

We hear the sound of helicopter blades off in the distance.

"You better get inside," I say. "This will bring in more rotters." I walk away from them and get into the van before anyone protests. Then, I call out the window. "Check her for a tracking device. Rob knows where to look."

"Will do," Aisha says.

As I pull away, I watch them in the side mirror. They're working on getting the drugged sour woman into the hospital, and she'll get her first dose of suppressant tonight.

twenty-one

Dean

A FEATHERED DARK FRIEND
WATCHES FOR LURKING DANGER
HE HELPS ME DEFEND

I leave the van in Fells Point in case anyone is tracking me. My leg burns and aches with every step, but I manage to get over the tracks and through the woods toward the house I stay at with Pizza every few days. This injury will force me to stay in one location.

A trickle of blood runs down my leg. I need to slow down, or I'll reopen the wound, and healing will take longer.

Before I forget, I text Dr. Warren my exact coordinates and tell her I need the food dropped off as close as possible without anyone seeing it. I haven't been hurt this badly since my stab wound, and Dr. Warren was here to operate and speed the recovery.

Once at the house, I find a towel and place it over the bedsheet, so I don't make a mess of this stranger's bed. They may return at some point, and I can't imagine what it would be like to find a pool of dry blood on the bed.

I fold my arms over my chest and fall asleep as soon as I'm vertical.

What seems like a minute turns into several hours. There's a tapping at the window, and I stir awake to find it's bright as fuck. Pain shoots through my eyes. I cover them with my arm and try to bend my leg. It's itchy and hot. This will take longer than I thought, and not having food will be a factor.

With one arm in front of me, I steer into the closet, hoping to find a hat. There are no baseball hats, but I do find a woman's beach hat with a large rim, so I put that on and cover my face as best I can. I'm able to open my eyes enough to search the room. There's a leather purse on the ground near the dresser, and inside I find sunglasses. They aren't as dark as I need, but it's better than nothing.

The tapping continues. I follow the noise, half expecting to find a tree blowing against the window, but instead, it's Pizza. He must have memorized the houses we stayed at and checked them until he found me.

If he's looking for a free meal, today won't be the day. My phone has a text from Dr. Warren telling me a time and location for my food drop off, and it's under the cover of night to be less conspicuous. I call her since it's been a while, and she may have heard about what happened yesterday.

It rings, and she answers quickly. "Mr. Kaplan, I was getting worried. Your last text was incoherent. Then I spoke with Mr. Foley, and he told me you were shot?"

"Jason filled you in? Well, the bullet went clean through the calf, and it's healing. It missed the artery since I'm not dead. Hurts like hell, though." I look at the wound, and it's scabby and pink. My body would fight off an infection, I think. Right now, it looks like dried cranberry sauce stuck in my hair.

"Have you dressed it?" she asks.

"Um, no. I suppose I should look for some first aid. Last night I was too tired to do much. That food coming this evening will be everything I need." I wander out of the room and then remember Pizza. The back kitchen door is where he knows to come in, so I let him through. The little black bird walks through instead of flies like he's the home's resident back from work. As I search the kitchen and bathroom for first aid materials, Dr. Warren goes on about the cured mission.

"They have begun taking the cured out of the city. It's remarkable how quickly this is going. The convention center is a well-functioning operation, though I hear things went poorly last night." I can hear her clicking her pen. A nervous habit that drives me crazy.

"Things going poorly would be an understatement. I told you I was shot, right? Then we killed two sours, drugged one, and the big one got away. What do you know about a sour named Omar? This guy is determined that I go with him." I hope he's down for the count, given the damage I caused. Maybe I'll get lucky and he'll die.

"I'm not sure of individuals specifically, but I understood there were special agents coming in to track the infected." Dr. Warren is concerned, and she feels out of touch with the operations within city limits. As someone who pushed the suppressant and cure, she's had little say in the way of implementation.

"Well, he got the wrong memo or something." I locate bandages and antiseptic. This is going to hurt, but it's a must, so I lift my leg over the tub and dump the brown bottle over my wound. It fizzes and stings. The pain is so bad I grit my teeth and hold the phone away from my face, so she doesn't hear me cry.

"—end the target," she says. I must have caught her mid-thought, but she continues. "The suppressant will work on them, and Jason confirmed the one you sedated is going through the process now."

"Shit, I forgot. How is Jeronimo?"

"They operated for several hours, but he should recover. It'll be impossible to airlift people out again, so make sure there isn't a need."

"That wasn't my call."

"I was saying," she continues, "the suppressant should work on sours, but I'm at a loss for what to do for your type. There is a chance I've found something that would decrease your symptoms, but I can't be sure without you here."

My leg is pulsing, but I'm able to put ointment on the wound and wrap gauze around it. My arms are tired, and so is my body. I need to get this woman off the phone and go back to sleep.

"Can we talk about the impossible cure another time?"

"I'm working on it, Mr. Kaplan. I want to assure you that I'm doing all I can." Her frustrated voice concerns me. She's been working on this for years, and I she's probably exhausted. There may not be an answer out there. One of us is willing to accept this, and the other is not.

"Right now, I need to stay alive."

"Yes, you do. I will continue to provide food and information. I'm working on something to get you on the train, but we need to mask your symptoms, so you'll pass the screening process."

"I need to focus on being in here a little longer, and with that, I need to go. There's planning I need to do. Thanks for the food."

"You're welcome, and good luck." Dr. Warren ends the call.

Last night, I killed people. It's been years since I had to do that, but the instinct to defend myself returned quickly. It felt good because I'm reminded my abilities aren't always a curse. If I almost took down Omar once, I can do it again.

"Pizza," I call. "I need to get some sleep, so I need you to watch the house." He marches over to the counter and flies up, gawking out the window with his beak parted, readying the alarm call at the first sign of danger.

The bathroom is a mess, but I leave it for another time. In the bedroom, the curtains allow too much light in. So I throw another sheet over the rod to darken my sleeping quarters. This will enable me to lie down in comfort and let my mind spin about Omar.

twenty-two

Shelby

TAKE ME TO CAMDEN
BODIES LAY LIKE MYSTERIES
I CAN'T ABANDON

The papers are coordinated by date and topic, stacked neatly, and put in order according to relevancy. I've skimmed them dozens of times with Angela. The woman, Beth Jackson, from the apartment where we discovered her and her niece, Viola, told us she used to work at Johns Hopkins but left for a smaller lab. She was working on performance vitamins for athletes unrelated to anything like a deadly virus.

Viola appears to be a sour like Dean. The others saw it too, but since Jeronimo was hurt, this mission lost steam.

I'm helping Sinai most by talking to the cured when they're ready for transport to the train station. The cured are confused, their brains reforming, and sparks are connecting that haven't been in a long time. I try to explain what happened, but often it's better to be vague and stick to what the future holds. Their pasts are holey, and it'd be impossible to guess what they went through.

They weren't coherent for the damage they caused and the horrible elements they endured. Yet these are the lucky ones because many have died or cannot be cured.

Angela knocks on the door and opens it. "You at this again?"

"I can't stop. There aren't any connections. And I've searched every single paper from the office and lab. I need another clue." I shuffle some papers and stare at the words.

It's been four days, and Dean is staying off the grid somewhere. He assures me he's healing, but I'm not sure he'd tell me the truth if he weren't.

"How is Jeronimo?" I ask.

"He's awake and taking liquids, but he's in a lot of pain. This is going to take him a long time. Maybe months." She sits on the bed, looking down at me and my paperwork mess.

"When we get home, we'll have to see what we can do for him. Between the two of us, we can take care of him."

"I think so, too," Angela says. She picks up a stack of papers and thumbs through them. "We didn't go to all the places on your map."

She doesn't have to remind me. It's constantly on my mind, tangled with everything else, including Jason, who's become distant and shut off since Jeronimo was taken. There's never a good time to sneak away, and the other locations are further than the last. Though we have yet to make it to Hopkins.

"I'm not sure if it's possible to leave again," I say. "I was hoping Dean would get involved when he's better, but it's been a slow process for him. Ivan has gotten too involved here to be torn away. I think he'll do anything Aisha says."

Angela giggles. "He's struck by the bug, that's for sure."

"Love bug?" I grin. It's good to see him so happy, but I also worry he's forgotten all the reasons we're here. We understand Dean needs time, so we're backing off, but there was the map to consider. "Do you think Jason could get us into Hopkins?"

"Good luck. He's been working harder than anyone. I suppose we find ways to calm our emotions when we're freaking out. Anyway, that place is huge. What could you possibly learn from going back there?"

She's right. Johns Hopkins is a massive hospital complex with hundreds of rooms, maybe even thousands. They have a specialty in everything, and each one has a floor or wing.

"What kind of lab do you think it is?" I ask. Noting the name on the lab forms gives little away.

"Epidemiology, maybe? Or whatever it is that studies contagious diseases."

"Hmm." I tap the pen against my lip. What brings these three stars together? A woman who worked on performance vitamins, a lab with dead chimpanzees, Hopkins. Viola's last name is Jackson, but there isn't anyone at the lab that matches.

"I have an idea," I mumble. "Beth said Viola was her brother's daughter, but what if Viola's mom didn't take her husband's last name? That's common for people who have a doctorate. Especially if they maintain publications." Renee, my sister, who is also a veterinarian, told me she would never change her name for this reason.

The gears are turning for Angela because she doesn't speak for another minute. "You have Beth's number. Text her and ask for her sister-in-law's name."

"Of course." I reach for my phone to send Beth a text message. We've kept in touch off and on since I want to know if Viola returns.

> **Me**
> Checking in. Is your sister-in-law's last name Jackson like Viola's?

> **Beth**
> She took my brother's last name in theory but kept her maiden name for professional reasons. I'm sorry I didn't think of that. Her name is Flora Ross, and she was a doctor.

> **Me**
> Was she at Hopkins?

> **Beth**
> No. She did research for colon cancer and worked outside the beltway.

My heart sinks, and the connection that bloomed dies instantly. Angela grabs my phone, pretending to be me.

> **Me**
> What was the name of the company?

> **Beth**
> Colon Squared.

I look at Angela for an answer, but she's on her phone plugging something in. Then she holds it up to me, and we see our first break. Colon Squared is a subsidiary and often a satellite office of Johns Hopkins located in Pikesville. A suburb next to Baltimore but on the other side of the beltway, so they wouldn't have been affected by the quarantine.

"Look her up in the Hopkins system," I suggest.

Angela does but frowns. "Nothing is coming up."

Before I leave my conversation with Beth, I thank her and ask if she needs anything from us. She's leaving the city tomorrow, and her thoughts are heavy on Viola. While she's reluctant to go, I let her know I'll search for her, and we'll leave my contact information and location for Viola to find if she returns. There is little more we can do. Beth needs to be on that train, or she could face incarceration for missing her departure window.

Angela is sitting on my bed while I'm on the floor in front of all my papers. "What are you thinking?" she asks.

"Recheck the paperwork from the lab. Is Flora's name there?" I hand her a stack to go through, and right away she speaks up.

"Doctor Flora Ross sat on a board for performance enhancement ethical protocol. It's on this contact sheet. Let me call the number." Angela dials the number on the form, but her smile quickly fades. "Disconnected. Now what?"

"It's a lead. Flora is connected to Beth and Hopkins." I let the web of connections become a visual in my mind. Then I say, "What if we don't need to go to Hopkins? It could be a hint, but there isn't a house number or office suite for reference. We should investigate these two stars." I point at the stars near Camden Yards, the baseball stadium, and the last one over by The Domino Sugar Factory, which is where Fat Man used to be headquartered. This star is in the residential area and not on the water like the factory.

"Those are far away."

"I have to go, and today." I've wasted enough time. "Are there any bikes here?"

"I can't go with you today. There's too much happening here."

The papers in front of me aren't helping anymore. I grab my backpack and put food, water, and a change of clothes inside. My charger, extra ammunition, and the map are carefully added. I fit myself with a holster and two guns. The days of not being armed in this city are long behind me. At one time, all I had were rusty knives, but today we're rationed bullets, and I plan to use them.

"This cannot wait. Cover for me if anyone asks where I went." Before my nerves get the best of me, I pull Angela in for a hug.

Reluctantly, she says, "I'll show you where the bikes are."

The muggy air is like the inside of a dog's mouth, and even flying down a hill, there's little relief from the breeze. The roads are bumpy from random weeds with the strength of twenty men. There are tufts of grass poking out of drain spouts, in windowsills, and piercing cracks in the sidewalk.

My mind plays little tricks, and I imagine I'm having a conversation about unimportant things like grass growing in odd places when, in fact, I'm coming to terms with the fact that I'm alone.

I am one hundred percent alone.

Even at the house, when my roommates weren't home, I knew someone was next door or walking down the street. There was a human connection within minutes, maybe even seconds. I haven't been this disconnected from others in a long time.

The trees have thick leaves swaying in the breeze and the hot sun burns my nose and cheeks.

I check in with myself to see if I'm scared, and the response is yes, but I'm also excited. There isn't someone telling me I can't do something. I can go down any path without checking in. Sure, I'm going to make some people worried and angry, and that's not fair to them. But for once, I'm choosing to think about myself and what drives me.

The first and closest stop is Camden Yards, which is also the most intimidating. This is where it all started. Dean was torn away when a stampede of survivors clashed with the infected inside the stadium. I've never been back. There's been no reason to.

Could this star suggest another clue and not one that necessarily needs investigating on the ground? It could be. The ride is relatively easy and mostly downhill since I take route 83. My bike gets me there, I think over and over. Angela and I used to use this little motto when we were runners with the Rec Pier. Our bikes were our horses, and we were the messengers. We traveled to several points in the local area to keep up with other survivors who needed us.

Pulling off route 83, I ride down an exit ramp. Then I cut past the old police station, ironically next to a place called *The Block,* which hosted strip clubs.

The signs once lit with women's legs kicking into the air and neon pink signs beckoning patrons inside are now dark. These blocks are forgotten. There aren't any residences or resources other than a police station that has probably been looted more times than I can count.

The soaring brick buildings around Camden Yards are ahead. My heart races as if old memories could become real again. This is where the SWAT team took down the infected while I watched in horror. Dean was lost, and I had to push through the chaos to get home. I pedal until I find the tall wrought-iron gates open and the stadium full of debris and trash.

We came here, hand in hand, along with thousands of people waiting for their ration cards. It was a massacre. Carefully, I make a complete loop around the stadium as quickly as possible and listen for any trouble. It's dead silent.

There's nothing here. Curious, I park my bike and walk to the rows of seats to see the field. The air flows differently as it tunnels through the openings between cement walls.

I want to see the field. In my most profound naïve state of hope, I imagine a perfectly green baseball field with crisp white lines and thousands of fans. The smell of beer and hot dogs should be in the air.

The tunnel is short, and the light at the end brings me to the rows of seats. Unfortunately, down below no longer resembles a baseball field.

Bodies.

Dried, decayed humans huddled in tall, gorgeous green grass. Some are missing limbs, and a few are without heads. The infected tore through here three years ago, and all that's left are decomposed corpses baking in the sun.

It's so much worse than I expected. No one cleaned this out, and animals didn't drag them away. Even the rats don't want to eat the infected.

I quickly run back to the bike to leave this deathscape. The beauty that once was here is gone, and I'll never be able to look at the baseball field again without seeing everyone who died.

Without waiting, I swiftly return to the gates and exit the stadium. If there's something here worth finding, I didn't see it.

There are a few blocks that I'm familiar with once I get to Federal Hill. I recognize the path we'd take to the Domino Sugar Factory when we faced off with Fat Man. It's to the right, and I'm thankful I can avoid it. There have been enough bad memories stirred today.

As I get deeper into the residential area, the streets stop making sense, and each block crosses another with no rhyme or reason. I stop to check my map. When I do, I get the feeling someone is watching me.

My brow sweats. I slowly turn to look behind me, but no one is there. There are no sounds that would indicate someone is with me. I pull my bag in front of me and search the map for my location compared to the star, which has a number and a street name. It's not far, so I put everything away and get off the block that gives me the creeps.

Soon, I'm in front of the row home marked by a star. I wonder if this is Viola's home. The stars took me to Beth Jackson, so this could be her relatives' home. It's three stories tall, with a curved front where narrow windows sit in a row. There are marble steps leading to the door and dried flower baskets hanging in the windows. It's a nice house, but sadly, the door is broken, and it's clear, even from out here, that someone trashed the place.

I park my bike and walk up the steps to figure out how long ago this happened. There are water stains on the door and wall and leaves blown throughout the main level; it's been this way for a while.

There must be something worth discovering—old mail, photo album, or anything identifying who lived here. Stepping over broken tables and what looks like rat droppings, I gag at the smell. Every window in the back is broken, and mildew is growing on the carpet. It smells of mushrooms, even in this heat. The kitchen doesn't have an address book or mail, and the living room has no old magazine subscriptions or anything useful. There are nails on the wall, but no pictures hanging. Everything is gone. Disappointed, I open the door to the basement. There's water covering the floor and items floating in the stillness. Anything down there is ruined.

Upstairs is my last chance, and I'm becoming more hopeless with every step. I take the wooden stairs, each creaking, warning me I'm not welcome. When I reach the top, I notice it's very different from downstairs. The window in the first room is intact, and the bed has a layer of dust settled on the quilt. The dresser and closet don't have any personal items, and even the medicine cabinet doesn't have a prescription bottle. It's so strange. This house had to be lived in by someone.

There are two more rooms to look through, and when I get to the last one, I find it reminds me of my room as a teenager. The bed is messy, and there are posters of hip-hop bands and a desk with sports trophies, Barbies, and hand-drawn pictures on the wall. This person will never experience those awkward teenage years when we think we're finally adults.

Something in the closet catches my eye. A box with picture frames peering out of the top. I walk over and slide it out. Inside are all the articles I'd been searching for: mail, photo albums, and pictures from the wall.

"What the hell?" I say.

"Don't touch my things," a scared young voice comes from the doorway, but when I look, no one is there.

"Hello?" I search the room, and when I step away from the closet, the floor squeaks, causing me to jump. "I heard you. Come out."

No one speaks. I know there was a voice. My hand goes to one of my guns, and I pull it out of the holster. The safety is off, and I walk forward. A young Black girl steps in front of the door, so I can't leave. She lives here, I'm sure of it. I would guess she's thirteen, petite, and very fit. Her arm muscles are tight and defined.

"I'm not here for trouble. I was looking for something."

"What is it?" The girl draws up her gun and points it at me. We're in a standoff, but there's no part of me that wants to shoot this person.

"My name is Shelby, and I'm on a mission to cure survivors and get them onto the trains. You want to leave here, don't you?"

She keeps her distance, staying in the hallway and the shadows. I want to coax her forward to get a better look at her face. Is she a cured sour or infected, or maybe she's one of the few survivors who never left the city?

"I'm never leaving this city." She says calmly and almost adult-like. How bad has it been for her? Is she alone?

"I've met others who didn't think they could leave. Baltimore was their only home, and they were scared. But there are resources on the outside. Do you have any family to contact? Or maybe you know someone on the outside I can find for you?" I'm rambling to keep her attention. She could sprint, and she's closer to the stairs than me.

"I'm not scared," she huffs out.

"The military will come for those who don't leave. We don't want them to do that. You can come with me now."

"They'll never find me. I'm faster than them."

I holster my gun and put my hands up. "I am not going to hurt you. Can you come closer so we can talk?"

The girl shakes her head no. I'm unsure what to do to get out of this situation. She should come with me so I can get her to the trains, but it's clear she's settled in this decaying house.

"I have food. Are you hungry?" I offer, hoping to get her attention.

"No." Her one-word answer strikes a nerve.

"I told you my name. How about you tell me yours?"

"Why?"

"Because I want to help you."

"No, you don't!" she shouts. "Everyone wants to see what's wrong with me, but no one can do anything about it. Get out!" She steps forward, and her eyes are black as night.

I stumble back and hit the bed with my heel. Pain shoots up my leg. "Shit!" Then I look at the girl and find the need to apologize. "I'm sorry. I didn't mean to swear."

She freezes and stares at me. "I've heard the word shit before."

"Oh. I'm guessing you're thirteen?" Again, I take in her height. She has long braids down her back, and someone is clearly caring for her. "You're not alone. If you already have help, I'll leave. I'm worried about you, that's all."

"You guessed correctly. I'm thirteen. You do need to go." She steps back into the dark hallway.

"The light hurts your eyes?"

Her head wipes in my direction. "What did you say?"

"You can run fast? Your scene of smell is so good you probably knew I was coming before I walked through the front door. This house was marked for me. I'm looking for something." If this is above her head, I'm about to find out. This could be Viola, and if it is, and this is her house, I might find a clue to what Mona was trying to tell me.

"I'm not a freaking mutant!" She grows defensive again, and I know I need to change tactics. That gun in her hand has not dropped.

"If you're a sour, that means you are stronger than me, a salt. Do you know those terms?"

The gun shakes in her hand. "I do."

She may have been part of Dean's community. Someone who fell under the radar when most of them were cured or died. "How about you put that gun away, so you don't accidentally shoot me?" I smile, hoping to get through.

"I'll hold it until you leave."

My chances of getting her on my side are sinking drastically. "I'm going to tell you a story, and at the end, if you don't trust me, then I'll leave."

"Fine." She lowers the gun a few inches.

"I'm married to someone like you. His name is Dean." I tell her about his condition and the trials for a suppressant and a cure, using a very abbreviated version and one a child could follow. Then I tell her about what I did at the Rec Pier and how brilliant Mona was. "This map in my bag took me to a lab, and I identified a woman named Dr. Flora Ross."

When I say this name, the gun droops, and she begins to cry. "That's my mom. She didn't do this!"

"Are you Viola? Were you at your aunt's home when we arrived? You jumped out that window, didn't you?" I try not to press her, but her tears won't stop.

Then, without warning, she runs away. I sprint after her, down the steps and to the front door. Outside, I catch the soles of her shoes moving so fast she's nearly a blur. And there goes my chance.

"Please, come back!" I shout in her direction, but she's gone.

All is not lost. I send Dean a text to see if he's well enough to meet me, and I send him the address. While I wait for his response,

I venture inside to search the house more thoroughly. Viola's closet is where she put all her personal belongings. I pull out a box and a laundry basket full of papers, picture frames, and other household items.

I carefully pick each up and examine it. The first is a picture of a man and woman standing behind Viola. They're an attractive Black family with bright smiles and interlocking hands. The love for one another is heartbreaking, making me yearn for my sisters and parents back home.

I pull out more documents and find junk mail, birthday cards, magazines, and other notices. I flip open the birthday card wishing Viola a happy tenth birthday. She's been in this city for three years. How much of that time was spent without her parents?

A piece of mail catches my eye. It has colorful graphics and an emblem. When I pull it closer, I notice Flora's name on it. It's an invitation to a professional event. By skimming the paper, I can confirm that Flora is a scientist, but not the type Beth suggested. Is Beth covering something up, or was she wrong?

The letter indicates it's for internal medicine and specifically infectious diseases. I jump to my feet and take the paper to the window for more light.

Slowing down, I read the letter from top to bottom. Doctor Flora Ross is the guest speaker for this event, and it's letting her know she has a table for guests.

I text Angela to research the name so I can continue looking through the house. There are a other papers with Flora's maiden name on them. Could Beth have forgotten, or is she protecting Viola?

There's a lot of uncertainty. There must be more, but not in Viola's room. Her parent's room is in good condition, so I search the closet, dresser, and under the mattress.

"Bingo."

A stack of brown envelopes with red letters contains confidential markings on the front.

The first set of documents is entirely above my head with medical jargon. There are numbers and letters that I think are associated with drugs.

I call Dean because he didn't respond to my text, and I could use another brain. One who knows about sours.

He answers, groggily. "Shelby? Is everything okay?

"How are you?"

"Resting up but doing okay. How is Jeronimo?"

"Okay, but it'll be a long recovery." I feel bad leaping into my current problem of the day, but I can't slow down. "Is there any chance you can make it to Federal Hill? I'm in someone's house, and you need to meet this person."

"Why are you being vague? Is someone trying to hurt you?"

"Not at the moment. I'd rather explain in person. Are you able to move around yet?" It's been a few days since his leg wound, but I'm not exactly sure how long he needs to heal.

"I was going to move out tonight. It's stiff but much better. This one took longer than I imagined." I hear him shuffling as if he's getting out of bed. "Send me the address. I'll eat and be on my way."

"Check your text messages. And please don't tell anyone about this." It needs to be Dean. Viola might be like him, and he'll be the only one who understands what that all means.

"Who would I tell?" he chuckles and hearing him in good spirits eases the worry I've carried.

"Dr. Warren, Alicia, Ivan, anyone really! See you soon," I say, without feeding into his lone wolf status.

twenty-three
Shelby

THEY'RE NOW TOGETHER
BONDING LIKE LOST FAMILY
FARING THE WEATHER

The silence breaks when Dean calls to me. "Shelby?"

"I'm up here."

His clunky feet run up the steps. When he comes in, he takes his time lowering himself down.

"Whatcha got here?"

The papers are spread in front of me as I sit cross-legged. "There's a girl who lives here, and I think she's like you. Her name is Viola Jackson. Do you recognize the name?"

He shakes his head. "Some sours were spread out around the city and didn't want much to do with us. I didn't get to know them. We had a census, and she might be on there. It's at the zoo if you want me to check."

"You shouldn't go back there. We'll find another way."

"Did the map lead you to her?" He takes some of the papers I'm holding and scans them. "What are these about?"

"This is one of the map's locations, and I'm also confused by the papers, but look, they're from that lab that Angela and I found." I point to the logo.

"Can I send a picture to Dr. Warren?" Dean readies his phone.

"Oh, um." I trail off because I don't want outside influencers interfering with my research. "Can we cover the name on the forms so she doesn't know who they're from?"

"Sure. I guess you haven't told Mike about this?"

"No. And I'm not sure I will." I fear being pulled off this and shoved aside. Mona said it should be me. So it will be me.

"I don't blame you. Let me give her a call about what I'm sending. I'll leave you out of it." He dials her number and turns away from me.

I leave the room to give him privacy and to search the house further. There isn't much else up here. The home office has bills and an old calendar which I flip through, but the computer is missing. While Dean is on the phone, I hear steps coming from downstairs.

Viola has returned. I try not to act surprised when I meet her in the stairwell. She's wearing a hat pulled low, and two pairs of sunglasses duct taped together to protect her eyes.

"My aunt is leaving tomorrow," she says. "And she vouched for you. Said you could get me out too?"

This is no place for a young girl. The front door is broken, mold is sprouting throughout the home, and I can't imagine where she's getting food from. "I'll do everything I can to see that happen. If you trust me, there's someone I want out you meet."

She walks past me in the hall and pauses when she hears Dean's voice. With her nose in the air, she breathes deeply. "Who is that?" She panics and runs toward the stairs.

"Viola, wait. That's Dean, and he's sour like you!"

Her feet stop on the last step, and she turns slowly toward me. "This is who you were talking about."

"Yes. I want you to meet him. Did you ever talk to the group that calls themselves sours?" I watch her walk up the steps carefully. My heart thumps with each step.

"My mom and I are alike. A man they called Lion at the zoo would have someone check in on us sometimes, and Dean is familiar. He stopped by here with others once or twice. For the most part, we stayed away. They were nice, though."

"Dean was a liaison with that group. He and Lion are good friends. I promise we're not the bad guys."

"That's what a bad guy would say." She's not joking.

"Come with me?" I ask, as sweetly as possible. She agrees, and when we walk into the master bedroom, we find Dean taking pictures of the paperwork.

"What are you doing?" Viola asks him.

Dean shoots up. His nostrils flare, and I know he's taking her scent in. "Sour?" He steps forward and puts out his hand. "I'm Dean."

Viola does the same but eyes him carefully. She could flee at any minute, and with Dean's leg healing, he may not be able to catch her.

"My name is Viola, and I asked what you're doing." She directs her attention to the papers on the bed and drops Dean's hand.

Dean and I speak over each other, but I take the lead. "We think your mom has information about the virus and how it got put in Baltimore. This paperwork is interesting."

"Where did you find that?" Viola circles around Dean so she can see the paperwork more clearly.

"Under the mattress," I say.

Her shoulders sink as if it's a place she knew she should have checked but didn't. "It won't tell you anything."

Dean arranges the papers and takes more pictures. "If we can stop this virus from getting out of the city, then we need to try. Some of this paperwork is for a conference for epidemiology, but another packet details a diagnosis similar to sours." He jabs his finger at a graph. "These are white blood cell counts compared at different time intervals."

Viola walks out of the room as if she's heard enough. I give her space to figure things out. I quietly ask Dean, "Can you be a little easier on her? Her parents are dead, and her aunt is leaving the city tomorrow."

"Easier on her? Have you told her Omar is tracking people like us? How can we be sure she's like me and not the other sours?" He continues going through the paperwork; there must be fifty pages.

"We're getting close to something, aren't we?"

"Dr. Warren will tell me more about this."

Viola speaks to us from her room down the hall. "I can hear you. My mom and I turned early you know? She died at Fort Meade with all the others. There was no food or water. That was two years ago." Her words tumble out slow and sad.

Dean stops what he's doing and whispers, "When Nick and I found the bodies, one person was left alive, but they ran off. We assumed it was a salt because they survived. That must have been her. Her mom may have been like me, but starvation took her. Maybe it took all of them before the deterioration of our disease did."

"She was trapped with all those people?" Her mother and many more sours were sick and lost their lives days before Dean and Nick discovered them. Dean's community buried them at the location because there were too many to move. So Viola has been alone for a long time. She's just a girl.

Viola returns to our room with a bag around her shoulder. "Well, I can't stay here." Tears drip to her chin. I've no doubt she's looking for someone to hang around, and I wish it could be me.

"She can't come back to Sinai," I say. "It's not safe." I turn to Viola and address her family situation. "I'm sorry about your mom."

She shrugs uncomfortably, and I decide I'll leave it alone.

"Right." Dean takes more pictures while he sorts out more ideas.

"The map is complete. I've got no more stars to investigate, so whatever is in this house must have some answers. I'm going to call Mike and tell him we're together. Maybe he has a way out."

"Whatever," Dean says, dismissing me. I'm not sure what happened between them or if Dean doesn't trust Mike. His idea of what Mike is capable of is farfetched.

"What's your deal with Mike?"

He returns to the paperwork to put it back in order. "I only met the guy once, and he knew who I was. Later, I got the sense that he also knew we were married but kept that information from you."

"The trial was intense. He was being protective."

"Maybe. Dr. Warren won't tell me anything about Mike. If you need to talk to him, then do what you want."

Mike could get Dean and Viola out of here, and it's worth exploring even with Dean's trust issues. "I'll be right back." I exit the room for privacy, and I send Mike a text.

> **Me**
> Mike. I'm with Dean again. We're in Federal Hill. Can we get out of here soon?

> **Mike**
> Send me your address.

> **Me**
> Ok. The military is more active. Let's get out soon to be safe.

> **Mike**
> I have a location in mind, but need a driver. You'll have to take the train, so it's less suspicious.

> **Me**
> Okay.

I send him our location, and the pit in my stomach grows. I thought we would be leaving this city together. Hopefully, he'll be okay with an extra passenger. I'm keeping Viola as a surprise because I want to be sure she'll go with Dean. I check the time, and it's mid-afternoon. I have a few hours to move, or I'll have to stay here tonight, which isn't ideal given there's no front door.

When I return to find Dean, he's no longer in the master bedroom. Voices fill the hall, and I take a minute to listen to his conversation with Viola.

They're laughing and sharing stories about their abilities. He's building her trust. Dean needs this to pull him back from his lonely ways. The two of them are sitting on the bed when I poke my head around the door. Viola is smiling at Dean as if he told a joke.

"Hi," I say. "It's getting late, and I'm not sure if I should stay here. Mike is seeing if he can get you out soon."

"Dr. Warren says they can't fly helicopters over the city walls, and they got in a lot of trouble for aiding Jeronimo." Dean's happy voice turns hostile whenever I bring up Mike.

"Air isn't the only way out," I say.

"True. Anyway, Viola and I are going to go for a run. I want to show her a few things. Can we meet up with you tomorrow?" Dean stands from the bed, and Viola follows. "I got the kid."

"Hey!" Viola interjects. "I'm not a kid." She elbows past him and stands by the door. "But running with a sour again would be cool."

"Look, kid," he shakes his head. "I mean, Viola. There are people after me. We'll need to talk about that."

"I'm not scared." Her lip pouts out, and she lifts her fists.

"Good!" Dean says.

I interject. "Wait! Mike might have a way out soon. We can't be far from each other. Where are you going?"

"To the zoo to see if I can learn anything more about Viola's family."

"Is it safe?" We just talked about how insecure that location is. I can't run as fast as them, and I'd make it there after dark.

"Go to Jason at the convention center. You can hang out with him for a while, right?" Dean is pushing me off on Jason, and I have to shut my gaping mouth in disbelief. It's actually a good idea, and I should have thought of it.

I don't have much choice. Staying here alone isn't an option, and Dean and Viola are bonding over their disease. "I'm taking the papers with me." Each folder is carefully put in my backpack.

Dean can tell I'm disappointed we have to split up. "Can you figure out what Omar and the sours are up to? He's disappeared, and I want to be careful with Viola."

"I'll check into that and look through these papers more." Some quiet time to study these will be perfect.

"Let's meet back here if we need to." Dean taps the hatchet on his hip. "You're armed, right?"

"Yes."

Viola wiggles excitedly for the field trip. I suppose she hasn't wandered far in this city since her mother died. I won't step out completely, but I'll give them the distance to do whatever they need to do as sours.

Dean leads the way and asks her, "Do you want to meet my crow? His name is Pizza."

"Pizza? That's a funny name for a pet," Viola giggles. She's laughing with him. The two loneliest people in the city may find comfort in one another.

twenty-four

Shelby

DODGING AS I GO
THE NEWS I'VE BEEN WAITING FOR
KEEPING MY HEAD LOW

Jason meets me outside, where Ivan and I snuck into the convention center. I wasn't sure if it was safe, but it turns out there are bigger problems this operation is facing than two missing soldiers.

"We're bringing in people faster than we have beds ready. They're leaving the infected drugged and gagged in hallways until we can take them." Jason stands on the sidewalk beside me. Behind us is a variety of staff moving indoors for the night.

"Can I stay here tonight?" I ask.

"Yeah, but it's not glamorous. Where are you coming from?"

"I was with Dean, and there's something I need to tell you."

Jason and I walk up the steps to the center. Hundreds of people are moving around inside. With the sun setting soon, I wonder how quiet this building is after dark. Tall windows bring in the light from outside, and there are no blinds to block the infected from noticing movement. Someone makes an announcement, and I take Jason's hand, so I don't lose him in the shuffle.

A man's voice carries throughout the building. "Team Night Hawk, report to the lower level at 1900 hours for your shift. Mandatory quiet hours begin."

I whisper to Jason. "What is 1900 hours?"

"Seven at night. I'll take you to my cot, but I have to do something before quiet hours." Jason leads me up a flight of stairs to a banquette room with purple swirling carpets. There are temporary walls set up with curtains for privacy. Several rows are jammed in, and each cubical has a number I assume we're assigned to.

"This isn't very private." I brush my hand over the curtain so it parts for me.

"I said it wasn't glamorous. I'll be back in fifteen minutes." He points at the ground. "Stay here. I want to hear what's going on." Then he disappears before I can ask questions.

He was quick with me, and cold. We're all reeling from Jeronimo's close call, and I've hung on to messages from the team with updates. The city is under a lot of pressure to get the infections cured.

And there's me. It isn't fair to bring him into my mess when he's dealing with so much. We've joined forces over the same worries repeatedly. Those haven't vanished, but how far can one man stretch?

I want to mention Viola and our suspicions about her mother. He'll understand my need to protect Viola along with Dean. How involved he'll want to be is something I can't gauge. His expression reads like it did when April shot him in the leg and the electricity ran out. It took weeks to coax him out of a gray, murky state of mind.

The walls are white with silver hinges keeping them together. Sounds of others in cubicles beside me become more apparent as each minute passes. There are no windows near us. Will we be able to talk?

My phone vibrates, and it's Mike calling to check in.

"Hi, Mike," I whisper.

"I have a way out for Dean. Tonight he'll need to catch a boat from Fort McHenry. Can you be certain he's there at 3 am?"

I slump on the bed to steady my shaking knees. This is it. Dean's leaving. "We're not together right now, but I'll make sure he's there." I want to tell him about Viola, but there are parts of this story I'm putting together. "Who's picking up Dean?"

"The boat will look like it's the coast guard."

"Good. I'll get the message to him."

We hang up and the guilt for withholding Viola from Mike sits in the pit of my stomach. It's not fair, of course. She needs to leave. The convention center's windows are bright when I leave the room. The curfew is 8 pm, but I can't leave Jason without telling him where I'm going. He would be furious if I disappeared.

I pace the hallway near the sleeping quarters, and I wait for longer than he said it would take. Time is wasting away.

Should I stay, or should I go? Having back-up at this hour would be nice. I had no problem getting to the stadium. And Dean left me to fend for myself early on. I survived. Why do I continuously need to have an accomplice?

"This is stupid!" I say to no one. Jason gave me a timeframe, and he didn't stick to it. The building is loud, as others ensure they're in before curfew.

I take the steps to the front doors, dodging others as I go and trying to keep my head low in case anyone recognizes me. Something pulls my attention as I hold the door open. It's almost as if I can feel someone watching me. Cold eyes burrow into me from a hidden place. I hesitate to leave. The sun is going to sink soon, and the bike I brought may not reach our safe house in time.

A tingle on my back that rides up my shoulders suggests someone has caught me. Someone dangerous. I slowly lift my head and search the room. People continue to shuffle in different directions, and I catch the sound of wailing from the basement level. The infected are being cured. Their bodies are being put to the test as they are brought back to reality.

Who's watching me? It's not the infected.

A tall Black man, with eyes of ink standing in a darkened corner. His hair is buzzed off, and he has sharp, handsome facial features. This man is seven-feet-tall, and his weight is mostly composed of muscle. Why is he staring at me?

I get the urge to raise my middle finger and dart out the door.

"He's a sour. Stop looking at him." Jason catches my elbow and leads me outside in a hurry. "What the fuck are you doing? I pointed at the fucking ground, so when I said stay here, you knew where here was."

"Mike called with the news I've been waiting for." I scramble to get out words as Jason brings me around the corner, away from others moving through the doors.

"Mike?" His face is pinched with confusion. "You're still working for that guy?"

"I'm working *with* that guy, yes."

"Dr. Warren said they'd parted ways, and he's her brother. I'm not sure you should trust him."

I don't want to argue, so I twist from his grip. "Mike got me in here, and he wants to help Dean."

"Help him with what? Where's he taking Dean when he gets him out?"

"I—I didn't get that far," I stumble.

"Well, when your head catches up to reality, consider what Mike's plans are with Dean. That sour you saw in there? He attacked Dean the other night. Nearly got Jeronimo killed. They're writing it off as a rotter's attack, but we know the truth." Jason rubs the back of his neck, then checks his watch. "You shouldn't stay here tonight. Omar recognized you. I'm pretty sure he has Dean's entire profile."

I let the name Omar roll around in my head. "There's somewhere else I can go. You don't have to come." I walk away from him with a sudden urgency to find shelter before it's too dark. Why haven't I thought more about what Mike wants with Dean? I assumed he would get Dean out, and then Dean would work with Dr. Warren. If Mike and Dr. Warren aren't working together, then what's Mike's motive?

"Where are you going?" Jason follows me to the sidewalk.

"A lot happened in twenty-four hours."

"Fuck. I'm coming with you. Shit. Something is happening every time I see you. Every time!" He keeps up. Despite having paperwork in his hand, and his glasses on his head.

"You're not ready to go anywhere."

"It's clear you're not staying here, and I'm sure you've found some sort of trouble. It's probably worth it, though." His suggestion makes me smile through the fear turning my thoughts.

I come up on my bike and he stomps his foot. "A bike?"

There isn't one for him, and he knows I've got him beat. "Jason, Mike said he can get Dean out at Fort McHenry." I swing my leg over the bike and get ready to pedal away. "There's another sour. She's a teenager, and she's the one that jumped through the window when we met Beth. She's like Dean."

"Wait. Another sour didn't need the suppressant?"

"Yes."

He throws up his hands. "Wait! This is a lot to process. Fuck."

"Jason, I can't stay here."

"Shit!" he continues to swear, torn about what to do next.

I pedal, but he catches the back seat, forcing me to stop. "They're in danger, and you need all the help you can get."

"Can you keep up with the bike?"

"I have a bike too. Meet me two blocks south of here." He folds and tucks the paperwork he'd been holding into his back pocket.

"Um," I stare at him. My sense of direction is by sight. I could guess where south is.

"That's two blocks that way." He points to his left.

"Got it. Don't take long!"

"I won't," Jason jogs away, and I ride in the direction he suggested. While I hate needing him with me, his speech made me realize I can do this alone, but it's good to have assistance when it's available.

In less than a minute, I'm at the spot where he told me to wait. While there, I text Dean to meet me back at the safe house by midnight. I don't get an immediate response and assume he and Viola are taking a much-needed nap before their regular wake time.

While tucking my phone back into my bag, I get the sense that someone is watching me again. There's an office building to my right and past it is an open green space running into a parking lot.

The brush is significantly overgrown, and one tree has rotted and fallen onto a bench. On my other side is groups of row homes. Each is empty, and no one is around. I listen carefully, but I find nothing. The windows are dark. Every alley is empty. Every car abandoned.

In the distance, I see Jason pedaling to catch up. He's got a backpack on, and he's wearing a black hat like he would when he was a runner.

He says, "Let's go by the house we stayed at before you left. I moved our weapons there."

We bike down a deserted street and turn into Fells Point at the end before the harbor.

"That sour, Omar, was big." I say.

"That's why we need the extra protection."

"Do you think he's following us?" If it is a sour, he's faster and stronger than I am. And when it's dark, he'll be at an advantage with his night vision.

"I saw their plans tonight. They're sweeping the west near the highway wall. That will lead them far from us." Jason slows as we come to the block near our house, and I convince myself that no one is watching us. It's nerves and my anxiety playing evil mind games to confuse me.

A small tree grows where the steps meet the sidewalk. The paint around the windowsills is peeling, but the entrance is intact. Jason sweeps his hand over the top of the door frame for a key. He unlocks the door and steps in.

"Anyone around?" he says to the dead space.

No one answers, and we split up to check for break-ins. He goes upstairs, while I run to the back of the house. Besides more dust, it's the same as it was the day I left. Jessie was here that day. Angela helped me and Jason get her to the train. She was scared when they took her from me to quarantine. It was a hard day that threatens tears.

"Clear down here," I call out.

"Clear up here. Check the basement?"

It's dark and dingy, but nothing is amiss. Jason hasn't come back down, so I go upstairs.

On our old bed is a black bag of guns, with Jason checking the inventory. Then a notion strikes me. I move away from Jason and walk to the closet. The door creaks open easily. Dust floats around the room, causing my eyes to itch. I sneeze three times, and Jason responds with "bless you," each time I do.

I reach my hand up and feel for what I left here. Yeji's gun. It's wrapped in a t-shirt and shoved to the side, making it hard to reach. I hop up and down until my fingers can grab a piece of the fabric and pull it toward me. The shirt smells of oldness as I pull it from its spot. It plops in my palm, and I gently fold back the corners to reveal the black metal that meant so much to me.

This was Jeronimo's gun that my old roommate stole from him when they had a romance. Yeji kept their relationship hidden, and I didn't realize how much they meant to one another until after she was gone. Jeronimo is my roommate. It would have shocked anyone as much as me, but after Jason and I split, he fell in as the big annoying brother that pushed me upright again.

Jeronimo is hurt, and not able to return. That has to be hard on him. Yeji was killed by an infected we were treating, and this gun failed to protect her. It, however, saved Jason when April was threatening our lives. She wanted my map for the enemy. An enemy that had already killed our friends, tortured the sours, and burned the infected to the ground.

"Is that what I think it is?" Jason asks.

"It's Jeronimo's, really. Not Yeji's. I'd like to take this with me. He deserves to have it back." I check and find it's not loaded. "Do you have anything for this?"

Jason pulls another two boxes from under the bed. "I'm sure we can find something. There's more in the kitchen."

There are guns of various sizes and a few boxes of ammunition. There are other supplies I can't name, and even bullet-proof vests. I pull one out and find it's small enough to fit me. "Can I have this?"

"Please." Jason takes it from me and slips it over my head. "Here is how you fasten it." He uses the Velcro straps to keep it in place. It feels stiffer and heavier than I expected.

"I can't wear it all the time," I tease.

"Sure you can." Jason smiles but gets me out of it with a loud yank of the Velcro. "Those sours aren't good people. Or at least, they're very mission focused and sure as hell won't let us stand in their way. Let's take what we can."

The sun is not in our favor, and we need to hurry. Each of us unzips bags and pairs weapons with bullets. We stuff our packs and strap as many things to our body as possible while riding a bike.

As I sort through the bag, I find a hard plastic box. "What's this?" I try to open the clasps, but they're hard to move.

Jason reaches for my hand to stop me. "Grenades."

I quickly withdraw from him, place the box on the bed, and step back to distance myself from it. "Grenade? Why?"

"Ya never know when you might need a grenade, right? Too bad it's too big for the pack." Jason closes each black bag and puts them back where they were.

Before we leave, I have a minute to appreciate the house we lived in together. It wasn't for long, but it was the first time we were on our own. Of course, Angela was our roommate, but the three of us worked together well. Then I was summoned to the train. There was an entire chapter to the end of their sentence in Lazarus City that I missed.

"Jason?" I turn my attention to him as he secures a small knife inside his boot. "What'll happen to Dean when he gets out? It'll be hard for him to work or be social during the day. Is he going to be stuck wandering the streets at night forever?" What a terrible life. In here he has the freedom to go where anywhere without judgment. What if he's caught?

"You haven't gotten that far? Fuck, Shelby. I wanted a chance to build a life with you, and you wanted to make sure Dean had the same freedom as you. Now you get it. He'll never have that, even if he's out." Jason stands with sympathy painted on his face but bitter words.

"That hurts." I elbow past him and run down the stairs. He's right about the fantasy I was living in, and I hate him for breaking that image. Dean will be a sour forever.

Jason runs down the steps and grabs me from behind before I can get out the door. "Shelby, I'm sorry. I have a lot of shit bottled up from what happened between us."

I relax in his arms and cry. I ruined my engagement to Jason by trying to live in an impossible marriage with Dean. What's wrong with me? Why can't I break away from this heavy guilt surrounding Dean?

"I wish I could be more for you," I say through tears. "When Dean went missing during the stampede at the stadium, a part of me broke. I miss who I was when I was with him. I love you, Jason, but I'm not sure who I am without Dean. There's no fair amount of time to ask you to wait for me." I rub my eyes and sniff to keep my sentences straight. "I've lost sight of what I want, and what is reality."

Jason releases me, and I turn to him. "I love you too," he says. "And Dean is a good man. There will always be a connection there; I see that. I've never wanted to replace him. If I could carry your pain, I would."

I don't deserve his understanding, patient nature. A small laugh escapes me. "No one can carry this but me. I love that you want to."

He cups my cheeks and brings me to his lips. "I'd do it over again if you let me." His mouth is warm and welcomes me back to the sensual moments we shared. It's so easy to let him touch me and bring me close. My body warms to his finger trailing down my chin, to my sternum, then to my navel.

I gasp and pull away. "This is not a good time."

"Shelby," he acts surprised. "I have about thirty pounds of guns on my back. How could you consider sex right now?"

My mouth drops open, wanting to argue, but nothing good comes to mind. Jason laughs as my cheeks warm. I mutter, "Thank you."

And he knows I'm not talking about sex. "We need to get closer to Federal Hill."

"It's dark enough for the infected to come out. Let's be quick about getting there."

twenty-five

Dean

**WE SHARE THE VIRUS
OUR ABILITIES BINDING
NO SOURS LIKE US**

Has it been a few weeks since I left the zoo? Being on the run changes how I view time. Viola is a bright girl, but her behavior shifts from being warm and funny to standoffish all too quickly. She remembers me from my days as a liaison within our sour community, but I can't say I recall seeing her. Perhaps her mother kept her away from our social gatherings and community events, where information was shared.

I remind myself she isn't my second chance. Viola is not Skiddle. Nevertheless, I have this immediate desire to protect her and show her all the things I've learned about the city and our kind. She's eager too. Living with her aunt for the past few months has brought her some sense of reality, but that was only after Beth was captured by Aisha's team and cured. Beth may have been someone I drugged and dragged in.

I understand Beth is preparing to depart. What would happen to us outside those walls? I must convey our situation to her so she can keep herself safe if I can't. If we don't leave the city, we'll inevitably be caught along with others left behind.

We end our brief tour of the zoo when I get a text from Shelby asking us to meet her. She provides a few details about Mike bringing a boat. This could be it, my last day in Lazarus City. I've never been sure about Mike, but he's come through. I send a text to Dr.

Warren to provide an update on my status. It's the middle of the night, so I don't expect a response, but at least she'll learn of my exit, and we can meet up on the outside.

"We might have a boat ride out of the city," I say to Viola as we leave the zoo.

"I've never been on a boat. Oh wait, that's not true. I took the water taxi a few times, but I was little." She keeps up with my quick jog, and it's time to tell her about VioTech.

We keep to wider paths through Druid Hill Park where the weeds haven't encroached on the pavement. A nice breeze keeps at our back on this warm night.

"I need to tell you something, but I'm afraid it will scare you," I say to her.

"Nothing scares me anymore."

"Well, sometimes fear is a good thing. We may be the only two sours who didn't decompose like the others."

"Like my mom?" she asks.

"I'm not sure. Your mom may have been like us, but we can't survive without food or water. Our body can only heal so much." I start from the beginning with the most abbreviated version I can muster because of our time constraint. The first battle with Fat Man's army, and the snowy tree covered area we fought. It was the morning, so the sun was high, bouncing off the white surroundings. So many of us died that day. I don't lie to her. I tell her the truth. She listens intently, taking it in.

"I heard about the fight, but I didn't know it was that bad. My mom kept me away from other sours, but we checked in with a liaison who stopped by sometimes. Once or twice it was you, but usually someone else."

"That sounds right. I never ran those routes unless I was filling in." I continue by sharing details about Marcus, the original leader at the aquarium, and I share Skiddle's death, painfully. "His body wasn't what I expected," I tell her. "It was warm when I brought him home, but the life left him so quickly. This made little sense in my mind."

Her lip trembles, and I regret taking this conversation too far. I shouldn't be telling her these details, but part of me wants her to hear what our people have been through. There's so much more she needs to understand.

"We made a plan to attack Fat Man and brought him to the zoo. I'm not proud of everything we did, but we had to find those missing sours." Our pace has slowed by the time we hit the exit ramp for Route 83. The highway allows us to walk down the middle uninterrupted by cars or people.

"Don't stop," she says. "I want to know." Her pace matches mine, yet she doesn't look at me while I speak.

"My friend Nick, he was like us. A sour that hadn't lost his ability. We found the missing sours, but they were all dead." I rub my fingers over my eyes, holding back the emotion and anger I felt that day. So many carelessly murdered. No food, air, or comfort.

"I saw you at Fort McHenry. They had me in there too. I almost died because there wasn't any food, but I ate mice and roaches. Then I held my mom's hand while she shivered. They all died around me. Sometimes they didn't take turns, and people died all at once." She stops walking and gazes up at the sky. "I hate all of this."

I'm not sure if I can hug her. How long does it take a frightened teenager to warm up? We stop and hold our position while I wait to see if she has more.

"What have you been doing since the trains stopped?" I ask.

She kicks at the ground. "Not much. What did you do?" I consider her vague answer as territory I'm not permitted in yet.

"There was this guy who was a friend for a while. His name is Rob, and he became a sour the summer the trains first ran. We were good friends for a year, but he got sick and needed the suppressant." My relationship with Rob was like the best summer camp I knew would end. Rob would leave and go somewhere different from me, so we wouldn't talk as much, and with time, we both became busy with our lives. Or he became busy with his life, and I shut everyone out.

"I heard you at night sometimes. But I was too scared. After what happened to my mom, I didn't talk to anyone until I found my aunt."

If I had been looking for sours before, I could have met Viola much sooner. "How did you find your aunt?"

"She actually came to the house expecting to find my parents. That was the happiest day of my life. Aunt Beth wasn't too sure about my condition at first. It took some convincing that I wouldn't bite her."

"The cured rotters have been through hell. She remembers nothing?" I ask.

"Nope. Nothin'. And I'm glad about that."

"Me too." I'm building up to it. My palms sweat as I prepare myself to tell her we're being hunted.

"What's wrong?" she asks. Her innocent face turns toward me, and I see Skiddle again. A young life teetering between death or survival.

"There are sours created by a company named VioTech. They've been brought in to track me down. It's possible I'll get out tonight and away from VioTech. I'm going to take you with me, so you'll be safe." It comes out in a rush. Was it too much?

"Oh."

"Viola, staying here will get us caught. It's a giant cage, but it's still a cage. If we leave, we'll have more control over what happens to us."

We continue moving in silence until the next exit ramp. I point to the left, and then follow her through downtown. The harbor is ahead. It's inky waters sparkling with the moon's reflection. This city has worked hard to keep me, but tonight, if all goes to plan, I'll be free.

"My mom trusted the leaders at the zoo. So I'll go with you."

"Good. We really need to get going. Can you run the rest of the way?" I secure the straps on my backpack one more time and touch the hatchet on my hip.

Viola checks her weapons and gives me a thumbs-up. She has a gun holster around her back with two pistols at her ribs. We fired a few rounds at the zoo so she would know how it feels because she admitted they were more for show.

"How do you feel about all this? One minute you're living with Aunt Beth, and the next you're strapped up like Rambo, ready to face anything," I joke.

"Who's Rambo?"

"What?" I stagger backwards in shock. "Who is Rambo? Kids these days don't respect the classics."

She grins. "When we get out, you can show me all the classics you want."

"That's a promise."

We take off, and she keeps up with me, so I try to move quicker.

"I can go faster," she says. Viola takes off and I step it up to keep pace.

"Have you found your strength has grown over time?" I ask.

"Heck yeah, it's sick!" Viola jumps and gets an easy five-foot lift.

"Oh, now we're showing off?" I do the same, and for the rest of our run, we show off our tricks. She runs up a building's wall and does a flip. I climb the rocky wall of a church like Spiderman. Viola jumps over a parked car in one bound.

I ask, "How long have you been a sour?" Her moves impress me, and I clap to show my appreciation.

"It was about six months before my mom injected herself after I did. By then, I was homeschooled."

"Why did you infect yourself?"

"Dunno," she says, but I don't believe her. I was her age once, doing things that didn't make sense, unable to grasp the serious-ness of my actions. Her response protects her, and for now, I'll leave it alone.

Viola continues her story. "Then my dad was convinced everything was working, and soon after, he injected himself too. But that's when we had to go to the stadium, and things got bad there." She lowers her gaze. This must have been where her father died.

"Was your dad like you?"

"He was starting to turn at the stadium, but I don't think he was like me. Can we talk about something else?" She crosses her arms and rubs her elbows.

"Sure, sorry about that. Let's see how fast we can run. I'll count to three. Ready?"

"Yes!" Her smile returns. We'll dredge up the past another day. I wonder, though, if her father was the one who bit me. Part of the original family who contracted the virus, it may have been him.

I count down, and we're off!

We've run for miles without breaking a sweat or needing to rest. I'd miss this. But this strength comes with a price.

I trip on my next attempt at a trick and fall face first on the road. Because I was going so fast, I slide a few feet before stopping.

Viola makes an empathetic noise from behind me. "Oh, ouch. You okay?" I can tell she's holding her laughter to make sure I'm not hurt first.

I raise my hand and peel my cheek from the yellow line. Blood runs down my face and it instantly itches as it repairs. "I can't let Shelby see this blood. She'll freak out. Stay here while I run into one of these houses for a new shirt?"

Viola bends over, giggling, unable to stop. My skin is hot and tender. I must have scrapped an entire layer off my face.

I wave my hand to brush her off and head to the nearest row home with a broken lock. Inside, the air is humid and musty. Nothing living here. I run upstairs and find several of the same shirts in different colors. They're all golf shirts, with an athletic material, and a few buttons.

Preppy.

I take off the one I had, which is stained with blood. Before I toss it, I dump water on it from my drinking bottle and clean off my face and neck. The skin is pink, but it's healed. My eyebrow has lost a bit of shape, though.

A navy-blue polo shirt looks great with my hiking shorts. I smile at myself at how ridiculous this is. Shelby will have a good laugh with Viola when we meet up.

I bound down the steps and freeze before I walk outside.

Sour.

Not Viola, but someone else.

I backtrack slowly into the shadows of the house and listen.

There are people talking up the block. Viola should have heard or smelled them too. She'll be hiding. I search the street as best I can without sticking my head outside, and she's nowhere.

I remember seeing a rooftop deck on the home next to this one, so I run up the steps, crawl out the back window, and climb onto the roof by grabbing the downspout. From here, I locate Viola across the street, looking back at me from the roof. Smart girl. Get above them so they can't smell us.

The people walking grow quiet as they cross into view. There are six of them, and by their size and scent, I identify them as sour. We're up high, so they may not detect us if our scent didn't remain down below. There's enough of a breeze that we should be safe. I squat down, and Viola mimics me.

Sours, the ones trying to capture us, walk down the street in a V shape being led by Omar. His voice booms even when intended as a whisper. He instructs his team to check the doors of houses as they go. They'll find the house I'm in, and if they go inside, they'll smell me.

I'm not waiting for that.

When I stand, I back up to ensure the sours can't see me. Then I push my hands down to tell Viola to stay where she is. She nods, and I carefully walk over the black and silver tarred roofs so I can get to the front of the block where Omar already passed. Only, the last roof is squishy.

I take a step forward and instantly realize it was a dangerous move. It's slow at first, but if I jump, I'll add more pressure and then I'll be in real trouble. I distribute my weight by laying down and rolling to the other side.

It supports me enough to stand until I step backwards to reassess my exit, and with a loud crack, I fall through. My feet hit the plaster ceiling below and for a few seconds, it holds me. But with so much water damage, this too gives, and I land onto a bed with chunks of roofing, wood, and ceiling raining down on me.

Coughing out the dust, I get my bearings. That was less than subtle, and it's time to run.

I dash down the steps, through the back door, and into the alley in seconds. To confuse them, I run east a few blocks, then I zigzag around buildings. It's working, because the sounds of their boots slapping the pavement lead them in the wrong direction. It won't last for long.

I circle a few blocks and backtrack so Viola is up ahead. I find a tiered deck that allows me to climb up quickly. I run to her and grab her hand.

"We need to run!"

She's breathing heavily from nerves, so I take a second to let our eyes lock. "Nothing will happen to you." I've made this promise before and failed. Not tonight. Never again.

"Okay," she whimpers.

"Stay close, but if we separate—"

"Separate? No! I'm not doing that." Viola's words trigger the hidden memories of Shelby saying this when we left for the stadium on day one. She was petrified of being alone, but I told her where to meet if we couldn't stay together.

"We shouldn't, but if we do, go to where Shelby is." I nod quickly, and she eventually agrees. "Let's move!"

Together we take several paces back, and then run with all our strength until we can jump the narrow street between city blocks in this part of town. We do this for several blocks until it's no longer possible, then we climb down and take an indirect route to our meeting spot with Shelby.

twenty-six

Dean

SORROW FALLS AROUND
FACING WHAT I CAN'T ESCAPE
REGRET HAS THIS SOUND

Viola and I are fried when we make it to the row home. We lost them. I searched behind us several times and made sure the wind was at our front so I could catch their scent.

At the house, Shelby runs up to us. "What took so long? Did something happen?"

Viola and I get inside, and we close the broken door to the best of our ability.

"Sours were onto us, but we got away," I tell them.

Jason is standing in disbelief. He has a small flashlight pointed at the ground to keep attention away from the windows, but he can tell what Viola is.

"Another one," is all he says.

Shelby steps in. "This is Viola. We almost met when we were at Beth's house."

"You jumped out the window. It was two stories high." Jason tries not to stare, but he's not doing a good job of it.

"I shouldn't have run. I realize that now," Viola says.

"Enough," Shelby interrupts. "I'm sorry, but we have possible sours chasing you, a boat waiting at Fort McHenry, and it's nighttime, so rotters will be out for Jason and me. Dean, Mike says he can bring you out tonight, but I don't know what comes next." Her eyes find me in the dark, and she reaches for my hand.

I let her palm rest in mine. "I guess I'll figure that out." She knows how I feel about him, but if Mike is the first person who can get me out of here, it's hard to turn away. "Can he take Viola too? We need to be together."

"I didn't mention her. I'm sure he will, though."

Her answer surprises me, but I appreciate there are things she keeps to herself. "Who knows about her?"

"Only the people in this room, and her aunt. I didn't tell Mike because there are too many questions about the map still. Why did Mona want me to find Viola, or did she even know she existed? I'm not done looking for what brought me here. If you're on the outside, that's one worry I can put to rest."

"Maybe I can answer questions?" Voila asks. "What map are you talking about?"

Shelby scrambles to pull the map from her backpack and she gestures for us to follow her to the kitchen, where the moonlight is seeping through the window. It casts a blue glow, providing enough light for everyone to be comfortable.

"These stars were supposed to lead me to clues. I think it's about how the virus started." Shelby trails her finger over the map, counting every star in the order she visited them. "Here is Hopkins. We didn't get inside, but we found a lab over here." She points at each star. "Then we visited your aunt. Later I checked the stadium."

"You went to the stadium?" I ask. "I've been there. It's ugly."

"Horrible that no one could bury the dead there. I couldn't stay to look around, so I went to your house, Viola. What do these things mean?"

Viola steps away from the table. "My mother wasn't the only one in the medical industry. My father was a pharmaceutical rep for sports medicine."

"Like a personal trainer?" Jason asks.

"Not really," Viola continues. "If I tell you something, how will it affect me and my aunt?"

Those of us bending over the table stand straight and look at her. "What is it?" I ask. "Did your father do something?"

Viola's face goes hard, and she juts out her chin. "No. It wasn't him; he was a good man. I did something stupid."

"Can you tell us? No one is going to hurt you here." I assure her and give her the space she needs to address the group.

"My dad was working with the Orioles, Ravens, and other sports teams that performed in Baltimore. I overheard someone say he was selling performance drugs. You know, like steroids. I was so mad at him, but also curious because it didn't sound like a steroid to get bigger muscles."

Viola steps away from the table and walks over to the kitchen sink, blocking the moonlight from hitting the map. She continues, "I think my mom was working on a stronger drug for him but didn't tell me. I can't say for sure, but my mom's work supported what my dad did. And I destroyed it."

"How did you destroy it?" I ask.

She shuffles her stance and keeps her eyes out the window. "I found the safe in their room. The code was their anniversary. How dumb is that? The vials of drugs inside looked like steroids, and I was curious, I guess. I shot myself with one, but nothing happened right away."

Shelby steps forward and places her hand on Viola's shoulder. "Go on. What was next?"

"I woke up feeling sick, like the flu. My dad stayed home with me, but then they discovered the vial and freaked out. Mom took me to the lab to run tests. I spent the next few weeks between there and the house. They were mad. Lots of yelling. I couldn't go to school or do anything."

"Stop." I raise my nose to the air and find the unmistakable scent of sour. "They're here," I whisper.

The door implodes, and in comes Omar, followed by his sours. There's no hesitation from them. They storm in with lightning force and within seconds they're upon us. Shelby grabs the map and tries to fold it, but one sour has her wrist and is twisting her arm, so she falls to the ground screaming.

Someone slams into my side, causing me to bang my head on the wall. I crumple to the floor and a man falls on top of me. It's Omar, and he's pissed as hell. His nostrils flair as he hangs over me.

"Time to get even for hitting me with that axe!" His head draws toward mine, ready to head butt me. My knee comes up fast, striking his nuts right where I needed it to land. He wheezes, and he flushes a dark red, but he doesn't get up. I knee him three more times, and he grits his teeth, taking my blows.

"You're fucking crazy," I tell him, and then I bring my head up, smashing his nose, and ruining the surprise he had for me.

He falls off and grabs his face. Viola screams when a woman grabs her by the hair. I whip out my hatchet and crack the sour on the head so she releases Viola. Her body drops limp next to us. Viola takes out her gun to shoot, but I hold her hand down.

"Be careful who you hit." Then I let her do what she needs to. She jumps on the back of a sour woman strangling Jason and then twists the sour's neck until a juicy cracking sound lets us know the neck is broken. Another body hits the ground.

Before I can talk to Jason, he's swept to the floor by a sour. This one is a tall man who easily overpowers him. I can't get a grip on Jason as he's dragged out of the kitchen by his ankles.

"Shelby," I yell, while scrambling to get ahold of Jason. I can't find Shelby anywhere. The house grows quiet as the fight falls out to the street. The sour yanks Jason away and his head bobs down the marble steps. I take a step to follow, but someone wraps their arm around my neck and pulls me back.

Omar and I stumble into the kitchen, where I grab a pot and throw it over my head at his face. The kitchen is compact and cluttered with furniture and a fallen sour. I'm able to wiggle free by elbowing Omar in the stomach.

The scent of rotters fills the air.

From the inside of the house, I see rotters circling Jason and Shelby on the street. Jason has his gun, and fires at those getting too close. When he runs out of bullets, he pulls another gun from his backpack. But how long will that last?

Shelby has what looks like a broken chair in her hand. She bats at the rotters closing in, and the sours stand on the sidewalk laughing.

I leave Omar in the kitchen and push through the rotters, making my way to Jason and Shelby. By moving rotters away, I create a path for us to escape.

"Run!" I tell them. "Where's Viola?"

Shelby throws her backpack on the ground and takes out another gun to hand to Jason. He fires immediately at the rotters.

Fresh salts. I bet the rotters can't contain themselves.

Their whines and groans pierce the air. Shadows from the moon silhouette on the road as several more shamble into view.

"More are coming," I warn them. My nose tells me this isn't the end, either. "Get out of here now. Go hide!" I grab Shelby and pull her off the ground when I notice something in her fist. "What is that?"

"Grenade," she says, quick and mean. "Get the hell out of my way." She pushes past me while tossing another gun to Jason who follows her to where the sours are standing with satisfied grins on their faces. "Hey, assholes!" The sours turn away from Omar coming out of the door, and Shelby pulls the pin. She throws the bomb at their feet and dives toward Jason.

How long does a hand grenade take to go off? This one took five seconds, and the sours didn't understand what was happening. The explosion shakes the ground and knocks me back. Pieces of stone and asphalt pelt me as I cover my head. My ears ring, but not for long.

Through the dust I find fallen sours, and Omar stomping out of the house toward me. He's got Viola next to him. Her hands are bound and there is a cloth stuffed in her mouth.

"Stop this!" Omar shouts. "This will not end well if we keep going. Dean Kaplan, come with me, and I let the girl go." He has her by the back of her shirt and shakes her to make a point.

"If I don't?" I muster as I stand to face him.

"I can crack her head like a watermelon. You want to see me try?" He brings Viola in front of him and places his large palms on both sides of her head. Viola tries to scream, but the towel in her mouth stops her.

"No. I'll go with you!" To show good faith, I undo the hatchet at my hip and drop my backpack to the ground. "I have no other weapons."

The rotters are dazed after the explosion. Their senses thrown as they wander around, smacking into buildings and light posts. Jason and Shelby have guns locked on Omar.

He sees them and shakes his head. "You think I'm the only one they made? Or the biggest? If you kill me, there's another ready to take my place. Get this over with now, Dean."

"I said I'll go. Shelby, Jason, lower your guns. Take Viola and keep her safe."

Shelby refuses. "No. He's going to come back for her. I won't keep losing to VioTech."

"I'll make you a deal." Omar drops his hands from Viola's head. "Dean comes with me right now, and I'll keep this girl a secret. My mission was clear. I don't need to say more." His nostrils flare, convincing me he knows exactly what he has in his grasp.

I point at the sour standing behind him, the last one other than Omar. "What about that guy?"

Omar pulls a gun from his waist and shoots the other sour in the head. "No problem. See?"

Shelby jumps back, and Jason moves to stand next to her. Who kills their own team member? A maniac, that's who. How could we trust this man?

"My nerves don't do well when you do shit like that, Omar." I slowly walk closer to him.

"I'll let the girl go if you put this on." He grabs a pair of plastic handcuffs that look like zip ties. They use these on the rotters too. They'll cut me if I try to get out.

"Fine."

He throws them at my feet, and I pick them up.

"No! Dean, don't do it." Shelby screams, her voice shaking. "Please."

Jason pulls her back so she can't interfere. "Let him go, Shelby. Dean knows what he's doing."

"He doesn't. This won't protect anyone, Dean. They're going to kill you!"

Omar shakes his head. "Such bad ideas about what we do. Dean is helping us."

I wrap the handcuffs around my wrists and use my teeth to tighten them. Then I hold my hands out so Omar can see what I've done. "Now let the girl go."

He holds up his end of the deal. "There you go, little bird, back to your nest. Come, Dean. We have a boat to catch."

A boat, he says. Could this be the same boat that Mike was bringing? These two aren't playing for the same team, are they? I glance at Shelby, who must have heard it too. She yanks the rag out of Viola's mouth and unties her wrists. Viola cries so hard she can't speak, but she keeps me in her sight, mouthing words I can't understand.

We just found each other; two of a kind. I made her a promise I'm already breaking. I can't keep her safe if I'm not with her. Shelby will have to take over.

Omar grabs my elbow and walks me past Shelby, Jason, and Viola. They stay where they are supposed to, stunned, unable to do anything. In my head, I plead they'll let me go. This is the end. I'm getting out of this city right now, and while it's not how I envisioned it, it's still a chance to be free from Lazarus City.

The rotters behind us figure out what happened, and I can hear Jason instructing the others to move out of the area. There are a few pops of a gun. I shudder. They'll be okay. This isn't their first time.

There's a pier located past Locust Point right before Fort McHenry. It's so overgrown with bushes and weeds, the trails are hardly recognizable. Above are tattered remains of the American flag that have been waving for three years. Mostly the red stripes remain, making it a blue box with red licorice ribbons floating in the sky.

"The boat is here." Omar has not let go of my arm, and he pushes me toward the dock. There's a boat that looks like a coast guard vessel with a deep cabin. We get closer, and I expect to see Mike. However, I do not. There are strangers on board. All of them keep their eyes on me when I board. Omar leads me below deck and takes another hand cuff making sure there are two on my wrists, and another around my feet.

I'm oddly calm, and I wonder if this is the next level of panic. A calm ending when I recognize loss. There will be no welcome team waiting for me. Restraints are the beginning of this new life unless I escape.

Omar opens a small fridge in the compact kitchen. He pulls out a white container and opens it. My nose immediately finds meat. Deer meat, if I'm not mistaken.

He shoves a large piece in his mouth. "Want some? My friends didn't make it, so I've got extra." He grins, his white teeth with a pink hue from the meat.

"Sure. I never turn down food."

Omar looks surprised, but he shrugs and holds out the container for me to take. I pull up my hands, defeated. This makes him laugh.

"Sorry, brother." He opens the container and uses his fingers to get a piece out for me. Then he handfeeds me like I'm a baby bird. The meat is tender, and I'm going to need my strength. I thank him, and he feeds me this way until there's none left.

Then he sits back and finishes his portion. This giant has a soft spot. I'm not sure where it is exactly, but if he sticks around, I plan to find it. He's military by his actions. Though killing his soldier was different. He'll follow orders, but not go outside of those. Ivan would say going off orders causes a ripple effect. You think you're helping someone, but you might get shot.

Shit, Ivan. I remember my phone in my back pocket and wonder how long I'll be able to keep it. Shelby is going to have to tell him what happened tonight, and he'll be furious about not being there. I hope I get to see him again so I can explain why I did this.

"Can I ask you something?" Omar says.

The boat lurches forward and we're on the move. This is it. I'm actually leaving the prison I've been kept in for three years. A strange excitement comes over me. I'm leaving, handcuffed by the enemy, but leaving.

"Ask me anything." I try to sit back and play it cool, like I have no worries about what's coming.

"The drug that'll get rid of this virus for rotters would also work on me? And if I don't use it, I'll die?"

"Oh, that. Yeah, that's how it works." I'll spare him the history of the sours Fat Man killed. The public only knows of rotters, so I see where his confusion lies.

"They told me I could get sick after a few months."

I wonder if Dr. Warren's suppressant and the cure are accessible to VioTech. It's probably patented, but I know nothing about this.

"You need to ask more questions. Whoever is telling you this is leaving something out," I assure him.

"How long have you been a sour?"

"Three years."

"You didn't die." Omar analyzes me.

"Not yet."

"Why not?"

"I'm a fucking freak, I guess." I change the subject. "Where are they taking me?"

"Oh, you, my friend, are getting the royal treatment. First stop, VioTech's lab in Wilmington, Delaware. We can get there by boat. It's going to take a while, so get comfortable."

If by comfortable, he means to get used to the cuffs digging into my wrists and wondering if the food he gave me was drugged, then I'm doing great.

twenty-seven

Dean

SURVIVAL IS BLEAK
CAPTURED, SCARED TO SEE WHAT'S NEXT
AS I GROW MORE WEAK

I came to realize that Omar intended for me to be comfortable, because he stuck a needle in my arm. The room went fuzzy, and I was out.

A few hours later and I'm awake in a studio apartment. It has four walls and a fake window. A door at the corner probably leads to a place I don't belong. Then there's a sofa, a bed with a nightstand, and a change of clothes. The front of the room has a small refrigerator and a table without chairs.

The ceiling is twenty feet, with a tinted window above the door. If I were to strip down, how many people up there would see my birthday suit?

My head throbs, which is an unusual sensation for me. I haven't had a headache unless it was from a fall or thump. Those cleared quickly. This is different. I'm lying on a bed made of cotton sheets that smell like linen and artificial lilac. Everything is clean. Everything but me.

I sit up to see what else is around. There's a pair of slippers on the floor, and my shoes are missing. I slip them on and wiggle my toes.

The pounding in my head decreases as I move around. I haven't been drugged since Dr. Warren sedated me when Fat Man stabbed me. I woke up groggy, but not sore like this.

How long have I been out? I've no access to a real window or clock. When I pat my back pocket, my phone is gone too.

"Hello?" I holler.

No one responds.

What else should I do? I change my clothes, giving anyone behind the window a good show.

I should panic, but I'm not sure what my situation is yet, so I'm reserving that. The conclusion I have so far is I've been given a clean room, clean clothes, and I'm being monitored by someone behind the mirror.

Then, I notice there's tape over the crease in my elbow. Someone took my blood. I didn't notice it before. Maybe I am groggier than I thought.

My nose picks up things other than the fake lavender coming off the sheets. There is plastic, chlorine, and something else that's hard to say. Air that's been recycled too many times comes to mind.

Within a few hours, I grow tired and allow my eyes to close while I rest on the couch. I'm startled when someone knocks on the door.

"Who is it?" I ask, confused.

"Dean?" a small voice whispers, and I recognize it right away.

"Lion?" I rush to the door and try the lock, but it shocks me when I touch it. "Fuck!" I shake my hand.

"They put a volt on the knob to keep you from trying to get out." Lion's voice is muffled. How is he here? Are they using him to get to me? I want to trust my old friend, but for now, I'm keeping my distance. Still, it's good to hear his voice.

I ask an obvious question. "Can you get me out?"

There's a pause. "I'm working with the lab animals, and I have limited access. Those windows in there are monitored pretty heavily, but I called in a fake emergency, so I have about three minutes until they return. Listen quick. Don't trust anyone in here."

"Already done."

"They're going to run tests on you, but you're not in immediate danger. Try to keep a low profile and do what they ask."

"That's exactly what someone working for VioTech would say." My fists tighten at my side. Lion and I were as close as brothers, and now he's turned on me.

"What?"

"You heard me."

"Dean. I would never." Lion stutters his words. "We don't have time for this! Listen to me. Dr. Warren knows you're in here, and we're working to get you out, but security is tight, and we can't get the police involved. The public can't know about sours." His whisper is fast and jittery, as if he's afraid he'll be discovered. Before I can respond, Lion says, "I have to go."

I'm not sure what to make if it. Did Lion get a job here to spy for Dr. Warren, or is he working for VioTech because they know his history and they're using him?

I back away from the door, staring at the knob one more time. The shock wasn't too bad, if I'm expecting it. So I reach over and grab it again. A jolt vibrates through my body, but I hold on long enough to feel the knob is locked well, and there isn't any wiggle. I let go and tighten my fist. Could I punch through?

"I wouldn't do that, sir." A woman's voice comes from an intercom on the wall. Her voice returns. "Hello, Dean." It's rich, and she sounds like someone around my age, perhaps slightly younger.

"Who are you?" I ask.

"You can call me Courtnay, but at one time you knew me as Courtnay Baby, right before you killed my husband."

A shiver drips down my spine. Courtnay was Fat Man's wife. Roger was his real name, and we found out who she was when we were torturing him for information. "I didn't kill him." The truth is revealed. "He ran away from us and into a group of rotters. I tried to save that asshole, actually. He refused my help."

She scoffs. "I believe you. Roger wasn't great at making formulated decisions. That's why he was on the inside, and I stayed here."

"Sounds like a great marriage." She used him and sent him to a place he could, and did, die.

"So, Dean. Do you wish to know why you're here?"

"I'm pretty sure I can guess." I walk around the room, exploring as we talk. They've kept the lights dim, but I wonder how many devices in here could quickly make my life miserable.

She urges me to continue. "Well, go ahead."

"Ah, well, you think I'm the only sour who didn't lose his abilities and die off, so you sent Omar after me. He dragged me here so you can begin your tests. I imagine the blood you took isn't enough. There'll be countless studies until you get your hands on a stable virus. Then you'll sell it, exposing everyone to the Lazarus virus, and ultimately destroying the world." I give the mirror a thumbs-up and smile. "Sound about right?"

She grumbles. "We're not destroying the world, but we cannot pass up a virus that provides super strength to those it infects."

"But it won't affect everyone the same way. I bit someone, and he turned into a sour, which was a surprise."

"True. Not everyone can be given the gift you have, but we have already identified the markers with eighty percent accuracy."

"Do you have the cure?"

"No," she's quick to answer.

"So you kill anyone who turns into a rotter?"

"No. We keep them for further study in the lower level. They're cared for appropriately, I assure you." Her assurance means very little to me. "Well," she pauses for a few seconds, "I'll expect your cooperation when we come for you in an hour."

"Do I have a choice?"

"We always have choices, Dean."

The radio is silent, and I expect she's done talking, but still observing. Does she know Lion was one of us? How far did Marcus's information fly when he worked with Fat Man? Hopefully, I killed him before he told Fat Man too much.

I circle the room, missing Shelby, Ivan, Viola, and Pizza. I even miss Aisha and Rob.

The hour goes by slower than anything.

Finally, there's a knock at the door, and a group of men in white lab coats enter. I don't recognize any of them until a man with a thick beard and a missing finger steps past them.

"Sorry you had to find out this way, friend," Mike says.

"How could you turn on your sister? Or does she know about this?" Shelby trusted him, but I never did. That boat was his, and Omar made sure I was there.

And that's exactly who walks through the door next. He's so tall he has to duck. "Are we going to play nice or not nice?"

I wonder how many sours are behind him. When I test the air, there's a potent scent of them.

"Do you have to cuff me?" I ask.

Omar brings up padded restraints. "We can, but I don't have to." Then, in his other hand, he shows me a taser gun.

"I get the picture. I'll go willingly."

Mike smiles. "Very good."

He never answered my question about Dr. Warren. Everything I've worked for is in question. But Courtnay, who didn't give me a last name, told me she doesn't have the cure. That would mean Dr. Warren is not part of her team. The lines of betrayal blur. How long has Mike been working for VioTech?

I follow Omar past white-coated people and realize almost all of them are sour. Mike stays immediately behind me. I want to jab my elbow into his teeth, but I resist.

We walk through a maze of hallways, and I do my best to memorize them. Doors are marked with numbers, and there are other people moving around the dimly lit hallway. Is it shaded because sours work here? Everywhere we turn, I smell more of what is so familiar; turned lemons, fruit about to go bad.

If they've been this way for a while, they'll start dropping. Each person we pass looks me over with no expression. Do they know they're going to die without the suppressant?

We come to a room with a large, cushioned chair straight from a horror movie with restraints for the wrists and ankles.

"Sit here," Omar gestures, and I do as I'm told.

"What are we doing here?" I ask.

"It won't be comfortable, but you heal fast."

That sounds less than promising. "Bad like you're going to make me eat weird food, or bad like you're going to press lit cigarettes into my chest?"

"Oomph, what an imagination." Omar laughs. "Nothing like that. We'll take more blood and run some tests."

"Will you stay here?" I choose my words carefully. Friendly, even.

His black eyes catch mine, and his lips turn up in the corners ever so slightly. "Dean, I'm your guard. They've put me on you." He laughs a little. "We're going to be together a lot."

"Good, because one day this might be you in this chair. They'll be curious, right? Stick you with needles and test your pain threshold. Maybe put burning acid in your eyes to see if you recover. When they do that, I hope I'm here."

He leans close to me. "What makes you think they didn't already do that to me?"

I nearly lose my breath. Omar is a test subject, a lab rat, just like I am, and he's doing it willingly.

Mike steps up along with a group of others in white coats. I search their faces, finding most of them are sours wearing contacts. I'm among my people, so why do I feel like they prefer to see me die?

"This is going to give you a strange sensation," Mike says with a grin. "It shouldn't hurt. We're testing the effects of certain drugs running through your system. Do you want to know what they are?"

"Sounds like a fun game. How about I guess?"

Mike's eyebrows perk. "That sounds interesting. Okay, here is the first one."

A woman with black hair walks up and injects a needle into my arm. The solution feels cool, and my body instantly goes numb and heavy. Omar steps in to catch my head as I lose control of my posture.

"We should restrain him for safety," someone says. I think it's Omar, but I'm too sleepy. The floating feeling takes over, and I hallucinate for a short time.

Clouds.

A bright light that doesn't hurt.

Brown. Maybe pink?

"I can smell colors."

There is laughter so far away it must be across the moon. Things return slowly, gray, then objects appear.

Finally, I'm back. "What the fuck was that? Heroine?"

"It's a medical form of morphine, but yes, it has similar effects," Mike says. He turns to someone standing at a kiosk on wheels. "Did you mark the time and dosage?"

"Yes," they say. "Next dosage is ready in three minutes. His blood pressure is almost normal."

"Blood pressure?" I lift my arm and find there is a cuff around it, a finger monitor for my heart rate, and I'm restrained. "I thought I wouldn't be restrained?"

Omar answers me. "You almost fell out of the chair. Don't worry, Dean, I made sure you didn't hurt yourself."

I smile, lazy and unsure. "Thanks."

Another syringe is prepared and injected into my arm. This one is hot and burns as my veins welcome the drug. It courses through my heart, causing it to race so quickly, I see stars. I grit my teeth and tense my muscles as blood flows too fast and the pressure in my head becomes unbearable. I try to calm myself, to count, to focus on anything else, someone. Shelby? I can't though. There is only pain and a furious heartbeat that sends my blood speeding through my body.

"Speed?" I say through my clenched jaw.

Mike nods with a smirk. "Impressive."

This goes on for several more shots. I lose track. My body is high, then low. I crash, speed, burn, grow cold, pass out, all within the next few hours. They space them out as time goes on. When they're done, I'm spent. I dribble spit from my lip and cannot wipe it away because my hands are tied to the chair. The guessing game ended after four syringes.

Omar undoes my straps and offers his hand to help me stand. I push him away sluggishly.

"I don't." My words aren't keeping up with my thoughts. "I don't." I try again but fail.

"Let me help you. This was a hard day." Omar reaches for me again, but I bat at him.

When I stand, my legs go limp, and I fall to the cold floor. Omar stands over me. "Dean, can I step in now?"

It's because I realize I've pissed myself. My pants are wet, and I wonder at what point that happened. How long have I been sitting in urine?

"Shower." I manage the word, and he nods. Then Omar brings over a wheelchair and lifts me like a pet.

No one in the room says anything as he takes me away. The halls are dark, and people avert their eyes as we pass.

"That wasn't good," he says. "I did that same thing, but they spaced it out a few days. Not all at once."

"They assume I'm stronger." My breaths are catching up, and vision is returning to normal.

"Are you?"

While I suspect I am, I'm sure as hell not going to share. "Not sure."

He takes me to a locker room. It has lockers, bathroom stalls, sinks, and to the back is a row of showers.

"I can walk." Though struggling, I make it to a long bench and remove the slippers they gave me. They smell, and I toss them to the corner.

"Stay in here. The door will be locked, and I'll be back with clean clothes." Omar takes the wheelchair and locks the entrance behind him.

There are no mirrors in this room, but I suspect there's a microphone or something recording my every move. I sit for a few minutes, waiting for my strength to improve.

Then I slowly peel off my socks, pants, and underwear, embarrassed that someone will collect this and wash it for me. Did Omar piss himself too, or am I the only one? What would that say about my condition? I'm not as inferior as they expect.

I strip my shirt away and notice there are little discs stuck to my chest. They must have monitored my heart at some point. I peel them off, and they take bits of chest hair with it.

The water runs hot. I allow it to wash over my short hair and soak into my beard. Will every day be like this? Lion wants me to lie low and be the good boy, but I can't. I can't be in this place under these terms.

They can hear me. I'm sure of it. Even with the exhaust fan, and the water running, someone will hear. I rub my eyes with my right hand, and let the tears fall freely. Let them hear me cry. Let them see that I'm not inhuman and what they're doing to me is cruel.

Shelby. What does she think happened to me? If she saw me now, I wouldn't be able to hide the fear rumbling in my head. Is death what's waiting for me after this is over? I play strong; I play it like I'm funny, and this is a game. But it's far from that.

twenty-eight

Shelby

WOMEN ARE TEAMING
RUNNING MISSIONS TO THE STARS
AGAINST YOUR SCHEMING

"What do you think has happened to him?" I ask Jason. At Sinai I keep to myself. Viola has the room next to me, but we've hardly spoken, and I try to keep her away from others.

"Dr. Warren is trying to reach out to Mike for answers, but he's being a dick about getting back to her." Jason sits on the bed I lay on and rubs my shoulder.

"He's upset that Dean didn't get on his boat. I'm sure he wants nothing to do with me now," I say weakly.

"Are you going to get out of bed?"

"Where's Ivan?"

"Probably with Aisha."

I roll over so I can look at Jason. "I guess there's no reason for me to be in here, either. Jeronimo is on the outside, recovering. Dean is missing. I haven't finished the job Mona tasked me with." That stupid fucking map. It's stuffed in my backpack waiting for me to do something.

What does it all mean? I've battered my head around this for days. There's something missing. Viola's dad was part of this, and her mother too. Viola might be one of the first infected, but that doesn't explain how the virus was spread after the city walls went up.

A conspiracy theory that Mike shared with me when we first met. He said someone spread lies about the virus, which caused the government to wall in the city at lightning speed. Then the infection was released. He suggested it was bio-warfare and Baltimore was a big testing ground.

Some of this makes sense.

Who got ahold of the virus after Viola's parents were involved?

Jason shakes my shoulder. "Are you okay? You're staring into space."

"There must be a connection to someone in their lives." I sit up and stretch. I realize I'm being vague with Jason. Lying around for a few days stiffened my grieving body, but thinking of Dean caged in some underground lab being poked and god knows what else has a way of sapping all my energy. I need to get back to what I was doing because it could bring me closer to VioTech.

"Hungry?" Jason asks, ignoring my random speech.

"Not really, but I want to talk to Viola. Can I meet up with you later?"

"I have to go to the convention center today, but Angela and Rob are around. Don't shut everyone out right now, okay?" Jason leans in and kisses me on the head.

I grab him by the shirt and pull him closer for a longer kiss. "I won't. There's something I'm missing, and once I find it, I'm going to expose VioTech. Then Dean will be set free."

"Let's hope you're right." Jason steps out of my way as I wander out of my room and over to Viola, who is sitting on her bed and looking out the window. Both of us have needed time to process the events.

"Viola?" I wait at the door for her to respond. "Do you think we could talk?"

"What about? I'm the only sour left in here that hasn't died yet." She folds her arms across her body and makes eye contact.

I remain still. "We can talk about that too. Can I come in?"

"Nobody's going to stop you."

She's not hostile, but she's also not warm. "Have you spoken with your aunt since you've been here?"

"Yes. She's in quarantine and has friends to stay with later."

"I'm working on getting you out of here too."

She whirls in my direction. "I don't want your help, Shelby. Look what it did to Dean. They dragged him away, and we have no idea where he is. You're like an adult on a stupid treasure hunt."

"Hey!" I raise my voice. "This treasure hunt could prevent the virus from spreading to millions of people outside this wall. If we expose VioTech, we can shut down their study and turn their research over to the government for safekeeping." I walk into the room and stand in front of her, so she has to pay attention.

"The government?" She scoffs. "What do you think they can do?"

"Control this dangerous virus better than a company hellbent on making a profit from other people's suffering."

Viola holds her breath before speaking in defeat. "We're just two people. That's not enough."

From the doorway, Jason pokes his head in. "We are much more than two people."

How long has he been listening? I return my attention to Viola. "He's right, you know. We have another organization backing us, and the government is working hard to get survivors out of Baltimore."

I don't have the patience to wait for Viola to warm up. She could have information that will lead us to an answer. I realize she's a child, and it isn't fair to put her under this much pressure.

That's not an option now that Dean and I are on opposite sides of these walls again. I'm embarrassed and frustrated at not following Mona's clues better.

"Wait." I run from the room and come back with my backpack. The map wasn't finished. I didn't look at all the locations.

"What are you doing?" Jason looks at his watch. "I have to go soon. Will you be okay?"

I wave him away. "Yeah, fine." The map comes out, and I smooth it over Viola's bed at her feet. Then I point to Hopkins. "We didn't search there because it was too big."

Jason agrees. "There must be hundreds of rooms in that place. Most are locked up for good."

"It's the only hospital that remained open when the outbreak happened. We must have missed something."

Viola's eyes scan the map. "That's a lot of notes. What are you looking at?"

I show her the map and point out all the key locations. Our old headquarters, where I used to live and work, the stars. I'm not sure why I do, but this aerial view of the city makes it feel as though we can reach every corner. The fact is, the city is crumbling, and the infected own the streets.

"Do you know any connections between your parents and Johns Hopkins?" I ask.

"Not my parents," Viola says.

I slouch in defeat. They must be connected.

She continues, "But my Aunt Beth worked with clinical trials in some department there."

My jaw drops, and I hear the air rush out of Jason. He gets excited quickly. "Do you know what division or floor?"

"I could show you, but I don't remember what it's called. There were times I'd visit for lunch. You got keys?" She asks.

"No, but I know who might," Jason says. "Call Aisha."

I've held onto this number for this long, and the reason finally presents itself.

Angela follows me down the sidewalk with Aisha by our side. Apparently, Aisha and Rob have access to Hopkins now that everyone has left. They use it for extra supplies.

"So, tell me why we're doing this again?" Aisha asks after I gave her the abbreviated version of Mona's stars and what we might be searching for. A connection that runs from Viola's family to the virus to VioTech. I didn't tell anyone that Viola was a sour in case it changes their decision to help us.

"I'm not exactly sure." I wish this woman didn't intimidate me so much. She walks with such confidence and maturity. If she's Dean's new type, I clearly missed the mark.

"That's not helpful," Aisha says bluntly.

Angela rolls her eyes and gives me a light punch in the arm. The door leads us to a lobby with a welcome center. Viola, who is wearing sunglasses provided by Dr. Warren, points us down the dark hallway.

The hospital looks like it did the day I left. We follow Viola to a set of elevators. While we're standing next to them, Aisha backs up and takes another look at Viola.

"Why are you wearing sunglasses inside? It's dark." Then Aisha's eyes grow wide. "Holy mother. You're like Dean, aren't you? Nobody told me there's another sour like Dean." Her voice rises and Angela joins her in confusion.

"This chickadee is a sour, and nobody told us?"

Viola, confused and scared, tries to walk away, but I grab her arm. "Yes," I say. "And it's possible there's a connection between her family and VioTech."

"Did her family make the virus?" Aisha steps closer to Viola, but I get between them and hold my ground.

"Back off. We all want the same thing here, okay? To figure out if VioTech is at fault or if something else happened. If you don't want to keep going. Then leave!" I snatch the ring of keys from her hand, but she yanks them back.

"I didn't say I wasn't invested in whatever this is," she huffs, "but I would appreciate if you were more upfront with me. If Viola is a sour, and she's like Dean, you're putting us in danger by being together."

Angela laughs coldly. "Are you scared?"

"No!" Aisha's eyes burn through Angela. "I've seen more shit in here than you have, okay? While you all got out on that train, we cured rotters who hadn't received care for years. We had to learn how to control them and keep our staff safe. That virus can't get out of the city, ever."

"Too late," I remind everyone. "Dean is out there, and its further proof they're using the virus. You should have seen Omar. He doesn't care about anything but getting Dean into VioTech's hands."

Aisha agrees. "I've seen those sours, and they aren't part of the military. We need to stay together."

I turn to Viola, who's standing against the elevator door as if she were trying to hide. "What floor did you take it to?"

"The seventh," she murmurs.

Without another word, I push through the door to the stairs. We fall in line, our footsteps louder as we go up. Everyone is taking their time, panting at the top, except for Viola who ran ahead.

She calls to us, and her voice echoes off the walls. "It's this floor." Her promise gets us moving a little faster.

"I miss being a sour sometimes," Aisha says.

The floor she's on isn't one I've seen before, and I did a fair amount of exploring when I lived here.

Viola is standing next to her aunt's office. "We need a key," she says.

Aisha tries every key. There must be fifty on the ring, but we wait patiently. By the end, her hands are shaking. "None of these are working." She kicks the wall in frustration. "Now what?"

Viola rushes past us with her shoulder slamming into the door. It flies open, and she crashes to the ground.

I run to her to see if she's okay, but she's laughing and holding her arm. "You should have seen your face," she says. "Ouch, my arm feels weird." Viola is wearing a white tank top with jean shorts. Her shoulder is sagging, and a knobby point is where it doesn't belong.

"Gross!" Angela says.

Aisha walks over to us. "You could have warned me. That shoulder is dislocated. Come here."

"Won't I heal?" Viola asks.

"Your body heals off if we don't pop it back in. We should hurry or it will set like this." Aisha takes a hold of Viola's arm and then turns to us. "You might want to look away."

She doesn't need to tell me twice. Angela and I stare at one another with our lips tight and our eyes pinched. There's a scream, and then a popping noise that makes my skin crawl.

Aisha takes control of the room and distracts me from the over-turned stomach feeling I have. "Let's get to work. This place is untouched, and it's not big. We should be able to comb through it pretty easily." Each of us sets off to a different area.

We're not destructive. We carefully take out files and sort through them. Then we put them back where they belonged. I search the hiding places I've learned while here. Taped to the wall of drawers, under seat cushions, and the underside of any furniture.

Nothing.

I pick up a dead potted plant to look under it. Angela stares at me oddly. "Really?"

"You never know!" As predicted, we don't need long. All we've found are papers with no importance. There's no computer. Did she take it home when we were forced to leave our workplace? Or was it stolen?

"I give up," Angela says. "None of this makes sense. I found paperwork on clinical trials, but they're for learning disabilities and other mental health things that affect the brain." She holds up printed maps of the brain with colorful graphs and diagrams.

"This infection affects the brain," I say.

"Yeah, but this is specifically about memory loss. It's not what we're looking for." Angela puts everything back.

I sit at the desk, trying not to be frustrated. "How can we come this far and come up empty-handed?"

Viola is sitting in the office chair, silently sobbing. In her grip is a framed picture of her parents, her, and her aunt. "You should take that," I tell her.

"Will I ever see Aunt Beth again?" She wipes her eyes with the back of her hand. "Am I going to live here forever, alone? Like some monster that comes out at night?"

"Absolutely not," I say. "I will not leave you here." I swing the office chair so she's facing me. "Promise!"

She nods and her tears drip down her cheek. When I rub her shoulder, she rests her hand on mine and smiles.

"Who are these people?" Aisha grabs a different frame from the desk to show us.

It's a picture of Beth at a work function. Everyone is in a hardhat, and they hold a sign that says *Habitat for Humanity*. It's a company that fixes up houses in the area for low incomes residents, or even builds homes from the ground up.

There are two faces I recognize in that picture. One is her aunt, and the other is, "Fat Man!"

"Which one?" Aisha asks. "I've never seen him."

I point at the man with a wide smile and perfect teeth. He has sandy blond hair and a clean-shaven face. "His real name is Roger. I don't know anyone else in the picture, but if she's standing with him, that's a clue we're in the right direction."

Angela plays devil's advocate. "So we show someone a picture with Fat Man and then we have proof? I don't think so. We need more."

"Well," I say, "who else is in this picture?"

Aisha holds it so Viola can take a better look, but she says she doesn't know anyone else.

"Who can we ask?" Angela says.

"Let me take a picture and forward it to Mike. He's upset Dean never got on the boat, and he may not respond to me." I follow through anyway, understanding he may not help me now that Dean is missing, but I'm hopeful our friendship goes deeper. His personality changed after the attack, and his desperation turned into anger.

"I'll ask Dr. Warren too." Aisha takes a picture and sends it off. Then together we search the office once more. An hour goes by before Aisha's phone vibrates with a phone call. She looks at us and then puts her finger up to have us quiet down. "Hello?"

We stare at her, so she leaves the room for privacy.

"Do you think it's Dr. Warren?" I ask the others.

The search continues, but we're touching the same piles of papers several times over. Nothing makes sense.

Then I notice something I hadn't before. There's a thick top that resembles the same wood grain as the desk. I run my fingers around the edge and find hinges on the back.

"I think I found something. Let's clear her desk."

Viola and Angela clear the desk and place her things on the floor and on shelves behind us. I pull up the top and it lifts to reveal a hidden compartment.

"That's a nice hidey hole," Angela says. She lifts out the first envelope and pulls the documents out. There are prints of a map spread over several pieces.

"It's a puzzle!" I say. "Lay them on the ground and we'll put it together."

The three of us clear space in the small office to lay out the white papers. There are dark lines showing borders, and tiny red dots in concentrated areas. At first, I think this is showing the denser populations in Baltimore. But areas around the harbor have no redness, so that can't be right. We take a few minutes, but we lay out a map that covers five square feet. It's a view of inside the beltway. The border has fences and areas that are walled off and patrolled.

"It's the wall," I say. The others agree. "But these red dots?"

They're focused on areas that don't have a lot of residents. The streets aren't labeled, so I'm having a hard time getting my bearings.

Angela groans. "I know what this is. Look here." She points to the cluster in the heart of the map. "That's the stadium district.

That's where the infected attacked hundreds of people. Then over here is the hospital that fell first, Mercy General."

"Oh, my god! You're right." The red areas are specifically placed where people were told to go to collect ration cards. They had us line up inside the stadiums in alphabetical order to serve a large population. Or that's what they told us. Now I see what really happened.

"Do you think VioTech knew the city was going to shut down, and where the highest concentration of people would be?" Angela asks the very question in my head.

Aisha walks into the room, and her gaze falls on the map. Without another word, she snaps pictures of it and sends it to someone. "That was Dr. Warren, and she said one person in that picture is Dr. Courtnay Nowak. That's Fat Man's wife!"

"She works for Hopkins?" Angela walks over to the map to get closer to Aisha.

"Dr. Courtnay Nowak is a department head over at VioTech's bioengineering division." Aisha smiles as if she's won the million-dollar question. "She wants us to search for documents outlining how the virus was manipulated and bought by VioTech early on. So she's having your aunt investigated. Sorry." Aisha's face pinches uncomfortably.

"There's no way Aunt Beth did this. She would never have gotten so many people sick!" Viola steps into the middle.

I raise my hands, trying to keep the room calm. "She didn't say that. Remember, your aunt was infected for years. If she was part of this, someone would have protected her."

"Maybe." Viola's tears have left her eyes and cheeks red.

"Let's take pictures, gather what we can carry, and get out of here," I suggest.

This may not be everything, but it's closer than we've been before. I'm hopeful Dr. Warren can step in if Mike is going silent on me. Why hasn't he returned my text message? I wanted him to get me out of the city without a quarantine.

"Aisha," I say. "Can you tell Dr. Warren about Viola? Tell her we need to get on the next train. We can't stay in here anymore." The map is now complete, and I suspect we're carrying enough documentation to move us forward.

She raises her cell to her ear, and when Aisha says, "Hello, Dr. Warren. I have Shelby here, and she needs to talk to you." Aisha reaches toward me. "You can do this. Tell her everything."

I pick up the phone and say, "We have another Type B like Dean. She needs protection, and a way out right away. This isn't a request."

twenty-nine
Shelby

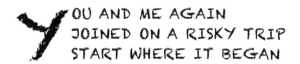

YOU AND ME AGAIN
JOINED ON A RISKY TRIP
START WHERE IT BEGAN

Dr. Warren has instructed me to prepare for departure. Viola and a few others can join me. Aisha has indicated she can't go before they close the hospital and move everyone to the convention center. Ivan sits melancholy at the foot of my bed while I pack the few things I came with, and Yeji's gun.

"You can stay for Aisha," I assure him. "She could use it. And I'm going to find Dean with Lion and Dr. Warren's assistance."

He fiddles with the hem on a blanket, lost in thought. "Dean isn't in a good place."

"I don't believe he is."

Aisha steps into the room. "That's not true," she says. "We have a friend on the inside with Dean. Lion says Dean is doing okay, but they're running tests on him."

Ivan rubs his eyes with his fingers. "Is he with VioTech?"

"Yes," she says.

I'd expected this all along, and so has Dr. Warren, and Mike hasn't answered my calls.

"How did we let this happen?" Ivan rises from the bed. "I should have been with you!" Ivan would blame himself even if he were there.

"Over the last few weeks, you've integrated yourself into the hospital. I had Jason with me, and I thought we could handle it."

Ivan connected with something he can be more passionate about than rebuilding cars. I believe he's found a comfortable place here.

"I'll admit it's nice to engage here, but my brother comes first." He walks over to Aisha. The two lock gazes, and I'm instantly the third wheel. "I need to go. You understand?"

Aisha reaches for Ivan's hand and holds it. "I wouldn't expect it any other way. I'll shut down Sinai and leave on a train soon."

I interrupt. "Dr. Warren can get a few people out tomorrow. Anyone else who wants to leave later will go through quarantine." To exit, survivors register at the train station or convention center. Survivors are given a date to leave right away. The military examines everyone, and a two-week quarantine follows departure.

"Is Angela joining us? It would be cool to have more backup." Ivan is already formulating a plan in his head but locating Dean and breaking him out won't be easy; VioTech is a giant company.

"I need to talk to her, but I agree another person or two would be ideal." I return to packing so Ivan and Aisha can begin their long goodbyes. She leads him out of the room for privacy. He's falling in love with her. Anyone around them would agree. Could it be the forever type of love that only comes once in a lifetime? I thought I had that with Dean, and I'd be willing to risk everything to find him. Even my second chance with Jason.

Ivan doesn't return, so I finish packing and leave my room to find Rob and Angela. Viola remains asleep in her room. She's like Dean in her preference to be up at night.

The patient floor is busy. They haven't moved the recently cured to their recovery beds yet but are making plans to do it soon. This frees up more beds for the infected to get the suppressant, followed by the cure serum. I'm not sure they're bringing in new patients.

I walk through the hallway searching for Angela, but I find Rob first. He's in a room with a middle-aged Black woman, and he's calling her Pearl. The woman smiles at him and pats his hand.

He lifts the blanket covering her feet to reveal her left foot has been removed. She grins graciously despite her injury. Rob asks her a few questions and tells her she'll be fitted for a prosthetic once quarantine is complete. "I'd like to get you on a train as soon as possible, Pearl."

She says, "Has anyone told my husband that I've been found?"

"I'm not sure, but I'll find out."

"Thank you, hon." The woman yawns, and Rob turns out the lights and leaves the room slowly.

When he turns to find me standing there, he jumps. "Shelby, dang. Don't sneak up on someone."

I won't admit it, but that fear is going to follow him out of this city. It will fester and breed into anxieties he can't reason with.

"Sorry about that. I didn't want to bother your patient."

"That's Lion's wife. Did you know that?"

"Oh! I didn't. How is she?" It's a miracle they make these connections for people. Lion had searched for his family for months, and Dean continued the search. I'm certain Rob has looked for his wife too, but after so much time passes, they lose hope.

"Pearl will make a full recovery. She'll learn to walk on her prosthetic foot with time, but she'll be okay. They never remember a thing, which is probably for the better. It's like surfing through television shows and every channel in the middle is black." Rob lifts his chin to suggest we walk together.

"Who'll tell Lion?"

"I need to find Aisha so that call can happen soon. We wanted to be sure she recovered so she could identify herself." Rob stops at the next door and whispers. "This guy is mean. You don't need to come in. They're doing a psychological evaluation. If they can't return him to society, he'll become a ward of the state. Yesterday he bit his lip so he could spit blood at me."

"That sounds horrible for everyone." I lean around the doorway to discover an older Hispanic man with restraints on his wrists.

Rob responds to the human tied to the bed. "We had a shitty incident when we first started doing this. What follows some back is paranoia and rage."

"I've heard others talking about this." The news doesn't report on it, but we see much more than outsiders. Those who are cured grow confused. Some wake up lost and forgetful. Others are angry, aggressive, and disoriented. It'll take them hours, days, weeks, or a lifetime to recover and understand what happened to them.

Rob sighs heavily. "Some are locked in their rooms until the military takes them in restraints. They need security and sedation."

"Nothing can be done for them?" I ask.

"Maybe on the outside, but in here, we're in crisis mode. Shelby, I'm acting like a nurse, and I have no professional training. We're limited to what we can do."

"Then come out with me. I can take you with me and Viola." We hover near the door so I whisper my intent.

"That's the other sour Aisha told me about?" He avoids eye contact when he responds. "I can't be around others like that again."

"Why?" This is the first time he's mentioned this. I thought Dean and Rob had a good relationship.

"Imagine you have the strength of five people. Then you get sick, and it's stripped away. Poof. You're weak again. The only time in my life I wasn't scared was when I was a sour."

The man inside the room groans and calls out to Rob, "You coming in here or what, cunt?"

I shiver at the patient's response to us.

"There you go with the pet names again. I'm coming, sweetheart." Rob smiles before going into the room. "I like what I do, but when they close this hospital, I'm leaving and never turning back. Dean was like a brother to me when we were sours. Then we became strangers again. Save him. He needs you more than he needs me."

Rob leaves me stranded in the hallway. I move past the room, unable to hear the patient's rude remarks and taunting slurs. He's right though, I'll never understand the power of a sour. It's piqued my curiosity, and I've laid in bed imagining what it would be like to run as fast as Dean or be so strong. Then I also consider how difficult it is to be in the sunshine and eating nothing but raw meat.

My search for Angela takes me upstairs to the rooms she's preparing. She waves me in and then throws a pillowcase at me.

"Perfect timing. I have twenty rooms left."

As she makes the bed, I prepare the pillow and make sure the bathroom is clean. "All good in here," I say.

Angela pushes a cart with more laundry, and we leave one room and move into another. "What are we discussing?" she asks directly.

"Dr. Warren is getting me and Viola out without quarantine. There's room for more, and I'm hoping you'll consider coming with us." Again, I do the pillow and check the bathroom. This one needs wiping down, so I gather spray and a towel to clean the toothpaste off the sink and mirror.

"I can't leave yet. Dean is important, but so are hundreds of infected who need cures. This is why I came here. You have Dr. Warren helping you, and I've no doubt she'll get Dean away from VioTech." She uses her hand to tuck the blankets under the mattress. It seems everyone knows where Dean is, but we can't pluck him out. "Now that's a hospital corner." She gleams over the tightly made, fresh bed.

"How can you be so sure?" I'm bewildered by her overconfidence. I haven't worked directly with Dr. Warren. And truth be told, she intimidates me.

"Between Dr. Warren and Mike, you should be able to get Dean out of whatever cell they have him in. And we found the answers you were looking for." She tidies up the cart and we shove on to the next room.

"What do you mean?"

"Beth is working for VioTech, or she sold the virus to them in return for them paying her a ton of cash. She's the missing link. Not Viola."

"Maybe. I'm not too sure, and she's in quarantine on the outside now. I plan to talk to her more."

"Shelby, you have what you need to get Dean out. The infected need us. I know you can do this, and you have a strong team behind you." Angela stops making the bed to make sure I'm paying attention to her.

"It's not that simple! VioTech isn't going to just hand over Dean. He's exactly what they've been searching for." Why aren't the others as worried about him as me?

"Talk to Jason. That's who you should take," Angela adds. "He's been in a funk since Jeronimo was hurt and is dying to see him. Plus, the convention center needs more hands-on people like us, not more leaders like Jason. If I were you, I'd take him."

"Jason?" My cheeks flush with heat. I have considered asking him, but it's too big of an ask.

"Go talk it out with him. This is about who *you* could use. Who is the most valuable resource? Don't leave it up to others to decide."

She's right. Jason has more connections than anyone. He's been involved with these companies and their missions in the past. He knows Dean, and he and I work well together. It should be him.

"I have to go," I say, dropping the pillow in my hand.

"Yeah, you do. Go figure this out before some weakling like Rob agrees to go." She musters a laugh as she shakes out a sheet over the mattress.

"He's not weak, and he already said he wasn't interested."

"There you have it. Two of us are off your list. Talk to me before you go, dummy?"

I run up to Angela and give her a hug. "I will. Thanks for the advice."

There are uncertain butterflies in my stomach whispering for me to slow this down. Jason has met Viola and understands how special she and Dean are. He will help if he can.

The entire walk back to my room, I play how I'll ask Jason to leave with me. My words are childish and small. *Jason, I have this problem... I mean... Jason, Dean needs us... Jason, let's be friends and save Dean.*

When I get to my room, the door is open. That's the problem with hospital doors that don't lock.

"Hello?"

No one answers. I step into the room and notice the bathroom door is closed with the shower running. Who would break into my room for a shower? I reach for a boot next to the bed. I didn't pack it because it's too heavy. With it raised in the air, I open the bathroom door.

Steam rolls out, and the white curtain hides someone behind it.

"Be warned, whoever you are. I'm prepared to fight!"

A hand reaches around the curtain and yanks it back. Jason's eyes fall on the boot raised above my head. "What are you doing with that? Where's your knife and gun?"

"It's packed in my bag! I shouldn't need them in my room. What are you doing here?" I lower the boot and toss it under the sink. Jason's wet, naked body is two feet away. I avert my eyes, but my gaze switches back to him, and I follow the drips of water as they trail down his chest to other areas.

"My shower is broken, so I came here. You weren't home. I thought I would be in and out before you noticed." He reaches for a towel and rubs it over his head, then ties it around his waist.

I refocus my energy on the intrusion. "There are hundreds of rooms in this hospital."

"I didn't mean to scare you." He reaches past me to where his clothing hangs behind the door. "You can stay for the show if you want."

My cheeks burn in embarrassment. "I'll wait outside." I shut the door behind me and busy myself with something, anything, but truly I've already packed, and there's nothing more to do. We wait for a package from Dr. Warren with medical solutions Viola needs to pass inspection at the train station. Once that's received, I'll be on the next train out.

The package was intended for Dean, though that plan was regrettably lost when Omar took him.

I need to convince Jason to come with me. It makes the most sense. Ivan will be relieved to have a partner like Jason with us.

Jason exits the bathroom with a cloud of steam dissipating behind him. "You're leaving tomorrow," he says. "Are you and Viola ready?"

"Almost. Someone should arrive with a package soon. There's something I want to ask you." I take a seat on the bed, and he sits next to me, bending down to put his socks on.

"Sure. I was hoping we could talk about what comes next. I've spoken to Dr. Warren, and we have a few ideas where they might keep Dean. She's vague about Mike's involvement, and I'm not sure they're working together. How much has Mike told you?"

Not as much as I'd like, but I don't tell Jason because I realize how naïve I've been. Mike is my best chance of getting to Dean. "He hasn't told me everything, but I'll make him when I see him in person." Mike is probably more involved than I have imagined. When we were at Johns Hopkins together, I discovered how deeply invested he was in the trial and Dr. Warren's mission. I know he's keeping something from me.

"We'll find out for sure," Jason says.

"This brings me to what I wanted to ask. Dr. Warren said I'm able to bring a few people with me. I've got Ivan, but the others aren't able to..." I trail off, hoping he'll figure it out.

"But?"

I guess he won't. "You, Jason. I want you to come with me."

"Oh."

He looks out the window, then to the ground, and finally directly at me. I'm asking for his help to save the person who tore us apart. Will he want to come because he needs to protect and control situations? Or will this be too much?

"Jason, you can say no."

"No," he answers too quickly. "I'm sorry Shelby. I love you, but I'm fighting this virus from a different angle. I'm on the inside here, and I can't stop what I'm doing." Jason stands and grabs his shoes from under my desk. "Take Ivan." Before he leaves, he walks to me and runs his hand over my hair. "If things were different, and we met on the outside with no one holding us back, do you think we would have made it?"

My mouth parts, searching for words. "I don't know. I'd like to believe we would have. If everything were different. It scares me how easy it is to love you, and confusing too."

He kisses me, and I grab his hand so he can't walk away. This might be the last time I see him. For certain, it'll be our last moment in Lazarus City. He saw me out once, and this time I'll need to go without him. I'm suddenly torn with regret and fear. Tears drip down my cheek, and I kiss him harder.

Jason Foley said no. My heart aches to find reason.

When I pull away, he uses his thumb to wipe my tears. "Be safe," he says. Then he's gone all over again, and words saying *I love you* never leave my lips.

thrity

Dean

WHISPERS FROM A FRIEND
I THOUGHT WE'D BE TOGETHER
HERE UNTIL THE END

There are sensations I've grown out of as a sour. The lingering pain of a headache and indigestion, for example. That's changing as VioTech rips me apart. They've done injections, electrocution, and today I was introduced to a tank of cold water. A pulley system took me to the bottom and monitored my body's temperature, as well as how long I could hold my breath. This was repeated in hot water. Not hot water as in Jacuzzi temperature. Hot as in my skin stung, like needles were trying to pierce through and touch my bone. They discovered that my body temperature regulates once I'm removed from the element, and that I can hold my breath for an extreme amount of time. The world record is just over twenty-two minutes, they told me. It was fifty-three minutes before my body shook and bubbles escaped my lips, no matter how hard I pinched them together. For the first time, I discovered what it was like to drown when my chest filled with water.

Recovery from several experiments in a row takes its toll. I don't bounce back as fast. Maybe those assholes learned I can't breathe underwater. Of course I can't breathe underwater, mother fuckers!

Anger gets me nowhere. Omar grows quieter as he escorts me to the next torture device. I'm being put through more tests, and he might find it unsettling. There isn't an end to what they can conjure up.

My life cannot continue this way. I've lost track of time, but I'm convinced it's been a week. Or is it two? The amount of blood samples they've taken makes ill.

If I'm strong enough, I'm going to fight the next person who walks through that door. I'll punch them in the nose, and then the stomach. Then an elbow to the back of the neck, followed by several rapid punches to the kidney. I could kill them if no one stops me. Nothing would be more satisfying, and truly, it could be anyone from VioTech.

The bed welcomes my wet, tired body. They've allowed my room to grow dark, even though it's the middle of the day. I lie there, waiting for my body to heal, and hoping they bring more food.

Food that doesn't smell like it's been tampered with. It's been a guessing game.

A gentle knock at the door does nothing to gain my attention. It's a passing noise. One I'd like to forget while I rest.

"Dean?" Lion calls softly from the other side. "You holding up?"

"Let me rest," I mumble, sucking in the drool that drips onto my pillow.

"I have to tell you. Someone told them we used to work together, and I think I'm being let go. I guarantee they'll move you somewhere else."

"It's Mike."

"Mike, who?" Lion asks. I haven't told him anything, and he never met Mike. Before I can explain, he continues, "Today's my last day, but I'll keep trying." He's speaking rapidly, as if someone is coming.

I've not laid eyes on him or been convinced he has my best interest in mind.

"Mike. Is. Is Warren's brother," I stutter. The exhaustion is overwhelming, and my body tingles from head to toe as it tries to repair the damage.

"I need to leave," Lion continues, ignoring my warning. "Before I go, you should know Shelby left the city. She's looking for you."

My muscles tense, and I try to sit up in bed, but the room blurs. "Where is she? Tell her not to come here!"

There's no response.

"Lion? Tell her!" I shout. "Tell her I'm fine. There's nothing she can do. Keep her away from here!" Panic fills raw throat, pained from water scratching places it shouldn't.

He's gone.

Shelby. God, what is she doing now? Dr. Warren has to intervene. Mike. Mike will draw her in and then use her against me. The reason to fight my way free becomes clearer. If I don't escape, Shelby will break down doors to find me. Then we'll both be dead.

thirty-one

Shelby

T'S NOW OR NEVER
LAYING ON THE CONCRETE FLOOR
COOLING THE FEVER

"We'll be fine with just the three of us," I tell Ivan as we hide inside a dark parking garage close to the train station.

"You're right. Aisha could use my help, but she also has her team around her. They're better skilled than me." His response is quiet. Ivan found me in my room yesterday, emotional from Jason's rejection. I laid my head on his shoulder and cried until the tears wet his shirt.

It's early morning and the first train will leave in an hour. Viola jogs in circles. She's antsy and quiet.

"Hold still, Viola." A pair of contact lenses will make her brown eyes appear less dilated and will provide shade from the sun without her needing to wear sunglasses.

"I've never worn something like this before," she murmurs.

"If you can hold your eye open like this, I can do it." I use my thumb and pointer finger to pry my eyelid wide. She nods and after several attempts, we get both in place. "Test them out in the sun."

Though she squints as a natural reaction, they work. Viola giggles delightfully. "This is sick!"

Ivan and I grin at one another. There are also pills that will lower her heart rate, and we're instructed to cover Viola with cold packs for ten minutes before she goes through the checkpoint. This will wear off, so we have to time it right.

"What about the finger prick?" Ivan asks.

"Dr. Warren said they won't prick you unless you fail the other tests."

Viola steps up. "What happens if I fail?"

I catch myself from speaking abruptly. Viola deserves the truth, but there's no simple way to put it. "They will have you undergo the suppressant, and then the cure, before they release you."

"But that would kill me!"

"It won't happen, though. Dr. Warren has made sure of it. Trust the process, stay close to me, and act as calm as possible. If your heart rate spikes, all these drugs will run through your system too fast." The amount of pressure we're putting on a child is uncomfortable.

Ivan looks at his watch. "We need to lower her body temperature. Here are packs to cool her down, and a drug they call cool aid, which helps the process. I'll go stand in line to save our spot."

"Okay." I take the cold packs from him, and Viola swallows her first pills. "I'll come find you in ten minutes."

The parking garage is cooler in an underground corner, so we settle there. Viola lays down on the oil smudged concrete, and I cover her in cold packs.

"Never thought I'd do something like this," she says.

"How are you feeling?"

"Like cold water is running through the inside of me. It's in my chest but spreading all around." Viola wiggles her fingers. "This won't last long?"

"No. We'll need to move fast."

"You scared?"

Her question surprises me, and I stammer. "No, we'll be fine." I lay more packs along her arms and one on her forehead. Her brown eyes are full of worry. I'm certain mine match and there's no use lying. "Actually, I'm scared shitless."

Viola smiles. "Me too." Her hand brushes my foot, and I take it to squeeze. Four times. One for each of my sisters, and I add an extra for her.

"I'm sorry. This is too much to put on a girl your age. I wish there was another way."

"It's okay," she says in that dismissive way teenagers respond to things. Her face is tight, and brows furrowed, telling me she's truly not okay.

At the ten-minute mark, I'm supposed to give Viola another pill of the cool aid as well as a beta blocker to lower her heart rate. The dosage level is three times what the average person would need. Her body shivers, and I worry we've given her too much.

With chattering teeth, she lifts her arms so I can pull her to stand.

"I'm a walking snowman in summer. Can we go now?"

"Try to act normal. You've got this!"

We venture into the sunshine, holding hands. We've no reason to lie about our identity because they're desperate to get people out. In the back of my mind, I've replayed the worst-case scenario. They recognize Ivan and me as trespassers and arrest us, and Viola fails her test. Dr. Warren doctored the records on file, but is that enough? My heart thunders in my chest, and I wish for a drug to calm my nerves.

Ivan waves at us from his place in line. When we join him, I notice those around us are all cured. It's easy to tell because of their dental hygiene, scars, and overall disheveled appearance.

"We stand out," I whisper to Ivan just as the line moves.

"I thought of that. Tell them you aren't a cured, or they'll never believe you. Say we're survivors who lived at the hospital and your services aren't needed any longer. You both got that?" He looks convinced this will work, and what choice do I have?

The line is moving, and within a minute, we're providing our information at the desk, just as I did the first time I left. What a distinct feeling it was then. I was scared and sad. Guilt riddled me as I was getting a ticket out while others left behind were continuing our fight. This is different. Fear grips my entire body, and my anxiety is like static electricity feeding through my veins. My palms sweat, and my head spins.

Ivan nudges me. "Shelby, he asked you a question."

"Sorry, I'm a little excited to leave," I say convincingly enough.

The man behind the counter smiles. "We get that a lot. I'll make this as easy as possible. Provide me with your name, please."

"Shelby Bolger."

"Date of birth, address inside the city, and the place you will stay when released from quarantine."

"The three of us work at Sinai." I provide him with the information he asks for. Beside me, Viola and Ivan are doing the same. Each of us keeping our stories short. Voila is having little shivers that crawl through her at unexpected times, but she's holding it together.

The man's comments on Sinai. "They're closing down that location. I guess we'll be seeing a lot of you. Thank you for serving this assignment. Go on through that door for your exam." He hands me a printout and politely waves me away.

Viola is quick to follow, and then Ivan, who is breaking into a sweat.

"First part done," I assure them.

We walk through the doors and are escorted to individual curtains inside the train station. Behind each is a private stall for the exam. I sit on the table and go through temperature taking, blood pressure, several questions about my mental and physical health, and then an eye exam to test my dilation.

Viola.

She may not pass this test with her contacts. I need to leave so I can interrupt her or put myself between her and the doctor. Or, I don't know what to do, but there has to be something!

"You're ready. Please take this with you and wait to board the train." The nurse hands me another form and whips the curtain open. Standing patiently are Ivan and Viola.

"How did you?" I point to my eye.

"I'm not sure. The nurse was confused and asked me additional questions about my contacts. I told her they were prescription and the hospital could provide them. I kept talking and making up more lies until she put up a hand and told me to go."

"Let's hope it works."

Together, we sit and wait until it's time to load the train. Viola is close to me, and the warmth of her skin changes soon after we sit down. The drugs lasted just long enough.

We're on the train a short time later. Viola sits next to the window and watches as the wrecked row homes flash by. The overgrowth in the city shows nature wrapping itself around the city, one vine at a time.

"When we get home, I'll contact Mike. We won't waste any time."

"I want to call my aunt," Viola says.

"We should wait. Remember everything we found?"

"She would never hurt me. Please, I have to call to tell her I'm out. She'll be with friends I haven't seen in years. They're all I got left." Viola's lips tremble.

"Let's get home first, and then we'll figure out what's best. We're not out of harm's way yet." I sound like a parent blowing off their kid because the answer will be no.

"We can wait, but I am going to call her. You can't stop me from doing it."

Ivan nudges me. "You're going to have to let her talk to her family."

"Can we make it to your house first?" The two of them seem sure we're going to skip the exiting process. Once the train stops, we'll be interviewed, and they'll try to get us on a bus to a hotel for quarantine. Dr. Warren has told us to bypass the line, walk to Ivan's car, and leave.

It can't be that simple.

Only, it is that simple. The train stops, and we leave through an emergency exit. We walk straight to Ivan's car, which is where he left it when we came into the city. Then he drives us to his house. Once inside, we turn up the air conditioning and settle into the living room.

"We made it," I say. A rush of relief fills me. I've gotten Viola out of Lazarus City and into a safe place with no one detecting us. This plan would have worked for Dean if I'd been able to use it.

"Does your family know you're out?" Ivan asks.

"No. I'm not ready to tell them either. Viola, call your aunt, but please don't tell her where you are until we figure this out."

She leaps from her seat, taking the cell phone from my hand. "Promise!" Viola says as she dashes down the hall for privacy.

"Here we are," I say. "When she hangs up, I'll call Mike to figure out when we can meet. Maybe even today. I should call Dr. Warren too."

Viola bounds down the hall, holding the phone in front of her. "Aunt Beth wants to talk to you."

I take the phone from her and hold it against my chest. "What have you told her?"

"That you got me out, but Dean is missing, and you want to find him. I may have mentioned we visited her office and found some stuff." Her face pinches into a guilty frown.

"So you told her everything?" I should have been there when she called. She'd only stepped out for two minutes. How much could have been leaked?

"Not in detail," Viola squeaks.

"I'm taking this call outside." I turn away and head through the door to Ivan's front yard. Tall pine trees shade Ivan's cabin. The leaves rustle when a breeze hits them, giving me the sense of space and freedom.

When I pull the phone to my ear, I can hear others in the background with Beth. "Hello."

"Shelby, dear. Thank you for getting Viola out of the city! I'm in awe of what you could do. How did you do it? When can I see her?" Beth is talking as if I've picked her niece up from summer camp to bring home. Doesn't she suspect we're in quarantine?

"Viola told you we went to your office. Did she mention the map of the city outlining the virus exposure?" I launch into my interrogation, hoping it'll shake loose more information. "Her father was manufacturing a drug that was intended to be a performance miracle for athletes. Am I close? VioTech got wind of this and bought it, but only after Viola tested it on herself." I've been stringing this together but saying it aloud for the first time brings new aspects to light. The story is snapping into place.

Beth's voice changes. She's more direct this time. "That drug was not for sale. VioTech bribed my brother. They threatened him. Her name is Doctor Courtnay Nowak, and she promised if we cooperated, she would help us leave the city before it was released. Only that didn't happen. The governor was on board, also bribed, of course. That's why the walls went up quickly. So what's next?"

My knees lock as I try to stay upright. "What's next? Thousands of people died!"

"I didn't want this!" Her voice shakes and the background noise on her end dies.

"Where are you?"

"What do you mean?" Beth becomes defensive.

"Where the hell are you, Beth?"

She clears her throat and remains silent. There are footsteps and a door slams in the background. "I'm at VioTech. They had me under contract since before the infection was released. It's all my brother's doing," she says flatly.

"You told them about Viola!" I bark, disgusted she has turned on her family.

"Never! I would not put her in danger." Her voice quiets. "They have what they need already. Dean is here."

"You're with him?"

"I've seen him. Shelby, the experiments they're conducting are painful. I would never put Viola through this."

A sob breaks through my otherwise composed front. "Can you get me in?"

"Who are you working with?" Beth asks.

"Mike Gillespie." It spills out when a ticket to Dean flashes before me. I'm so close that I can't resist taking this leap of faith.

"Oh."

There is silence for a moment.

"Do you know him?" I ask.

"Tonight. Just you. I'll text you details."

She hangs up.

Mike and Dr. Warren will need to wait. I'll let them know I've gotten out, and that we're lying low at Ivan's for a few days. This will buy me time. Mike may not reach out for a little while, so avoiding him won't be difficult. Ivan and Viola will jeopardize this opportunity if I include them. I'll make an excuse to leave so they won't suspect anything.

The only thing I need is Yeji's gun nestled inside my backpack.

thirty-two

Dean

LET US PLAY A GAME
WHERE I CAN ASK THE QUESTIONS
WITHOUT ANY SHAME

There has been no interaction today. Only a few plates of food come from a small opening in the door. After a sniff test, I've eaten everything. They're giving me a break because I'm at a new location. To get more here, they had to sedate and restrain me. My new room is the mirror opposite of my old, minus the electric volt on the doorknob.

My aches from the day before had dissipated but I'm still weak. I'm afraid to do any sort of exercise knowing they're watching me. Will they move quicker if they observe one hundred pushups in under five minutes?

I'm sure of one thing. The next person through that door will die. If it's Omar, I'll have to work harder because of his size. I'd rather it not be Omar, because there's something sad and desperate about him. He understands the consequences of becoming a sour, but it's as if he'd given up long before his transition. VioTech changes people into sours, but they can't change them back. Omar won't talk about it when I ask him how many people died.

He may not believe me when I tell him I have access to the cure. I wonder why Mike doesn't have access to it, or if he does, but he's keeping it from them. There's no doubt Mike has turned on his sister and the rest of us, but I don't know his motivation.

Hours creep by, and I play my life's story, starting the day I was ripped away from Shelby. I'm trying to figure out what I could have done differently, and if it would have made a difference.

My childhood was terrific. Happy. My parents loved one another and supported us. They expected good grades, and for us to make moral decisions, which is impossible to live up to all the time. We make poor decisions to test our success. Failure has more lessons than wins most often. They didn't see it that way. They wanted us to get it right the first time.

Hours slip by when the loudspeaker crackles to life. "Hi, Dean. It's Doctor Courtnay Nowak. We've had little time to connect, and I'm sorry for that."

"You're busy operating an evil lab. I get it," I push.

"Ha. Ha. Ha. You're clever," she draws out. "We're giving you a few days off, so we wanted to provide something to occupy your time. So, are you a book man, or television, cards, exercise equipment? Just name it."

"A bottle of whiskey, and a shotgun should do it."

"Again, you're entertaining when you want to be. I'm extending a gift to you. If you don't choose, you'll get nothing. So, what will it be?" The speaker switches off.

Does she expect me to come up with fun games to keep me busy while I await my next deadly encounter? How can I choose? It's as if she's asking me for my last request.

"A phone call," I say.

"I can't do that. Choose again."

"I'd like to play cards with Omar. And a bottle of tequila. And a radio." I could listen to music or a baseball game. That would be comforting, but that's just it; I don't want to get comfortable.

"Omar?" she asks, surprised. "You want to play games with Omar?"

"He gets me; what can I say?"

She's silent for a moment. "If that's what you want, I'll see if he's available. But trust me on this, Dean. If you try anything, your living situation here can get abruptly worse."

"Clean sheets and clothing for my new room. I'd like to add those. Something athletic."

A laugh comes from the speaker. Let her think I'm eating up her favors. I may not kill Omar, but I have another plan in mind. The radio should drown our voices enough for a conversation I've been holding back.

"That can be done. Good day." Courtnay signs off.

I'll have a visitor. Before Omar comes, I take a few moments to stack the dirty dishes, strip the bed preparing for new sheets, and sponge myself off, noticing the smell rolling off my pits. A shower would be nice, but I suppose they considered the dunking booth from hell enough.

The door swings open without a knock or warning. Omar is standing there with a large cloth bag in his hands.

"Now I'm the maid," he jokes with a grin so wide it reaches the edges of his cheeks. "I hear we're playing cards." Omar throws the bag at me, and I catch it in the chest.

"Oomph! Thanks," I wheeze.

Omar retrieves a deck of cards from his back pocket and shows me a radio. It's a small one with two speakers, silver push buttons, and a fake wood appearance.

"It's old, but it has a plug, and it works," Omar assures me before closing the door behind him.

"Let me make my bed and stuff the dirty sheets in here. You can sit on the couch and start shuffling. Wait, didn't I say a bottle of tequila?"

His grin returns, and he wiggles his brows. "Yes. But they turned you down because I can't drink on the job."

"It burns through us faster than we can get drunk."

"Not my call, but it would have been nice. I didn't know we could drink."

I'm reminded of Nick bringing tequila over when Aisha and I broke up. He was a good friend. Always with a joke, and I'm myself around him. Rob was the same way. As much as I try to convince myself that I'm a loner, the truth is I prefer companionship. Even if it's a crow.

I make the bed while Omar rattles off several card games he knows how to play. We settle on Texas hold'em even with nothing to bet with.

"Bragging rights," he says.

The radio gets three stations, and two are preachers raving about the sins of others. Sounds of the fifties and sixties fill the room with occasional scratches and hiccups.

I begin the conversation easily. Asking him about his time in service, and what he does outside of work. Omar doesn't have much of a life outside of these walls, and in fact, he vaguely suggests he lives here full time. This makes my goal more stressful.

"You never leave here?" I ask.

"I don't mind. This is what I signed up for. Our country will be stronger if we can maintain these powers."

Bile builds in my throat when he calls our disease *powers*. "When are they going to cure you?"

Omar shrugs, and I've found the touchy spot I'd hoped to. "This is my assignment. When it ends, I'll deal with what comes next."

I lean over and turn the radio up to a song I don't recognize. "But it doesn't have to end with death. Others have gone through this, and today they're cured."

The cards in front of us become a motion more than a strategic game.

He scoffs. "There is no help here."

I wave my hand to call. The cards I've been dealt are horrible. "I can get you what you need."

"Is that why you called me here? To trick me?" His sight stays on his cards.

"Omar, I'm not tricking you. There are dozens of sours who were cured, and some are free now."

"Can they be turned into a sour again?" This is a question I wasn't prepared for, but I can relate. The powers, as he calls them, are a total turn on. Strength comes to me easily, the ability to heal, and speed is better than any high.

"I suppose they could," I admit.

"You don't change or get sicker like others?"

"They aren't sure why I'm this way. I'd rather be dead than live in here for the rest of my life." My words grimly haunt me as they're spoken. Being tortured every day is no way to go on. This is why they don't allow me to have shoelaces or a belt.

"VioTech might take it too far." Omar throws down his hand to reveal a pair of queens and a pair of sevens.

"Nothing," I say in response to his win. My mess of cards flops on the table.

"I'm not someone they listen to."

I take up the cards and reshuffle. "You would be if you were under the care of someone else. I have good people who wouldn't hurt us."

"Let's not talk about this anymore. Not now."

"Sure. What do you want to talk about?"

"Tell me about your wife? Do you miss her?"

"Ouch," I respond, trying to be funny. The sudden reminder of Shelby, wandering somewhere outside of Baltimore, doing god knows what, brings on an angry curiosity. She's going to do something stupid.

"Sorry," Omar says.

"No, it's okay. Um, Shelby is perfect. She's hilarious, kind, and a pain in the ass." I laugh and deal us another hand. "She's hard-headed and takes chances before she thinks them through. But she's also nervous as hell and has a hard time pushing herself even when she can handle it."

"You sound frustrated with her." Omar picks up his cards and arranges them in his hand.

"That's part of the draw, I guess. Things are never dull. She has a way of seeing the big picture and dragging me into it. Without her, I'd be a lonely hermit."

"I hope you see her again," Omar says. "The only woman I ever loved turned me away, so I turned to my work. Before I knew it, I was an older guy with few choices." His eyes flicker across the cards as if they were the most interesting thing in the world, when it was so obvious he's replaying his painful past.

"You're not the only one with regrets."

thrity-three

Shelby

SUNSET FULL OF PINK
I'LL NEVER GIVE UP THE SEARCH
VERGING ON THE BRINK

This is my least favorite time to travel. The evening is bright because of the summer sun, but twilight happens in a blink. I'll never make it home before darkness falls.

Viola and Ivan are easily convinced that I want to check on my house that sat abandoned for three months. I ran by the house, as I promised, and leave a note detailing where I'm going. This will buy me time and provide back-up in case something happens.

The directions Beth provided take me an hour around the Baltimore beltway to the north. The area is full of office structures, warehouses, and other featureless buildings. No company name is advertised on the outside.

An unnerving sensation sits heavy on my shoulders. This could be VioTech's underground facility. Where else would she be taking me?

Dean could be behind one of these doors, and Beth the key to finding him.

"But then what?" I ask myself as I pull up to the security gate she directed me to.

A bulky man, too muscular to fit into the small office, leans his head out the window. "Identification, please." He has a mustache that twists when he talks. There's something off about him, but I can't place it.

I pull out my license and hand it over to him. "Beth Jackson is expecting me. I have an appointment."

The man's face is expressionless as he folds back into the small building and taps his computer. The screen flashes to life, casting a blue glow over his face. That's when I figure out what's different. His eyes are dark like Dean's. They have sours working in this facility.

He hands me my license and the gate swings open. "Suite 502. Go to the left where it's marked visitors."

I return my license to the wallet and throw it into my purse. "Thank you."

The sky is spectacular, with pinks and purples hovering over the setting sun. I find a parking spot where he said I would and exit my car. Yeji's gun is tucked in my waistband, though I'm not sure how far I'll get with it.

Anxiety shakes me as a million worse case scenarios run through my mind. Dean is dead. There's an ambush waiting for me. I'll be arrested for interfering with a government project. This is the last sunset I will ever see. Then a sliver of hope tries to call for attention. Dean is alive and well. We'll be reunited. I'll take him to Ivan's, and everyone will be happy.

I try to tell myself Beth is waiting inside to talk to me, and then I'll go home to determine what her information means.

Yes, that's what's going to happen.

The parking lot is full of cars at almost 8 pm, and upon closer inspection, the building is one of several in a row. They're all the same color, beige. The outside is clad in vertical siding, and the rusted nails holding it together suggest the buildings are old. A few rows over is a taller building with a large glass front. I feel more drawn to that area, but Beth and the guard said building 502.

There is an intercom to announce myself.

"Can I help you?" a voice I don't recognize answers.

"I have an appointment with Beth Jackson in suite 502."

"And what is this about?" It's clear she doesn't want to deal with me.

"A family member who is not well." I'm not lying. Hopefully, this gets her attention.

"Let me ring her," she says.

My hands won't stop sweating no matter how many times I wipe them on my pants. If Jason were with me, he'd tell me what to do. We'd already be inside, getting offered a bottle of water while we wait for Dean to be escorted in.

No. This isn't his fault. I can make the right decisions and see this through. Dean is my responsibility, and I'm doing this for him.

"You may enter. Go straight through the lobby, then stay to the left." The door buzzes, and I pull it open.

Inside, the floor is concrete, and I'm in a sparse lobby with a few metal chairs. A white table sits in the middle with nothing on it.

I go through the door on the other side and come into a wide hallway; the layout is similar to a hospital. There's a meeting room with glass walls, and people that don't look up as I pass. The floor is now tiled, walls are painted a pale yellow with artwork of fields and landscapes. It's peaceful, and a stark change from the lobby.

Each office I pass has a glass door with someone working inside or a dark desk. Nothing out of the ordinary. In fact, my sense of dread lessens. I'm in a normal office building. Familiar almost, like any office I've typically been in.

I find a name tag that says Dr. Bethany Jackson, and Beth is sitting at her desk. She waves at me to come in, so I do. Then I take a seat across from her. My gun pokes into my back as I do.

"Can I get you anything?" Beth gestures to a mini fridge behind her.

"I'm okay. Thanks."

"How is Viola? I can't wait to see her." Beth is carrying on like we didn't have our last conversation.

I put on a smile while I scan the office for a security camera. "It hasn't even been a day yet. We all need time to adjust." I pause, look at her deeply, and whisper, "Are we okay to talk here?"

"Of course, dear. VioTech isn't the monster you're making them out to be. My brother worked with them and got himself in a terrible situation. We graduated from the same university, with the same degree. Did Viola tell you that? My brother and I shared so many things."

"Including the Lazarus virus?" I question. Why is Beth speaking so differently than when we were on the phone?

"Well, not necessarily. I didn't understand the gravity of his research. Even now, I'm discovering new things. We all are. Dean's unique viral structure is what the virus was intended to do. Viola and Flora were doing well, so we thought. When Curtis took the drug, it reacted differently. He couldn't control it."

My fingers hover in front of my lips. "They infected themselves?"

"Yes. He wanted to be like Flora and Viola. He was sick for a week, and at the stadium, he lost consciousness. I had to leave him." A tear hangs in her eyelashes, and she quickly swipes it away. They were at the stadium where the majority of the virus spread.

"You said Viola and her mom were sick, like Dean?" I'm calm, but I have the strong desire to shake the truth from her lips.

"Viola wasn't old enough to understand the consequences of her actions. I'm not sure how she got ahold of the drug, but Curtis told me she injected herself. He said to keep it quiet, so we told no one else. Flora freaked out and injected herself so her and Viola could go through it together. Or that's what Curtis told me."

Beth is leaving out details, and I'm nervous about pushing her so early. "And what about VioTech?"

Beth crosses her arms and stares at me. "VioTech wanted to protect Baltimore. They purchased the drug from Curtis months before all this." Her lips are thin and tight, as if the truth is hiding within.

"How could it have spread so quickly?" I change my tactic, because it's clear she's trying to protect VioTech and possibly Viola, her only living relative. "Is Dean here or not?

"Dean was infected at the stadium, correct?" Beth avoids my probe about Dean's whereabouts. I try to respond calmly, but my nerves are pushing me too far.

"Yes."

"VioTech didn't realize how unstable the infection was. To test the consequences on a mass scale would provide VioTech and our national defense with a firsthand review of the Lazarus virus's capabilities. Remember, they were hoping for advanced capabilities from day one. Lazarus virus can do good, but it needs adjustments."

This entire time, I expected the virus intended to turn people into rotters was their goal. That's what's been shared with me, and we all bought this story. It's not true. Sours are what they wanted from the beginning.

"It does a lot of bad too. Were you at the stadium?"

She mutters a yes under her breath. Then continues, "I was with Viola and her parents to get ration cards like everyone else. Curtis was so ill; he could hardly walk. The riot brutally changed our lives forever. Curtis turned on others, biting them until someone killed him. Viola and her mother separated, and I was infected. It's the last thing I remember until a few months ago."

"Why would VioTech want this? They set up an entire city to be destroyed. This could have taken over the world." My heart is pumping enough adrenaline that I could flip her desk and throw it out the window. She's retelling me this part of history as if it weren't fatal to hundreds.

She rests her hands on the table, and they shake. "VioTech reported the outbreak to the CDC before they needed to. They threw my brother's name out like it was trash." Everything Mike told me when we first met falls into place. VioTech wanted to infect thousands, and they made it look like the pandemic had already begun. Only, the result was far worse than they anticipated.

VioTech created a threat before the virus was spread.

Then, like caged animals, chaos ensued. Survivors were trapped with the infected as they spread through crowds of people.

My throat runs dry. "What sick person would do this?"

"Oh, honey." Beth rips a tissue from the box and hands it to me. "It's not one person. This is too big for that. This is a weapon of mass proportion. Everyone wants it."

A man's voice surprises me from the doorway. "It's true. People want a part of the Lazarus virus for different reasons." Mike enters the room. His beard has grown in thick, and some of his stocky weight has returned. "Dean is special. He could be the only one."

I bite the inside of my cheek and look at Beth for assurance. Viola remains a secret. If I can't save Dean, I can save this girl from VioTech.

"You're working here?" I ask, stupidly. "Mike, tell me you're connected to Dr. Warren, and this is a ruse? Please!"

"My sister is brilliant. Brilliant and extremely private. She cut me off after Hopkins, at least as far as the trial for a cure goes." His voice grows angry, and he steps closer. "Do you know how I found out about the cure? On the goddamn news with everyone else! Who does that to their brother?"

"I confided in you. Trusted everything you said! All so I would lead you to Dean? I hope someone is paying you a lot of money." Springing from my seat, I move around the desk to Beth.

Mike grabs my arm and twists me toward him. "It's always about money and power, Shelby." To get away from him, I elbow him in the gut, knocking the air from his lungs.

Then I pull the gun out and aim it back and forth between Beth and Mike. Anxiety and adrenaline battle for attention. By now, others have come to the office. Security reaches for their weapons, and I feel the barrels of their guns directed at me. An invisible beam seeps from them and lands heavy on my chest. I'm going to die.

A peaceful, cool wave runs through me. It catches in the corners of my mind screaming at me to drop the gun and surrender. If this is how it ends, I've met this minute with purpose. Fighting for someone I love, and something I believe in.

"Shelby," Mike says, raising his hands as if he's given up. "You can't win this way. There are over a dozen people with guns in the hallway, and I promise they have better aim than you."

"We were friends once. Weren't we?" I grasp at the days we'd drink moonshine in the hospital's basement. He and I have shared so much. "You used me this entire time?"

"The suppressant needed to be tested, and it's true I may have planted that idea in you. But what happened there was devastating. I don't want the infected to die." He rubs his chest as if his heart needs calming. "I don't want anyone to die. What I want is for people to live longer, be stronger, faster, and eliminate foreign threats. The United States could be the richest and most well-off country in the world, and Dean is going to get us there."

I've been a pawn of Mike's this entire time. Someone to stick blame on when things got twisted and ugly. He's preyed on me, and he's doing the same to Dean. A part of me suggests I knew this about Mike all along but went along with this plan because he made me feel important.

"Mike, do you recognize this gun?" I hold it higher so he could see.

He squints at it, trying to place it. Then he shrugs.

"You've been shot by it once," I murmur, glancing at his deformed finger that Joi bit off when she was infected. The suppressant wore off, and there was no cure for Joi. This is his fault.

"Yeji's?" His voice hushes when he realizes what I'm capable of. If they're going to take me down, I'll do it with him lying next to me.

"Take me to Dean and let us go. You don't own him. He's a goddamn human being!"

Beth gasps and sobs frantically.

"Shelby." Mike is whispering now. "If you kill me, there are others who are worse than me. I would never hurt you."

"You already have."

271

"No, that's not true. I have Dean. He's here." Mike stammers, and the guards step closer to me, but he waves them off. "You can see that he's unharmed. I can't let him go, but you can talk to him."

Mike will never let me leave. These are words of a desperate man imagining his life before he dies. Sweat rolls down my back, and I'm so angry my teeth are clamped and ready to break.

"There's no freedom with you alive."

His expression drops. "I have no power here, Shelby. No one in this room can meet your demands. My job was to get Dean into this facility, which I did successfully. "

"You're a liar who betrayed his family and friends."

I pull the trigger, shooting Mike. He drops in an awkward way. He said it himself. He's got no power, so he's useless.

The end to his manipulation is now.

Then, I'm tackled to the ground with so much force, I black out.

thirty-four

Dean

CAN'T SLEEP TONIGHT
ECHOES OF TORMENT REMAIN
NIGHTMARES UNTIL LIGHT

VioTech tortures me during the day and leaves me alone at night. The two-sided window has no light coming from the other side. They watch me rest, eat, and scratch my ass like a chimp in the zoo.

There's a bathroom in my room. No need to worry about me hiding there because it has a toilet, sink, and no space to turn around.

My bed has fresh sheets, thanks to Courtnay. I receive this gift with caution because I know she'll want favors. Or she's trying to buy my trust, which will never happen. The new space is probably because they figured out my relationship with Lion. I hope he's okay, and that someone has told him about Pearl. The reason I held onto that information was because I worried something happened to her when she was being cured, or I had mistaken her identity.

I try to sleep.

My body is tired and wants to, but something keeps me up. An uneasiness hangs heavy in the air, though I can't smell anything different.

How long until they come for me? What pain will tomorrow bring? Omar could be my way to break this cycle. I'm not stupid enough to think we're friends. His employer comes first, and that's clear. But he has taken an interest in what I say about the cure. Sours have limited days until they deteriorate and die. He's seen it; I'm confident he has.

There's a thump outside the door. I assume it's Lion for a moment, but then I recall he's been dismissed. It was only a matter of time before they connected us.

A jiggle of the knob gives way to Omar. His forehead creases with concern, and he squints through a frown.

"Dean, are you awake?" he walks closer to my bed in my dark room.

"Yeah. I can't sleep. What's going on?" I sit up and reach for my shirt. Before I can put it on, Omar is beside me, his eyes already pleading before he tells me what's wrong.

"Mike is dead."

I stand so we're facing one another. Dead? "Was there an accident?"

"Someone shot him." Omar grinds his teeth, chasing his thoughts. "They caught the person who did this, and I hear they're bringing them here."

I put on my shirt, shorts, and sneakers as the tension rolls off Omar. Mike is the reason I'm here, so I can't say I'm sorry he's gone. Dr. Warren will be upset her only sibling died, but she's suggested they're not working together.

"Omar, where did this happen?" I breathe in, trying to catch gunpowder, but come up with Omar's soured sweat.

"A building down the street has offices. It's where the corporate people sit. I never go there. We have specific jobs and instructions to follow."

He's panicking. Was he closer to Mike than I imagined?

"I'm sorry if he was your friend. But he's the reason I'm a prisoner here."

Just then, the lights flash on, blinding Omar and me. There are three settings in my room: dark, comfortably dim, and florescent hell. Omar doesn't have his contacts in. Did this event wake him from his sleep? I reach for the sunglasses on my nightstand, but Omar has nothing for protection.

"Turn off the light!" He shouts.

A woman with reddish-blond hair steps into the room. We've never met this close before. Courtnay's younger than I thought she would be. Fat Man must be at least ten years older than her. How could this woman in her mid-twenties end up managing such a deadly operation?

"Omar, what are you doing here?" she questions. "Go back to your room. This does not concern you."

"Yes, boss." Omar keeps his hand over his eyes and leaves. That's how easy it is to manipulate him when he's got nowhere to go. This is his home. His prison is the same as mine.

"Now, Dean. Where to begin?" She claps her hands together, and a security team enters the room behind her.

"It's a little late for your wacky experiments, right?" I step back. I need more time to heal between these.

"That's not why we're here. I need to ask you a few questions. Please sit." She gestures to the couch, and I have no choice but to agree. I sit with the security team standing around me; they have the upper hand.

"I heard Mike was shot," I say, pleasantly.

"Do you know who shot him?" Courtnay squints, anticipating I'm the mastermind behind Mike's death.

"No. But he deserved it." I'm not playing her guessing game, so I lean back on the couch and act calmly to annoy her.

"Mike was a valuable member of this team." She shows no remorse because she's made of stone.

"Err. I'm being held against my will. I've got no sympathy for you or him. What do you want from me? Does his death affect me in any way?" I try not to raise my voice, but being hungry and tired is a rough combo. "What cruelty are you going to put me through next? How many times will my heart stop for your gain? How much blood will you take? Mike will not prevent you from doing any of those things! Who cares if he's dead?"

"Mike provided assistance that will now be impossible."

I lean my head back, and it hits me. "He was a direct line to Dr. Warren. So now he's dead, and you're hoping I'll help you? Is that your angle?" A laugh burst out in surprise. "You think I'm going to help you? My days are numbered here. No matter what I do, a body bag is my only way out. So, torture away! I'm not talking to Dr. Warren for you. Now get the fuck out of here!"

She crosses her arms over her chest. Then her lips pucker into a sinister smile. "I think you'll do whatever I tell you to." Courtnay turns to the guards behind her. "Subdue him."

I throw up my hands and kick the coffee table at the people approaching me. They're sour, with more energy because they've rested, eaten, and not gone through the trials I've been subjected to.

When I try to break their grasp, they're too much.

A needle goes into my neck, blurring the room, and my limbs dangle like noodles. "What. Was. It?" I slur.

"Just a sedative that will wear off in a few minutes. Secure him."

They bind my arms and legs in restraints that are made of heavy fabric and leather. Drool drips from the corner of my mouth, and I clumsily rub my lips against my shoulder. "Asshole," I say.

"Can you understand me?" Courtnay says.

"How did you become a giant bitch in this fucked up company? Is your dad in charge of something? Maybe it's your mom. Did you even go to college?" I snicker and shake my head as the drugs wears off.

Courtnay grumbles. "Dean, I have a surprise for you, but I need you to focus." She slaps me on the face a few times.

"Yes! I hear you."

The room is less blurry, and the tightness of my binding bites into my skin as the feeling returns. I'd rather stay numb.

Courtnay signals for the guards outside of the door. "Bring it in."

This room is too small to hold a dozen guards, plus the gurney they bring in. Will they strap me to this and wheel me away?

I realize the gurney isn't for me. There's someone at the table. Is it not for me?

Feet first, I glimpse dirty sneakers and then a pair of faded blue jeans. The body's shape registers before I notice her face, and any upper hand I may have gained is gone. They've got me. I'll do anything now.

"What is she doing here?" I pull at my restraint as Shelby is wheeled into view.

"How advanced are Dr. Warren's studies? Has she stabilized the infection? Tell me, or your wife will find out if she's a sour or a rotter." Courtnay walks up to a woman in a white jacket holding a silver case. "Inside here is the virus."

The woman in the white coat whispers to Courtnay.

"What is it?" I ask. "Do nothing to her!"

"The nurse reminded me we don't have Shelby's DNA results to see if she'll be a rotter or a sour, and I like those odds." Courtnay takes a syringe from the case and holds it in the air for me to see. "Tell me about Dr. Warren's trial."

"What can I say? I'm a freak, okay? I'm not like the others, but we're not sure why." My skin perspires, making the restraints slide. If I try hard enough, I might free one hand.

"Shelby killed Mike. There's no room to negotiate. Tell me what you know." Courtnay steps closer to Shelby, and there's nothing I could tell her that would stop this.

"I'm not a scientist or a doctor. There's no formula in my head. The cure doesn't work on me!"

She plunges the needle into Shelby's arm without warning. "Fine, let's see what happens. Leave her here and leave him like that. Go!" She shouts her orders to everyone in the room, and I'm frozen in fear.

What did she do?

"Shelby, wake up! Can you hear me?" Why would she come here? Mike led her here with false promises, but he wasn't prepared for her to be armed. A price I'm glad he paid.

She could be a rotter. The chances of her turning into a sour are rare. I'll need to take her to Dr. Warren so she can be cured.

My thought stops.

VioTech is working with the military. They should have the cure. It's public knowledge that the cure is effective. So, if they have it, why aren't they using it? Shelby could be saved no matter what direction she takes.

Is Courtnay holding this from her people? Why would she do that? I must be missing a connection between VioTech and the military. Could the drug be locked down so she can't access it? I don't believe it.

She's manipulating every sour in here to believe there is no hope. Or she doesn't want the cure. She wants to grow this virus and change into what serves her.

Super soldiers that go on forever.

I pull against my restraints again, noticing the one around my left wrist is loose. It's not my stronger dominant hand though. I groan and twist. It gives a little more. I slide the restraint closer to my palm and use spit to lubricate my skin.

"Come on," I whisper, aware that someone is watching me from the window.

A groan escapes from Shelby. She's waking up.

"Shelby, it's Dean."

Her head rolls around, but she doesn't open her eyes. Would she come here alone? Jason has to be close by. Someone knows she's here. Ivan. It could be him, or one of her friends. They wouldn't let her do this alone.

"What's happening?" she moans. When she tries to sit up, she loses her balance and falls from the gurney. Her body smacks the ground, and she curls into a ball. Crying now, she remains where she is.

"Hey. It's okay. I'm over here, and if you get me free, I'll help." I'm not sure she understands me or even recognizes my voice.

The restraint slides over my hand after I spit on my wrist.

"Where?" she murmurs, unable to complete her thought. That single word stabs me with more pain than I could imagine.

My cheeks grow red, and fire races through my skull, trailing into my arms and back. I growl and tug against the bonds restraining my body. The rip of fabric and groan of resistance fuels my anger.

"Get me out!" I scream, and the tether holding my wrists breaks. Those around my ankles remain too hard to pull apart, but I'm able to unclasp the thick bands with my free hands. I fall to my knees and crawl to Shelby.

"It's me," I say. "Do you hear me?" I reach out and touch her shoulder, as she convulses in tears.

I maneuver to get in front of her. Then I pry her hands away from her face. Her long brown wavy hair tangles around her, making it hard to move her without pulling it.

"Shelby, try to relax."

Her breathing is rapid. "What's going on? I don't feel right," she sobs. "I can't see anything!"

"Can you sit up?" I have to lift her head up. It's been a while since I've seen someone turn, but I remember some were faster than others.

"I'm tired. Can I sleep here?" Her panicked crying ceases, and her body relaxes.

"No, you can't sleep here. You need to get up!" I force her to a more upright position, but she's growing hot to the touch, and she wants to melt to the floor. "Stay awake!" I shout, but it's no use. The virus is taking her, and I can only wait.

I lift Shelby into my arms and carry her to the bed. The covers will be too much. Her head is already forming beads of sweat as the fever takes over. It could be days or hours until she returns, and when she does, she'll be one of us or one of them.

I shift her to the middle of the bed so she can't roll off. Then, I look up at the window.

"You did this. You have the cure, don't you? Why won't you use it then? Why are you making your sours suffer and die? Criminals! That's what you are."

The lights darken, and the red beeping lights on the cameras go off.

I hadn't noticed the static coming from these places until they were gone. I've said too much, and Courtnay doesn't want her secret out.

"Murderer!" I shout again. The sound echoes off the walls and sits in my gut. This is the most alone I've been since arriving.

Courtnay probably has stockpiles of the cure and suppressant. That was an act. Begging me for information from Dr. Warren. Maybe I told her one thing she didn't know; that the cure won't work on me. I hope I didn't give her any ideas about what my next test will be.

God, Shelby. What are we going to do? I can try to keep her safe in here but seeing her as a rotter is something I only imagined in nightmares.

There's a knock at the door.

I stand but remain by the bed.

Omar enters and searches the room.

"What do you want?" I sneer.

He reaches out a hand, but I step away. "This is Shelby?"

"They gave her the virus."

From where he stands, he examines her. "Fever set in. I looked something up in the system. They tested her."

"What do you mean?"

"I know what she'll turn into."

thirty-five

Dean

FEVER RUNNING HOT
RED SKIN IS WET WITH BLISTERS
A ROTTER OR NOT

They haven't come for me in twenty-four hours while Shelby remains unconscious. They bring me food, clothing, and a bucket to bathe in, but even Omar makes himself scarce.

Her fever is hotter than seems possible. The redness in her cheeks is blotchy and capillaries come to the surface begging for relief. When I open her eyelids, there's a flash of white when her eyes roll back.

They have provided a saline bag that feeds into her arm, so she receives nourishment, but it's once a day. No one has been out this long. What if the fever kills her before I can do anything?

If I could wear a track on the linoleum floor, it would show my pacing marks. I circle my small room. For distraction, I search the radio for songs Shelby likes in case it soothes her. We talk too. Well, I talk to her, and she lays there with her chest rising and falling. How much longer can I stand this?

My plan to get Omar to aid in our escape grows further from reality. He's avoiding me. Or he's been forbidden to see me since my outburst.

They could save Shelby from this pain by giving her the suppressant and cure before she turns. But they choose not to. I can only take wild guesses on Courtnay's motivation. What is her goal? Why is she keeping the sours sick when she could cure them?

The window and buzzing of surveillance equipment remain quiet. Idle worrying is the worst way to pass the minutes.

Another day goes by, and her fever continues. It's boiling her from the inside. A nurse joins me in the room. She provides a chilled solution and takes her vitals, but it remains the only help. The nurse is a sour. She's quiet, but I can smell it on her.

She's writing notes on a small notepad. Before she leaves, she tries to give me a faint smile, so I take it upon myself to ask.

"How long will she be like this?"

"It varies, but I think she'll wake up soon." The nurse turns to leave, and before she exits, she asks, "You know what will happen to her? The test is eighty percent accurate."

"I do."

The nurse nods and closes the door behind her.

I'm alone with Shelby again.

I want to throw more questions at her. Will they give me food for Shelby? She'll be hungry. She'll be confused and in pain.

While I try to predict what will happen next, I can't be sure how hard this will hit her.

So I pace again.

My feet follow the trail around my room. Sometimes I break into a jog to push out jitters and let my mind rest. The streets call me. Running at night alone was the best escape when living in solitude.

After several minutes of this, I grow bored, so I give myself a bucket bath with warm water from the sink. Then I ring out a washcloth with cold water for Shelby's fever. When I leave the bathroom, she's sitting straight up in bed.

Her erectness shocks me, and I stumble backward, nearly falling over. I drop the washcloth and push myself out of the bathroom by grabbing the wall.

"Shelby, you're awake." I want to reach for her, but her posture is so rigid, and her eyes are pinched shut. Sweat rolls down her forehead, sticking to her brow. "Shelby?"

Her eyes flash open, and they're dark as night. I'm not sure what she's focusing on, but it's not me. Her eyes remain locked straight ahead as she sways.

"Are you awake?" I ask, no longer sure if this is a sleepwalking episode.

Then she turns her head toward me with a cold and unnatural expression. I'm twice her weight and more than half a foot taller than her, but the uncertainty of what will happen next sends a chill down my spine.

"Um, Shelby?" I wave my hand in front of her face.

Her eyes snap shut, and she falls back into her usual position in the middle of my bed.

"What in the hell was that?" I've a sudden urge to not be alone.

"Mmmmm," she mumbles.

I keep my distance, at the very least to avoid her head butting me if she sits up again.

More groans, and a tear traces down her cheek, falling into her hair.

"No," I whimper. This isn't what they promised. "Shelby?" I shuffle closer to the bed, hiding at the end like a child playing a game. "Talk to me, please."

Her mouth parts, and she gasps, then a terrible gurgle rumbles from her lips.

I pull the sheets into my fists. They made her sick. I bury my face into the blankets I've wadded up and let them absorb my hidden crying. So many things could have made this different. If I'd only held onto her longer at the stadium, this wouldn't have happened. If I'd found her earlier instead of running away.

"I'm so sorry," I say. "God, what will I tell your parents?"

"Hungry?" A woman's voice pulls me from my sorrow. "Dean? What's happening? My head hurts so bad and," she removes a sheet from her legs, "is that a catheter?"

"What? Jesus, Shelby!" I spring from my location and wrap her in my arms. "They told me you had the genetic marker, but it's not a guarantee."

"I can't breathe," she says, pulling away from me. "Slow down, please." Her hand goes to her head.

"Yeah, that's gonna hurt for a while, but it'll ease when you eat." I go to pound on the door. "Hey! She's awake, and we need food."

"Please be quieter. Feels like sludge is moving through my body. I'm heavy, and I want this catheter out of me. I can walk, right?"

"Sludge, that's what I called it!" I don't mean to sound proud of this connection, but if anyone would understand how I felt when I changed, it would be her.

The bed sinks when I crawl over to support her while she's sitting up. For the first time, I notice the sour mixing with her signature smell. She sways again, so I hold an arm behind her to steady her.

"Is someone coming? Where am I?" She glances around.

"What do you remember last? You've been asleep for three days."

"Three days?" she gasps.

"They said you shot Mike."

"I killed him. Is this my punishment? He betrayed me and brought you here. If I didn't stop him, he'd discover," she lowers her voice to whisper, "her. And I couldn't let that happen. What are they doing with us?" Her fingers make small circles on her temples.

This isn't the time to tell Shelby about the experiments they've been doing on me. They'll do something to her too, and it's a thought I've been pushing aside.

"We'll talk about that later, after you get rest and food." I knock on the door lightly. "Is anyone out there?"

The door swings open, and Omar enters with a plastic container. "I brought food as soon as I heard. How is she?"

Shelby curls into herself and covers the sheet over her body. "Who are you?" She squints, trying to place him.

Omar and I walk to the coffee table where Omar puts the food down. "I'm Omar, and I work for VioTech."

"He's a sour, like we are," I say.

Her face flushes pink. "Did you say I'm a sour? I thought I had a fever or was waking up from whatever drug they gave me. Sour? I'm *infected*?"

We have a lot to cover, but food is what she needs to feel herself. "You should eat." I reach for the container and show her the meat inside.

"Oh, my god." She bursts into tears, hard and fast.

Omar, overwhelmed by what's happening, gives my shoulder a squeeze before turning around and leaving.

I take the food to Shelby. "This will make you feel better."

"Raw meat? I can't eat that. Dean, I can't!"

"That feeling won't last. If you don't eat, you won't build your strength. And Shelby, the strength you have will be like nothing you've ever experienced."

Inside the container of food is red fleshy meat, like steak. I hold a grape-size piece in my hand and push it to her.

She slaps it away, and the food flies across the room.

"Ok, maybe I'm rushing this. I didn't eat for a few days. Your need for sustenance could come later." I stand to retrieve what fell on the floor and toss in the trash. Then I put what's left in the mini fridge with the bottles of water. When I offer Shelby water, she doesn't refuse.

"Water is okay?" she asks before unscrewing the cap and guzzling it down. "This thing needs to be out!" She gestures to her lap where the catheter is. "Help me stand."

"Um, yes, water is okay, and yes, I will help you stand. What are you going to do?" I reach for her and let her brace herself against me as she slips off the bed to her feet.

285

Shelby is firmer in her stance than she expected. "I'm pulling this thing out." I can't see much with the hospital gown, but I imagine she has a bag taped to her leg, and tubes going to uncomfortable places. She rips out her central line connected to saline bags. It bleeds, stopping quickly.

"Do you need me?" I ask, hoping she doesn't. This is out of my comfort zone.

"Stay here." Shelby steps away from me and goes into the bathroom. "There's no door?"

"Nope." They monitor me. Though the camera isn't angled in that general direction, and I convince myself I have some privacy.

To give Shelby privacy, I pace the room again. She grunts, and curses, and then I hear the ripping of something sticky being pulled from flesh.

"Oh, my god! That hurts." There's a long pause, and I remain against the door on the opposite side of the room. "Now it itches."

"You're healing."

She comes out of the bathroom, her blue gown loose around her. "Do you have any spare clothes?"

I sort through my pile of laundry and give everything a quick smell test. I locate a t-shirt clean enough, and clean boxer briefs for her.

"Can someone see me if I change here?" she asks, looking at the window.

"I'm not sure if anyone is watching anymore. I'd use the bathroom, even though it's small. I've lost any modesty I had after I pissed myself during one of their experiments." It slips out before I can pull it back.

She pulls the gown up and over her head, revealing her body. I try not to look at her familiar nakedness. Her stomach is flatter, and her ribs more pronounced. She'd been on rations in Baltimore again, but I wanted things to be better for her. I'm the reason they're not.

When she pulls on the shirt, she sees me staring. "I'll get the weight back."

"It's difficult as a sour. Your metabolism is fast."

Without warning, the door shoots open and several guards come in. Shelby is mid-way through, pulling her legs into the boxer briefs.

Courtnay walks past the others and over to us. "I never would have believed you'd both be so special. This is something else. I wish we could test your siblings to see what would happen."

My fists tighten at my side, but if I strike, I'll be taken down by the guards. They're holding rods that shoot electricity out of the tip.

"What do you want, Courtnay?" I cross the room, so I'm closer to Shelby. "She hasn't eaten yet. She's too weak for whatever you have planned."

Shelby grabs my arm. "Who is this?"

"Fat Man's wife."

Courtnay grumbles. "Call him Roger. I've always hated that nickname. We're taking you to a monitoring station, and we need a blood sample to see if you're like Dean. We used his blood to change you, after all."

Shelby holds onto me tighter. "I'm not going anywhere."

The lights in the room flash on, blinding Shelby and me. She drops to the ground and covers her face, screaming.

I find my way to the glasses and hand them to her. "Put these on." My eyes are pinched shut, so it's hard to find her again.

There is a scuffle and Shelby shouts. "Get off me!" The glasses are knocked from my hand, so I bend down, searching for them.

Then there's a crunch.

Courtnay says, "We'll get you another pair. Don't wait up for her."

I stretch out my arms and run, trying to contact someone, but I only hit the wall. A jab in the back delivers a bolt of energy. I shake and convulse, falling to the ground. The effects of the taser ringing in my ears.

The room goes dark.

—

An hour later, I'm awake and changing my pants because the electrocution makes me piss myself. Only Shelby took my last pair of drawers, so I'm wearing hospital pants alone. The scratchy material does nothing good for my tender areas.

I bang on the door until Omar answers.

"Dean, you're going to make this worse for you and her. Try to stay calm." He shuts the door, leaving me alone, and I know an escape would be reckless.

"That's my wife they're torturing!" I shout.

He answers me from the outside, prepared to leave. "I was watching them. She's hooked up to a bunch of monitors, and they drew her blood. Courtnay is asking her questions. That's it."

Those questions could turn into interrogation tactics. "I want her brought back. She'll need to eat."

"Give it time."

I run my fingers over my beard, playing my next words carefully. "There's no way any of us are leaving here alive."

Omar walks through the door, closing it behind him. "Don't speak that way." His eyes flash around the room, landing on the window. "They aren't recording you after your outburst."

I step closer. "What do you know about that?" The cure and suppressant are in this building, but Omar isn't important enough to get access.

"Nothing. That's the first time anyone suggested the drugs were here. I suppose most of us thought they were for rotters in the city, but that doesn't make sense." He's seeing reason, but it's not the picture he wanted.

"Did you ask Courtnay about it?"

"Hell yes, I did. She told me there's no access to that because it's a controlled substance."

"You believe her?"

"Not sure," Omar says.

How can I get this guy to help me? "Do you want to die?"

He bites back words before I can figure out what brought him here. Then he changes the topic. "Shelby is like me. She's not like you."

I should have guessed that. I turned Rob, and he was a normal sour, not some super freak. That means her time is limited. A year would be the max until her body couldn't live with the Lazarus virus any longer. Then she'll deteriorate and die. But that's only after they abuse her.

"Get us away from here." He needs to see me as his equal. "We can save you and every sour in here."

Dr. Warren would cure them. After that, she'll shut this place down and lock away the research forever. I have to get her in here.

"Dean, you're asking too much," Omar says.

"No, I'm not. We're talking about people's lives."

"I know that, Dean! There is more to VioTech than experiments. What they are creating could put the United States at the top of the world's defense." He raises voice and paces away from me in frustration.

I punch the door, leaving a dent in the metal. My hand prickles as it repairs. "If this broke out, the entire world would collapse. How equipped are we for that? Countries with no protection would be demolished."

"VioTech would ensure that won't happen. That's why they're running tests and doing all the lab work. They want a virus that isn't transmittable." As he speaks, his voice quavers with uncertainty.

Shocked, I rock back on my heals. "That's impossible."

"I'm not an expert, Dean."

I hate the way he uses my name when he's trying to win a conversation. Could it be possible that I could protect others from my condition? Does Dr. Warren have access to this technology? "If they figured it out, then why are sours dying?"

He chuckles. "They haven't figured out how to sustain us."

My gut rolls, realizing I'm too important. The missing link: they can't keep their super soldiers alive, and having a bunch of dead heroes isn't what the government would sign up for. Let alone a lot of volunteers.

"I'm not the key. They'll kill me before they figure it out."

"You might be right." Omar circles back to realizing my death is in his hands. "I don't want them to keep hurting you or Shelby. I regret that's happening." That says a lot, given he shot his own man in front of us. I suppose there are parts to Omar I'll never understand, though he did mention a chance at love that was lost. Does that change how he sees Shelby and me? We'll have no future if I stay here.

He walks to the door, but I put my hand on it to keep it closed.

"They have all the DNA and blood needed for whatever science stuff they need. If I left, their research would continue, and I would live. You are all I have, Omar." I use his name as a weapon, the same as he's been doing.

"I'll think about it." He places his hand on the doorknob but pauses until I step away. "I'll make sure you get food and clothing for Shelby. Eat what I brought earlier. That hand of yours will need it."

He leaves, and I'm alone again. Sitting, wondering what they're doing to Shelby. What information will they be able to pull from her? She's got secrets I haven't cracked into. Jason has his hands in so many pockets, I can't imagine what he's told her.

They have to be looking for Shelby. Whoever she came out with will be searching for her. They'll tell Dr. Warren. It might take time, but someone cares enough to escalate this. They need to find us before it's too late.

thirty-six
Shelby

WOKEN AND CONFUSED
WHAT HAPPENED TO MY BODY
IT'S BATTERED AND BRUISED

My veins carry fiery blood through my body, and I focus on the swooshing feeling of it gushing from heart to toe. This woman is attempting to interview me, but I can hear my blood flowing. It pulses and quits. Then does it again.

The ache in my head grows, so I have a hard time hearing. Is it possible to have a headache so bad that my ears are clogged with pain?

I rub my sweaty hands on my pant leg.

"What is your response?" the woman sitting across from the table asks. Courtnay is her name. I've only heard a few things about her, and it appears she's in charge.

Mike's death hasn't fully registered. No one should end up like Dean and me. He won't prey on people who need help. Could he have prevented Yeji's death? How much of this is his fault?

"Shelby?" the woman raises her voice.

"Can I have an aspirin?" The joints in my body hurt when I move, and sweat periodically drips down my nose, landing on my lips. "I don't feel well." I state the obvious.

The woman waves for someone to come get me. "Take her back and feed her."

Strong hands wrap around my arm and jerk me out of the chair. I stumble as they drag me from the office and down the hall. It's a man leading the way, pulling me with him, and two women dressed in blue following behind.

They smell like old apples, or another fruit about to turn. I'm one of them. Do we all carry the scent?

The halls go on forever, and while I've tried to memorize the halls, it all blends together. We stop at a room where one goes in, returning with a plastic container. I can smell it from here. It's meat. Specifically, beef. Visions of a steak rolls into my mind. Dean explained this to me once. Each scent brings up a visual reminder of where he's seen it before.

I imagine my dad flipping steaks on the grill. He's smiling. The sun is high, and the meat is red with white fatty lines running through it. I want it.

My stomach turns, expecting food, but my instinct twists into disgust.

We walk to another door, and a guard unlocks it so they can push me through. Then the container is tossed on the floor next to me. This room is dim, so I see better.

Dean rushes to me. "Shelby, are you okay?"

"No!" I scream like a beast, unsure of where it came from. "I'm not okay, Dean. I can't eat that!" My head pounds with every word.

Dean opens the package and puts his nose to it. "It's safe. You should try to eat. You'd feel a lot better." He rubs my back with his hot and heavy hand.

I squirm from his touch.

He tries to show me he isn't hurt or frustrated, but I can tell Dean's temper is catching up. Nothing I haven't handled in the past. We all have our moments. "Dean, please don't make me."

"You think I want this? When I wasn't eating, I was tempted to eat Jessie's tail. In a desperate stupor, I tried to convince myself that she wouldn't miss it. You're not acting rational. Eat this damn food, Shelby!" He grabs the meat and holds it under my nose.

It makes me shake. My saliva glands drip. The urge to take a bite is too great. I lean forward, like a kid licking an ice cream, and let my tongue run over the steak. My shoulders surge forward, and my hands act without my doing. I rip and tear at the meat, hardly chewing each bite until it's gone.

The heat in my body cools, and a jittery, amped feeling takes over.

"Wow," I mumble. Parts of me tickle in an uncomfortable hard to reach kind of way. I get off the floor, only after checking the container for more meat. My belly is puffed out with the food now gurgling inside.

Dean is trying to busy himself by folding a few pieces of laundry, but I can tell they've already been folded. I place my hand on his, and our body temperature matches.

"We're the same now." I whisper. "I never thought I could touch you without you jumping or hesitating."

"Why did you come here?" He sounds so tired; ready to give up.

"I couldn't let them take you."

He shakes his head and stops pretending to do his laundry. "You don't owe me anything."

"It's not up for you to decide. I can't move on if you're suffering, and I can prevent it." I try to step around him, so he'll look at me, but he refuses.

"It took two years to separate myself from anyone who needed me. Then you bully your way through those boundaries like they don't exist."

"You closed me out!" I pull at his shirt to get him to face me. "When I left Lazarus City the first time, I was terrified of the night even in a safe place. Every noise freaked me out! How can I live knowing you're part of the night? It was almost as if I feared you. I don't want to feel that way." Stories from the days when we were a happily married couple twist into view. Long walks with Jessie in Patterson Park, picking crabs at Captain James, sitting with other Oriole's fans with peanuts from the outside vendors, and him. Just him. I breathe Dean in to sense what's beyond the sour smell, and it stirs a thousand memories.

I reach around his torso, and he leans his head against mine, but then pulls away. "I know what you're thinking, and it's the new strength coursing through your body, so give yourself time to figure that out."

My cheeks burn with embarrassment. "I'm not trying to do anything." What am I saying? Suddenly awkward, I back off.

He leans closer, even though I've put a few feet between us, and whispers, "What we need is a plan, and I'm working on one. Until it's figured out, lie low, and do what they ask you to. You'll eventually need the suppressant."

There's going to be pain in my future. Courtnay doesn't care about my wellbeing. Dean walks over and turns the radio on.

I look at the two-way mirror and intercoms in the room. We're never really sure if we're being watched. "Tell me what you're thinking. We were always a team."

Dean gestures to the couch, where he fills me in on his idea of getting Omar to help us. Given I don't know Omar other than when he kidnapped Dean, I'm not sure I like this plan, and I share my concern.

"Lion used to have access to my old room, but they moved me. I've no idea where he is anymore," Dean says.

I speak in code, hoping Dean picks up what I'm saying. "Do you remember that person that left someone behind? Someone you became friends with?" Dean acknowledges that I'm talking about Beth and Viola with a nod. "That person set a trap when I figured out they had a connection to VioTech. But I left a note at my house for someone to find. Someone will find it, and they will rescue us."

He shakes his head in frustration. "That's your plan? Waiting for people to come for us? We could be hours away from where we started."

"I've just got here. Let me figure out alternative ways in case we need them, but we need to work together." I can't take another person hiding truths from me because they assume it's the only way to keep me safe.

"Okay," he answers without hesitation.

I look around the room, getting my bearings, which I hadn't done yet. My head hurts, but my fever is improving.

"No television? What do you do with yourself?" I spot the radio and a deck of cards, but there's nothing else.

"They keep me pretty busy during the day. We should get some rest before they come for us tomorrow."

Anxiety and curiosity ruin any chance of sleep. Dean won't go into details, but he will with time. I want a layout of this building. Figure out who I'll see more often, and where the exits are.

"I could try to sleep," I say. "More food would be nice."

"Don't get your hopes set on that." Dean walks over to the bed and gestures to it. "Do you want your regular side? I can sleep on the couch." I think he blushes, but turns away before I'm sure.

"You don't have to sleep on the couch." Incredibly unsure of what to do next, I go to the bed and pull off the socks Dean gave me. I hope they bring me more appropriate clothing tomorrow. "If they don't give me a toothbrush by tomorrow, I'm using yours."

"That's gross." Dean falls into bed beside me and it's all I can do not to roll closer to him to figure out who wants to be the big spoon. I haven't had a moment with him in five years.

"I've used your toothbrush before," I admit. "When we went skiing at Wisp, I forgot mine, so I used yours."

"You held that in for this long?"

"It was torture to keep that secret from you." I laugh and roll on my side so I can look at him. "I miss you, and even though I'm infected and our situation is terrible, I'm glad I'm here with you."

He exhales and groans. "I never wanted to see you in here. If you get out, and I don't, promise you won't come back without backup."

"I'm an adult who's been through hell and back. If I get out, you'll be with me." These words aren't bitter. I'm not trying to assert myself over him or undermine his reaction to my doings. I'm going to do what's best. It may not hurt to slow down before I act, and this situation proves that. "I'll try to be more thoughtful about my actions."

"And I can treat you like an equal. Especially now that you have sour abilities." He puts up his hand playfully, asking for a high five.

I slap his palm and grin. "Good deal." Before I can sleep, there's something else I need to mention. "I learned that VioTech's intention was to create sours like you this entire time. Our young friend's dad created a performance drug. He marked it to VioTech, and they bought it. But the research wasn't complete because he turned himself into a rotter. Dean, he may have infected you at the stadium."

"He's dead?" Dean becomes somber, and I wonder how much of this he'd put together.

"Yes."

Dean is silent for well over two minutes. His gaze moving from one corner of the room to the other absentmindedly. "I wonder if Marcus was working with VioTech since before the walls went up. He turned on us so quickly and reported our conditions to them. Then he tried to convince us to work with VioTech. When we turned him down, he became irritated and violent."

The sour community always seemed tight and organized. I only know so much about the former leader at the aquarium. "Was anyone else?"

"Probably Mike."

I twist away from him in bed. "I'm so stupid."

Dean rests his hand on my shoulder and guides me back to him. "We were given impossible odds and had to create reason as we went. You're not stupid, you were hopeful. So was I."

"Thank you for saying so." I place my hand over his and Drew yawns.

"Let's get some rest."

For the next few hours, I try to sleep. I'm not sure what time it is, but my body's internal clock suggests it's late. We've got no windows or natural light. The couch is plain, like one from a waiting room.

Dean rests beside me, his eyes pinched, and his breathing steady. At least one of us can sleep.

thrity-seven
Shelby

ALL I NEED TO DO
STAY ALIVE WITHIN THIS CELL
I CAN'T WITHOUT YOU

What I assume is morning is disturbed by someone entering. She carries shackles for me or Dean.

"I'm not doing that until you give me more food," I say. This is the first day I feel capable of communicating. However, my head aches and I still have a fever.

A tall Black man I recognize steps past the woman sneering at me. "I'm Omar, we've met before." He lifts his hand to me.

I want to kick him, or spit in his face. He's the one who leads Dean away. "Excuse me while I don't shake your hand."

Omar frowns and lowers his arm. "I should have expected that."

Dean comes forward. "Hi, Omar. What's on the agenda for today? Something easy, I hope."

"I can't be sure, but we're taking you to the lab." Omar attempts to smile, but it looks like a lie to me.

We're being held prisoner and I'm hungry. Not a normal hungry that makes me a little shaky or grumpy, the hunger I could hurt someone over if they don't feed me.

Dean smiles and throws his arm over my shoulders. "She's hungry. Got anything for us?"

The woman with the shackles steps forward, but Omar raises his hand. "Do we need to use these?"

"Not on me," Dean says.

I grumble, but I want my hands free to pick up weapons if I find any. "I'll behave." My smile is as fake as the others'.

Omar grins with acceptance. "Come, then. I'll take you to the kitchen before the lab. Your friend is going to join us, and be warned, she has one of those electric probes on her belt."

The woman moves her shirt, showing off the top of her baton that extends into a taser. She wears a wicked grin, and her point is made.

Before we leave, Omar hands us a pair of sunglasses. I notice he isn't wearing any, so I ask him. "You're a sour, so what's up with your eyes?"

"Contacts." Omar points to his eyes and bends down so I can see them more clearly. There's a disc that has a dark gray tint to it.

"Oh, interesting." It's similar to what Dr. Warren provided Viola, and I wonder if there's any information sharing between her and VioTech.

Omar grins, as if he can hear my thoughts. "That was something Mike brought from his sister."

I'm sick and angry all over again. "Mike betrayed his sister, and those of us who trusted him."

"You're glad you killed him?" Omar has no expression that suggests he's invested in Mike, but he tilts his head to the side curiously.

I hesitate before I tell him I've killed before, and if needed, I'd do it again. Even if the disgust and regret rests like incurable decay in my heart. Instead, I offer something softer because Dean has suggested Omar will be on our side. "I thought he was my friend. Despite what happened, Mike had been there for me. I'm trying to decide if it was all a lie, or if he actually cared."

Omar nods, and we follow him down the hall. I search for anywhere leaking natural light that might be a way out. I was brought here unconscious, so I'm not sure if we're underground or if there are stories below us. They could have driven me miles away, or even flown me to another state. The halls are lit with florescent lighting, with no signs of what I need.

The kitchen is also dark and artificially lit. Omar provides us each with a white plastic container of pre-cut meat. I let my fingers slip around it. I wish it were warm and not cold. Yet I eat it faster than is polite.

There is little conversation between the four of us. The woman with the taser continues to tap it whenever I look at her. So I pretend she's not there.

We go further into the building, taking stairs down a level. This means more than one level.

I catch Dean watching me and I shrug, assuming he's done all this before. It's possible I'll find something he hasn't. I sniff the air, catching elements I never would have before. Pinesol, dust, rubber, and, of course, the sour coming off the four of us.

Each scent sparks a memory. Some so real they're raw and painful. My mom cleaning the kitchen with pine fresh Pinesol, the dust of my childhood room when I visited from college, and the rubber on my bike tires that would carry me to work. Tiny movies dance by faster than I can hold them.

Dean takes my hand and asks, "Are you okay?"

"These senses are intense." I flex my toes, letting my muscles contract up through my legs and to my abs.

"The food is getting you past the uncomfortable phase. You're not experiencing its full effects yet."

My eyes widen. "There's more?" This comes with relief, given what VioTech may do to me. I'll heal faster, and I'm stronger. I squeeze Dean's hand, and he grins.

"Strength is coming in I see," Dean says.

"Hey," Omar interjects. "This is where you two say bye-bye."

I pull on Dean, and he says to Omar, "Stay with Shelby."

The taser wielding guard says, "We'll tell you where to go. Not the other way around."

Omar doesn't appreciate her bossing him. "I'll stay with Shelby," Omar says. "It's her first time in a situation like this. Wouldn't want her getting lost." He grimaces, and the guard backs down.

"Um, thank you?" I pose it as a question.

"See you in the room," Dean says, and then follows the woman away from us.

We watch them turn the corner and leave our sight. I get the sense Omar wants to speak to me, but he doesn't say a word when he turns in the opposite direction.

"We're underground, aren't we?" I ask, keeping up with him.

Omar clears his throat before answering. "How did you know?"

"Unlucky guess." I wonder how deep we are, and if Omar sleeps here or has a home to return to. I suspect he lives here with the other sours. They'd be a liability on the street. We share this prison, but he has more leeway.

"This way," Omar points to the end of the hall.

"You're familiar with these halls. How do you keep it straight?" I catch up to him and stop at the door he gestures to.

"I've been here a long time."

"How long?"

"Long enough that I'm not feeling great." When he says this, I study him more closely. He's a tall man who is broad and square like a tank.

"Your health is deteriorating? I heard that happens after a while. It will happen to me."

He nods but won't verbalize an answer. There's pain behind his eyes. Did he willingly sign up for this death sentence?

I want to tell him everything at that moment. Share things I promised myself I wouldn't. "You can be cured," I whisper. "You're no different from the infected in the city."

"I've heard."

"Then why not go into the city and get the medication you need?"

"It's not that simple." Omar pulls up his pant leg, and I see an ankle monitor.

"They're keeping you here? They don't have any right."

"Shelby, I was dying before they turned me. They presented me with an offer, and let's just say this year was better than it could

301

have been. I'm a veteran; a soldier by nature. Reliving that makes up for the life that's being cut short."

My thoughts wander to other sours in here. "Is everyone like you?"

"Pretty much. Some are terminally ill like me, some volunteers with a few screws loose."

"They won't cure you?" I ask, mulling it over as I do. He signed up to be infected and agreed it would take him to life's end.

"I thought it was impossible, but now I see it's the contract I signed. It wouldn't matter if they cured me. Death is coming."

Fearful to push or pry too far, I hold off asking what type of terminal illness he has. The virus must act as a temporary cure, but in time, it wears off. Does Dean know this about Omar, or has he saved the grizzly details for me?

"I'm sorry, Omar."

"The woman who escorted you here is in the same position. Anyone you smell sour on agreed to these terms. It is for a good cause, they told us. Their presentation is very convincing." He smiles softly. "Don't worry about me. Inside, they're going to test a few drugs on you. Dean went through this on his first day. It will not be comfortable."

Bile creeps up my throat. "I'm not built for this sort of thing."

"There's no choice today. Put on a brave face."

Omar leads me through the door, and there is a team of scientists in lab coats. A chair is covered with a rubber sheet.

I cry hard, and faster than I expect. "Please don't do this."

Someone grabs my arms and pulls me to the chair. My newfound strength is nothing compared to the strong sours. I kick one of them in the chest and he falls backward, taking a monitor on wheels with him.

"Strap her down," a man in the corner shouts.

The next several hours are the worst I've ever lived. They inject me with different solutions and monitor my vitals while I struggle to breathe or stay conscious. My heart races until I'm sure it will stop. I black out a few times. There is pain. Chaos is ingested and works its way out in grotesque, spastic ways.

I wish I'd lose consciousness for good, but my prayer is not answered.

Hours later, I wake up in a new set of clothing. I'm stiff, my memory is scattered, and I can smell dry urine on my legs. Tears roll down my face. This is what it's like to live here?

They've abused the sours here one experiment at a time, pretending it's for the greater good of the world, when really, it's malicious.

Dean is not in the room when I arrive, and I'm thankful because I don't want him to see me this way. I sit on the couch, wrapping my head around what happened. Dry sweat clings to my skin, and I cringe at the smell rolling off me. I walk to the door and bang on it. "I need a shower and new clothes!"

He's done a good job of hiding the truth of our situation. We're test animals with no rights or say in our treatment.

The door is unlocked, and Omar holds out a change of clothing and a towel. "I'll show you to the shower." He walks down the hall, and I can smell something changing in him. This is what it's like to be a sick sour. Their scent fades, and I can't put a finger on what replaces it.

Close to the sleeping quarters is a locker room. The woman's space is separate, but he goes inside and points to the curtains.

"I'll wait here."

"You're going to be with me? While I shower?" He was in the room when I peed myself after the injections, and when someone stripped and redressed me. But I was unconscious, and now I know fully that he's infringing on my soon to be naked space.

Omar's cheeks turn red. "I'll wait over by the lockers."

Damn straight, he will. Before I push the white curtain aside, I scan the room, searching for leverage. There is a vent above the sinks. It's large enough for me to crawl through but screwed shut. Next, I look for weapons, but turn up nothing. Inside the shower are three dispensers labeled soap, shampoo, conditioner. The water is warm, and I take a minute to let it run over my hair before I use my fingers to spread the soap over my body.

"Hey, Omar?" I call.

From a distance, he answers. "Yes?"

"Do you miss being able to run around Lazarus City? You had the freedom to move outdoors while you chased Dean." He has a soft spot somewhere; everyone does.

"Sure. It was nice."

"Will you go back there?"

There's silence before he responds. "This is the last home I'll know."

"How are you feeling?" I ask.

"I've been better. Why are you asking?" His voice sounds suspicious.

"I wish there was another way. I don't mean to pry." My fingers run through my hair with the cheap conditioner, and then I wash it out. The warm water invites me to stay, but I want to see how Dean fared. I dry off and change into the clothing provided.

Then I ask Omar, "Where do I put my dirty clothes, and do you have a brush?"

Omar appears from around the corner. He points to his shaved head and smiles. "I don't have a brush, sorry." But then he does something unexpected. He reaches out his hand with a slender metal tool that looks like a nail file and a badge. "Careful with this. There're rumors that someone is coming for you and Dean. Did you tell someone about our location? Courtnay is on edge."

I take the tool and hide it in the waistband of my sweatpants. "I left a note saying I was coming to see Beth Jackson. Do you know her?"

"What department does she work in?"

I think of the office Beth was tucked away in. Her name was on the door, but I don't remember her title. "She had an office in building 502, and I think she was a scientist, but I'm not sure."

"Well, I'm sure she'll deny ever speaking to you. That's how they do things around here. We should get going." His lips pucker into a question that never comes.

My note has been found. That means Angela or Jeronimo went by the house. Beth will lie to keep me in here, and my efforts to alert anyone might be lost. If Omar is stepping in, maybe we have a chance. "If we break out, will you come with us?"

"Oh, I don't know. Things aren't what they seem here. I'm not sure I have many choices."

I reach to hug him, but he steps away. I've taken it a step too far. Our relationship isn't about us, it's about what's better for the infected.

Before long, we return to my room and Dean is lying in bed. Omar shuts the door without coming in, and I hear the familiar sound of it being locked.

"Dean?" I walk to him and sit down.

He wakes up and reaches for me. "I wasn't sure if they were bringing you back."

When I pull away, he notices my wet hair and better fitting clothing.

"Today was awful." I fight back the tears that want to rain down. Without asking if it's okay, I crawl next to him and curl up. To his surprise, I bring his hand under the sheets, and let his fingers touch the items Omar gave me. "Something good happened though." I bring myself closer to his ear. "It's a tool to pick locks and a security card to get access to different locations. Do you know what floor we're on?"

Dean lifts himself to his side so he's facing me. His hand brushes the wet strands of hair behind my ear, and he whispers, "We're three floors below ground level. They had me on the main floor in a conference room today. It was to take a lie detector test, which didn't work because my pulse is quicker than normal. They gave up pretty fast, but before they blindfolded me again, I saw natural light, and in the elevator, I heard three dings as we descended."

"Wow," I respond. "That's impressive. Could you get us to the elevator?"

"Yes."

"We need Dr. Warren to expose what's happening here. Omar and the other sours can be cured." I try to keep my voice down, but the possibility of saving ourselves and others is overwhelming.

"Shelby, don't get your hopes up."

"Don't do that," my voice shakes. "I will not allow them to do god knows what to me over and over again. We're getting out of here tomorrow."

"Slow down." He wraps his arms around me and pulls me closer. "We need a plan because we only get one shot at this. If we screw it up, they'll separate us, or worse."

My anxiety seems less pronounced with the virus, but my ability to reason is a factor I can't ignore.

Unfortunately, fighting our way to freedom after one day of their tests is quickly demolished. Each test leaves me weaker.

Even the worst of times inside Lazarus City couldn't have prepared me for this prison. The days roll by, stretching into a third week. I'm antsy and angry. The tests are not every day, but when they happen, they are merciless. Drugs, physical pain, drowning, stamina tests, and providing them with samples of every bodily fluid imaginable.

Omar continues to deteriorate, and I hold on to what he said. People were coming for us. But where are they? Each day, I wait for someone to burst through the door and rescue us.

No one comes.

thirty-eight

Dean

BREAK ON THROUGH WITH ME
LOST IN THIS DARK HIDDEN LAB
WE NEED TO BE FREE

Yesterday they did a lab with us together. We had to guess what the other person was thinking or receive an electric shock. I was impressed by how often we got the answer right, but with each volt, our spirits sunk.

"Today they'll leave us alone," she says after what we recently endured. We're given time off between sessions. "And I've waited long enough. Let's leave this place."

"Omar hasn't brought us the clothes we need."

"Why are you fighting me on this? How can you be here another day?"

The door opens, and someone pushes two food containers into the room. "Breakfast," I say, avoiding her question.

We get the food and sit on the couch. I smell it before I eat to make sure there is no additive. Today, something is off. The red meat comes off more of a mineral, mixed with pepper, and metal.

"Don't eat it," I say to Shelby, but I'm too late. She already has half the food down. "Didn't you smell that?"

"I was too hungry, and I forgot. It tastes mostly okay." She frowns, realizing how careless she's been.

"Go throw up."

Shelby pushes the container away and walks to the bathroom. I hear her gag, but nothing comes up.

"Throwing up is not my thing. I'm sorry." With more coughing and a growl, she quits. When she leaves the bathroom, her eyes are red and watery from trying to vomit.

"Who knows what's in it?" I lift the meat to my nose again, but it gives nothing away. "Sit on the couch so I can monitor you."

She obeys, and we listen to the radio for ten minutes before she giggles.

"I don't think they'll kill meeee." She sings her last words and sighs. "It's not a terrible drug. It's a gooooooooood one."

"Oh, fucking great!"

Shelby takes a bite from my container I left in front of us. "It tastes flowery, Dean. Springtime."

"You're high. That's perfect." I move the food to the door before she can eat more. "Let's see how long this lasts." When I turn around, Shelby has removed her shirt. My eyes widen as I watch her naked body. While I've been sleeping next to her, we've been well behaved regarding personal space. It hasn't been easy, but our marriage is a strange place.

"It's hot in here." Shelby fans her fingers in front of her face. "My mouth feels sticky. Sticky. Icky. That's a weird word. English is sooooo weird." She smacks her lips and sticks out her tongue.

"Um." I will myself not to look at her, but she pants.

"Can I remove my socks?" she pleads.

"Yeah. You need a shirt and some water. It shouldn't take long to wear off."

I guide her to the couch and insist she put a t-shirt on to cover herself.

"Dean, you are the smart one. You're so handsome!" She jabs her finger at my chest. "I miss us together, doing the fun stuff, doing the city thing, going to baseball games, eating crabs, happy hour."

A smile glides over my lips. The drug only makes her high and ridiculous.

"I miss all of that too."

"And sex."

"What?" I nearly trip over myself.

"I miss sex with you."

"Okay, let's drink more water." I hand her a cup and she takes tiny sips. Then she leaps up and runs to the containers of food.

"It's wearing off, and this is the most fun I've had in here. Let's eat it all and be stupid for a few minutes. Please?" She pops open the food and takes another piece.

"I'm not sure that's a good idea." I make my way over to her, but she finishes her portion. "They want to know what happens when we ingest something addictive."

"You're a downer," Shelby throws her container at the door. Then she turns to whisper. "It's fun, and we don't get that. So eat your psychedelic meat and enjoy yourself before we..." she holds her fists up and pretends to box the air in case someone is paying attention.

I take a breath in, defeated, hopeful, confused, and then I eat the drugged meat because what the hell?

The drugs slur my words in five minutes, which is faster than I expected. Warmth clouds my cerebrum.

How do I know that word?

The walls breathe.

Corners of the room cast rainbows that slide onto the floor and run for my feet. I let the colors catch me. They ooze into my toes similar to soda, prickling my skin with tiny bubbles. And then I'm gone.

Neither of us remember the next hour or more. It's hard to tell how much time passed. Sprawled on the couch, we wear boxer shorts, and play with socks on our hands. Sweat drips from my forehead.

"I think we were dancing," I say. The radio blasts rock-n-roll from the fifties. "Was I on the coffee table?"

Shelby pulls the socks off her hands, and wobbles over to her pile of clothing on the floor. "I remember dancing too. We need more water. I could drink a lake." She walks into the bathroom and drinks from the faucet.

"What the hell was that?" My muscles are tense as the drug leaves my system. It's working its way out as quickly as it came on.

"I remember doing the twist, and something about shaking, rattling, and rolling. I think I actually rolled across the floor. My hair is a mess." She bursts out laughing. "Were they watching us?"

I laugh too. "I think we gave them a sock puppet show. God, that's embarrassing." My jaw itches as it repairs from laughing and grinding my teeth.

Shelby walks over to me, now fully dressed, and pulls me closer to her. "They won't expect us to escape tonight." Then she kisses me. "I wanted to do that before I can't."

Her eyes are dilated, making it hard to see the chestnut brown and dark flecks that used to call me home. I want things between us to be as they were.

I caress her face, gently tracing her lips with my index finger. There was a time when I could touch her whenever I wanted. I lean in, worrying I'll love her more before it needs to end. Breathing in, I lift her scent into me, hoping to keep it locked inside forever. I press my mouth to hers, kissing her softly.

She runs her nails up my back, and I trail my teeth down her neck, bringing on a shiver. Her skin feels smooth under my mouth and tongue. I want to taste every part of her.

Our hands grasp for one another, and I lift her so she's straddling me. I carry her to the bed only a few feet away. Despite my limbs being strained from dancing and being drugged, I'm able to lay her beneath me. Does she recognize how much I need to feel this again? This awakening among the doom and sorrow following me. Could there be hope for us after she's cured? This could be the only chance I have to be with Shelby.

Her toes curl, and her fingers run over my scalp, resting on the back of my neck.

"Don't think," she sighs, reading my mind. We both understand what will happen if we leave here. She'll eventually return to work a normal life with salts. I'll be sick forever. I don't belong anywhere in this world.

I hold back the threat of crying over her and lower myself closer to her body. She struggles to take off the shorts she's wearing, so I help her before undressing myself.

Falling between her thighs, Shelby shows me she wants me by pulling my hips until I'm inside her. We gasp, moving the way lovers do, slowly regaining trust and affection. I pull her hands above her head, and she crosses her legs over my back the way she used to. I push further into her and roll us over so she's on top and I can run my hands over her shape. Our strength is similar, and she uses it to grab my wrist and bring my hand to her breast.

I take it into my mouth, and Shelby groans breathlessly. My fingers wrap in strands of her hair to pull her closer so I can look at her pale skin contrasting with flushed cheeks. She's beautiful. My heart pangs, desperate to reconnect with what was once ours.

The night falls over us, and we continue to touch each other, making up for the years apart. At one point, more food is pushed into the room, but we ignore it. Even if the drug has vanished from our system, the effects remain vivid. We danced tonight, we laughed, and we felt each other again.

Hours later, when we're tangled in the sheets, and half asleep, Shelby leans over and kisses me.

"We have to go," she whispers.

The expiration of our lives is unknown. I nestle my nose beside her ear and kiss her neck.

"Let's get dressed."

I use the tool Omar provided to unlock the door. It took several attempts, and a few bloody knuckles because I kept slipping.

Shelby clings to my shirt when I open it. "I thought an alarm would go off."

"I know where the stairs are. Follow me." Together we walk down the hallway holding our shoes, so our socks pad our footsteps. Each door we pass is dark underneath. We would be foolish to think no one is in the office or lab.

I tilt my head to the left, toward the stairs. "You have the key fob?" I ask her.

She pulls it from her pocket to show me, then places it away.

Squeaky footsteps come from behind us. "Shit," I whisper. "Pick up the pace."

We're at an intersection in the hallway. There's a sign of a man walking upstairs.

A black box indicates we need the key fob to go further.

"What if it beeps when I unlock it?" Shelby asks.

"Then we move faster. Climb the stairs until you see an exit or the third floor. One of those will lead us out." Sweat is pooling down my back. If we're caught, we won't have another chance at this.

Someone is coming closer, and we have little time before they're upon us. I grab Shelby's shaking hand and make her hit the security box.

It beeps, and the red light turns to green.

We slip through the door, and I make sure it closes quietly. There's a small click, but we're successful.

Up the steps we go, taking them slow rather than running so we can hear if anyone is around.

"Shhh." I raise my fingers to my lips. "Someone is talking."

A group of people walk onto the landing on the floor above us. They're in deep conversation, so they don't notice when we sneak through the door closest to us.

We are one flight up, with two more to go.

"Um, Dean." Shelby pulls on my shirt while I catch the door, so it shuts silently. "Dean."

"What?" I turn to find Omar and several other sours standing in the hallway. They're in their pajamas, unarmed, and a woman has a towel on her head as if she just showered.

My gaze switches between Omar and the others.

"Lost?" Omar asks.

I'm sending out false hopes that they won't recognize us. We'll continue on our way, pretending nothing happened.

"Yes. Thank you. We were looking for..." What the hell should I say?

"The food bank?" Omar does his best to cover our blunder, but those behind him look confused. A familiar guard pushes her way into view.

"That's Dean and Shelby, idiots! Don't let them leave this floor." She stomps toward us, and I catch the sour perspiring off her panicked body.

Shelby shoves the woman to the ground. She holds up the small tool Omar gave us as if it were a mighty weapon.

"No! I did not survive a year in Lazarus City, go back in to pull Dean out, only to be captured by a bunch of sours who are prisoners at VioTech! If anyone tries to stop me, I will slit your throat." She grits her teeth, and the wild look in her eye falls hard on those circling.

The woman she pushed composes herself and folds her arms over her chest. "You don't know what VioTech has promised."

The mob grows larger, and we step back until we're against the door. I pull the key fob carefully from Shelby's pocket and prepare to open the door when Omar's haunted face catches my attention. He's scared for us and for himself.

I swipe the fob and hear the beep. We rush through, dropping our shoes as we run up the steps. Omar is in the lead, but he's chasing us along with the others.

"One more flight," I tell Shelby as we round the corner.

The third floor isn't locked, and we burst through. We're in a large lobby with a ceiling over two stories tall. There are elevators, a front desk, and the exit is a wall of glass peering out into the dark sky. The incoming sun casts a blue glow into the area.

Shelby says, "I remember seeing this building when I got here."

We run to the door, but it's locked with nowhere to use the fob. I punch it and my knuckles crack. This isn't ordinary glass. Those chasing us run into the room. We're outnumbered by at least twenty people.

"Shelby, I'll distract them while you find a phone. You remember Jason's or Dr. Warren's phone number? We need to contact someone and let them know where we are. Can you do that?"

She uses her newfound strength to run away from everyone and up a flight of curved stairs. A few follow her, but Omar distracts them by having them focus on me.

"She won't get far. Get Dean before he breaks the window." That leaves me, with about fifteen sours, a glass wall behind me, and nothing as a weapon. I instinctually reach for my absent hatchet, cursing myself.

The group rushes me, and hands are pulling on me, grabbing, trying to take me to the ground. I throw elbows, knocking a man in the jaw. Then I reach for a short woman to use as a shield to ram through the others. When I punch the glass door, it spiderwebs but doesn't break. As I go to punch again, someone grabs my arm and drags me away.

I come around, swinging at anything within reach. Omar grunts. I must have slugged him, but he falls back more dramatically than he needed to and takes down several of his peers.

There is space between sours that might allow me to run. I take a few steps and hear Shelby call my name.

"Dean!" She's on a catwalk above the reception desk. "Throw me the fob."

I toss it to her. The white plastic square pivots through the air until it reaches her hand. As soon as she has it, she's tackled to the ground. They're struggling, but I can't get to her.

Fight, Shelby. Give them hell!

There are bodies surrounding me again, this time some wait, while others jump me. I can tell they're losing their abilities, because I am stronger than three of them trying to pin my arms behind me. When they have me tight, I use them as a chance to leverage myself and kick at those close enough. I hope their healing process has slowed down.

I'm taken to the cold tiled floor, and they have me in a position I can't wiggle out of. A tall man with an electric probe comes toward me.

"I won't fight anymore," I assure him.

He zaps me as soon as the others let go, and my body convulses. It's not as strong as it could have been, thankfully.

"Get him back to his quarters. Where is the girl?" the man asks.

"Upstairs," Omar answers.

Everyone looks to the catwalk. Shelby is cursing, but I can't find her.

thirty-nine

Shelby

WARM FEELING RUSHES
HAS HARM COME TO ME AGAIN
MY PALE SKIN BLUSHES

My head cracks down on the woman's nose as she tries to hold me to the floor.

"Bitch!" she screams in pain as blood gushes over her lips.

"Try again," I dare her.

And she does, but I'm too quick, and I punch her in the throat, causing her to buckle and gag. There are three sours behind her, but one appears too timid to fight.

"I meant what I said. There is too much to lose. If you let me go, I'll bring help."

They stand frozen over me. One woman and two men. Each bigger than me.

"What do you mean you can save us?" a man asks. "We agreed to this. There's a contract."

"You signed a contract that allows VioTech to take your life?" I stand, trying to get myself aligned with the next office door.

"When you have a death sentence already, a few extra months sounds nice. I have pancreatic cancer. When this infection wears off, I'll die immediately. They've given me a chance to protect our country before I go." He stands taller, prouder, as if he has any idea what he's talking about.

"Protect the country? No one had me sign an agreement. I'm being held against my will!" I manage another few steps back, and

I'm almost there. His severe illness triggers a sorrow. He is a man suffering and searching for redemption before death.

His shoulders sink. "I didn't realize that. Sometimes sours act badly with their new abilities and need to be restrained."

"I want to call a doctor who I trust to cure me. The infection was not my choice, like it was yours." My voice quavers, but I hold my ground.

They look to one another for guidance. While they hover, trying to figure out if they want to hurt me or let me go, I use the fob to gain access to the office next to me.

I slip in and slam the door shut, using a chair against the door-knob to buy me time.

They aren't banging or trying to break it down. At least, not yet.

The office is nicely furnished with a large cherry wood desk and plush blue chairs for visitors. I reach for the phone. When I pick it up, there isn't a dial tone.

"How do I dial out?" I ask the empty room. Nine was the magic number in past jobs, and when I try, I'm able to dial Jason's number.

A clock on the wall shows its quarter to six in the morning. I thought it was closer to the middle of the night, but this explains why sours were awake.

"Hello," he answers groggily.

"Jason!" I burst into tears. "I'm being held here. Courtnay. VioTech!"

"Shelby, fucking god it's so good to hear your voice. Slow down. Where the hell are you? Everyone is searching for you and Dean." He's much more clear now, and I can hear him jumping from bed and stumbling over furniture.

"Where are you?" I ask in return. Please don't be in Lazarus City anymore.

"I'm at your house with Jeronimo and Angela. Where are you?" He demands, angrier this time.

I search the office for mail or something that gives me a loca-tion. "Wait!" I find a stack of envelopes with an address. I read it aloud quickly. "They're keeping us underground. We are three floors down. They will deny we're here! Bring the police."

"Let me record your voice." Jason taps his phone, and an automatic voice lets us know the recording has begun. "I'm coming for you." Then he shouts away from the phone. "Jeronimo, Angela! Get up! We're coming! Stay with me and tell me everything you can."

Jason's voice is muffled as he yells orders to Angela and Jeronimo. Tears won't stop streaming down my cheeks, but somehow, I tell Jason as much as I can, starting with the hardest part.

"They infected me. I'm a sour." I explain what Courtnay has done to us, and the sours living here. A jarring thump on the door interrupts my story.

He hears it too. "Who is that?"

"I got a head start, but I can't be on here long. Get the police. Get Dr. Warren!" I put the phone down but keep it on speaker so Jason can understand what happens next.

"Are you there?"

"They're coming through now. Stay quiet so they don't know you're on."

"I will," he says. These are his last words before the door crashes open, and the chair splinters.

"I'll go easily. Please don't hurt me," I say. The woman with the taser walks forward. She raises the black rod and smacks me in the head.

Stars burst through my vision, and I fall to the ground. Another crack hits me in the side, causing me to gasp and choke in pain.

"Get her to her quarters, and keep them sedated," she instructs.

A pinch in the neck suggests they've injected something into me, and my surroundings fade.

The dream state I find myself in is confusing. I'm aware of those moving past, and voices telling others what to do, but I'm also alone in the darkness. I think I'm here for a long time. My body is moved, and I go through hot and cold periods, bright and darkness, too. There is a sense that I'm no longer occupying the space that contained me, but I have nothing to base this on.

"Shelby?" A man's voice hovers over me. I suspect it's Omar.

My shoulders are being pushed, and a cold rag pressed to my forehead. The room is well lit. I can tell because my eyelids appear pink and are not full of darkness.

Only, it doesn't hurt as I expect.

"What's happening?" I ask. My mouth is tacky with spit that hasn't been swallowed in hours or days.

"You're breaking your fever now. You can wake up," the voice says. It's not Omar.

My eyes flutter open, and Jeronimo is next to me, holding my hand. "How did you get here?"

This is not VioTech. It's a hospital room with mauve walls and a window. My sense of smell is no longer what I had as a sour.

"Am I cured?"

"Yeah," Jeronimo says. "And so are those sours who worked at VioTech. Pretty messed up, if you ask me." He releases my hand and reaches for his phone. "We've been sitting with you since you were brought here. They did a number on you, but you're a tough chick. Doctors thought it be better if you healed and stayed under for the cure. I'll be right back." He stands and smiles softly.

"Where's Dean? Is he okay?"

"I'll let Dr. Warren explain. He's safe. I can tell you that much." Jeronimo closes the door as he leaves.

My fingers graze my forehead, and the fever is evident from how achy my body is. I was a sour for just enough time to understand what Dean lives with.

I wiggle my toes and yawn. How can I have slept for so long and still be tired?

The door opens and Dr. Warren steps in. I've never been so happy to see her. She's as I remember. Thin, petite, her blonde hair is streaked with gray and tied in a tight bun at the nape. There's a pair of dark-rimmed glasses hanging on her white doctor's jacket, and she's wearing black heels.

Her smile comforts me. "Hello, Mrs. Bolger."

"Hello, Dr. Warren. I guess the vaccine doesn't last as long as I'd hoped."

"No, it's good for six months, and then you need it again. Similar to the flu shot. That's why you were infected. You've had the suppressant and cure cocktail, so you should be yourself soon. Anyone who went into the city was required to have a recent dose of the vaccine, but you bypassed that."

"How is Dean?" I ask.

Before she can answer my question, Jason, Angela, Jeronimo, and my mom enter the room. My mom is hysterical.

"Shelby! Oh, baby. God, I thought I lost you for good this time." She throws her arms around me and pulls me close to her chest, rocking me. "I love you so much. Don't go back to that city ever again. What would your father and I do if you were hurt or worse?"

I wipe tears off my face and pull away. "Mom, please calm down."

Her fingers glide over my cheek, tucking my hair behind my ear. She shakes as she holds my shoulders and looks at me. "Never again. You're done with all this. Dean is out. That's what you needed."

Jason shifts in his stance, making me uncomfortable. "What's going on with Dean?" I address Dr. Warren over my mom's shoulder. There's no chance she's letting me out of her sight.

"I've worked with Mr. Kaplan, and the child he is caring for."

"Viola? Her aunt can't watch her?" I ask.

Jason runs his hand over the back of his neck and frowns. "We have some catching up to do. VioTech's employees overseeing that division have been incarcerated. That includes Beth and Courtnay."

Mike. Will I be held responsible for what I did to him? Jason and the others may not know. His sister, Dr. Warren, who is standing at the foot of my bed, has lost her brother because of me.

"I should tell you what happened to Mike," I say.

Dr. Warren puts up her hand. "I am aware. He was a troubled man, and I'm sorry for what transpired. I want to believe things could have been different, but we have no control over the past."

"I'm sorry," I offer. The story between Mike and I will replay for eternity. Dr. Warren will go through the same.

"Me too. And Mr. Kaplan and Viola Jackson have taken residence with Dean's brother. We agreed on outpatient treatments. I was treating the virus as a whole, which wasn't working. To pivot, I've been treating one symptom at a time. Their vision should return to normal in a few months. Then we'll go from there."

Jason interrupts. "They can infect people, Shelby. It's important to understand that."

My mom gasps. "Dean is sick? Is it the Lazarus virus?"

"Mr. Foley is correct," Dr. Warren continues despite my mother's shock. "But we have medical advances that treat and suppress symptoms. I hope that Dean and Viola will live full lives with intervention."

Normal is farfetched, but I smile. "I see." Viola won't be able to kiss anyone, which teenagers often do, and my one night with Dean remains just that; one night.

My mom stops fidgeting over me. "I hope Dean gets better," she says as if it's a cold. "When can she come home?"

Dr. Warren answers by clicking her pen and looking at a tablet she carries. "All drugs have been administered. We're monitoring her to ensure her fever is under control before she leaves."

"Can I get a hug?" Angela lightly bumps my mom away and wraps her arms around me.

It's so tight I can't breathe, but a giggle chokes its way out and she releases me.

"Missed you too, Angela."

"Missed you more, stupid." She punches my leg and winks. "We'll get Jessie from your sister. You're moving back in, right?"

My mom's hands go to her chest, and she turns a few shades lighter.

"Mom, I want my bed. You can visit me every day. Promise."

She sniffles but agrees.

Dr. Warren steers us back. "The police will talk to you. They've confiscated a map and materials you've collected. I'll make them aware that you're awake but resting."

"Oh, it's so soon," my mom protests.

"I want to." I've risked everything going back into Lazarus City to follow Mona's blue stars on an old map. It led me to Viola and Beth. The information we gained could be vital in shutting down VioTech.

"This is what I worked for. No company should have that much power."

After a few minutes of everyone fussing over me, I tell them I'm tired and politely kick them out.

Everyone leaves except for Jason.

"Hey." He sits on the bed next to my legs. "I'm a dick for not going with you." His eyes well up with tears that he rubs away with his palm.

"Jason, don't do that to yourself. I would have ditched you the same way I did to Ivan and Viola." He never would have been able to stop me. The pain and guilt I caused. It makes me wish I'd told them my plan before I left.

"Why did you go alone?"

I blow out a long breath of frustration. "For the past few years, I've needed someone to tell me what to do or support me. It's prevented me from making decisions. Finding Renee, for example. I could have gotten to her without the Rec Pier, but I was scared. Letting Mike pull me into his conspiracy is another example. I wanted to believe him because I didn't know how to push back or question him. Beth said she knew where Dean was. I've put so many people in danger, I couldn't do that again."

"I understand," he says. "We contacted Beth, of course. She admitted to seeing you and talking about Viola, but they shared footage of your car leaving the parking lot."

"That must have been staged. Thank you for coming after me. You know, to keep me safe you often leave me out of your plans. It

322

made me resent you for excluding me." I allow my voice to be accusatory because it's not often I'm able to face my grudges.

"I wish I hadn't. All it did was drive you away when I could have been helping you." Jason kicks at the floor. "Will we ever be *us* again?"

There are too many parts to this narrative. When can I see Dean? Will we be able to touch the way we did? I don't think so, but that won't push me back to Jason.

"I want to go home. Hug my dog. Drink coffee, and maybe eat a donut or something that isn't raw. Is there a future for us? Jason, I can't answer that right now." I come off frustrated, and I am. It's not about if we will rekindle our love affair. The idea intrigues me, and I'm not prepared to shove him away, but I need space.

Jason leans over to kiss me. His soft lips brush mine, and warmth flutters in my stomach, telling me this story isn't finished. Will he always be the one that got away? Perhaps it's me who got away from him. I put him through more than he should have endured; guilt follows this thought.

I wish I took in his scent as a sour, so I could bottle that memory forever.

"I'll leave so you can rest," he says. Then he's gone and the room grows silent.

The first time I exited Lazarus City, it wasn't a new beginning. My goal was to stay tapped into Fat Man's mission, even when he died. I was connecting with survivors and working alongside Mike until he moved on when we had no leads. Then there was Jason. The day he got out of quarantine marked the end of my waiting. He was free to be with me, and we tried so hard to make our relationship work on the outside. I was stranded between finding momentum to rebuild my life and the man who was my husband. Dean was always at the forefront of my mind. Every decision I made reminded me of his absence, and what would have happened if he wasn't sick.

He's out here now. I'm able to push off into whatever comes next. The ingredients for the future don't need to involve Jason or Dean. I've given them what was required of me.

For Jason, it started with the map. New territories around the city he hadn't seen. Dr. Warren was searching for doctors for the hospital, so I delivered Renee and Thomas. Of course, I didn't realize this, but Mike needed a scapegoat for testing the suppressant on the infected, and I stepped in. I sought these people too. I won't pretend otherwise.

Dean never asked for my help. He didn't expect it, but I had to deliver what my heart wanted, knowing he'd never have given up on me either. Now he's free.

Therefore, I'm free.

forty

Dean

**NOT ONE BUT TWO YEARS
A LOT HAS CHANGED IN THAT TIME
SAID GOODBYE TO FEARS**

"Check that out!" Viola slaps a packet of papers on the table in front of me. She's breathing heavy in excitement and from running from the bus to the cabin.

"What's this?" I ask, as if I don't know.

Viola shouts with enthusiasm. "You said if I got an A on my geometry test, I could try out for the tennis team." She grins and wiggles her shoulders in a happy dance. "A promise is a promise, right?"

This young lady was out of school for five years. When I enrolled her, she tested at a seventh-grade level when she should have been a freshman. I'm not sure I've met someone so competitive in my life. By tooth and nail, she drove herself to grade level, and I made a promise.

"I'm proud of you for working so hard. We have ground rules to follow."

She interrupts me by saying, "I know. I know! We have to tell people we have a blood disease if we're injured, I have to wear my medical band, keep my skin covered during sports, I need to play down my strengths and take it easy on others, and take my medication."

The medication Dr. Warren constructed keeps our viral loads nearly undetectable, yet most of our strengths remain only weaker.

Light sensitivity is better, but not resolved. Contacts offer relief, though we stay out of the sun whenever possible.

"It's important Viola."

"Yeah! I got it, and I'll be so careful." Her hands fold in a prayer pose as she begs me to keep my promise.

"Okay. Tennis isn't a contact sport, so you can do it."

She shrieks, throwing her arms around my neck. "Thank you. Thank you!"

I'm ridden with sorrow that her family can't be with her. Beth is in prison, along with other members of VioTech's team for their hand in the Lazarus virus. VioTech has made their records open to the public so they could continue operating other divisions. It's one of the largest pharmaceutical and household medical companies in the United States. In other words, they have good lawyers.

Ivan and Aisha come into the kitchen. Aisha's pregnant belly makes her walk like a penguin. The timeline for Viola and me to find our place has come to an end, and we move into our new house next week.

"What's all the screaming for?" Aisha grins, hoping for something she can celebrate. She runs her hand under the water and slathers it with soap to get her wedding ring off her swollen fingers again.

"Dean's letting me try out for tennis!" Viola claps and spins, unable to contain herself. I'm not sure we even have a tennis racket. "I'll text my friends!" She bolts from the room, already typing in her phone.

"Will you miss having a teenager in the house?" I joke.

Aisha tears up. "These hormones are the worst! Yes, I'll miss you both, but you'll be only a few miles away. Perfect location when Viola needs to babysit." She groans and yanks her ring off her finger. "I can't put it on again," she sniffles.

Ivan rubs her stomach and kisses her on the head. "A little privacy might be nice. No offense."

"Get a room!" I stand from the table and close my computer. "You can be here for Viola tonight? I have those plans after I stop at work."

"She's old enough to stay here alone." Aisha steps in, acting motherly quite often. At first, we hovered over Viola because of the situation with Skiddle. But we realized Viola wasn't the type that wanted this sort of attention, so we slowly allowed her the space to be a teenage girl. Which, I discovered, can be really moody.

Skiddle was stubborn, but nothing like this. I'm thankful Aisha has been around tending to areas I'm completely incapable of. This is another reason I chose to stay close by.

"Okay, love birds. I'll be back later." I wave them goodbye and go to my truck. Before I do, a familiar friend eyes me from the shadowy woods. There are always treats in my car, and he waits for them.

The can of unsalted peanuts sits in my cup holder. I put some in my palm.

Pizza flies over, landing on my flannel shirt. He gently takes each nut from my hand and turns to walk up my arm to my shoulder.

"You're going to make me late."

He makes a clicking sound deep in his throat. It's ridiculous, but I returned for him, so he'd know where I was. I risked being discovered and arrested for this bird. Pizza followed me to Ivan's home and has made a nest somewhere in the woods. I'm not sure if he's been a country bird before, but he's adjusting.

"Remember when I found you?" I say to Pizza, reliving the story.

Omar wanted to see where I lived. His days to survive his life-threatening condition were numbered once he got the cure. So I invited him to go on an adventure. Most sours under VioTech's care were cured and released with fines or penalties. Many died during the process; their bodies were too weak. Omar survived long enough for our little adventure, but soon after, he died peacefully in hospice care.

VioTech preyed on sick people with few options. Mostly those who were dying from various conditions, with no support from family or friends. Omar had undiagnosed testicular cancer that metastasized, and no family or close friends to care for him. He was the perfect target.

With the city empty, we found a way in that was less guarded. I've never heard it so quiet. The rotters and survivors were gone. It's hard to imagine VioTech's intention was to create people like me from the beginning. I'm not anti-science, despite what I've been through, but I have a better understanding of what can go wrong on a catastrophic level.

The government did what they said they would. Cured as many as they could. Humanely euthanized whoever couldn't be saved and made arrests for those refusing to leave. With heat sensors and drones patrolling the area, there was no hiding.

I took Omar to the zoo. Pizza was waiting by the door, expecting me, or using some bird intuition I don't understand. Together the three of us toured the rundown space, searching for animals left behind. From what I understood, they caught the chimpanzees and moved them to a facility in Florida. They were the only creatures to survive. And the only reason we didn't eat them is because they resembled humans too much. I spent a lot of time with those chimps, and I relied on them to alarm me when rotters or intruders approached. In return, I fed them whenever I could, and made sure they had a warm place in the winter.

Pizza squawks, pulling me from my time warp. "Sorry. I can't help myself." He flies over to a low branch after I give my shoulder a shrug. "I gotta drop something off at work, then I've got big plans. You'll never guess what today is."

His black eyes blink at me, and I grin.

My truck is clean and organized how I want it. I start it up and head down Ivan's long driveway. A reminder dings on my phone, and I see tomorrow is my appointment with Dr. Warren. Viola and I go every two weeks for injections and viral checks. She's stopped promising us a cure, but she has expressed hope in discovering something for our future partners so we can be intimate. The vaccine is hopeful but may not offer full protection. Also, I'd prefer Viola doesn't get the green light to do things that teenagers find interest in.

At our last meeting, Dr. Warren said, "Mr. Kaplan. The virus is smarter than me, dare I admit it. The instant I make progress, its components change. You're constantly in a state of flux with this variant. VioTech had no idea how unstable it truly was."

I can handle this sort of news because I've made a new life for myself. A job, a house, a family with Ivan, Aisha, and Viola. Not to mention the support group around us. Cured sours have kept in touch, and my relationship with Rob is mended.

The highway takes me to the job site I've been working on, and I hop out to drop off keys to the future owner.

We're building a veterinarian center called The Lion's Den Rescue, and my friend is overseeing the doctors and scientists who will rescue lab animals, rehabilitate them, and use relocation when possible. It's also a place for locals to bring their sick animals.

Lion steps out of the trailer where his temporary office is. "Dean, good to see you. Thanks for bringing this by." He takes the keys from my hands. After VioTech fired him, he began working with local animal activists. Losing the zoo defeated Lion in ways our war against VioTech and Fat Man never touched.

"I can't stay, but I didn't want to get into the weekend without passing these to you. I'll be back early on Monday."

From the doorway appears his wife, who has a prosthetic foot from her days as a rotter. Pearl has become his business manager, and the two never leave one another's side. I wave and she responds with a smile.

"Where are you going?" Lion says.

"You know what today is, right?"

He slaps his hand over his chest. "Of course! We're going to watch it on television at home. Though Pearl doesn't watch that sort of thing."

She fusses. "It's a milestone. I'll be watching it today."

"I think the entire world will be," I say, thankful this early April day is warm and cloudy.

"Have a great time," Lion waves me away, knowing I have plans that can't wait. "Bring Viola by for dinner next week. I have those tennis shoes she wanted."

Lion and Pearl never located the rest of their family. It's given them all the more reason to spoil Viola.

"I just approved her trying out for tennis. How come you already have shoes for her?" I ask suspiciously.

Pearl interjects. "We knew that bright girl would get what she's after. That's why she'll be working with us once this clinic is open."

"Until college," Lion adds.

"College?" The thought of her leaving makes me uneasy. We're not like the others. One stupid mistake could cause an outbreak. "Let's take it one day at a time. A job at the clinic is a good start."

I marvel at the work we've done together. This project is one thing, but also preserving the sour community is another. Between our crew from Baltimore and the survivors at VioTech, we have nearly a hundred of us. They're required to check in with Dr. Warren every so often, but not as much as Viola and me. At first, I didn't want to see anyone from the past, but that changed.

Lazarus City wasn't all bad. We grew into our new bodies side by side, creating a community that stood for something. We fought next to each other and mourned when fellow sours died.

Too many people were lost.

Kenny and I remain close, but only virtually. He's graduated college and has a career with a large investment firm. As the youngest recovered sour, excluding Viola, he has attempted to move beyond the disease. His parents were on the outside, so he was met with open arms.

I don't marvel at the strengths left with me. In fact, I try to hide them. While our community remains close, we prefer privacy about our experience. There are plenty of *I Survived Lazarus City* books and docuseries on television, but not a single one is from a sour.

We had the threat of being exposed and we were tested in a lab. It was enough to keep our mouths shut.

What Shelby and I endured was evil. The sours at VioTech underwent similar experimentation. Some died early, and VioTech cremated them, leaving them in unmarked graves until the police intervened. There's a plaque honoring them in their lobby, a place I never want to see again. The rotters they stored in the lower levels were cured, but again, most had serious illnesses that claimed them soon after.

Back on the road, I turn the music up and reflect on my life. Today is monumental for many. There are fears I'll face, but not alone. There will be thousands of survivors present, and I look forward to a united front. The past won't take us down. We can overcome together.

forty-one
Shelby

UNCERTAIN IF HERE
IS WHERE THE STORY SHOULD END
BUT THAT'S NEVER CLEAR

Carley and Anne pack the last of the tools they brought over. My new kitchen table and shelves are in place, and I'm thankful they've given me the space to make this decision.

Anne loads up the trunk of her car, and Carley nudges me.

"You're really doing this? It's kind of crazy."

We turn to look back at my row home. A brass crab knocker is fixed to the red door, the shutters repainted, screens replaced, and windows cleaned.

"This is my home."

"Well, I'm glad your roommates followed you here. I wouldn't want you living here alone." Carley and Anne lift a table saw into the car. We built plant boxes in the backyard that I'll fill with flowers.

"Actually, I decided to live by myself." I hold my breath, preparing for the questions to be hurtled at me.

"Do Mom and Dad know?" Carley's eyes widen, and Anne is by my side as well. "Shelby, you can't! Renee and Thomas got as far from the east coast as possible."

Anne interjects. "I don't think Texas is as far as possible. They could have gone to California or another country."

"You're not helping, Anne!" Carley continues to huff, her cheeks growing red.

I look up at my house on Patterson Park Avenue, remembering the man who spat in my face when I tried to reclaim it. Dean maintained it, and now it's mine again. "This is why I didn't tell you. Mom and Dad are aware, if that makes a difference." I walk back inside with my sisters hot on my heels.

They'll never understand why I've done this. Dean's name is no longer on the house, and we're officially divorced. I continued working but returned to school to earn my social administrators license, and I've taken a job in the city with the senior population.

"The commute from my old place was far. Anyway, Jeronimo is getting married, and Angela will move on to a program out of state for EMTs. They're moving on with their lives, and so am I."

The curved wall that meets the wooden stairs wraps up to the second and third floors. I repainted every inch, and it was painful. There were other things I did to reclaim this space, such as bringing in new furniture, changing the locks, and cleaning the backyard. I built scaffolding, cleaned up the messes I made, chose a color without asking others for input, and stocked the fridge. This place feels like home.

"Jessie is too old to protect you!" Carley sways her hand to my white fuzzy friend, who lays in a ball on the couch. Her tail wags when she hears her name.

She's not able to go for long walks in the park, and her bark has lost its sharpness. I've resolved that her end is likely a few months away, and I'll make her comfortable until that time. Renee has prescribed me medication that eases her pain and keeps her hungry for soft food.

Her dark eyes tell me there's life there, and my happy old lady brings me comfort.

"I have an alarm, a permit to carry a weapon, and I'm always cautious. Carley, take it easy." Everyone is always excited when they hear I have a twin. They remark on how close we must be, and they aren't wrong. But Carley was born first, and that gives her the right to be bossy. Only I don't listen when fear is driving her emotions.

Anne smiles and shrugs. "You've got it worked out. We're close enough if you need us. Tonight is one of many, but we're going to be worried. I wish you had at least one roommate."

"Like a man?" I question.

"Like anyone!" Carley claps to make her point. "Anyone besides Jessie, who is a hundred and twenty in dog years." Jessie's tail wags again.

"I need to take her out and feed her," I tell them. "Thank you for helping me put a few things together. I can move the last boxes from Angela and Jeronimo's house."

"Are you going somewhere?" Carley looks at me suspiciously.

"Rob and I are going out tonight. We're only friends! Before you get weird."

Carly groans. "I know Rob is your friend, and he moved back here too. You're both nuts. Lindsay and Chad got away from here, like normal people. Doesn't this city give you the creeps?"

Her question is beyond loaded, and she's overstayed her welcome. Anne senses this and pulls on Carley's arm. "Time for us to go. I need to be home for the kids. Dinner won't make itself." Then she turns to me and reaches for my hand, squeezing it four times for each of my sisters, and possibly to remind me that Carley loves me, and this is her way of showing it.

I squeeze back. How do I tell her I don't need anyone's watchful eye? I want to be released from that responsibility. It should be reversed, right? The person protecting someone is responsible, but that's not entirely true. Needing protection comes with a price. I'm done positioning myself for others, listening to them, and halting my train of thought to consider them. I'm in charge of that now.

"Love you," I say, hugging them.

Carley's shoulders cave, and she resigns to keeping her opinions to herself. I'll take that as a win. After I see them to their car, I walk Jessie across the street, feed her, and go upstairs to change before Rob gets here.

I thought he would leave the area, and he questioned it, too. When we were allowed back into Baltimore, something shifted in him. Rob retook what was lost. Judy, his wife, was found, but she couldn't be saved because of serious injuries to her abdomen. He said goodbye all over again.

Rob has a job and purpose. A lot of us have this story. Lazarus City has done things to us we can't change. It's nestled deep inside our psyche, rearing its ugliness at unexpected times.

The city was empty for years. It was scoured by the military and scientists before the walls came down. VioTech, being held responsible for the outbreak, paid million-dollar fines too high to imagine, which caused them to claim bankruptcy. Regretfully, it didn't put them out of business.

A knock at the door sends Jessie to her feet, and she barks as loud as she can at the window overlooking the front stoop.

I rush down the steps, noting Rob is early. When I go outside, I'm surprised it's not Rob standing there.

"Hey, Shelby. Is this a bad time?" Jason's curly hair is cut short, and he's cleanshaven.

"I can't talk long. Rob is on his way to pick me up. Are you going tonight?" I let him pass me in the vestibule and walk into the living room.

He pats Jessie on the head. "Sure am. I have an extra ticket too, but I guess you don't need it." His grin fades. There's been no intent on avoiding Jason. Our lives drifted in different directions.

Our relationship only existed inside Lazarus City, and now we're here again. Could Baltimore ignite the passion we once shared? The days of his warm body next to mine at the Rec Pier have long passed. It's undergoing heavy reconstruction, and they've talked about making it into a restaurant and hotel. I hope they can bring it back.

"I'm going with Rob, but we can walk together if you want to join." Rob and Jason were never close after Rob flipped to Fat Man's team during his darker moments, but the two are friendly enough.

"No. You stick with your plans. I'm meeting people from work, and maybe Jeronimo after. Is Angela coming?" he asks.

"She's going with her girlfriend. I'll meet up with everyone if I can, but it'll be difficult. Can I leave you for a second? I need to finish getting ready."

"I won't keep you. There is something I wanted to mention. I've bought a place in Fells Point, right on the water."

"So, you're staying?" My heart thunders in my chest. He'll be a few blocks away.

"Returning to this fucking city is a mind trip." He rubs his hand along the back of his neck and stares out the window searching for words.

"I listen for them." I'm referring to the infected. They haunt me, along with the creaks and unidentified noises in the house.

"Me too. Might never lose that instinct. Do you talk quietly at night?"

"Only sometimes. Group therapy has been good for me. Want to come sometime?" I lead, hoping he'll reach out if he needs to.

He snickers. "Thank you. I may take you up on that, but I'm doing okay." Jason prefers to go at it himself. He's not one for opening up and reaching out.

"Well, then, I guess I'll see you around." I walk him to the door and open it. When he passes me, he stalls. His fingers brush against my hand, sending warm tingles up my arm. It would be easy to fall for him again.

"I came here to ask you out on a date. See if we could start over. Little Italy has a few restaurants open." His green eyes with flecks of gold lock on mine, and I can almost taste his lips.

Warmth rides up my neck, settling on my cheeks, and I say, "Maybe."

"Maybe? Well, that's not no." He grins.

I curl my arms around him and rest my head on his chest. "Give me time to feel out this city again. I have to be alone before letting someone in."

He kisses my forehead. "I can understand that."

My words hang in my throat. I want to tell him yes, but also, he shouldn't wait for me. The opportune time may never come, but the offer sits sugary on my tongue.

"I'll call you soon," I offer.

"Yeah, that would be nice. See you around then." He lets his arms slip from our embrace, and he walks down the steps to the sidewalk. I half expect him to turn back while he makes his way to the end of my block, but he doesn't.

"Okay," I say, and close the door. That cut into my time to get ready! Dry shampoo to the rescue.

Jessie's white eyebrows roll up and down before she rests her head on the armrest of the couch. Her favorite spot is right by the window where she monitors the world.

I take quick care of myself. Pulling on a hat and zipping a sweatshirt to adorn the appropriate attire for the event.

Another knock at the door suggests Rob is here. I'm as ready as I can be.

Rob and I link arms, and walk down the street toward Fells Point, where we've decided to get a drink. He's filling me in on the renovations to his row home.

"The roof was leaking next to mine, so it caused the bricks to fall inward. They're going to shore it up with steel beams and giant screws. It's intense, but should do the job," he says.

Dean kept the house in good shape while he could. I'm luckier than many. Some tried to return only to find one of Fat Man's fires took down their block, or the flooding was so bad that mold mitigation would cost thousands of dollars.

"We're keeping the construction and home modeling companies in business, aren't we?" I say, trying to make light of a difficult situation.

"I need my contractor license so I can cash in!"

"I'd hire you. The rooftop deck is wobbly, and a lot of the wood needs to be replaced. The toilet in the backroom froze and a pipe burst, and I found a nice family of bats living under the cornice."

We walk into a bar and quickly order beers. I take a sip to celebrate. We're going to be okay even with challenges ahead.

He raises his glass, and I clink it with his. "Cheers to the death of Lazarus City, even if we'll rebuild for years."

We finish our drink and move on toward our destination. There are hundreds of people dressed in similar colors to honor this monumental day. The atmosphere shifts and takes on an energy of cheer as we march towards the place that started it all.

I grip Rob's arm tighter.

"Over there. We need to make that stop." Rob points to the famous area where everyone will meet before our final destination. Pickles Pub.

The bouncer checks our licenses and waves us in. The crowd hums around us with chatter, while the air smells of beer and fries.

"I'll get us beers and meet you back here," Rob motions to the bar.

"We're missing the National Anthem."

"Sorry, I know you wanted to hear that. Just one drink and we'll go in," he assures me.

"Okay."

The crowd is mostly survivors because today is ours. Their eyes flash with panic, but they're keeping it together. The swirl of emotions and inhibitions being shed breathes through everyone.

Someone taps me on the shoulder. When I turn, I find Dean behind me. He's wearing a black hat, orange Orioles t-shirt, and has a beer in his hand.

"Enjoying that?" I ask, pointing at his drink.

"Sure am. Where's Rob?"

"Getting me a beer. He's a good friend."

"That he is." Dean takes a long sip, and the froth sticks to his beard.

People push past us, trying to make their way to the bar. Dean and the stadium are a combination I never wished for again. Being here now shows me how wrong I was. Survivors can have these moments.

It's opening day. The first game the Baltimore Orioles have played in Camden Yards since the outbreak. We may lose. In fact, we probably will. The team has been rebuilt and relocated several times.

One thing is for certain: our pride is intact. We're going to fight for this city and bring back its people. Most importantly, I'm doing this with Dean. The large televisions hung on the surrounding walls show the baseball field with players lined up. Their hats are on their hearts. The crowd at the bar falls silent while the National Anthem plays. Rob makes his way over with two overly full beers sloshing over the rim. He tips his head with a smile, acknowledging Dean.

Those around us grow louder as we sing every word and mark the traditional spot of the song where Orioles fans shout, "Ohhhh!"

When the song is over, people become antsy to get to the game. There are so many bodies moving in different directions, and my anxiety sends an unwelcome message. Run. I need to get away from these people. They're too close, and someone might attack.

Dean rests his hand on mine. His smile reassures me that the story in my head is old news. "If we get separated," he says.

I fill my lungs with a deep breath, refusing the old stories swimming through my head. Lazarus City released us. We beat it, and we are free to move on. I squeeze his hand and say, "We won't."

Acknowledgements

This is the final book in the Lazarus City series. Will there be a spin-off? Your guess is as good as mine! Let's see where my muse takes me. I started this journey almost six years ago when I found myself jobless and thrust into a stay-at-home life with my three kids. This was a good thing, and all the roads leading me here were necessary. Today I tell people I have two jobs. Back in the workforce part time, and doing this author gig. My kids are getting older and busier, which makes me and my husband also busier. I'm still writing through. And I have a few new stories planned for you. I hope you've enjoyed Lazarus City, Sour Moon, Salt Rush, and Rotters End. Thank you for giving these books a chance. Please leave a review! This helps the robots catch hold of my books and shoot me out to more readers.

Special thanks to my family, who continue to support and encourage me. Especially my husband for understanding my need to hide in the basement office away from everyone. And for accepting the costs that goes into publishing. That reminds me. Hey, Netflix. If you want to make a series out of Lazarus City, my contact information is below.

The life of an author, rather it be full time or part time, can be rather lonely. I'm thankful to have a team of talented humans reviewing my work and answering questions on a daily and weekly basis. Here is a list of a few of them: Rissa, Kasey, Robin, Ariele, Rachael, and our amazing Discord group. Beth for her hard work on the interior designs. Ivan for the gorgeous cover. And Jenny, who combed through my manuscript for copy edits.

Connect with
Melisa Peterson Lewis

facebook.com/melisapetersonlewis

instagram.com/melisa.peterson.lewis/

melisapetersonlewis.com

fingerstosky@hotmail.com

Printed in Great Britain
by Amazon

32979518R00195